EVERYMAN,

I WILL GO WITH THEE,

AND BE THY GUIDE,

IN THY MOST NEED

TO GO BY THY SIDE

DOG STORIES

EDITED BY DIANA SECKER TESDELL

EVERYMAN'S POCKET CLASSICS

Alfred A. Knopf New York London Toronto

THIS IS A BORZOI BOOK
PUBLISHED BY ALFRED A. KNOPF

This selection by Diana Secker Tesdell first published in
Everyman's Library, 2010
Copyright © 2010 by Everyman's Library
A list of acknowledgments to copyright owners appears at the back
of this volume.
Third printing (US)

US website: www.randomhouse.com/everymans

ISBN: 978-0-307-59397-9 (US)
978-1-84159-606-8 (UK)

A CIP catalogue reference for this book is available from the
British Library

Typography by Peter B. Willberg
Typeset in the UK by AccComputing, North Barrow, Somerset
Printed and bound in Germany by GGP Media GmbH, Pössneck

DOG
STORIES

Contents

O. HENRY

MEMOIRS OF A YELLOW DOG

I DON'T SUPPOSE it will knock any of you people off your perch to read a contribution from an animal. Mr Kipling and a good many others have demonstrated the fact that animals can express themselves in remunerative English, and no magazine goes to press nowadays without an animal story in it, except the old-style monthlies that are still running pictures of Bryan and the Mont Pelée horror.

But you needn't look for any stuck-up literature in my piece, such as Bearoo, the bear, and Snakoo, the snake, and Tammanoo, the tiger, talk in the jungle books. A yellow dog that's spent most of his life in a cheap New York flat, sleeping in a corner on an old sateen underskirt (the one she spilled port wine on at the Lady Longshoremen's banquet), mustn't be expected to perform any tricks with the art of speech.

I was born a yellow pup; date, locality, pedigree and weight unknown. The first thing I can recollect, an old woman had me in a basket at Broadway and Twenty-third trying to sell me to a fat lady. Old Mother Hubbard was boosting me to beat the band as a genuine Pomeranian-Hambletonian-Red-Irish-Cochin-China-Stoke-Pogis fox-terrier. The fat lady chased a V around among the samples of gros grain flannel-ette in her shopping bag till she cornered it, and gave up. From that moment I was a pet – a mamma's own wootsey squidlums. Say, gentle reader, did you ever have a 200-pound woman breathing a flavor of Camembert cheese and Peau d'Espagne pick you up and wallop her nose all over you, remarking all the time in an Emma Eames tone of voice: 'Oh, oo's um oodlum, doodlum, woodlum, toodlum, bitsy-witsy skoodlums?'

From pedigreed yellow pup I grew up to be an anonymous yellow cur looking like a cross between an Angora cat and a box of lemons. But my mistress never tumbled. She thought that the two primeval pups that Noah chased into the ark were but a collateral branch of my ancestors. It took two policemen to keep her from entering me at the Madison Square Garden for the Siberian bloodhound prize.

I'll tell you about that flat. The house was the ordinary thing in New York, paved with Parian marble in the entrance hall and cobblestones above the first floor. Our flat was three – well, not flights – climbs up. My mistress rented it un-furnished, and put in the regular things – 1903 antique upholstered parlor set, oil chromo of geishas in a Harlem tea house, rubber plant and husband.

By Sirius! there was a biped I felt sorry for. He was a little man with sandy hair and whiskers a good deal like mine. Henpecked? – well, toucans and flamingoes and pelicans all had their bills in him. He wiped the dishes and listened to my mistress tell about the cheap, ragged things the lady with the squirrel-skin coat on the second floor hung out on her line to dry. And every evening while she was getting supper she made him take me out on the end of a string for a walk.

If men knew how women pass the time when they are alone they'd never marry. Laura Lean Jibbey, peanut brittle, a little almond cream on the neck muscles, dishes unwashed, half an hour's talk with the iceman, reading a package of old letters, a couple of pickles and two bottles of malt extract, one hour peeking through a hole in the window shade into the flat across the air-shaft – that's about all there is to it.

Twenty minutes before time for him to come home from work she straightens up the house, fixes her rat so it won't show, and gets out a lot of sewing for a ten-minute bluff.

I led a dog's life in that flat. 'Most all day I lay there in my corner watching that fat woman kill time. I slept sometimes and had pipe dreams about being out chasing cats into basements and growling at old ladies with black mittens, as a dog was intended to do. Then she would pounce upon me with a lot of that drivelling poodle palaver and kiss me on the nose – but what could I do? A dog can't chew cloves.

I began to feel sorry for Hubby, dog my cats if I didn't. We looked so much alike that people noticed it when we went out; so we shook the streets that Morgan's cab drives down, and took to climbing the piles of last December's snow on the streets where cheap people live.

One evening when we were thus promenading, and I was trying to look like a prize St Bernard, and the old man was trying to look like he wouldn't have murdered the first organ-grinder he heard play Mendelssohn's wedding-march, I looked up at him and said, in my way:

'What are you looking so sour about, you oakum trimmed lobster? She don't kiss you. You don't have to sit on her lap and listen to talk that would make the book of a musical comedy sound like the maxims of Epictetus. You ought to be thankful you're not a dog. Brace up, Benedick, and bid the blues begone.'

The matrimonial mishap looked down at me with almost canine intelligence in his face.

'Why, doggie,' says he, 'good doggie. You almost look like you could speak. What is it, doggie – cats.'

Cats! Could speak!

But, of course, he couldn't understand. Humans were denied the speech of animals. The only common ground of communication upon which dogs and men can get together is in fiction.

In the flat across the hall from us lived a lady with a black-and-tan terrier. Her husband strung it and took it out every evening, but he always came home cheerful and whistling. One day I touched noses with the black-and-tan in the hall, and I struck him for an elucidation.

'See here, Wiggle-and-Skip,' I says, 'you know that it ain't the nature of a real man to play dry nurse to a dog in public. I never saw one leashed to a bow-wow yet that didn't look like he'd like to lick every other man that looked at him. But your boss comes in every day as perky and set up as an amateur prestidigitator doing the egg trick. How does he do it? Don't tell me he likes it.'

'Him?' says the black-and-tan. 'Why, he uses Nature's Own Remedy. He gets spifflicated. At first when we go out he's as shy as the man on the steamer who would rather play pedro when they make 'em all jackpots. By the time we've been in eight saloons he don't care whether the thing on the end of his line is a dog or a catfish. I've lost two inches of my tail trying to sidestep those swinging doors.'

The pointer I got from that terrier – Vaudeville please copy – set me to thinking.

One evening about 6 o'clock my mistress ordered him to get busy and do the ozone act for Lovey. I have concealed it until now, but that is what she called me. The black-and-tan was called 'Tweetness'. I consider that I have the bulge on him as far as you could chase a rabbit. Still 'Lovey' is something of a nomenclatural tin can on the tail of one's self-respect.

At a quiet place on a safe street I tightened the line of my custodian in front of an attractive, refined saloon. I made a dead-ahead scramble for the doors, whining like a dog in the press despatches that lets the family know that little Alice is bogged while gathering lilies in the brook.

'Why, darn my eyes,' says the old man, with a grin; 'darn my eyes if the saffron-colored son of a seltzer lemonade ain't asking me in to take a drink. Lemme see – how long's it been since I saved shoe leather by keeping one foot on the foot-rest? I believe I'll—'

I knew I had him. Hot Scotches he took, sitting at a table. For an hour he kept the Campbells coming. I sat by his side rapping for the waiter with my tail, and eating free lunch such as mamma in her flat never equalled with her home-made truck bought at a delicatessen store eight minutes before papa comes home.

When the products of Scotland were all exhausted except the rye bread the old man unwound me from the table leg and played me outside like a fisherman plays a salmon. Out there he took off my collar and threw it into the street.

'Poor doggie,' says he; 'good doggie. She shan't kiss you any more. 'S a darned shame. Good doggie, go away and get run over by a street car and be happy.'

I refused to leave. I leaped and frisked around the old man's legs happy as a pug on a rug.

'You old flea-headed woodchuck-chaser,' I said to him – 'you moon-baying, rabbit-pointing, egg-stealing old beagle, can't you see that I don't want to leave you? Can't you see that we're both Pups in the Wood and the missis is the cruel uncle after you with the dish towel and me with the flea liniment and a pink bow to tie on my tail. Why not cut that all out and be pards forever more?'

Maybe you'll say he didn't understand – maybe he didn't. But he kind of got a grip on the Hot Scotches, and stood still for a minute, thinking.

'Doggie,' says he, finally, 'we don't live more than a dozen lives on this earth, and very few of us live to be more than 300. If I ever see that flat any more I'm a flat, and if you do you're flatter; and that's no flattery. I'm offering 60 to 1 that Westward Ho wins out by the length of a dachshund.'

There was no string, but I frolicked along with my master to the Twenty-third Street ferry. And the cats on the route saw reason to give thanks that prehensile claws had been given to them.

On the Jersey side my master said to a stranger who stood eating a currant bun:

'Me and my doggie, we are bound for the Rocky Mountains.'

But what pleased me most was when my old man pulled both of my ears until I howled, and said:

'You common, monkey-headed, rat-tailed, sulphur-colored son of a door mat, do you know what I'm going to call you?'

I thought of 'Lovey', and I whined dolefully.

'I'm going to call you "Pete",' says my master; and if I'd had five tails I couldn't have done enough wagging to do justice to the occasion.

JONATHAN LETHEM

AVA'S APARTMENT

PERKUS TOOTH, the wall-eyed former rock critic, awoke the morning after the party he vowed would be his last, the night after the worst blizzard of the winter, asleep on a staircase, already in the grip of a terrific cluster headache. He suffered these regularly, knew the drill, felt himself hunkering into the blinding, energy-sapping migraine by ancient instinct. Nobody greeted him, his hosts asleep themselves, or gone out, so he made his way downstairs, groped to locate his coat in their closet, and then found his way outdoors.

Perkus's shoes were, of course, inadequate for the depth of freshly fallen snow. He'd have walked the eight blocks home in any event – the migraine nausea would have made a cab ride unbearable – but there wasn't any choice. The streets were free of cabs and any other traffic. Some of the larger, better-managed buildings had had their sidewalks laboriously cleared and salted, the snow pushed into mounds covering hydrants and newspaper boxes, but elsewhere Perkus had to climb through drifts that had barely been traversed, fitting his shoes into boot prints that had been punched knee-deep. His pants were quickly soaked, and his sleeves as well, since between semi-blindness and poor footing he stumbled to his hands and knees several times before he even got to Second Avenue. Under other circumstances he'd have been pitied, perhaps offered aid, or possibly arrested for public drunkenness, but on streets the January blizzard had remade there was no one to observe him, apart from a cross-country skier who stared mercilessly from behind solar goggles, and a few dads here and there dragging kids on sleds. If they noticed him at all they probably thought he was out playing, too. There was no reason for someone to be making his way along impassable streets so early the day after. Not a single shop was open, all the entrances buried in drift.

When he met the barricade at the corner of Eighty-fourth, he at first tried to bluster his way past, thinking the cop had misunderstood. But no. His building was one of three the snowstorm had undermined, the weight of the snow threatening the soundness of its foundation. He talked with neighbors he hadn't spoken to in fifteen years of dwelling on the same floor, though gripped in the vise of his cluster headache he barely heard a word they said, and he couldn't have made too good an impression. *You need to find someplace to sleep tonight* – that was a fragment that got through to him. *They might let you in for your stuff later, but not now. You can call this number* . . . but the number he missed. Then, as Perkus teetered away: *Get yourself indoors, young man.* And: *Pity about that one.*

Perkus Tooth had already been at a watershed, wishing to find an exit from himself, from his life and his friends, his tatter of a career – to shed it all like a snakeskin. The city in its twenty-first-century incarnation had no place for him, but it couldn't fire him – he'd quit instead. For so many years he'd lived in his biosphere of an apartment as if it were still 1978 outside, as if placing the occasional review in the *Village Voice* or *New York Rocker* gave him credentials as a citizen of the city, but the long joke of his existence had reached its punch line. The truth was that he'd never thought of himself as a critic to begin with, more a curator. His apartment – bursting with vinyl LPs, forgotten books, binders full of zines,

VHS cassettes of black-and-white films taped from PBS and 'Million Dollar Movie' – was a cultural cache shored against time's indifference, and Perkus had merely been its caretaker, his sporadic writings the equivalent of a catalogue listing items decidedly *not* for sale.

And his friends? Those among whom he wasted his days – the retired actor, now a fixture on the Upper East Side social scene; the former radical turned cynical mayor's operative; the once aspiring investigative journalist turned hack ghost-writer – had all used up their integrity, accommodated themselves to the simulacrum that Manhattan had become. Perkus had come to an end with them, too. He needed a new life. Now, incredibly, the storm had called his bluff. This was thrilling and terrifying at once: who would he be without his apartment, without that assembly of brunching mediocrities?

There was only one haven. Perkus had one friend who was unlike the others: Biller. (Perkus had never heard a last name. Biller was just Biller.) Homeless in a Manhattan that no longer coddled the homeless, Biller was crafty, a squatter and a survivor, an underground man. Now, as if in a merciful desert vision, the information that Biller had once jotted on a scrap of receipt on Perkus's kitchen table appeared before him: Biller's latest digs, in the Friendreth Apartments, on Sixty-fifth near York. Perkus couldn't remember the numerical address, but he didn't need that; from Biller's descriptions of the odd building and its inhabitants he'd surely be able to find it.

Yes, Biller was the one he needed now. Trudging sickened through the snowdrifts like a Napoleonic soldier in retreat from Moscow, Perkus was adequately convinced. He had got complacent in his Eighty-fourth Street apartment. Time to go off the grid. Biller knew how to do this, even in a place like Manhattan, which was nothing *but* grid. Biller was the essential man. They could compare notes and pool resources, Perkus preferring to think of himself as not yet completely without resources. Perkus laughed at himself now: in his thinking, Biller was becoming like Old Sneelock, in Dr Seuss's 'If I Ran the Circus', the one who'd single-handedly raise the tents, sell the pink lemonade, shovel the elephants' shit, and also do the high-wire aerialist act. In this manner, dismal yet self-amused, Perkus propelled his body to Sixty-fifth Street, despite the headache's dislodging him from himself, working with the only body he had – a shivering, frost-fingered, half-blind stumbler in sweat- and salt-stained party clothes.

He trailed a dog and its walker into the lobby, catching the swinging door before it clicked shut, one last act of mastery of the mechanics of outward existence, and then passed out in a melting pool on the tile just inside. Biller would later explain to Perkus that another dog walker had sought Biller out, knowing that the tall black man in the spotted fur hat functioned as ambassador for the vagabond entities sometimes seen lurking in the building, and that this tatter-demalion in the entranceway was nothing if not one of those. Biller gathered Perkus up and installed him in what he would come to know as Ava's apartment. It was there that Perkus, nursed through the first hours by Biller's methodical and unquestioning attentions, his clothes changed, his brow mopped, his sapped body nourished with a simple cup of ramen and beef broth, felt his new life begin.

Perkus Tooth had twenty-four hours alone in the apartment before Ava arrived. Biller kept close tabs on all the vacancies in the building and assured him that this was the best way, the intended result being that Ava would take him for granted, detect his traces on the floors and walls and in the bed and then unquestioningly settle in as a roommate. So Perkus spent the first night by himself on the surprisingly soft bed, half-awake in the dark, and then was up to pace the rooms at first light. He dwelled in the space alone just long enough to posit some conjunction between his new self – shorn of so many of its defining accoutrements, dressed in an ill-fitting, lumpish blue-and-orange sports sweatshirt with an iron-on decal name, presumably of some star player, his right temple throbbing with cluster, a really monstrous attack, ebbing in its fashion but still obnoxious, yet his brain also, somehow, seemed to have awoken from a long-fogging dream, a blind spot in sight, yes, but peripheral vision around the occlusion's edges widened, refreshed – between this self and the apartment in which he'd strangely landed, the apartment that had been fitted, like his body, with hand-me-downs, furnishings that would have been rejected even by a thrift shop. The presumption was that if he puzzled at the weird decrepit prints hung over the decaying living-room set, the framed 'Streamers' poster, or the Blue Period Picasso guitarist sun-faded to yellow over the nonworking stove in the dummy kitchen, he should be able to divine what sort of person he'd become since the last time his inquiries had turned inward. Who he was seemed actually to have slipped his mind.

Yet no. The rooms weren't going to tell him who he was. They weren't his. This was Ava's apartment, only she hadn't come yet.

Perkus hadn't encountered another soul in the hours he'd been installed in the Friendreth, had only gazed through immovable paint-sealed windows at minute human forms picking through drifts on the Sixty-fifth Street sidewalk seven stories below, the city a distant stilled terrarium. This corner of Sixty-fifth, where the street abutted the scraps of parkland at the edge of Rockefeller University, formed an utter no man's land in the winterscape. He listened at the walls, and through the sound of spasmodic barking imagined he heard a scrape of furniture or a groan or a sigh that could be human, but no voices to give proof, until the morning, when the volunteers began to arrive. Perkus sought to parse Biller's words, a clustery confusion from the night before, working to grasp what form his new roommate might take, even as he heard the volunteers at individual doors, calling each apartment's resident by name, murmuring 'good boy' or 'good girl' as they headed out to use the snowdrifts as a potty.

Even those voicings were faint, the stolid prewar building's heavy lath and plaster making fine insulation, and Perkus could feel confident that he would remain undetected if he wished to be. When clunking footsteps and scrabbling paws led to his threshold, his apartment's unlocked door opened to allow a dog and its walker through. Perkus hid like a killer in the tub, slumping down behind the shower curtain to sit within the porcelain's cool shape. He heard Ava's name spoken then, by a woman who, before leaving, set out a bowl of kibble and another of water on the kitchen floor, and cooed a few more of the sweet doggish nothings a canine lover coos when fingering behind an ear or under a whiskery chin. Biller's words now retroactively assumed a coherent, four-footed shape. Perkus had never lived with a dog. But much had changed just lately, and he was open to new things. He couldn't think of a breed to wish for but had an approximate size in mind, some scruffy mutt with the proportions of, say, a lunch pail. The door shut, and the volunteer's footsteps quickly receded in the corridor. Perkus had done no more than rustle at the plastic curtain, preparing to hoist himself from the tub, when the divider was nudged aside by a white grinning face – slavering rubbery pink lips and dinosaur teeth hinged to a squarish ridged skull nearly the size of his own, this craned forward by a neck and shoulders of pulsing and twitching muscle. One sharp, white, pink-nailed paw curled on the tub's edge as a tongue slapped forth and began brutalizing Perkus's helpless lips and nostrils. Ava the pit bull greeted her roommate with grunts and slobber, her expression demonic, her green-brown eyes, rimmed in pink, showing piggish intellect and gusto, yet helpless to command her smacking, cavernous jaws. From the first instant, before he even grasped his instinctive fear, Perkus understood that Ava did her thinking with her mouth.

The next moment, falling back against the porcelain under her demonstrative assault, watching her struggle and slip as she tried, and failed, to hurtle into the tub after him, as she braced and arched on her two back legs, he saw that the one front paw with which she scrabbled was all she had for scrabbling: Ava was a three-legged dog. This fact would regularly, as it did now, give Perkus a crucial opening – his only physical edge on her, really. Ava slid awkwardly and fell on her side with a thump. Perkus managed to stand. By the time he got himself out of the tub she was on her three legs again, flinging herself upward, forcing that boxy skull, with its smooth, loose-bunching carpet of flesh, into his hands to be adored. Ava was primally terrifying, but she soon persuaded Perkus she didn't mean to turn him into kibble. If Ava killed him it would be accidental, in seeking to stanch her emotional hungers.

Biller had bragged of the high living available at the Friendreth, an apartment building that had been reconfigured into a residence for masterless dogs, an act of charity by a private foundation of blue hairs. Perkus's homeless friend had explained to him that though it was preferable that Perkus keep himself invisible, he had only to call himself a 'volunteer' if anyone asked. The real volunteers had come to a tacit understanding with those, like Perkus now, who occasionally slipped into the Friendreth Canine Apartments to stealthily reside alongside the legitimate occupants. Faced head on with the ethical allegory of homeless persons sneaking into human-shaped spaces in a building reserved for abandoned dogs, the pet-rescue workers could be relied upon to defy the Friendreth Society's mandate and let silence cover what they witnessed. Snow and cold made their sympathy that much more certain. Biller further informed Perkus that he shared the building with three other human squatters among the thirty-odd dogs, though none were on his floor or immediately above or below him. Perkus felt no eagerness to renew contact with his own species.

Those first days were all sensual intimacy, a feast of familiarization, an orgy of pair-bonding, as Perkus learned how Ava negotiated the world – or at least the apartment – and how he was to negotiate the boisterous, insatiable dog, who became a kind of new world to him. Ava's surgery scar was clean and pink, an eight- or ten-inch seam from one shoulder blade to a point just short of where he could detect her heartbeat, at a crest of fur beneath her breast. Some veterinary surgeon had done a superlative job of sealing the joint so that she seemed like a muscular furry torpedo, missing nothing. Perkus couldn't tell how fresh the scar was or whether Ava's occasional stumbles indicated that she was still learning to walk on three legs – mostly she made it look natural, and never once did she wince or cringe or otherwise indicate pain, but seemed cheerfully to accept tripod status as her fate. When she exhausted herself trailing him from room to room, she'd sometimes sag against a wall or a chair. More often she leaned against Perkus, or plopped her muzzle across his thigh if he sat. Her mouth would close then, and Perkus could admire the pale brown of her liverish lips, the pinker brown of her nose, and the raw pale pink beneath her scant, stiff whiskers – the same color as her eyelids and the interior of her ears and her scar and the flesh beneath the transparent pistachio shells of her nails. The rest was albino white, save a saucer-size chocolate oval just above her tail to prove, with her hazel eyes, she was no albino. At other times, that mouth was transfixingly open. Even after he'd convinced himself that she'd never intentionally damage him with that massive trap full of erratic, sharklike teeth, Perkus found it impossible not to gaze inside and marvel at the map of pink and white and brown on her upper palate, the wild permanent grin of her throat. And when he let her win the prize she most sought – to clean his ears or neck with her tongue – he'd have a close-up view, more than he could really endure. Easier to endure was her ticklish tongue bath of his toes anytime he shed the ugly Nikes that Biller had given him, though she sometimes nipped between them with a fang in her eagerness to root out the sour traces.

Ava was a listener, not a barker. As they sat together on the sofa, Ava pawing at Perkus occasionally to keep his hands moving on her, scratching her jowls or the base of her ears or the cocoa spot above her tail, she'd also cock her head and meet his eyes and show that she, too, was monitoring the Friendreth Canine Apartments' other dwellers and the volunteers who moved through the halls. (As Perkus studied the building's patterns, he understood that the most certain evidence of human visitors, or other squatters, was the occasional flushing of a toilet.) Ava listened to the periodic fits of barking that possessed the building, yet felt no need to reply.

Perkus thought this trait likely extended from the authority inherent in the fantastic power of her own shape, even reduced by the missing limb. He guessed she'd never met another body she couldn't dominate, so why bark? She also liked to gaze out the window whenever he moved a chair to a place where she could make a sentry's perch. Her vigilance was absolutely placid, yet she seemed to find some purpose in it, and could watch the street below for an hour without nodding. This was her favorite sport, apart from love.

Ava let him know they were to sleep in the bed together that first night, joining him there and, then, when he tried to cede it to her, clambering atop him on the narrow sofa to which he'd retreated, spilling her sixty or seventy writhing pounds across his body and flipping her head up under his jaw in a crass seduction. That wasn't going to be very restful for either of them, so it was back to the twin-size mattress, where she could fit herself against his length and curl her snout around his hip bone. By the end of the second night, he had grown accustomed to her presence. If he didn't shift his position too much in his sleep she'd still be there when dawn crept around the heavy curtains to rouse him. Often then he'd keep from stirring, ignoring the growing pressure in his bladder, balancing the comfort in Ava's warm weight against the exhausting prospect of her grunting excitement at his waking – she was at her keenest first thing, and he suspected that, like him, she pretended to be asleep until he showed some sign. So they'd lie together both pretending. If he lasted long enough, the volunteer would come and open the door and Ava would jounce up for a walk at the call of her name (and he'd lie still until the echoes of 'OK, Ava, down, girl, down, down, *down*, that's good, no, down, *down*, yes, I love you, too, down, down, *down* . . .' had trickled away along the corridor).

Though the gas was disabled, the Friendreth's electricity flowed, thankfully, just as its plumbing worked. Biller provided Perkus with a hot plate on which he could boil water for coffee, and he'd have a cup in his hand by the time Ava returned from her walk. He imagined the volunteer could smell it when she opened the door. Coffee was the only constant between Perkus's old daily routine and his new one, a kind of lens through which he contemplated his transformations. For there was no mistaking that the command had come, as in Rilke's line: You must change your life. The physical absolutes of coexistence with the three-legged pit bull stood as the outward emblem of a new doctrine: Recover bodily prerogatives, journey into the real. The night of the blizzard and the loss of his apartment and the books and papers inside it had catapulted him into this phase. He held off interpretation for now. Until the stupendous cluster headache vanished, until he learned what Ava needed from him and how to give it, until he became self-sufficient within the Friendreth and stopped requiring Biller's care packages of sandwiches and pints of Tropicana, interpretation could wait.

The final step between Perkus and the dog came when he assumed responsibility for Ava's twice-daily walks. (He'd already several times scooped more kibble into her bowl, when she emptied it, having discovered the supply in the cabinet under the sink.) On the fifth day, Perkus woke refreshed and amazed, alert before his coffee, with his migraine completely vanished. He clambered out of bed and dressed in a kind of exultation that matched the dog's own, for once. He felt sure that Ava was hoping he'd walk her. And he was tired of hiding. So he introduced himself to the volunteer at the door, and said simply that if she'd leave him the leash he'd walk Ava now and in the future. The woman, perhaps fifty, in a lumpy cloth coat, her frizzy hair bunched under a woollen cap, now fishing in a Ziploc of dog treats for one to offer to Ava, having certainly already discerned his presence from any number of clues, showed less surprise than fascination that he'd spoken to her directly. Then she stopped.

'Something wrong with your eye?'

He'd gone unseen by all but Biller for so long that her scrutiny disarmed him. Likely his unhinged eyeball signified differently now that he was out of his suits and dressed instead in homeless-man garb, featuring a two-week beard. To this kindly dog custodian it implied that Ava's spectral cohabitant was not only poor but dissolute or deranged. A firm gaze, like a firm handshake, might be a minimum.

'From birth,' Perkus said. He tried to smile as he said it.

'It's cold out.'

'I've got a coat and boots.' Biller had loaded both into the apartment's closet, for when he'd need them.

'You can control her?'

Perkus refrained from any fancy remarks. 'Yes.'

On the street, fighting for balance on the icy sidewalks, Perkus discovered what Ava's massiveness and strength could do besides bound upward to pulse in his arms. Even on three legs, she rode and patrolled the universe within the scope of her senses, chastening poodles, pugs, Jack Russells, even causing noble rescued racetrack greyhounds to bolt, along with any cats and squirrels foolish enough to scurry through her zone. Ava had only to grin and grunt, to strain her leash one front-paw hop in their direction, and every creature bristled in fear or bogus hostility, sensing her imperial lethal force. On the street she was another dog, with little regard for Perkus except as the rudder to her sails, their affair suspended until they returned indoors. That first morning out, the glare of daylight stunned Perkus but also fed an appetite he had no idea he'd been starving. The walks became a regular highlight, twice a day, then three times, because why not? Only a minority of female dogs, he learned, bothered with marking behaviors, those scent-leavings typical of all males. Ava was in the exceptional category, hoarding her urine to squirt parsimoniously in ten or twenty different spots. Biller brought Perkus some gloves to shelter his exposed knuckles but also to protect against the chafing of Ava's heavy woven leash, that ship's rigging, on his landlubber palms. Perkus learned to invert a plastic baggie on his splayed fingers and deftly inside-out a curl of her waste to deposit an instant later in the nearest garbage can. Then inside, to the ceremonial hall of barking from the Friendreth's other inhabitants, who seemed to grasp Ava's preferential arrangement through their doors and ceilings.

It was a life of bodily immediacy. Perkus didn't look past the next meal, the next walk, the next bowel movement (with Ava these were like a clock's measure), the next furry, sighing caress into mutual sleep. Ava's volunteer – her name revealed to be Sadie Zapping – poked her head in a couple of times to inquire, and once pointedly intersected with Perkus and Ava during one of their walks, startling Perkus from reverie, and making him feel, briefly, spied upon. But she seemed to take confidence enough from what she witnessed, and Perkus felt he'd been granted full stewardship.

Now the two gradually enlarged their walking orbit, steering the compass of Ava's sniffing curiosity, around the Rockefeller campus and the Weill Cornell Medical Center, onto a bridge over the Drive, to gaze across at the permanent non sequitur of Roosevelt Island, defined for Perkus by its abandoned t.b. hospital, to which no one ever referred, certainly

31

not the population living there and serviced by its goofy tram, as if commuting by ski lift. 'No dogs allowed,' he reminded Ava every time she seemed to be contemplating that false haven. Or down First Avenue, into the lower Sixties along Second, a nefariously vague zone whose residents seemed to Perkus like zombies, beyond help.

Perkus learned to which patches of snow-scraped earth Ava craved return, a neighborhood map of invisible importances not so different, he decided, from his old paces uptown: from the magazine stand where he preferred to snag the *Times*, to H&H Bagels or the Jackson Hole burger mecca. Perkus never veered in the direction of Eighty-fourth Street, though, and Ava never happened to drag him there. His old life might have rearranged itself around his absence, his building reopened, his paces waiting for him to re-inhabit them – but he doubted it. Occasionally he missed a particular book, felt himself almost reaching in the Friendreth toward some blank wall as though he could pull down an oft-browsed volume and find consolation in its familiar lines. Nothing worse than this; he didn't miss the old life in and of itself. The notion that he should cling to a mere apartment he found both pathetic and specious. Apartments came and went, that was their nature, and he'd kept that one too long, so long that he had trouble recalling himself before it. Good riddance. There was mold in the grout of the tiles around the tub which he'd never have got clean in a million years. If Ava could thrive with one forelimb gone, the seam of its removal nearly erased in her elastic hide, he could negotiate minus one apartment, and could live with the phantom limb of human interdependency that had seemingly been excised from his life at last.

* * *

Biller wasn't a hanger-outer. He had his street scrounger's circuit to follow, and his altruistic one, too, which included checking in with Perkus and, most days, dropping off donated items of food or clothing that he thought might fit. Otherwise, he left Perkus and Ava alone. When Perkus was drawn unexpectedly a step or two back into the human realm, it was Sadie Zapping who drew him. Sadie had other dogs in the building and still looked in from time to time, always with a treat in her palm for Ava to snort up. This day she also had a steaming to-go coffee and a grilled halved corn muffin in a grease-spotted white bag which she offered to Perkus, who accepted it, this being not a time in life of charity refused or even questioned. She asked him his name again and he said it through a mouthful of coffee-soaked crumbs.

'I thought so,' Sadie Zapping said. She plucked off her knit cap and shook loose her wild gray curls. 'It took me a little while to put it together. Me and my band used to read your stuff all the time. I read you in the *Voice*.'

Ah. Existence confirmed, always when you least expected it. He asked the name of her band, understanding that it was the polite response to the leading remark.

'Zeroville,' she said. 'Like the opposite of Alphaville, get it? You probably saw our graffiti around, even if you never heard us. Our bassist was a guy named Ed Constantine – I mean, he renamed himself that, and he used to scribble our name on every blank square inch in a ten-block radius around CBGB's, even though we only ever played there a couple of times. We did open for Chthonic Youth once.' She plopped herself down now, on a chair in Ava's kitchen which Perkus had never pulled out from under the table. He still used the apartment as minimally as possible, as if he were to be judged afterward on how little he'd displaced. Ava gaily smashed her square jowly head across Sadie's lap, into her cradling hands and scrubbing fingers. 'Gawd, we used to pore over those crazy posters of yours, or broadsides, if you like. You're a lot younger-looking than I figured. We thought you were like some punk elder statesman, like the missing link to the era of Lester Bangs or Legs McNeil or what have you. It's not like we were holding our breath waiting for you to *review us* or anything, but it sure was nice knowing you were out there, somebody who would have gotten our jokes if he'd had the chance. Crap, that's another time and place, though. Look at us now.'

Sadie had begun to uncover an endearing blabbermouth-edness (even when not addressing Perkus she'd give forth with a constant stream of *Good girl, there you go, girl, aw, do you have an itchy ear? There you go, that's a girl, yes, yessss, good dog, Ava, whaaata good girl you are!*) but another elegist for Ye Olde Lower East Side was perhaps not precisely what the doctor ordered just now. Perkus, who didn't really want to believe that when his audience made itself visible again it would resemble somebody's lesbian aunt, sensed himself ready to split hairs – *not so much Lester Bangs as Seymour Krim, actually* – but then thought better of it. He was some-what at a loss for diversions. He couldn't properly claim that he had elsewhere to be.

Sadie, sensing resistance, provided her own non sequitur. 'You play cribbage?'

'Sorry?'

'The card game? I'm always looking for someone with the patience and intelligence to give me a good game. Cribbage is a real winter sport, and this is a hell of a winter, don't you think?'

With his consent, the following day Sadie Zapping arrived at the same hour, having completed her walks, and unloaded onto the kitchen table two well-worn decks of cards, a wooden cribbage board with plastic pegs, and two packets of powdered Swiss Miss. Perkus, who hated hot chocolate, said nothing and, when she served it, drained his mug. The game Sadie taught him was perfectly poised between dull and involving, as well as between skill and luck. Perkus steadily lost the first few days, then got the feel of it. Sadie sharpened, too, her best play not aroused until she felt him pushing back. They kept their talk in the arena of the local and mundane: the state of the building; the state of the streets, which had borne another two-inch snowfall, a treacherous slush carpet laid over the now seemingly permanent irregularities of black ice wherever the blizzard had been shoved aside; the ever-improving state of Perkus's cribbage; above all, the state of Ava, who thrived on Sadie's visits and seemed to revel in being discussed. Perkus could, as a result, tell himself that he tolerated the visits on the dog's account. It was nearly the end of February before Sadie told him the tragedy of Ava's fourth limb.

'I thought you knew,' she said, a defensive near-apology.

He didn't want to appear sarcastic – did Sadie think Ava had told him? – so said nothing, and let her come out with the tale, which Sadie had spied in Ava's paperwork upon the dog's transfer to the canine dorm. Three-year-old Ava was a citizen of the Bronx, it turned out. She'd lived in the Sack Wern Houses, a public development in the drug dealers' war zone of Soundview, and had been unlucky enough to rush through an ajar door and into the corridor during a police raid on the apartment next door. The policeman who'd emptied his pistol in her direction, one of three cops on the scene, misdirected all but one bullet in his panic, exploding her shank. Another cop, a dog fancier who'd cried out but failed to halt the barrage, had tended the fallen dog, who, even greeted with this injury, wanted only to beseech for love with her tongue and snout. Her owner, a Dominican who may or may not have considered his pit bull ruined for some grim atavistic purpose, balked at the expense and bother of veterinary treatment, so Ava's fate was thrown to the kindly cop's whims. The cop found her the best, a surgeon who knew that she'd be happier spared cycling the useless shoulder limb as it groped for a footing it could never attain, and so excised everything to the breastbone. It was the love-smitten cop who'd named her, ironically, after his daughter, whose terrified mom forbade their adopting the drooling sharky creature. So Ava came into the Friendreth Society's care.

'She's got hiccups,' Sadie pointed out another day, a cold one, but then they were all cold ones. 'She' was forever Ava, no need to specify. The dog was their occasion and rationale, a vessel for all else unnameable that Perkus Tooth and Sadie Zapping had in common. Which was, finally, Perkus had to admit, not much. Sadie's blunt remarks and frank un-attractiveness seemed to permit, if not invite, unabashed inspection, and Perkus sometimes caught himself puzzling backward, attempting to visualize a woman onstage behind a drum kit at the Mudd Club. But that had been, as Sadie had pointed out, another time and place. For all her reson-ance with his lost world, she might as well have been some dusty LP from his apartment, one that he rarely, if ever, played anymore. If Perkus wanted to reënter his human life, Sadie wasn't the ticket. Anyway, this was Ava's apartment. They were only guests.

'Yeah, on and off for a couple of days now.' The dog had been hiccing and gulping between breaths as she fell asleep in Perkus's arms or as she strained her leash toward the next street corner. Sometimes she had to pause in her snorting consumption of the pounds of kibble that kept her sinewy machine running, and once she'd had to cough back a gobbet

36

of bagel and lox that Perkus had tossed her. That instance had seemed to puzzle the pit bull, but otherwise she shrugged off a bout of hiccups as joyfully as she did her calamitous asymmetry.

'Other day I noticed you guys crossing Seventy-ninth Street,' Sadie said. On the table between them she scored with a pair of queens. 'Thought you never went that far uptown. Weren't there some people you didn't want to run into?'

He regarded her squarely, playing an ace and advancing his peg before shrugging in reply to her question. 'We go where she drags us,' he said. 'Lately, uptown.' This left out only the entire truth: that at the instant of his foolish pronouncement a week ago, enunciating the wish to avoid those friends who'd defined the period of his life just previous, he'd felt himself silently but unmistakably reverse the decision. He found himself suddenly curious about his old apartment; he missed his treasure, his time machine assembled from text and grooved vinyl and magnetic tape. He even, if he admitted it, pined for his friends. Without Perkus choosing it, at first without his noticing, the dog had been making him ready for the world again.

So he'd been piloting Ava, rudder driving sails for once, uptown along First Avenue to have a look in the window of the diner called Gracie Mews. He was searching for his friend the retired actor, regular breakfast companion of Perkus's previous existence, the one with whom he'd sorted through the morning paper – Perkus even missed the *Times*, he was appalled to admit – and marvelled at the manifold shames of the twenty-first century. Of all his friends, the actor was the most forgivable, the least culpable in Manhattan's selling out. He was an actor, after all, a player in scripts that he didn't write himself. As was Perkus, if he was honest.

The hiccupping dog could tell soon enough that they were on a mission, and pushed her nose to the Mews's window, too, looking for she knew not what, leaving nose doodles, like slug trails, that frosted in the cold. It turned out that it was possible to wish to become a dog only exactly up to that point where it became completely impossible. Ironically, he was embarrassed to admit to Sadie Zapping, who was a human being, that he wished to be human again. With Ava, he felt no shame. That was her permanent beauty.

RUDYARD KIPLING

GARM –
A HOSTAGE

ONE NIGHT, a very long time ago, I drove to an Indian military encampment called Mian Mir to see amateur theatricals. At the back of the Infantry barracks a soldier, his cap over one eye, rushed in front of the horses and shouted that he was a dangerous highway robber. As a matter of fact, he was a friend of mine, so I told him to go home before any one caught him; but he fell under the pole, and I heard voices of a military guard in search of some one.

The driver and I coaxed him into the carriage, drove home swiftly, undressed him and put him to bed, where he waked next morning with a sore headache, very much ashamed. When his uniform was cleaned and dried, and he had been shaved and washed and made neat, I drove him back to barracks with his arm in a fine white sling, and reported that I had accidentally run over him. I did not tell this story to my friend's sergeant, who was a hostile and unbelieving person, but to his lieutenant, who did not know us quite so well.

Three days later my friend came to call, and at his heels slobbered and fawned one of the finest bull-terriers – of the old-fashioned breed, two parts bull and one terrier – that I had ever set eyes on. He was pure white, with a fawn-coloured saddle just behind his neck, and a fawn diamond at the root of his thin whippy tail. I had admired him distantly for more than a year; and Vixen, my own fox-terrier, knew him too, but did not approve.

' 'E's for you,' said my friend; but he did not look as though he liked parting with him.

'Nonsense! That dog's worth more than most men, Stanley,' I said.

' 'E's that and more. 'Tention!'

The dog rose on his hind legs, and stood upright for a full minute.

'Eyes right!'

He sat on his haunches and turned his head sharp to the right. At a sign he rose and barked twice. Then he shook hands with his right paw and bounded lightly to my shoulder. Here he made himself into a necktie, limp and lifeless, hanging down on either side of my neck. I was told to pick him up and throw him in the air. He fell with a howl and held up one leg.

'Part 'o the trick,' said his owner. 'You're going to die now. Dig yourself your little grave an' shut your little eye.'

Still limping, the dog hobbled to the garden edge, dug a hole and lay down in it. When told that he was cured, he jumped out, wagging his tail, and whining for applause. He was put through half a dozen other tricks, such as showing how he would hold a man safe (I was that man, and he sat down before me, his teeth bared, ready to spring), and how he would stop eating at the word of command. I had no more than finished praising him when my friend made a gesture that stopped the dog as though he had been shot, took a piece of blue-ruled canteen-paper from his helmet, handed it to me and ran away, while the dog looked after him and howled. I read:

Sir – I give you the dog because of what you got me out of. He is the best I know, for I made him myself, and he is as good as a man. Please do not give him too much to eat, and please do

not give him back to me, for I'm not going to take him, if you
will keep him. So please do not try to give him back any more.
I have kept his name back, so you can call him anything and he
will answer, but please do not give him back. He can kill a man
as easy as anything, but please do not give him too much meat.
He knows more than a man.

Vixen sympathetically joined her shrill little yap to the bull-
terrier's despairing cry, and I was annoyed, for I knew that a
man who cares for dogs is one thing, but a man who loves
one dog is quite another. Dogs are at the best no more than
verminous vagrants, self-scratchers, foul feeders, and un-
clean by the law of Moses and Mohammed; but a dog with
whom one lives alone for at least six months in the year; a
free thing, tied to you so strictly by love that without you he
will not stir or exercise; a patient, temperate, humorous, wise
soul, who knows your moods before you know them yourself, is not a dog under any ruling.

I had Vixen, who was all my dog to me; and I felt what
my friend must have felt, at tearing out his heart in this style
and leaving it in my garden.

However, the dog understood clearly enough that I was
his master, and did not follow the soldier. As soon as he drew
breath I made much of him, and Vixen, yelling with jeal-
ousy, flew at him. Had she been of his own sex, he might
have cheered himself with a fight, but he only looked wor-
riedly when she nipped his deep iron sides, laid his heavy
head on my knee, and howled anew. I meant to dine at the
Club that night, but as darkness drew in, and the dog snuffed
through the empty house like a child trying to recover from
a fit of sobbing, I felt that I could not leave him to suffer his
first evening alone. So we fed at home, Vixen on one side,

and the stranger-dog on the other; she watching his every mouthful, and saying explicitly what she thought of his table manners, which were much better than hers.

It was Vixen's custom, till the weather grew hot, to sleep in my bed, her head on the pillow like a Christian; and when morning came I would always find that the little thing had braced her feet against the wall and pushed me to the very edge of the cot. This night she hurried to bed purposefully, every hair up, one eye on the stranger, who had dropped on a mat in a helpless, hopeless sort of way, all four feet spread out, sighing heavily. She settled her head on the pillow several times, to show her little airs and graces, and struck up her usual whiney sing-song before slumber. The stranger-dog softly edged towards me. I put out my hand and he licked it. Instantly my wrist was between Vixen's teeth, and her warning *aaarh!* said as plainly as speech, that if I took any further notice of the stranger she would bite.

I caught her behind the fat neck with my left hand, shook her severely, and said:

'Vixen, if you do that again you'll be put into the veranda. Now, remember!'

She understood perfectly, but the minute I released her she mouthed my right wrist once more, and waited with her ears back and all her body flattened, ready to bite. The big dog's tail thumped the floor in a humble and peace-making way.

I grabbed Vixen a second time, lifted her out of bed like a rabbit (she hated that and yelled), and, as I had promised, set her out in the veranda with the bats and the moonlight. At this she howled. Then she used coarse language – not to me, but to the bull-terrier – till she coughed with exhaustion. Then she ran around the house trying every door. Then she went off to the stables and barked as though some one were stealing the horses, which was an old trick of hers. Last she returned, and her snuffing yelp said, 'I'll be good! Let me in and I'll be good!'

She was admitted and flew to her pillow. When she was quieted I whispered to the other dog, 'You can lie on the foot of the bed.' The bull jumped up at once, and though I felt Vixen quiver with rage, she knew better than to protest. So we slept till the morning, and they had early breakfast with me, bite for bite, till the horse came round and we went for a ride. I don't think the bull had ever followed a horse before. He was wild with excitement, and Vixen, as usual, squealed and scuttered and sooted, and took charge of the procession.

There was one corner of a village near by, which we generally pass with caution, because all the yellow pariah-dogs of the place gathered about it. They were half-wild, starving beasts, and though utter cowards, yet where nine or ten of them get together they will mob and kill and eat an English dog. I kept a whip with a long lash for them. That morning they attacked Vixen, who, perhaps of design, had moved from beyond my horse's shadow.

The bull was ploughing along in the dust, fifty yards behind, rolling in his run, and smiling as bull-terriers will. I heard Vixen squeal; half a dozen of the curs closed in on her; a white streak came up behind me; a cloud of dust rose near Vixen, and, when it cleared, I saw one tall pariah with his back broken, and the bull wrenching another to earth. Vixen retreated to the protection of my whip, and the bull padded back smiling more than ever, covered with the blood of his enemies. That decided me to call him 'Garm of the Bloody Breast', who was a great person in his time, or 'Garm' for short; so, leaning forward, I told him what his temporary name would be. He looked up while I repeated it, and then raced away. I shouted 'Garm!' He stopped, raced back, and came up to ask my will.

Then I saw that my soldier friend was right, and that that dog knew and was worth more than a man. At the end of the ridge I gave an order which Vixen knew and hated: 'Go away and get washed!' I said. Garm understood some part of it, and Vixen interpreted the rest, and the two trotted off together soberly. When I went to the back veranda Vixen had been washed snowy-white, and was very proud of herself, but the dog-boy would not touch Garm on any account unless I stood by. So I waited while he was being scrubbed, and Garm, with the soap creaming on the top of his broad head, looked at me to make sure that this was what I expected him to endure. He knew perfectly that the dog-boy was only obeying orders.

'Another time,' I said to the dog-boy, 'you will wash the great dog with Vixen when I send them home.'

'Does *he* know?' said the dog-boy, who understood the ways of dogs.

'Garm,' I said, 'another time you will be washed with Vixen.'

I knew that Garm understood. Indeed, next washing-day, when Vixen as usual fled under my bed, Garm stared at the doubtful dog-boy in the veranda, stalked to the place where he had been washed last time, and stood rigid in the tub.

But the long days in my office tried him sorely. We three would drive off in the morning at half-past eight and come home at six or later. Vixen, knowing the routine of it, went to sleep under my table; but the confinement ate into Garm's soul. He generally sat on the veranda looking out on the Mall; and well I knew what he expected.

Sometimes a company of soldiers would move along on their way to the Fort, and Garm rolled forth to inspect them; or an officer in uniform entered into the office, and it was pitiful to see poor Garm's welcome to the cloth – not the man. He would leap at him, and sniff and bark joyously, then run to the door and back again. One afternoon I heard him bay with a full throat – a thing I had never heard before – and he disappeared. When I drove into my garden at the end of the day a soldier in white uniform scrambled over the wall at the far end, and the Garm that met me was a joyous dog. This happened twice or thrice a week for a month.

I pretended not to notice, but Garm knew and Vixen knew. He would glide homewards from the office about four o'clock, as though he were only going to look at the scenery, and this he did so quietly that but for Vixen I should not have noticed him. The jealous little dog under the table would give a sniff and a snort, just loud enough to call my attention to the flight. Garm might go out forty times in the day and Vixen would never stir, but when he slunk off to see his true master in my garden she told me in her own tongue. That was the one sign she made to prove that Garm did not altogether belong to the family. They were the best of friends at all times, *but*, Vixen explained that I was never to forget Garm did not love me as she loved me.

I never expected it. The dog was not my dog – could never be my dog – and I knew he was as miserable as his master who tramped eight miles a day to see him. So it seemed to me that the sooner the two were reunited the better for all. One afternoon I sent Vixen home alone in the dog-cart (Garm had gone before), and rode over to cantonments to find another friend of mine, who was an Irish soldier and a great friend of the dog's master.

I explained the whole case, and wound up with:

'And now Stanley's in my garden crying over his dog. Why doesn't he take him back? They're both unhappy.'

'Unhappy! There's no sense in the little man any more. But 'tis his fit.'

'What *is* his fit? He travels fifty miles a week to see the brute, and he pretends not to notice me when he sees me on the road; and I'm as unhappy as he is. Make him take the dog back.'

'It's his penance he's set himself. I told him by way of a joke, afther you'd run over him so convenient that night, whin he was drunk – I said if he was a Catholic he'd do penance. Off he went wid that fit in his little head *an'* a dose of fever, an' nothin' would suit but givin' you the dog as a hostage.'

'Hostage for what? I don't want hostages from Stanley.'

'For his good behaviour? He's keepin' straight now, the way it's no pleasure to associate wid him.'

'Has he taken the pledge?'

'If 'twas only that I need not care. Ye can take the pledge for three months on an' off. He sez he'll never see the dog again, an' so mark you, he'll keep straight for evermore. Ye know his fits? Well, this is wan of them. How's the dog takin' it?'

'Like a man. He's the best dog in India. Can't you make Stanley take him back?'

'I can do no more than I have done. But ye know his fits. He's just doin' his penance. What will he do when he goes to the Hills? The docthor's put him on the list.'

It is the custom in India to send a certain number of invalids from each regiment up to stations in the Himalayas for the hot weather; and though the men ought to enjoy the cool and the comfort, they miss the society of the barracks down below, and do their best to come back or to avoid going. I felt that this move would bring matters to a head, so I left Terrence hopefully, though he called after me:

'He won't take the dog, sorr. You can lay your month's pay on that. Ye know his fits.'

I never pretended to understand Private Ortheris; and so I did the next best thing – I left him alone.

That summer the invalids of the regiment to which my friend belonged were ordered off to the Hills early, because the doctors thought marching in the cool of the day would do them good. Their route lay south to a place called Umballa, a hundred and twenty miles or more. Then they would turn east and march up into the Hills to Kasauli or Dugshai or Subathoo. I dined with the officers the night before they left – they were marching at five in the morning. It was midnight when I drove into my garden, and surprised a white figure flying over the wall.

'That man,' said my butler, 'has been here since nine, making talk to the dog. He is quite mad. I did not tell him to go away because he has been here many times before, and because the dog-boy told me that if I told him to go away, that great dog would immediately slay me. He did not wish to speak to the Protector of the Poor, and he did not ask for anything to eat or drink.'

'Kadir Buksh,' said I, 'that was well done, for the dog would surely have killed thee. But I do not think the white soldier will come any more.'

Garm slept ill that night and whimpered in his dreams. Once he sprang up with a clear, ringing bark, and I heard him wag his tail till it waked him and the bark died out in a howl. He had dreamed he was with his master again, and I nearly cried. It was all Stanley's silly fault.

The first halt which the detachment of invalids made was some miles from their barracks, on the Amritsar road, and ten miles distant from my house. By a mere chance one of the officers drove back for another good dinner at the Club (cooking on the line of march is always bad), and there we met. He was a particular friend of mine, and I knew that he knew how to love a dog properly. His pet was a big retriever who was going up to the Hills for his health, and, though it was still April, the round, brown brute puffed and panted in the Club veranda as though he would burst.

'It's amazing,' said the officer, 'what excuses these invalids of mine make to get back to barracks. There's a man in my company now asked me for leave to go back to cantonments to pay a debt he'd forgotten. I was so taken by the idea I let him go, and he jingled off in an *ekka* as pleased as Punch. Ten miles to pay a debt! Wonder what it was really?'

'If you'll drive me home I think I can show you,' I said.

So he went over to my house in his dog-cart with the retriever; and on the way I told him the story of Garm.

'I was wondering where that brute had gone to. He's the best dog in the regiment,' said my friend. 'I offered the little fellow twenty rupees for him a month ago. But he's a hostage, you say, for Stanley's good conduct. Stanley's one of the best men I have – when he chooses.'

'That's the reason why,' I said. 'A second-rate man wouldn't have taken things to heart as he has done.'

We drove in quietly at the far end of the garden, and crept round the house. There was a place close to the wall all grown about with tamarisk trees, where I knew Garm kept his bones. Even Vixen was not allowed to sit near it. In the full Indian moonlight I could see a white uniform bending over the dog.

'Good-bye, old man,' we could not help hearing Stanley's voice. 'For 'Eving's sake don't get bit and go mad by any measley pi-dog. But you can look after yourself, old man. *You* don't get drunk an' run about 'ittin' your friends. You takes your bones an' eats your biscuit, an' kills your enemy like a gentleman. I'm goin' away – don't 'owl – I'm goin' off to Kasauli, where I won't see you no more.'

I could hear him holding Garm's nose as the dog drew it up to the stars.

'You'll stay here an' be'ave, an' – an' I'll go away an' try to be'ave, an' I don't know 'ow to leave you. I don't think—'

'I think this is damn silly,' said the officer, patting his foolish fubsy old retriever. He called to the private who leaped to his feet, marched forward, and saluted.

'You here?' said the officer, turning away his head.

'Yes, sir, but I'm just goin' back.'

'I shall be leaving here at eleven in my cart. You come with me. I can't have sick men running about all over the place. Report yourself at eleven, *here*.'

We did not say much when we went indoors, but the officer muttered and pulled his retriever's ears.

He was a disgraceful, overfed doormat of a dog; and when he waddled off to my cookhouse to be fed, I had a brilliant idea.

At eleven o'clock that officer's dog was nowhere to be found, and you never heard such a fuss as his owner made. He called and shouted and grew angry, and hunted through my garden for half an hour.

Then I said:

'He's sure to turn up in the morning. Send a man in by rail, and I'll find the beast and return him.'

'Beast?' said the officer. 'I value that dog considerably more than I value any man I know. It's all very fine for you to talk – your dog's here.'

So she was – under my feet – and, had she been missing, food and wages would have stopped in my house till her return. But some people grow fond of dogs not worth a cut of the whip. My friend had to drive away at last with Stanley in the back seat; and then the dog-boy said to me:

'What kind of animal is Bullen Sahib's dog? Look at him!'

I went to the boy's hut, and the fat old reprobate was lying on a mat carefully chained up. He must have heard his master calling for twenty minutes, but had not even attempted to join him.

'He has no face,' said the dog-boy scornfully. 'He is a *punniar-kooter* [a spaniel]. He never tried to get that cloth off his jaws when his master called. Now Vixen-baba would have jumped through the window, and that Great Dog would have slain me with his muzzled mouth. It is true that there are many kinds of dogs.'

Next evening who should turn up but Stanley. The officer had sent him back fourteen miles by rail with a note begging me to return the retriever if I had found him, and, if I had not, to offer huge rewards. The last train to camp left at half-past ten, and Stanley stayed till ten talking to Garm. I argued and entreated, and even threatened to shoot the bull-terrier, but the little man was firm as a rock, though I gave him a good dinner and talked to him most severely. Garm knew as well as I that this was the last time he could hope to see his man, and followed Stanley like a shadow. The retriever said nothing, but licked his lips after his meal and waddled off without so much as saying 'Thank you' to the disgusted dog-boy.

So that last meeting was over, and I felt as wretched as Garm, who moaned in his sleep all night. When we went to the office he found a place under the table close to Vixen, and dropped flat till it was time to go home. There was no more running out into the verandas, no slinking away for stolen talks with Stanley. As the weather grew warmer the dogs were forbidden to run beside the cart, but sat at my side on the seat. Vixen with her head under the crook of my left elbow, and Garm hugging the left handrail.

Here Vixen was ever in great form. She had to attend to

all the moving traffic, such as bullock-carts that blocked the way, and camels, and led ponies; as well as to keep up her dignity when she passed low friends running in the dust. She never yapped for yapping's sake, but her shrill, high bark was known all along the Mall, and other men's terriers ki-yied in reply, and bullock-drivers looked over their shoulders and gave us the road with a grin.

But Garm cared for none of these things. His big eyes were on the horizon and his terrible mouth was shut. There was another dog in the office who belonged to my chief. We called him 'Bob the Librarian', because he always imagined vain rats behind the bookshelves, and in hunting for them would drag out half the old newspaper-files. Bob was a well-meaning idiot, but Garm did not encourage him. He would slide his head round the door panting, 'Rats! Come along, Garm!' and Garm would shift one forepaw over the other, and curl himself round, leaving Bob to whine at a most uninterested back. The office was nearly as cheerful as a tomb in those days.

Once, and only once, did I see Garm at all contented with his surroundings. He had gone for an unauthorized walk with Vixen early one Sunday morning, and a very young and foolish artilleryman (his battery had just moved to that part of the world) tried to steal both. Vixen, of course, knew better than to take food from soldiers, and, besides, she had just finished her breakfast. So she trotted back with a large piece of the mutton that they issue to our troops, laid it down on my veranda, and looked up to see what I thought. I asked her where Garm was, and she ran in front of the house to show me the way.

About a mile up the road we came across our artilleryman sitting very stiffly on the edge of a culvert with a greasy hand-kerchief on his knees. Garm was in front of him, looking rather pleased. When the man moved leg or hand, Garm bared his teeth in silence. A broken string hung from his collar, and the other half of it lay, all warm, in the artilleryman's still hand. He explained to me, keeping his eye straight in front of him, that he had met this dog (he called him awful names) walking alone, and was going to take him to the Fort to be killed for a masterless pariah.

I said that Garm did not seem to me much of a pariah, but that he had better take him to the Fort if he thought best. He said he did not care to do so. I told him to go to the Fort alone. He said he did not want to go at that hour, but would follow my advice as soon as I had called off the dog. I instructed Garm to take him to the Fort, and Garm marched him solemnly up to the gate, one mile and a half under a hot sun, and I told the quarter-guard what had happened; but the young artilleryman was more angry than was at all necessary when they began to laugh. Several regiments, he was told, had tried to steal Garm in their time.

That month the hot weather shut down in earnest, and the dogs slept in the bathroom on the cool wet bricks where the bath is placed. Every morning, as soon as the man filled my bath, the two jumped in, and every morning the man filled the bath a second time. I said to him that he might as well fill a small tub especially for the dogs. 'Nay,' said he smiling, 'it is not their custom. They would not understand. Besides, the big bath gives them more space.'

The punkah-coolies who pull the punkahs day and night came to know Garm intimately. He noticed that when the swaying fan stopped I would call out to the coolie and bid him pull with a long stroke. If the man still slept I would wake him up. He discovered, too, that it was a good thing to lie in the wave of air under the punkah. Maybe Stanley had taught him all about this in barracks. At any rate, when the punkah stopped, Garm would first growl and cock his eye at the rope, and if that did not wake the man – it nearly always did – he would tiptoe forth and talk in the sleeper's ear. Vixen was a clever little dog, but she could never connect the punkah and the coolie; so Garm gave me grateful hours of cool sleep. But he was utterly wretched – as miserable as a human being; and in his misery he clung so close to me that other men noticed it, and were envious. If I moved from one room to another Garm followed; if my pen stopped scratching, Garm's head was thrust into my hand; if I turned, half awake, on the pillow, Garm was up at my side, for he knew that I was his only link with his master, and day and night, and night and day, his eyes asked one question – 'When is this going to end?'

Living with the dog as I did, I never noticed that he was more than ordinarily upset by the hot weather, till one day at the Club a man said: 'That dog of yours will die in a week or two. He's a shadow.' Then I dosed Garm with iron and quinine, which he hated; and I felt very anxious. He lost his appetite, and Vixen was allowed to eat his dinner under his eyes. Even that did not make him swallow, and we held a consultation on him, of the best man-doctor in the place; a lady-doctor, who had cured the sick wives of kings; and the Deputy Inspector-General of the veterinary service of all India. They pronounced upon his symptoms, and I told them his story, and Garm lay on a sofa licking my hand.

'He's dying of a broken heart,' said the lady-doctor suddenly.

' 'Pon my word,' said the Deputy Inspector-General, 'I believe Mrs Macrae is perfectly right – as usual.'

The best man-doctor in the place wrote a prescription, and the veterinary Deputy Inspector-General went over it afterwards to be sure that the drugs were in the proper dog-proportions; and that was the first time in his life that our doctor ever allowed his prescriptions to be edited. It was a strong tonic, and it put the dear boy on his feet for a week or two; then he lost flesh again. I asked a man I knew to take him up to the Hills with him when he went, and the man came to the door with his kit packed on the top of the carriage. Garm took in the situation at one red glance. The hair rose along his back; he sat down in front of me, and delivered the most awful growl I have ever heard in the jaws of a dog. I shouted to my friend to get away at once, and as soon as the carriage was out of the garden Garm laid his head on my knee and whined. So I knew his answer, and devoted myself to getting Stanley's address in the Hills.

My turn to go to the cool came late in August. We were allowed thirty days' holiday in a year, if no one fell sick, and we took it as we could be spared. My chief and Bob the Librarian had their holiday first, and when they were gone I made a calendar, as I always did, and hung it up at the head of my cot, tearing off one day at a time till they returned. Vixen had gone up to the Hills with me five times before; and she appreciated the cold and the damp and the beautiful wood fires there as much as I did.

'Garm,' I said, 'we are going back to Stanley at Kasauli. Kasauli – Stanley; Stanley – Kasauli.' And I repeated it twenty times. It was not Kasauli really, but another place. Still I remembered what Stanley had said in my garden on the last night, and I dared not change the name. Then Garm began to tremble; then he barked; and then he leaped up at me, frisking and wagging his tail.

'Not now,' I said, holding up my hand. 'When I say "Go", we'll go, Garm.' I pulled out the little blanket coat and spiked collar that Vixen always wore up in the Hills to protect her against sudden chills and thieving leopards, and I let the two

56

smell them and talk it over. What they said of course I do not know, but it made a new dog of Garm. His eyes were bright; and he barked joyfully when I spoke to him. He ate his food, and he killed his rats for the next three weeks, and when he began to whine I had only to say 'Stanley – Kasauli; Kasauli – Stanley', to wake him up. I wish I had thought of it before.

My chief came back, all brown with living in the open air, and very angry at finding it so hot in the Plains. That same afternoon we three and Kadir Buksh began to pack for our month's holiday, Vixen rolling in and out of the bullock-trunk twenty times a minute, and Garm grinning all over and thumping on the floor with his tail. Vixen knew the routine of travelling as well as she knew my office-work. She went to the station, singing songs, on the front seat of the carriage, while Garm sat with me. She hurried into the railway carriage, saw Kadir Buksh make up my bed for the night, got her drink of water, and curled up with her black-patch eye on the tumult of the platform. Garm followed her (the crowd gave him a lane all to himself) and sat down on the pillows with his eyes blazing, and his tail a haze behind him.

We came to Umballa in the hot misty dawn, four or five men, who had been working hard for eleven months, shouting for our dâks – the two-horse travelling carriages that were to take us up to Kalka at the foot of the Hills. It was all new to Garm. He did not understand carriages where you lay at full length on your bedding, but Vixen knew and hopped into her place at once; Garm following. The Kalka road, before the railway was built, was about forty-seven miles long, and the horses were changed every eight miles. Most of them jibbed, and kicked, and plunged, but they had to go, and they went rather better than usual for Garm's deep bay in their rear.

There was a river to be forded, and four bullocks pulled the carriage, and Vixen stuck her head out of the sliding-door and nearly fell into the water while she gave directions. Garm was silent and curious, and rather needed reassuring about Stanley and Kasauli. So we rolled, barking and yelping, into Kalka for lunch, and Garm ate enough for two.

After Kalka the road wound among the Hills, and we took a curricle with half-broken ponies, which were changed every six miles. No one dreamed of a railroad to Simla in those days, for it was seven thousand feet up in the air. The road was more than fifty miles long, and the regulation pace was just as fast as the ponies could go. Here, again, Vixen led Garm from one carriage to the other; jumped into the back seat and shouted. A cool breath from the snows met us about five miles out of Kalka, and she whined for her coat, wisely fearing a chill on the liver. I had had one made for Garm too, and, as we climbed to the fresh breezes, I put it on, and Garm chewed it uncomprehendingly, but I think he was grateful.

'Hi-yi-yi-yi!' sang Vixen as we shot around the curves; 'Toot-toot-toot!' went the driver's bugle at the dangerous places, and 'Yow! Yow! Yow! Yow!' bayed Garm. Kadir Buksh sat on the front seat and smiled. Even he was glad to get away from the heat of the Plains that stewed in the haze behind us. Now and then we would meet a man we knew going down to his work again, and he would say: 'What's it like below?' and I would shout: 'Hotter than cinders. What's it like above?' and he would shout back: 'Just perfect!' and away we would go.

Suddenly Kadir Buksh said, over his shoulder: 'Here is Solon'; and Garm snored where he lay with his head on my knee. Solon is an unpleasant little cantonment, but it has the advantage of being cool and healthy. It is all bare and windy, and one generally stops at a rest-house near by for something

58

to eat. I got out and took both dogs with me, while Kadir Buksh made tea. A soldier told us we should find Stanley 'out there', nodding his head towards a bare, bleak hill.

When we climbed to the top we spied that very Stanley, who had given me all this trouble, sitting on a rock with his face in his hands, and his overcoat hanging loose about him. I never saw anything so lonely and dejected in my life as this one little man, crumpled up and thinking, on the great grey hillside.

Here Garm left me.

He departed without a word, and, so far as I could see, without moving his legs. He flew through the air bodily, and I heard the whack of him as he flung himself at Stanley, knocking the little man clean over. They rolled on the ground together, shouting, and yelping, and hugging. I could not see which was dog and which was man, till Stanley got up and whimpered.

He told me that he had been suffering from fever at intervals, and was very weak. He looked all he said, but even while I watched, both man and dog plumped out to their natural sizes, precisely as dried apples swell in water. Garm was on his shoulder, and his breast and feet all at the same time, so that Stanley spoke all through a cloud of Garm – gulping, sobbing, slavering Garm. He did not say anything that I could understand, except that he had fancied he was going to die, but now he was quite well, and that he was not going to give up Garm any more to anybody under the rank of Beelzebub.

Then he said he felt hungry, and thirsty, and happy. We went down to tea at the rest-house, where Stanley stuffed himself with sardines and raspberry jam, and beer, and cold mutton and pickles, when Garm wasn't climbing over him; and then Vixen and I went on.

Garm saw how it was at once. He said good-bye to me three times, giving me both paws one after another, and leaping on to my shoulder. He further escorted us, singing Hosannas at the top of his voice, a mile down the road. Then he raced back to his own master.

Vixen never opened her mouth, but when the cold twilight came, and we could see the lights of Simla across the hills, she snuffled with her nose at the breast of my ulster. I unbuttoned it, and tucked her inside. Then she gave a contented little sniff, and fell fast asleep, her head on my breast, till we bundled out of Simla, two of the four happiest people in all the world that night.

RAY BRADBURY

THE EMISSARY

MARTIN KNEW IT was autumn again, for Dog ran into the house bringing wind and frost and a smell of apples turned to cider under trees. In dark clocksprings of hair, Dog fetched goldenrod, dust of farewell-summer, acorn-husk, hair of squirrel, feather of departed robin, sawdust from fresh-cut cordwood, and leaves like charcoals shaken from a blaze of maple trees. Dog jumped. Showers of brittle fern, black-berry vine, marsh grass sprang over the bed where Martin shouted. No doubt, no doubt of it at all, this incredible beast was October!

'Here, boy, here!'

And Dog settled to warm Martin's body with all the bon-fires and subtle burnings of the season, to fill the room with soft or heavy, wet or dry odors of far-traveling. In spring, he smelled of lilac, iris, lawn-mowered grass; in summer, ice-cream-mustached, he came pungent with firecracker, Roman candle, pinwheel, baked by the sun. But autumn! Autumn!

'Dog, what's it like outside?'

And lying there, Dog told as he always told. Lying there, Martin found autumn as in the old days before sickness bleached him white on his bed. Here was his contact, his carryall, the quick-moving part of himself he sent with a yell to run and return, circle and scent, collect and deliver the time and texture of worlds in town, country, by creek, river, lake, down-cellar, up-attic, in closet or coalbin. Ten dozen times a day he was gifted with sunflower seed, cinder-path, milkweed, horse chestnut, or full flame smell of pumpkin. Through the looming of the universe Dog shuttled; the design was hid in his pelt. Put out your hand, it was there. . . .

'And where did you go this morning?'

But he knew without hearing where Dog had rattled down hills where autumn lay in cereal crispness, where children lay in funeral pyres, in rustling heaps, the leaf-buried but watchful dead, as Dog and the world blew by. Martin trembled his fingers, searched the thick fur, read the long journey. Through stubbled fields, over glitters of ravine creek, down marbled spread of cemetery yard, into woods. In the great season of spices and rare incense, now Martin ran through his emissary, around, about, and home!

The bedroom door opened.

'That dog of yours is in trouble again.'

Mother brought in a tray of fruit salad, cocoa, and toast, her blue eyes snapping.

'Mother . . .'

'Always digging places. Dug a hole in Miss Tarkins's garden this morning. She's spittin' mad. That's the fourth hole he's dug there this week.'

'Maybe he's looking for something.'

'Fiddlesticks, he's too darned curious. If he doesn't behave he'll be locked up.'

Martin looked at this woman as if she were a stranger.

'Oh, you wouldn't do that! How would I learn anything? How would I find things out if Dog didn't tell me?'

Mom's voice was quieter. 'Is that what he does – tell you things?'

'There's nothing I don't know when he goes out and around and back, *nothing* I can't find out from him!'

They both sat looking at Dog and the dry strewings of mold and seed over the quilt.

'Well, if he'll just stop digging where he shouldn't, he can run all he wants,' said Mother.

'Here, boy, here!'

And Martin snapped a tin note to the dog's collar:

> MY OWNER IS MARTIN SMITH
> TEN YEARS OLD
> SICK IN BED
> VISITORS WELCOME.

Dog barked. Mother opened the downstairs door and let him out.

Martin sat listening.

Far off and away you could hear Dog run in the quiet autumn rain that was falling now. You could hear the barking-jingling fade, rise, fade again as he cut down alley, over lawn, to fetch back Mr Holloway and the oiled metallic smell of the delicate snowflake-interiored watches he repaired in his home shop. Or maybe he would bring Mr Jacobs, the grocer, whose clothes were rich with lettuce, celery, tomatoes, and the secret tinned and hidden smell of the red demons stamped on cans of deviled ham. Mr Jacobs and his unseen pink-meat devils waved often from the yard below. Or Dog brought Mr Jackson, Mrs Gillespie, Mr Smith, Mrs Holmes, *any* friend or near-friend, encountered, cornered, begged, worried, and at last shepherded home for lunch, or tea and biscuits.

Now, listening, Martin heard Dog below, with footsteps moving in a light rain behind him. The downstairs bell rang, Mom opened the door, light voices murmured. Martin sat forward, face shining. The stair treads creaked. A young woman's voice laughed quietly. Miss Haight, of course, his teacher from school!

The bedroom door sprang open.

Martin had company.

Morning, afternoon, evening, dawn and dusk, sun and moon circled with Dog, who faithfully reported temperatures of turf and air, color of earth and tree, consistency of mist or rain, but – most important of all – brought back again and again and again – Miss Haight.

On Saturday, Sunday, and Monday she baked Martin orange-iced cup-cakes, brought him library books about dinosaurs and cavemen. On Tuesday, Wednesday, and Thursday somehow he beat her at dominoes, somehow she lost at checkers, and soon, she cried, he'd defeat her handsomely at chess. On Friday, Saturday, and Sunday they talked and never stopped talking, and she was so young and laughing and handsome and her hair was a soft, shining brown like the season outside the window, and she walked clear, clean, and quick, a heartbeat warm in the bitter afternoon when he heard it. Above all, she had the secret of signs, and could read and interpret Dog and the symbols she searched out and plucked forth from his coat with her miraculous fingers. Eyes shut, softly laughing, in a gypsy's voice, she divined the world from the treasure in her hands.

And on Monday afternoon, Miss Haight was dead.

Martin sat up in bed, slowly.

'Dead?' he whispered.

Dead, said his mother, yes, dead, killed in an auto accident a mile out of town. Dead, yes, dead, which meant cold to Martin, which meant silence and whiteness and winter come long before its time. Dead, silent, cold, white. The thoughts circled round, blew down, and settled in whispers.

Martin held Dog, thinking; turned to the wall. The lady with the autumn-colored hair. The lady with the laughter that was very gentle and never made fun and the eyes that watched your mouth to see everything you ever said. The-other-half-of-autumn-lady, who told what was left untold by Dog, about the world. The heartbeat at the still center of gray afternoon. The heartbeat fading...

'Mom? What do they do in the graveyard, Mom, under the ground? Just lay there?'

'*Lie* there.'

'Lie there? Is that *all* they do? It doesn't sound like much fun.'

'For goodness' sake, it's not made out to be fun.'

'Why don't they jump up and run around once in a while if they get tired of lying there? God's pretty silly—'

'Martin!'

'Well, you'd think He'd treat people better than to tell them to lie still for keeps. That's impossible. Nobody can do it! I tried once. Dog tries. I tell him, "Dead Dog!" He plays dead awhile, then gets sick and tired and wags his tail or opens one eye and looks at me, bored. Boy, I bet sometimes those graveyard people do the same, huh, Dog?'

Dog barked.

'Be still with that kind of talk!' said Mother.

Martin looked off into space.

'Bet that's exactly what they do,' he said.

Autumn burned the trees bare and ran Dog still farther around, fording creek, prowling graveyard as was his custom, and back in the dusk to fire off volleys of barking that shook windows wherever he turned.

In the late last days of October, Dog began to act as if the wind had changed and blew from a strange country. He stood quivering on the porch below. He whined, his eyes fixed at the empty land beyond town. He brought no visitors for Martin. He stood for hours each day, as if leashed, trembling, then shot away straight, as if someone had called. Each night he returned later, with no one following. Each night, Martin sank deeper and deeper in his pillow.

'Well, people are busy,' said Mother. 'They haven't time to notice the tag Dog carries. Or they mean to come visit, but forget.'

But there was more to it than that. There was the fevered shining in Dog's eyes, and his whimpering tic late at night, in some private dream. His shivering in the dark, under the bed. The way he sometimes stood half the night, looking at Martin as if some great and impossible secret was his and he knew no way to tell it save by savagely thumping his tail, or turning in endless circles, never to lie down, spinning and spinning again.

On October 30, Dog ran out and didn't come back at all, even when after supper Martin heard his parents call and call. The hour grew late, the streets and sidewalks stood empty, the air moved cold about the house, and there was nothing, nothing.

Long after midnight, Martin lay watching the world beyond the cool, clear glass windows. Now there was not even autumn, for there was no Dog to fetch it in. There would be no winter, for who could bring the snow to melt in your hands? Father, Mother? No, not the same. They couldn't play the game with its special secrets and rules, its sounds and pantomimes. No more seasons. No more time. The go-between, the emissary, was lost to the wild throngings of civilization, poisoned, stolen, hit by a car, left somewhere in a culvert. . . .

Sobbing, Martin turned his face to his pillow. The world was a picture under glass, untouchable. The world was dead.

* * *

Martin twisted in bed and in three days the last Halloween pumpkins were rotting in trash cans, papier-mâché skulls and witches were burnt on bonfires, and ghosts were stacked on shelves with other linens until next year.

To Martin, Halloween had been nothing more than one evening when tin horns cried off in the cold autumn stars, children blew like goblin leaves along the flinty walks, flinging their heads, or cabbages, at porches, soap-writing names or similar magic symbols on icy windows. All of it as distant, unfathomable, and nightmarish as a puppet show seen from so many miles away that there is no sound or meaning.

For three days in November, Martin watched alternate light and shadow sift across his ceiling. The fire pageant was over forever; autumn lay in cold ashes. Martin sank deeper, yet deeper in white marble layers of bed, motionless, listening, always listening. . . .

Friday evening, his parents kissed him good night and walked out of the house into the hushed cathedral weather toward a motion-picture show. Miss Tarkins from next door stayed on in the parlor below until Martin called down he was sleepy, then took her knitting off home.

In silence, Martin lay following the great move of stars down a clear and moonlit sky, remembering nights such as this when he'd spanned the town with Dog ahead, behind, around about, tracking the green-plush ravine, lapping slumbrous streams gone milky with the fullness of the moon, leaping cemetery tombstones while whispering the marble names; on, quickly on, through shaved meadows where the only motion was the off-on quivering of stars, to streets where shadows would not stand aside for you but crowded all the sidewalks for mile on mile. Run, now, run! Chasing, being chased by bitter smoke, fog, mist, wind, ghost of mind, fright of memory; home, safe, sound, snug-warm, asleep. . . .

Nine o'clock.

Chime. The drowsy clock in the deep stairwell below. Chime.

Dog, come home, and run the world with you. Dog, bring a thistle with frost on it, or bring nothing else but the wind. Dog, where *are* you? Oh, listen now, I'll call.

Martin held his breath.

Way off somewhere – a sound.

Martin rose up, trembling.

There, again – the sound.

So small a sound, like a sharp needle-point brushing the sky long miles and many miles away.

The dreamy echo of a dog – barking.

The sounds of a dog crossing fields and farms, dirt roads and rabbit paths, running, running, letting out great barks of steam, cracking the night. The sound of a circling dog which came and went, lifted and faded, opened up, shut in, moved forward, went back, as if the animal were kept by someone on a fantastically long chain. As if the dog were running and someone whistled under the chestnut trees, in mold-shadow, tar-shadow, moon-shadow, walking, and the dog circled back and sprang out again toward home.

Dog! Martin thought. Oh, Dog, come home, boy! Listen, oh, listen, where have you *been*? Come on, boy, make tracks!

Five, ten, fifteen minutes; near, very near, the bark, the sound. Martin cried out, thrust his feet from the bed, leaned to the window. Dog! Listen, boy! Dog! Dog! He said it over and over. Dog! Dog! Wicked Dog, run off and gone all these days! Bad Dog, good Dog, home, boy, hurry, and bring what you can!

Near now, near, up the street, barking, to knock clapboard housefronts with sound, whirl iron cocks on rooftops in the moon, firing of volleys – Dog! now at the door below. . . .

70

Martin shivered.

Should he run – let Dog in, or wait for Mom and Dad? Wait? Oh, God, wait? But what if Dog ran off again? No, he'd go down, snatch the door wide, yell, grab Dog in, and run upstairs so fast, laughing, crying, holding tight, that . . .

Dog stopped barking.

Hey! Martin almost broke the window, jerking to it.

Silence. As if someone had told Dog to hush now, hush, hush.

A full minute passed. Martin clenched his fists.

Below, a faint whimpering.

Then, slowly, the downstairs front door opened. Someone was kind enough to have opened the door for Dog. Of course! Dog had brought Mr Jacobs or Mr Gillespie or Miss Tarkins, or . . .

The downstairs door shut.

Dog raced upstairs, whining, flung himself on the bed.

'Dog, Dog, where've you *been*, what've you *done*! Dog, Dog!'

And he crushed Dog hard and long to himself, weeping. Dog, Dog. He laughed and shouted. Dog! But after a moment he stopped laughing and crying, suddenly.

He pulled back away. He held the animal and looked at him, eyes widening.

The odor coming from Dog was different.

It was a smell of strange earth. It was a smell of night within night, the smell of digging down deep in shadow through earth that had lain cheek by jowl with things that were long hidden and decayed. A stinking and rancid soil fell away in clods of dissolution from Dog's muzzle and paws. He had dug deep. He had dug very deep indeed. That *was* it, wasn't it? Wasn't it? *Wasn't* it?

What kind of message was this from Dog? What could

such a message mean? The stench – the ripe and awful cemetery earth.

Dog was a very bad dog, digging where he shouldn't. Dog was a good dog, always making friends. Dog loved people. Dog brought them home.

And now, moving up the dark hall stairs, at intervals, came the sound of feet, one foot dragged after the other, painfully, slowly, slowly, slowly.

Dog shivered. A rain of strange night earth fell seething on the bed.

Dog turned.

The bedroom door whispered in.

Martin had company.

P. G. WODEHOUSE

THE MIXER

LOOKING BACK, I always consider that my career as a dog proper really started when I was bought for the sum of half a crown by the Shy Man. That event marked the end of my puppyhood. The knowledge that I was worth actual cash to somebody filled me with a sense of new responsibilities. It sobered me. Besides, it was only after that half-crown changed hands that I went out into the great world; and, however interesting life may be in an East End public-house, it is only when you go out into the world that you really broaden your mind and begin to see things.

Within its limitations, my life had been singularly full and vivid. I was born, as I say, in a public-house in the East End, and however lacking a public-house may be in refinement and the true culture, it certainly provides plenty of excitement. Before I was six weeks old, I had upset three policemen by getting between their legs when they came round to the sidedoor, thinking they had heard suspicious noises; and I can still recall the interesting sensation of being chased seventeen times round the yard with a broom-handle after a well-planned and completely successful raid on the larder. These and other happenings of a like nature soothed for the moment but could not cure the restlessness which has always been so marked a trait in my character. I have always been restless, unable to settle down in one place and anxious to get on to the next thing. This may be due to a gipsy strain in my ancestry – one of my uncles traveled with a circus –

or it may be the Artistic Temperament, acquired from a grandfather who, before dying of a surfeit of paste in the property-room of the Bristol Coliseum, which he was visiting in the course of a professional tour, had an established reputation on the music-hall stage as one of Professor Pond's Performing Poodles.

I owe the fullness and variety of my life to this restlessness of mine, for I have repeatedly left comfortable homes in order to follow some perfect stranger who looked as if he were on his way to somewhere interesting. Sometimes I think I must have cat blood in me.

The Shy Man came into our yard one afternoon in April, while I was sleeping with Mother in the sun on an old sweater which we had borrowed from Fred, one of the barmen. I heard Mother growl, but I didn't take any notice. Mother is what they call a good watch-dog, and she growls at everybody except Master. At first when she used to do it, I would get up and bark my head off, but not now. Life's too short to bark at everybody who comes into our yard. It is behind the public-house, and they keep empty bottles and things there, so people are always coming and going.

Besides, I was tired. I had had a very busy morning, helping the men bring in a lot of cases of beer and running into the saloon to talk to Fred and generally looking after things. So I was just dozing off again when I heard a voice say, 'Well, he's ugly enough.' Then I knew that they were talking about me.

I have never disguised it from myself, and nobody has ever disguised it from me, that I am not a handsome dog. Even Mother never thought me beautiful. She was no Gladys Cooper herself, but she never hesitated to criticize my appearance. In fact, I have yet to meet anyone who did. The first thing strangers say about me is 'What an ugly dog!'

I don't know what I am. I have a bull-dog kind of a face,

76

but the rest of me is terrier. I have a long tail which sticks straight up in the air. My hair is wiry. My eyes are brown. I am jet black with a white chest. I once overheard Fred saying that I was a Gorgonzola cheese-hound, and I have generally found Fred reliable in his statements.

When I found that I was under discussion, I opened my eyes. Master was standing there, looking down at me, and by his side the man who had just said I was ugly enough. The man was a thin man, about the age of a barman and smaller than a policeman. He had patched brown shoes and black trousers.

'But he's got a sweet nature,' said Master.

This was true, luckily for me. Mother always said, 'A dog without influence or private means, if he is to make his way in the world, must have either good looks or amiability.' But, according to her, I overdid it. 'A dog,' she used to say, 'can have a good heart without chumming with every Tom, Dick, and Harry he meets. Your behavior is sometimes quite undog-like.' Mother prided herself on being a one-man dog. She kept herself to herself, and wouldn't kiss anybody except Master – not even Fred.

Now, I'm a mixer. I can't help it. It's my nature. I like men. I like the taste of their boots, the smell of their legs, and the sound of their voices. It may be weak of me, but a man has only to speak to me, and a sort of thrill goes right down my spine and sets my tail wagging.

I wagged it now. The man looked at me rather distantly. He didn't pat me. I suspected – what I afterwards found to be the case – that he was shy, so I jumped up at him to put him at his ease. Mother growled again. I felt that she did not approve.

'Why, he's took quite a fancy to you already,' said Master.

The man didn't say a word. He seemed to be brooding on

something. He was one of those silent men. He reminded me of Joe, the old dog down the street at the grocer's shop, who lies at the door all day, blinking and not speaking to anybody.

Master began to talk about me. It surprised me, the way he praised me. I hadn't a suspicion he admired me so much. From what he said you would have thought I had won prizes and ribbons at the Crystal Palace. But the man didn't seem to be impressed. He kept on saying nothing.

When Master had finished telling him what a wonderful dog I was till I blushed, the man spoke.

'Less of it,' he said. 'Half a crown is my bid, and if he was an angel from on high you couldn't get another ha'penny out of me. What about it?'

A thrill went down my spine and out at my tail, for of course I saw now what was happening. The man wanted to buy me and take me away. I looked at Master hopefully.

'He's more like a son to me than a dog,' said Master, sort of wistful.

'It's his face that makes you feel that way,' said the man, unsympathetically. 'If you had a son that's just how he would look. Half a crown is my offer, and I'm in a hurry.'

'All right,' said Master, with a sigh, 'though it's giving him away, a valuable dog like that. Where's your half-crown?'

The man got a bit of rope and tied it round my neck.

I could hear Mother barking advice and telling me to be a credit to the family, but I was too excited to listen.

'Good-bye, Mother,' I said. 'Good-bye, Master. Good-bye, Fred. Good-bye, everybody. I'm off to see life. The Shy Man has bought me for half a crown. Wow!'

I kept running round in circles and shouting, till the man gave me a kick and told me to stop it.

So I did.

I don't know where we went, but it was a long way. I had never been off our street before in my life and didn't know the whole world was half as big as that. We walked on and on, and the man jerking at my rope whenever I wanted to stop and look at anything. He wouldn't even let me pass the time of the day with dogs we met.

When we had gone about a hundred miles and were just going to turn in at a dark doorway, a policeman suddenly stopped the man. I could feel by the way the man pulled at my rope and tried to hurry on that he didn't want to speak to the policeman. The more I saw of the man, the more I saw how shy he was.

'Hi!' said the policeman, and we had to stop.

'I've got a message for you, old pal,' said the policeman. 'It's from the Board of Health. They told me to tell you you needed a change of air. See?'

'All right!' said the man.

'And take it as soon as you like. Else you'll find you'll get it given you. See?'

I looked at the man with a good deal of respect. He was evidently someone very important, if they worried so about his health.

'I'm going down to the country tonight,' said the man.

The policeman seemed pleased.

'That's a bit of luck for the country,' he said. 'Don't go changing your mind.'

And we walked on, and went in at the dark doorway, and climbed about a million stairs, and went into a room that smelt of rats. The man sat down and swore a little, and I sat and looked at him.

Presently I couldn't keep it in any longer.

'Do we live here?' I said. 'Is it true we're going to the country? Wasn't that policeman a good sort? Don't you like policemen? I knew lots of policemen at the public-house. Are there any other dogs here? What is there for dinner? What's in that cupboard? When are you going to take me out for another run? May I go out and see if I can find a cat?'

'Stop that yelping,' he said.

'When we go to the country, where shall we live? Are you going to be a caretaker at a house? Fred's father is a caretaker at a big house in Kent. I've heard Fred talk about it. You didn't meet Fred when you came to the public-house, did you? You would like Fred. I like Fred. Mother likes Fred. We all like Fred.'

I was going on to tell him a lot more about Fred, who had always been one of my warmest friends, when he suddenly got hold of a stick and walloped me with it.

'You keep quiet when you're told,' he said.

He really was the shyest man I had ever met. It seemed to hurt him to be spoken to. However, he was the boss, and I had to humor him, so I didn't say any more.

We went down to the country that night, just as the man had told the policeman we would. I was all worked up, for I had heard so much about the country from Fred that I had always wanted to go there. Fred used to go off on a motor-bicycle sometimes to spend the night with his father in Kent, and once he brought back a squirrel with him, which I thought was for me to eat, but Mother said no. 'The first thing a dog has to learn,' Mother used often to say, 'is that the whole world wasn't created for him to eat.'

It was quite dark when we got to the country, but the man seemed to know where to go. He pulled at my rope, and we began to walk along a road with no people in it at all. We walked on and on, but it was all so new to me that I forgot how tired I was. I could feel my mind broadening with every step I took.

Every now and then we would pass a very big house which looked as if it was empty, but I knew that there was a caretaker inside, because of Fred's father. These big houses belong to very rich people, but they don't want to live in them till the summer so they put in caretakers, and the caretakers have a dog to keep off burglars. I wondered if that was what I had been brought here for.

'Are you going to be a caretaker?' I asked the man.

'Shut up,' he said.

So I shut up.

After we had been walking a long time, we came to a cottage. A man came out. My man seemed to know him, for he called him Bill. I was quite surprised to see the man was not at all shy with Bill. They seemed very friendly.

'Is that him?' said Bill, looking at me.

'Bought him this afternoon,' said the man.

'Well,' said Bill, 'he's ugly enough. He looks fierce. If you want a dog, he's the sort of dog you want. But what do you want one for? It seems to me it's a lot of trouble to take, when there's no need of any trouble at all. Why not do what I've always wanted to do? What's wrong with just fixing the dog, same as it's always done, and walking in and helping yourself?'

'I'll tell you what's wrong,' said the man. 'To start with, you can't get at the dog to fix him except by day, when they let him out. At night he's shut up inside the house. And suppose you do fix him during the day, what happens then? Either the bloke gets another before night, or else he sits up all night with a gun. It isn't like as if these blokes was ordinary blokes. They're down here to look after the house. That's their job, and they don't take any chances.'

It was the longest speech I had ever heard the man make, and it seemed to impress Bill. He was quite humble.

'I didn't think of that,' he said. 'We'd best start in to train this tyke at once.'

Mother often used to say, when I went on about wanting to go out into the world and see life, 'You'll be sorry when you do. The world isn't all bones and liver.' And I hadn't been living with the man and Bill in their cottage long before I found out how right she was.

It was the man's shyness that made all the trouble. It seemed as if he hated to be taken notice of.

It started on my very first night at the cottage. I had fallen asleep in the kitchen, tired out after all the excitement of the day and the long walks I had had, when something woke me with a start. It was somebody scratching at the window, trying to get in.

Well, I ask you, I ask any dog, what would you have done in my place? Ever since I was old enough to listen, Mother had told me over and over again what I must do in a case like this. It is the ABC of a dog's education. 'If you are in a room and you hear anyone trying to get in,' Mother used to say, 'bark. It may be some one who has business there, or it may not. Bark first, and inquire afterwards. Dogs were made to be heard and not seen.'

I lifted my head and yelled. I have a good, deep voice, due to a hound strain in my pedigree, and at the public-house, when there was a full moon, I have often had people leaning out of the windows and saying things all down the street. I took a deep breath and let it go.

'Man!' I shouted. 'Bill! Man! Come quick! Here's a burglar getting in!'

Then somebody struck a light, and it was the man himself. He had come in through the window.

He picked up a stick, and he walloped me. I couldn't understand it. I couldn't see where I had done the wrong

82

thing. But he was the boss, so there was nothing to be said.

If you'll believe me, that same thing happened every night. Every single night! And sometimes twice or three times before morning. And every time I would bark my loudest, and the man would strike a light and wallop me. The thing was baffling. I couldn't possibly have mistaken what Mother had said to me. She said it too often for that. Bark! Bark! Bark! It was the main plank of her whole system of education. And yet, here I was, getting walloped every night for doing it.

I thought it out till my head ached, and finally I got it right. I began to see that Mother's outlook was narrow. No doubt, living with a man like Master at the public-house, a man without a trace of shyness in his composition, barking was all right. But circumstances alter cases. I belonged to a man who was a mass of nerves, who got the jumps if you spoke to him. What I had to do was to forget the training I had had from Mother, sound as it no doubt was as a general thing, and to adapt myself to the needs of the particular man who had happened to buy me. I had tried Mother's way, and all it had brought me was walloping, so now I would think for myself.

So next night, when I heard the window go, I lay there without a word, though it went against all my better feelings. I didn't even growl. Someone came in and moved about in the dark, with a lantern, but, though I smelt that it was the man, I didn't ask him a single question. And presently the man lit a light and came over to me and gave me a pat, which was a thing he had never done before.

'Good dog!' he said. 'Now you can have this.'

And he let me lick out the saucepan in which the dinner had been cooked.

After that, we got on fine. Whenever I heard anyone at the window I just kept curled up and took no notice, and every time I got a bone or something good. It was easy, once you had got the hang of things.

It was about a week after that the man took me out one morning, and we walked a long way till we turned in at some big gates and went along a very smooth road till we came to a great house, standing all by itself in the middle of a whole lot of country. There was a big lawn in front of it, and all round there were fields and trees, and at the back a great wood.

The man rang a bell, and the door opened, and an old man came out.

'Well?' he said, not very cordially.

'I thought you might want to buy a good watch-dog,' said the man.

'Well, that's queer, your saying that,' said the caretaker. 'It's a coincidence. That's exactly what I do want to buy. I was just thinking of going along and trying to get one. My old dog picked up something this morning that he oughtn't to have, and he's dead, poor feller.'

'Poor feller,' said the man. 'Found an old bone with phosphorus on it, I guess.'

'What do you want for this one?'

'Five shillings.'

'Is he a good watch-dog?'

'He's a grand watch-dog.'

'He looks fierce enough.'

'Ah!'

So the caretaker gave the man his five shillings, and the man went off and left me.

At first the newness of everything and the unaccustomed smells and getting to know the caretaker, who was a nice old man, prevented my missing the man, but as the day went on and I began to realize that he had gone and would never come back, I got very depressed. I pattered all over the house, whining. It was a most interesting house, bigger than I thought a house could possibly be, but it couldn't cheer me up. You may think it strange that I should pine for the man, after all the wallopings he had given me, and it is odd, when you come to think of it. But dogs are dogs, and they are built like that. By the time it was evening I was thoroughly miserable. I found a shoe and an old clothes-brush in one of the rooms, but could eat nothing. I just sat and moped.

It's a funny thing, but it seems as if it always happened that just when you are feeling most miserable, something nice happens. As I sat there, there came from outside the sound of a motor-bicycle, and somebody shouted.

It was dear old Fred, my old pal Fred, the best old boy that ever stepped. I recognized his voice in a second, and I was scratching at the door before the old man had time to get up out of his chair.

Well, well, well! That was a pleasant surprise! I ran five times round the lawn without stopping, and then I came back and jumped up at him.

'What are you doing down here, Fred?' I said. 'Is this caretaker your father? Have you seen the rabbits in the wood? How long are you going to stop? How's Mother? I like the country. Have you come all the way from the public-house? I'm living here now. Your father gave five shillings for me. That's twice as much as I was worth when I saw you last.'

'Why, it's young Blackie!' That was what they called me at the saloon. 'What are you doing here? Where did you get this dog, Father?'

'A man sold him to me this morning. Poor old Bob got

poisoned. This one ought to be just as good a watch-dog. He barks loud enough.'

'He should be. His mother is the best watch-dog in London. This cheese-hound used to belong to the boss. Funny him getting down here.'

We went into the house and had supper. And after supper we sat and talked. Fred was only down for the night, he said, because the boss wanted him back next day.

'And I'd sooner have my job than yours, Dad,' he said. 'Of all the lonely places! I wonder you aren't scared of burglars.'

'I've got my shot-gun, and there's the dog. I might be scared if it wasn't for him, but he kind of gives me confidence. Old Bob was the same. Dogs are a comfort in the country.'

'Get many tramps here?'

'I've only seen one in two months, and that's the feller who sold me the dog here.'

As they were talking about the man, I asked Fred if he knew him. They might have met at the public-house, when the man was buying me from the boss.

'You would like him,' I said. 'I wish you could have met.'

They both looked at me.

'What's he growling at?' asked Fred. 'Think he heard something?'

The old man laughed.

'He wasn't growling. He was talking in his sleep. You're nervous, Fred. It comes from living in the city.'

'Well, I am. I like this place in the daytime, but it gives me the pip at night. It's so quiet. How you can stand it here all the time, I can't understand. Two nights of it would have me seeing things.'

His father laughed.

'If you feel like that, Fred, you had better take the gun to bed with you. I shall be quite happy without it.'

'I will,' said Fred. 'I'll take six if you've got them.'

And after that they went upstairs. I had a basket in the hall, which had belonged to Bob, the dog who had got poisoned. It was a comfortable basket, but I was so excited at having met Fred again that I couldn't sleep. Besides, there was a smell of mice somewhere, and I had to move around, trying to place it.

I was just sniffing at a place in the wall when I heard a scratching noise. At first I thought it was the mice working in a different place, but, when I listened, I found that the sound came from the window. Somebody was doing something to it from outside.

If it had been Mother, she would have lifted the roof off right there, and so should I, if it hadn't been for what the man had taught me. I didn't think it possible that this could be the man come back, for he had gone away and said nothing about ever seeing me again. But I didn't bark. I stopped where I was and listened. And presently the window came open, and somebody began to climb in.

I gave a good sniff, and I knew it was the man.

I was so delighted that for a moment I nearly forgot myself and shouted with joy, but I remembered in time how shy he was, and stopped myself. But I ran to him and jumped up quite quietly, and he told me to lie down. I was disappointed that he didn't seem more pleased to see me. I lay down.

It was very dark, but he had brought a lantern with him, and I could see him moving about the room, picking things up and putting them in a bag which he had brought with him. Every now and then he would stop and listen, and then he would start moving round again. He was very quick about it, but very quiet. It was plain that he didn't want Fred or his father to come down and find him.

I kept thinking about this peculiarity of his while I

watched him. I suppose, being chummy myself, I find it hard to understand that everybody else in the world isn't chummy too. Of course, my experience at the public-house had taught me that men are just as different from each other as dogs. If I chewed Master's shoe, for instance, he used to kick me, but if I chewed Fred's, Fred would tickle me under the ear. And, similarly, some men are shy and some men are mixers. I quite appreciated that, but I couldn't help feeling that the man carried shyness to a point where it became morbid. And he didn't give himself a chance to cure himself of it. That was the point. Imagine a man hating to meet people so much that he never visited their houses till the middle of the night, when they were in bed and asleep. It was silly. Shyness had always been something so outside my nature that I suppose I have never really been able to look at it sympathetically. I have always held the view that you can get over it if you make an effort. The trouble with the man was that he wouldn't make an effort. He went out of his way to avoid meeting people.

I was fond of the man. He was the sort of person you never get to know very well, but we had been together for quite a while, and I wouldn't have been a dog if I hadn't got attached to him.

As I sat and watched him creep about the room, it suddenly came to me that here was a chance of doing him a real good turn in spite of himself. Fred was upstairs, and Fred, as I knew by experience, was the easiest man to get along with in the world. Nobody could be shy with Fred. I felt that if only I could bring him and the man together, they would get along splendidly, and it would teach the man not to be silly and avoid people. It would help to give him the confidence which he needed. I had seen him with Bill, and I knew that he could be perfectly natural and easy when he liked.

It was true that the man might object at first, but after a while he would see that I had acted simply for his good, and would be grateful.

The difficulty was, how to get Fred down without scaring the man. I knew that if I shouted he wouldn't wait, but would be out of the window and away before Fred could get there. What I had to do was to go to Fred's room, explain the whole situation quietly to him, and ask him to come down and make himself pleasant.

The man was far too busy to pay any attention to me. He was kneeling in a corner with his back to me, putting something in his bag. I seized the opportunity to steal softly from the room.

Fred's door was shut, and I could hear him snoring. I scratched gently, and then harder, till I heard the snores stop. He got out of bed and opened the door.

'Don't make a noise,' I whispered. 'Come on downstairs. I want you to meet a friend of mine.'

At first he was quite peevish.

'What's the idea,' he said, 'coming and spoiling a man's beauty-sleep? Get out.'

He actually started to go back into the room.

'No, honestly, Fred,' I said, 'I'm not fooling you. There *is* a man downstairs. He got in through the window. I want you to meet him. He's very shy, and I think it will do him good to have a chat with you.'

'What are you whining about?' Fred began, and then he broke off suddenly and listened. We could both hear the man's footsteps as he moved about.

Fred jumped back into the room. He came out, carrying something. He didn't say any more but started to go downstairs, very quiet, and I went after him.

There was the man, still putting things in his bag. I was just going to introduce Fred, when Fred, the silly ass, gave a great yell.

I could have bitten him.

'What did you want to do that for, you chump?' I said. 'I told you he was shy. Now you've scared him.'

He certainly had. The man was out of the window quicker than you would have believed possible. He just flew out. I called after him that it was only Fred and me, but at that moment a gun went off with a tremendous bang, so he couldn't have heard me.

I was pretty sick about it. The whole thing had gone wrong. Fred seemed to have lost his head entirely. He was be-having like a perfect ass. Naturally the man had been fright-ened with him carrying on in that way. I jumped out of the window to see if I could find the man and explain, but he was gone. Fred jumped out after me, and nearly squashed me.

It was pitch dark out there. I couldn't see a thing. But I knew the man could not have gone far, or I should have heard him. I started to sniff round on the chance of picking up his trail. It wasn't long before I struck it.

Fred's father had come down now, and they were running about. The old man had a light. I followed the trail, and it ended at a large cedar tree, not far from the house. I stood underneath it and looked up, but of course I could not see anything.

'Are you up there?' I shouted. 'There's nothing to be scared at. It was only Fred. He's an old pal of mine. He works at the place where you bought me. His gun went off by accident. He won't hurt you.'

There wasn't a sound. I began to think I must have made a mistake.

'He's got away,' I heard Fred say to his father, and just as he said it I caught a faint sound of someone moving in the branches above me.

'No he hasn't!' I shouted. 'He's up this tree.'

'I believe the dog's found him, Dad!'

'Yes, he's up here. Come along and meet him.'

Fred came to the foot of the tree.

'You up there,' he said, 'come along down.'

Not a sound from the tree.

'It's all right,' I explained, 'he *is* up there, but he's very shy. Ask him again.'

'All right,' said Fred, 'stay there if you want to. But I'm going to shoot off this gun into the branches just for fun.'

And then the man started to come down. As soon as he touched the ground I jumped up at him.

'This is fine!' I said. 'Here's my friend Fred. You'll like him.'

But it wasn't any good. They didn't get along together at all. They hardly spoke. The man went into the house, and Fred went after him, carrying his gun. And when they got into the house it was just the same. The man sat in one chair, and Fred sat in another, and after a long time some men came in a motor-car, and the man went away with them. He didn't say good-bye to me.

When he had gone, Fred and his father made a great fuss of me. I couldn't understand it. Men are so odd. The man wasn't a bit pleased that I had brought him and Fred together, but Fred seemed as if he couldn't do enough for me having introduced him to the man. However, Fred's father produced some cold ham – my favorite dish – and gave me quite a lot of it, so I stopped worrying over the thing. As Mother used to say, 'Don't bother your head about what doesn't concern you. The only thing a dog need concern himself with is the bill of fare. Eat your bun, and don't make yourself busy about other people's affairs.' Mother's was in some ways a narrow outlook, but she had a great fund of sterling common sense.

PATRICIA HIGHSMITH

THERE I WAS, STUCK WITH BUBSY

YES, HERE HE WAS, stuck with Bubsy, a fate no living creature deserved. The Baron, aged sixteen – seventeen? – anyway aged, felt doomed to spend his last days with this plump, abhorrent beast whom the Baron had detested almost since he had appeared on the scene at least ten or twelve years ago. Doomed unless something happened. But what would happen, and what could the Baron make happen? The Baron racked his brain. People had said since he was a pup that his intelligence was extraordinary. The Baron took some comfort in that. It was a matter of strengthening Marion's hand, difficult for a dog to do, since the Baron didn't speak, though many a time his master Eddie had told him that he did speak. That was because Eddie had understood every bark and growl and glance that the Baron ever gave.

The Baron lay on a tufted polka-dot cushion which lined his basket. The basket had an arched top, and even this was lined with tufted polka-dot. From the next room, the Baron could hear laughter, jumbled voices, the *clink* of a glass or bottle now and then, and Bubsy's occasional 'Haw-ha-*haw*!' which in the days after Eddie's death had made the Baron's ears twitch with hostility. Now the Baron no longer reacted to Bubsy's guffaws. On the contrary the Baron affected a languor, an unconcern (better for his nerves), and now he yawned mightily, showing yellowed lower canines, then he settled his chin on his paws. He wanted to pee. He'd gone into the noisy living room ten minutes ago and indicated

95

to Bubsy by approaching the door of the apartment that he wanted to go out. But Bubsy had not troubled himself, though one of the young men (the Baron was almost sure) had offered to take him downstairs. The Baron got up suddenly. He couldn't wait any longer. He could of course pee straight on the carpet with a damn-it-all attitude, but he still had some decency left.

The Baron tried the living room again. Tonight there was more than usually a sprinkling of women.

'O-o-o-oh!'

'Ah-h–h! There's the Baron!'

'Ah, the Baron!' said Bubsy.

'He wants to go out, Bubsy, for Christ's sake! Where's his leash?'

'I've just had him out!' shrieked Bubsy, lying.

'When? This morning? . . .'

A young man in thick, fuzzy tweed trousers took the Baron down in the elevator. The Baron made for the first tree at the curb, and lifted a leg slightly. The young man talked to him in a friendly way, and said something about 'Eddie'. The name of his master made the Baron briefly sad, though he supposed it was nice of people, total strangers, to remember his master. They walked around the block. Near the delicatessen on Lexington Avenue, a man stopped them and in a polite tone asked a question with 'the Baron' in it.

'Yes,' said the young man who held the Baron's leash.

The strange man patted the Baron's head gently, and the Baron recognized his master's other name 'Brockhurst . . . Edward Brockhurst . . .'

They went on, back towards the awning of the apartment house, towards the awful party. Then the Baron's ears picked up a tread he knew, then his nose a scent he knew: Marion.

'Hello! Excuse me . . .' She was closer than the Baron had

supposed, because his ears were not what they used to be, nor his eyes for that matter. She talked with the young man, and they all rode up in the elevator.

The Baron's heart was pounding with pleasure. Marion smelled nice. Suddenly the whole evening was better, even wonderful, just because Marion had turned up. His master had always loved Marion. And the Baron was well aware that Marion wanted to take him away to live with her.

There was quite a change in the atmosphere when the Baron and the young man and Marion walked in. The conversation died down, and Bubsy walked forward with a glass of his favorite bubble in his hand, champagne. The young man undid the Baron's leash.

'Good evening, Bubsy . . .' Marion was speaking politely, explaining something.

Some people had said hello to Marion, others were starting up their conversation again in little groups. The Baron kept his eyes on Marion. Could it be possible that she was going to take him away *tonight*? She was talking about him. And Bubsy looked flustered. He motioned for Marion to come into one of the other rooms, Bubsy's bedroom, and the Baron followed at Marion's heels. Bubsy would have shut the Baron out, but Marion held the door.

'Come in, Baron!' Marion said.

The Baron disliked this room. The bed was high, made higher still by pillows, and at the foot of it was the contraption Bubsy used when he had his fits of wheezing and gasping, usually at night. There were two chromium tanks from which a rubber pipe came out, flexible metal pipes also, and the whole thing could be wheeled up to Bubsy's pillows.

'. . . friend . . . vacation . . .' Marion was saying. She was pleading with Bubsy. The Baron heard his name two or three times, Eddie's name once, and Bubsy looked at the Baron

97

with the angry, stubborn expression that the Baron knew well, knew since years, even when Eddie had been alive.

'Well, no . . .' Bubsy went on, making quite an elaborate speech.

Marion began again, not in the least discouraged.

Bubsy coughed, and his face darkened a little. He repeated his 'No . . . no . . .'

Marion dropped on her knees and looked into the Baron's eyes and talked to him. The Baron wagged his cropped tail. He trembled with joy, and could have flung his paws up on Marion's shoulders, but he didn't, because it was not the right thing to do. But his front paws kept dancing off the floor. He felt years younger.

Then Marion began talking about Eddie, and she grew angrier. She drew herself up a little when she talked about Eddie, as if he were something to be proud of, and it was evident to the Baron that she thought, she might even be saying, that Bubsy wasn't worth as much. The Baron knew that his master had been someone of importance. Strangers, coming to the house now and then, had treated Eddie as if he were their master, in a way, in those days when they had lived in another apartment, and Bubsy had served the drinks and cooked the meals like one of the servants on the ships the Baron had traveled on, or in the hotels where the Baron had stayed. Now suddenly Bubsy was claiming the Baron as his own dog. That was what it amounted to.

Bubsy kept saying 'No' in an increasingly firm voice. He walked towards the door.

Marion said something in a quietly threatening tone. The Baron wished very much that he knew exactly what she had said. The Baron followed her through the living room towards the front door. He was prepared to sneak out with her, leap out leashless, and just stay with her. Marion paused to talk with the young man in the fuzzy tweed trousers who had come up to her.

Bubsy interrupted them, waving his hands, wanting to put an end to the conversation.

Marion said, 'Good night . . . good night . . .'

The Baron squeezed out with her, loped in the hall towards the elevators. A man laughed, not Bubsy.

'Baron, you can't . . . darling,' said Marion.

Someone caught the Baron by the collar. The Baron growled, but he knew he couldn't win, that someone would give him a warning slap, if he didn't do what *they* wanted. Behind him, the Baron heard the awful *clunk* that meant the elevator door had closed on Marion, and she was gone. Some people groaned as the Baron crossed the living room, others laughed, as the din began again, louder and merrier than ever. The Baron made straight for his master's room which was across the hall from Bubsy's. The door was closed, but the Baron could open it by the horizontal handle, providing the door wasn't locked. The Baron couldn't manage the key, which stuck out below the handle, though he had often tried. Now the door opened. Bubsy had perhaps been showing the room to some of his guests tonight. The Baron went in and took a breath of the air that still smelled faintly of his master's pipe tobacco. On the big desk was his master's typewriter, now covered with a cloth of a sort of polka-dot pattern like the lining of his basket-bed in the spare room. The Baron was just as happy, even happier, sleeping on the carpet here near the desk, as he had often done when his master worked, but Bubsy, nastily, usually kept the door of his master's room locked.

The Baron curled up on the carpet and put his head down, his nose almost touching a leg of his master's chair. He sighed, suddenly worn out by the emotions of the last ten minutes. He thought of Marion, recalled happy mornings when Marion had come to visit, and his master and Bubsy had cooked bacon and eggs, or hotcakes, and they had all gone for a walk in Central Park. The Baron had used to retrieve sticks that Marion threw into a lake there. And he remembered an especially happy cruise, sunlight on the decks, with his master and Marion (pre-Bubsy days), when the Baron had been young and spry and handsome, popular with the passengers, pampered by the stewards who brought whole steaks to his and Eddie's cabin. The Baron remembered walks in a white-walled town full of white houses, with smells he had never known before or since ... And a boat ride with the boat tossing, and spray in his face, to an island where the streets were paved with cobblestones, where he got to know the whole island and roamed where he wished. He heard again his master's voice talking calmly to him, asking him a question ... The Baron heard the ghostly click of the typewriter ... Then he fell asleep.

He awakened to Bubsy's coughing, then his strained intake of air, with a wheeze. The house was quiet now. Bubsy was walking about in his room. The Baron got to his feet and shook himself to wake up. He went out of the room, so as not to be locked in for the rest of the night, walked towards the living room, but the smell of cigarette smoke turned him back. The Baron went into the kitchen, drank some water from his bowl, sniffed at the remains of some tinned dog food, and turned away, heading for the spare room. He could have eaten something – a bit of leftover steak, or a lambchop bone would have been nice. Lately, Bubsy dined out a lot, didn't take the Baron with him, and Bubsy fed him mostly from tins. Now his master would have put a stop to that! The Baron curled up in his basket.

Bubsy's machine was buzzing. Now and again it made a

click-click sound. Bubsy blew his nose – a sign he was feeling better.

Bubsy didn't go to work, didn't work at all in the sense that Eddie had worked several hours a day at his typewriter, in some periods every day of the week. Bubsy got up in midmorning, made tea and toast, and sat in his silk dressing gown reading the newspaper which was still delivered every morning at the door. It would be nearly noon before Bubsy took the Baron out for a walk. By this time Bubsy would have telephoned at least twice, and then he would go out for a long lunch, perhaps, or anyway he seldom came back before late afternoon. Bubsy had used to have something to do with the theater, just what the Baron didn't know. But when his master had met Bubsy, they had visited him a couple of times in the busy backstage part of a New York theater. Bubsy had been nicer then, the Baron could remember quite well, always ready to take him out for a walk, to brush his ears and the clump of curly black hair on the top of his head, because Bubsy had been proud to show him off on the street in those days. Yes, and the Baron had won a prize or two at Madison Square Garden in his prime, so many years ago. Oh, happy days! His two silver cups and two or three medals occupied a place of honor on a bookshelf in the living room, but the maid hadn't polished them in weeks now. Eddie had shown them sometimes to people who came to the apartment, and a couple of times, laughing, Eddie had served the Baron his morning biscuits and milk in one of the cups. The Baron recalled that at the moment there were no biscuits in the house.

Why did Bubsy hang on to him, if he didn't really like him? The Baron suspected it was because Bubsy was thus able to hang on to his master, who had been a more import-ant man – which meant loved and respected by a lot more people – than Bubsy. In the awful days during his master's illness, and after his death, the person the Baron had clung to was Marion, not Bubsy. The Baron thought that his master wished, probably had made it clear, that he wanted the Baron to live with Marion after he died. Bubsy had always been jealous of the Baron, and the Baron had to admit that he had been jealous of Bubsy. But whether he lived with Bubsy or Marion, that was what the fight was about. He was no fool. Marion and Bubsy had been fighting ever since Eddie's death.

Down on the street, a car rattled over a manhole. From Bubsy's room, the Baron heard wheezing inhalations. The machine was unplugged now. The Baron was thirsty; thought of getting up to drink again, then felt too tired, and merely flicked his tongue over his nose and closed his eyes. A tooth was hurting. Old age was a terrible thing. He'd had two wives, so long ago he scarcely remembered them. He'd had many children, maybe twelve, and the pictures of several of them were in the living room, and one on his master's desk – the Baron with three of his offspring.

The Baron woke up, growling, from a bad dream. He looked around, dazed, in the darkness. It had *happened*. No, it was a dream. But it had happened, yes. Just a few days ago. Bubsy had waked him from a nap, leash in hand, to take him out, and the Baron – maybe ill-tempered at that moment because he'd been awakened – had growled in an ominous way, not raising his head. And Bubsy had slowly retreated. And later that day, again with the leash in his hand, doubled, Bubsy had reminded the Baron of his bad behavior and slashed the air with the leash. The Baron had not winced, only watched Bubsy with a cool contempt. So they had stared at each other, and nothing had come of it, but Bubsy had been the first to move.

Would he be able to get anywhere by fighting? The Baron's old muscles grew tense at the thought. But he couldn't figure it out, couldn't see clearly into the future, and soon he was asleep again.

In the evening of that day, the Baron was surprised by a delicious meal of raw steak cut into convenient pieces, followed by a walk during which Bubsy talked to him in amiable tones. Then they got into a taxi. They rode quite a distance. Could they be going to Marion's apartment? Her apartment was a long way away, the Baron remembered from the days when Eddie had been alive. But Bubsy never went to Marion's house. Then when the taxi stopped and they got out, the Baron recognized the butcher's shop, still open, that smelled of spices as well as meat. They *were* at Marion's building! The Baron's tail began to wag. He lifted his head higher, and led Bubsy to the right door.

Bubsy pushed a bell, the door buzzed, then they went in and climbed three flights, the Baron pulling Bubsy up, panting, happy.

Marion opened the door. The Baron stood on his hind legs, careful not to scratch her dress with his nails, and Marion took his paws.

'Hello, Baron! Hel-*lo*, hello! – Come in!'

Marion's apartment had a high ceiling and smelled of oil paint and turpentine. There were big comfortable sofas and chairs which the Baron knew he was allowed to lie on if he wished to. Now there was a strange man who stood up from a chair as they went in. Marion introduced Bubsy to him, and they shook hands. The men talked. Marion went into the kitchen and poured a bowl of milk for the Baron, and gave him a steak bone which had been wrapped in wax paper in the refrigerator. Marion said something which the Baron took to mean, 'Make yourself at home. Chew the bone anywhere.'

The Baron chose to chew it at Marion's feet, once she had sat down in a chair.

The conversation grew more heated. Bubsy whipped some papers out of his pocket, and now he was on his feet, his face pinker, his thin blond curls tossing.

'There is not a *thing* . . . No . . . *No*.'

Bubsy's favorite word, 'No.'

'That is not the *point*,' Marion said.

Then the other man said something more calmly than either Marion or Bubsy. The Baron chewed on his bone, sparing the sore tooth. The strange man made quite a long speech, which Bubsy interrupted a couple of times, but Bubsy finally stopped talking and listened. Marion was very tense.

'No . . . ?'

'No . . . now . . .'

That was a word the Baron knew. He looked up at Marion, whose face was a little flushed also, but nothing like Bubsy's. Only the other man was calm. He had papers in his hand, too. What was going to happen *now*? The Baron associated the word with rather important commands to himself.

Bubsy spread his hands palm down and said, '*No*.' And many more words.

A very few minutes later, the Baron's leash was attached to his collar and he was dragged – gently but still dragged – towards the door by Bubsy. The Baron braced all four feet when he realized what was happening. He didn't want to go! He'd hardly begun to visit with Marion. The Baron looked over his shoulder and pled for her assistance. The strange man shook his head and lit a cigarette. Bubsy and Marion were talking to each other at the same time, almost shouting. Marion clenched her fists. But she opened one hand to pat the Baron, and said something kind to him before he was out in the hall, and the door shut.

Bubsy and the Baron crossed a wide street, and entered a bar. Loud music, awful smells, except for a whiff of freshly broiled steak. Bubsy drank, and twice muttered to himself.

Then he yanked the Baron into a taxi, yanked him because the Baron missed his footing and sprawled in an undignified way, banging his jaw on the floor of the taxi. Bubsy was in the foulest of moods. And the Baron's heart was pounding with several emotions: outrage, regret he had not spent longer with Marion, hatred of Bubsy. The Baron glanced at the windows (both nearly closed) as if he might jump out of one of them, though Bubsy had the leash wrapped twice around his wrist, and the buildings on either side flashed by at great speed. Bubsy let out the leash a little for the benefit of the doormen who always greeted the Baron by name. Bubsy was so out of breath, he could hardly speak to the doormen. The Baron knew he was suffering, but had no pity for him.

In the apartment, Bubsy at once flopped into a chair, mouth open. The Baron's leash trailed, and he walked dismally down the hall, hesitated at his master's door, then went in. He collapsed on the carpet by the chair. Back again. How brief had been his pleasure at Marion's! He heard Bubsy struggling to breathe, undressing in his room now – or at least removing his jacket and whipping off his tie. Then the Baron heard the machine being plugged in. *Buzz-zz* ... *Click-click*. The groan of a chair. Bubsy was doubtless in the chair by his bed, holding the mask over his face.

Thirsty, the Baron got up to go to the kitchen. His leash, the hand loop part of it, caught under the door and checked him. The Baron patiently entered the room again, pulled the leash out, and went out with his shoulder near the right door jamb so the same accident wouldn't happen again. It reminded him of nasty tricks Bubsy had used to play when the Baron had been younger. Of course the Baron had played a few tricks, too, tripping Bubsy adroitly while he (the Baron) had been ostensibly only cavorting after a ball. Now the Baron was so tired, his hind legs ached and he limped. Several teeth were hurting. He had chewed too enthusiastically on that bone. The Baron drank all his bowl – it was only half full and stale – then on leaving the kitchen, the Baron caught his leash in the same manner under the kitchen door. Bubsy just then lurched out of his room, coughing, heading for the bathroom, and stepped hard on the Baron's front paw. The Baron gave an agonized cry, because it had really hurt, nearly broken his toes!

Bubsy kicked at him and cursed.

The Baron – as if a mysterious spring had been released – leapt and sank his teeth through Bubsy's trousers into his lower leg.

Bubsy screamed, and swatted the Baron on the head with his fist. This made the Baron turn loose, and Bubsy kicked at him again, missing. Bubsy was gasping. The Baron watched Bubsy go into the bathroom, knowing he was going to get a wet towel for his face.

The Baron was suddenly full of energy. Where had it come from? He stood with forelegs apart, his aching teeth bared, trapped by his leash which was stuck under the kitchen door. When Bubsy emerged with the dripping towel clamped against his forehead, the Baron growled his deepest. Bubsy stumbled past him into his room, and the Baron heard him flop on the bed. Then the Baron went back into the kitchen slowly, so as not to make his leash predicament worse. The leather was tightly wedged this time, and there was not enough space, if the Baron moved towards the sink, to tug it out. The Baron caught the leash in his back teeth and pulled. The leash slipped through his teeth. He tried the other side of his jaw, and with one yank freed the leash. This was the worse side of his jaw, and the pain was awful. The Baron cringed on the floor, eyes shut for a moment, as he would never have cringed before Bubsy or anyone else. But pain was pain. Terrible. The Baron's very ears seemed to ring with his agony, but he didn't whine. He was remembering a similar pain inflicted by Bubsy. Or was that true? At any rate, the pain reminded him of Bubsy.

As the pain subsided, the Baron stood up, on guard against Bubsy who might come to life at any moment. The Baron carefully walked towards the living room, dragging his leash straight behind him, then turned so that he was facing the hall. He sank down and put his chin on his paws and waited, listening, his eyes wide open.

Bubsy coughed, the kind of cough that meant the mask was off and he was feeling better. Bubsy was getting up. He was going to come into the living room for some champagne, probably. The Baron's hind legs grew tense, and he really might have moved out of the way if not for a fear in the back of his mind that his leash would catch on something again. Bubsy approached coughing, pushing himself straight with a hand against a wall. Bubsy made a menacing gesture with his other hand, and ordered the Baron to get out of the way.

The Baron expected a foot in his face, and without thinking hurled himself at Bubsy's waistline and bit. Bubsy came down with a fist on the Baron's spine. They struggled on the floor, Bubsy hitting and missing most of his blows, the Baron snapping and missing also. But the Baron was still on the living room side, and Bubsy retreated towards his room, the Baron after him. Bubsy grabbed a vase, and hit the Baron on top of the head. The Baron's sight was knocked out, and he saw only silvery lights for a few seconds. As soon as his vision came back a little, he leapt for Bubsy whose legs now dangled over the side of the bed.

The Baron fell short, and his teeth clamped the rubber tube, not Bubsy's leg. The Baron bit and shook his head. The tube seemed as much Bubsy and Bubsy's own flesh. Bubsy loved that tube, depended on it, and the thick rubber was yielding slowly, just like flesh. Bubsy, with the mask over his face, kicked at the Baron, missing. Then the tube broke in two and the Baron slid to the floor.

Bubsy groped for the other end of the tube, started to put it in his mouth, but the end was frayed and full of holes. Bubsy gave it up, and lay back on the bed, panting like a dog himself. Blood was trickling through the hair above the Baron's eyes. The Baron staggered towards the door and turned, his tongue hanging out, his heartbeats shaking his body. The Baron lay down on the floor, and his eyes glazed over until he could hardly see the bed and Bubsy's legs over the side, but the Baron kept his eyes open. The minutes passed. The Baron's breathing grew easier. He listened, and he could not hear anything. Was Bubsy asleep?

The Baron half-slept, instinctively saving every bit of strength that he had left. The Baron heard no sound from Bubsy, and finally the hackles on the Baron's neck told him that he was in the presence of something dead.

At dawn, the Baron withdrew from the room, and like a very old dog, head hanging, legs wobbling, made his way to the living room. He lay on his side, more tired than ever. Soon the telephone began to ring. The Baron barely lifted his head at the first ring, then paid no more attention. The telephone stopped, then rang again. This happened several times. The top of the Baron's head throbbed.

The woman who cleaned the apartment twice a week

arrived in the afternoon – the Baron recognized her step in the hall – and rang the bell, although she had a key, the Baron knew. At the same time, another elevator opened its door, and some steps sounded in the hall, then voices. The apartment door opened, and the maid whose name was something like Lisa entered with two men friends of Bubsy's. They all seemed surprised to see the Baron standing in the living room with his leash on. They were shocked by the patch of blood on the carpet, and the Baron was reminded vaguely of the first months of his life, when he had made what his master called mistakes in the house.

'Bubsy!'

'Bubsy, are you here?'

They found Bubsy in the next seconds. One man rushed back into the living room and picked up the telephone. This man the Baron recognized as the one who had worn fuzzy trousers and had aired him at Bubsy's last party. No one paid any attention to the Baron, but when the Baron went into the kitchen, he saw that Lisa had put down some food for him and filled his water bowl. The Baron drank a little. Lisa undid his leash and said something kind to him. Another man arrived, a stranger. He went into Bubsy's bedroom. Then he looked at the Baron but didn't touch him, and he looked at the blood on the carpet. Then two men in white suits arrived and Bubsy was carried out, wrapped in a blanket, on a stretcher – just as his master had been carried out, the Baron recalled, but his master had been alive. Now the Baron felt no emotion at all on seeing Bubsy depart in the same manner. The young man made another telephone call. The Baron heard the name Marion, and his ears pricked up.

Then the man put the telephone down, and he smiled at the Baron in a funny way: it was not really a happy smile.

What was the man thinking of? He put the Baron's leash on. They went downstairs and took a taxi. Then they went into an office which the Baron knew at once was a vet's. The vet jabbed a needle into him. When the Baron woke up, he was lying on his side on a different table, and he tried to stand up, couldn't quite, and then he threw up the bit of water he had drunk. The friend of Bubsy's was still with him, and carried the Baron out, and they got into another taxi.

The Baron revived in the breeze through the window. The Baron took more interest as the ride went on and on. Could they possibly be going to Marion's?

They were! The taxi stopped. There was the butcher's shop again. And there was Marion on the sidewalk outside her door! The Baron wriggled from the man's arms and fell on the sidewalk outside the cab. Silly! Embarrassing! But the Baron got on his wobbly legs again, and was able to greet Marion with tail wagging, with a lick of her hand.

'Oh, Baron! Old Baron!' she said. And the Baron knew she was saying something reassuring about the cut on his head (now bandaged, the bandage going under his chin, too), which the Baron knew was not serious, was quite un-important compared to the fact that he was with Marion, that he was going to stay with Marion, the Baron somehow felt sure. Marion and the man were talking – and sure enough, the man was taking his leave. He patted the Baron on the shoulder and said, 'Bye-bye, Baron,' but in a tone that was merely polite. After all, he was more a friend of Bubsy's than the Baron's. The Baron lifted his head, gave a lick of his tongue towards the man's hand, and missed.

Then Marion and the Baron walked into the butcher's shop. The butcher smiled and shook the Baron's paw, and said something about his head. The butcher cut a steak for Marion.

Marion and the Baron climbed the stairs, Marion going slowly for the Baron's sake. She opened the door into the apartment with the high ceiling, with the sharp smell of turpentine that he had come to love. The Baron ate a bit of steak, and then had a sleep on one of the big sofas. He woke up and blinked his eyes. He'd just had a dream, a not so nice dream about Bubsy and a lot of noisy people, but he had already forgotten the dream. *This* was real: Marion standing at her worktable, glancing at him now because he had raised his head, but gazing back at her work – because for the moment she was thinking more about her work than about him. Like Eddie, the Baron thought. The Baron put his head down again and watched Marion. He was old, he knew, very old. People even marveled about how old he was. But he sensed that he was going to have a second life, that he even had a fair amount of time before him.

MARK TWAIN

A DOG'S TALE

I

MY FATHER WAS a St Bernard, my mother was a collie, but I am a Presbyterian. This is what my mother told me; I do not know these nice distinctions myself. To me they are only fine large words meaning nothing. My mother had a fondness for such; she liked to say them, and see other dogs look surprised and envious, as wondering how she got so much education. But, indeed, it was not real education; it was only show: she got the words by listening in the dining-room and drawing-room when there was company, and by going with the children to Sunday-school and listening there; and whenever she heard a large word she said it over to herself many times, and so was able to keep it until there was a dogmatic gathering in the neighborhood, then she would get it off, and surprise and distress them all, from pocket-pup to mastiff, which rewarded her for all her trouble. If there was a stranger he was nearly sure to be suspicious, and when he got his breath again he would ask her what it meant. And she always told him. He was never expecting this, but thought he would catch her; so when she told him, he was the one that looked ashamed, whereas he had thought it was going to be she. The others were always waiting for this, and glad of it and proud of her, for they knew what was going to happen, because they had had experience. When she told the meaning of a big word they were all so taken up with admiration that it never occurred to any dog to doubt if it was the right one; and that was natural, because, for one thing, she answered up so promptly that it seemed like a dictionary speaking, and for another thing, where could they find out whether it was right or not? for she was the only cultivated dog there was. By and by, when I was older, she brought home the word Unintellectual, one time, and worked it pretty hard all the week at different gatherings, making much unhappiness and despondency; and it was at this time that I noticed that during that week she was asked for the meaning at eight different assemblages, and flashed out a fresh definition every time, which showed me that she had more presence of mind than culture, though I said nothing, of course. She had one word which she always kept on hand, and ready, like a life-preserver, a kind of emergency word to strap on when she was likely to get washed overboard in a sudden way – that was the word Synonymous. When she happened to fetch out a long word which had had its day weeks before and its prepared meanings gone to her dump-pile, if there was a stranger there of course it knocked him groggy for a couple of minutes, then he would come to, and by that time she would be away down the wind on another tack, and not expecting anything; so when he'd hail and ask her to cash in, I (the only dog on the inside of her game) could see her canvas flicker a moment – but only just a moment – then it would belly out taut and full, and she would say, as calm as a summer's day, 'It's synonymous with supererogation,' or some godless long reptile of a word like that, and go placidly about and skim away on the next tack, perfectly comfortable, you know, and leave that stranger looking profane and embarrassed, and the initiated slatting the floor with their tails in unison and their faces transfigured with a holy joy.

And it was the same with phrases. She would drag home a whole phrase, if it had a grand sound, and play it six nights and two matinées, and explain it a new way every time – which she had to, for all she cared for was the phrase; she wasn't interested in what it meant, and knew those dogs hadn't wit enough to catch her, anyway. Yes, she was a daisy! She got so she wasn't afraid of anything, she had such confidence in the ignorance of those creatures. She even brought anecdotes that she had heard the family and the dinner-guests laugh and shout over; and as a rule she got the nub of one chestnut hitched onto another chestnut, where, of course, it didn't fit and hadn't any point; and when she delivered the nub she fell over and rolled on the floor and laughed and barked in the most insane way, while I could see that she was wondering to herself why it didn't seem as funny as it did when she first heard it. But no harm was done; the others rolled and barked too, privately ashamed of themselves for not seeing the point, and never suspecting that the fault was not with them and there wasn't any to see.

You can see by these things that she was of a rather vain and frivolous character; still, she had virtues, and enough to make up, I think. She had a kind heart and gentle ways, and never harbored resentments for injuries done her, but put them easily out of her mind and forgot them; and she taught her children her kindly way, and from her we learned also to be brave and prompt in time of danger, and not to run away, but face the peril that threatened friend or stranger, and help him the best we could without stopping to think what the cost might be to us. And she taught us not by words only, but by example, and that is the best way and the surest and the most lasting. Why, the brave things she did, the splendid things! she was just a soldier; and so modest about it – well, you couldn't help admiring her, and you couldn't help imitating her; not even a King Charles spaniel could remain entirely despicable in her society. So, as you see, there was more to her than her education.

II

When I was well grown, at last, I was sold and taken away, and I never saw her again. She was broken-hearted, and so was I, and we cried; but she comforted me as well as she could, and said we were sent into this world for a wise and good purpose, and must do our duties without repining, take our life as we might find it, live it for the best good of others, and never mind about the results; they were not our affair. She said men who did like this would have a noble and beautiful reward by and by in another world, and although we animals would not go there, to do well and right without reward would give to our brief lives a worthiness and dignity which in itself would be a reward. She had gathered these things from time to time when she had gone to the Sunday-school with the children, and had laid them up in her memory more carefully than she had done with those other words and phrases; and she had studied them deeply, for her good and ours. One may see by this that she had a wise and thoughtful head, for all there was so much lightness and vanity in it.

So we said our farewells, and looked our last upon each other through our tears; and the last thing she said – keeping it for the last to make me remember it the better, I think – was, 'In memory of me, when there is a time of danger to another do not think of yourself, think of your mother, and do as she would do.'

Do you think I could forget that? No.

III

It was such a charming home! – my new one; a fine great house, with pictures, and delicate decorations, and rich furniture, and no gloom anywhere, but all the wilderness of dainty colors lit up with flooding sunshine; and the spacious grounds around it, and the great garden – oh, greensward, and noble trees, and flowers, no end! And I was the same as a member of the family; and they loved me, and petted me, and did not give me a new name, but called me by my old one that was dear to me because my mother had given it me – Aileen Mavourneen. She got it out of a song; and the Grays knew that song, and said it was a beautiful name.

Mrs Gray was thirty, and so sweet and so lovely, you cannot imagine it; and Sadie was ten, and just like her mother, just a darling slender little copy of her, with auburn tails down her back, and short frocks; and the baby was a year old, and plump and dimpled, and fond of me, and never could get enough of hauling on my tail, and hugging me, and laughing out its innocent happiness; and Mr Gray was thirty-eight, and tall and slender and handsome, a little bald in front, alert, quick in his movements, businesslike, prompt, decided, unsentimental, and with that kind of trim-chiseled face that just seems to glint and sparkle with frosty intellectuality! He was a renowned scientist. I do not know what the word means, but my mother would know how to use it and get effects. She would know how to depress a rat-terrier with it and make a lap-dog look sorry he came. But that is not the best one; the best one was Laboratory. My mother could organize a Trust on that one that would skin the tax-collars off the whole herd. The laboratory was not a book, or a picture, or a place to wash your hands in, as the college president's dog said – no, that is the lavatory; the laboratory is quite different, and is filled with jars, and bottles, and electrics, and wires, and strange machines; and every week other scientists came there and sat in the place, and used the machines, and discussed, and made what they called experiments and discoveries; and often I came, too, and stood around and listened, and tried to learn, for the sake of my mother, and in loving memory of her, although it was a pain to me, as realizing what she was losing out of her life and I gaining nothing at all; for try as I might, I was never able to make anything out of it at all.

Other times I lay on the floor in the mistress's work-room and slept, she gently using me for a foot-stool, knowing it pleased me, for it was a caress; other times I spent an hour in the nursery, and got well tousled and made happy; other times I watched by the crib there, when the baby was asleep and the nurse out for a few minutes on the baby's affairs; other times I romped and raced through the grounds and the garden with Sadie till we were tired out, then slumbered on the grass in the shade of a tree while she read her book; other times I went visiting among the neighbor dogs – for there were some most pleasant ones not far away, and one very handsome and courteous and graceful one, a curly-haired Irish setter by the name of Robin Adair, who was a Presbyterian like me, and belonged to the Scotch minister.

The servants in our house were all kind to me and were fond of me, and so, as you see, mine was a pleasant life. There could not be a happier dog than I was, nor a gratefuler one. I will say this for myself, for it is only the truth: I tried in all ways to do well and right, and honor my mother's memory and her teachings, and earn the happiness that had come to me, as best I could.

By and by came my little puppy, and then my cup was full, my happiness was perfect. It was the dearest little waddling thing, and so smooth and soft and velvety, and had such cunning little awkward paws, and such affectionate eyes, and such a sweet and innocent face; and it made me so proud to see how the children and their mother adored it, and fondled it, and exclaimed over every little wonderful thing it did. It did seem to me that life was just too lovely to—

Then came the winter. One day I was standing a watch in the nursery. That is to say, I was asleep on the bed. The baby was asleep in the crib, which was alongside the bed, on the side next the fireplace. It was the kind of crib that has a lofty tent over it made of a gauzy stuff that you can see through. The nurse was out, and we two sleepers were alone. A spark from the wood-fire was shot out, and it lit on the slope of the tent. I supposed a quiet interval followed, then a scream from the baby woke me, and there was that tent flaming up toward the ceiling! Before I could think, I sprang to the floor in my fright, and in a second was half-way to the door; but in the next half-second my mother's farewell was sounding in my ears, and I was back on the bed again. I reached my head through the flames and dragged the baby out by the waistband, and tugged it along, and we fell to the floor together in a cloud of smoke; I snatched a new hold, and dragged the screaming little creature along and out at the door and around the bend of the hall, and was still tugging away, all excited and happy and proud, when the master's voice shouted:

'Begone, you cursed beast!' and I jumped to save myself; but he was wonderfully quick, and chased me up, striking furiously at me with his cane, I dodging this way and that, in terror, and at last a strong blow fell upon my left foreleg, which made me shriek and fall, for the moment, helpless; the cane went up for another blow, but never descended, for the nurse's voice rang wildly out, 'The nursery's on fire!' and the master rushed away in that direction, and my other bones were saved.

The pain was cruel, but, no matter, I must not lose any time; he might come back at any moment; so I limped on three legs to the other end of the hall, where there was a dark little stairway leading up into a garret where old boxes and such things were kept, as I had heard say, and where people seldom went. I managed to climb up there, then I searched my way through the dark among the piles of things, and hid in the secretest place I could find. It was foolish to be afraid there, yet still I was; so afraid that I held in and hardly even whimpered, though it would have been such a comfort to whimper, because that eases the pain, you know. But I could lick my leg, and that did me some good.

For half an hour there was a commotion downstairs, and shoutings, and rushing footsteps, and then there was quiet again. Quiet for some minutes, and that was grateful to my spirit, for then my fears began to go down; and fears are worse than pains – oh, much worse. Then came a sound that froze me. They were calling me – calling me by names – hunting for me!

It was muffled by distance, but that could not take the terror out of it, and it was the most dreadful sound to me that I had ever heard. It went all about, everywhere, down there: along the halls, through all the rooms, in both stories, and in the basement and the cellar; then outside, and farther and farther away – then back, and all about the house again, and I thought it would never, never stop. But at last it did, hours and hours after the vague twilight of the garret had long ago been blotted out by black darkness.

Then in that blessed stillness my terrors fell little by little away, and I was at peace and slept. It was a good rest I had, but I woke before the twilight had come again. I was feeling fairly comfortable, and I could think out a plan now. I made a very good one; which was, to creep down, all the way down the back stairs, and hide behind the cellar door, and slip out and escape when the iceman came at dawn, while he was inside filling the refrigerator; then I would hide all day, and start on my journey when night came; my journey to – well, anywhere where they would not know me and betray me to the master. I was feeling almost cheerful now; then suddenly I thought: Why, what would life be without my puppy!

That was despair. There was no plan for me; I saw that; I must stay where I was; stay, and wait, and take what might come – it was not my affair; that was what life is – my mother had said it. Then – well, then the calling began again! All my sorrows came back. I said to myself, the master will never forgive. I did not know what I had done to make him so bitter and so unforgiving, yet I judged it was something a dog could not understand, but which was clear to a man and dreadful.

They called and called – days and nights, it seemed to me. So long that the hunger and thirst near drove me mad, and I recognized that I was getting very weak. When you are this way you sleep a great deal, and I did. Once I woke in an awful fright – it seemed to me that the calling was right there in the garret! And so it was; it was Sadie's voice, and she was crying; my name was falling from her lips all broken, poor thing, and I could not believe my ears for the joy of it when I heard her say:

'Come back to us – oh, come back to us, and forgive – it is all so sad without our—'

I broke in with *such* a grateful little yelp, and the next moment Sadie was plunging and stumbling through the darkness and the lumber and shouting for the family to hear, 'She's found, she's found!'

The days that followed – well, they were wonderful. The mother and Sadie and the servants – why, they just seemed to worship me. They couldn't seem to make me a bed that was fine enough; and as for food, they couldn't be satisfied with anything but game and delicacies that were out of season; and every day the friends and neighbors flocked in to hear about my heroism – that was the name they called it by, and it means agriculture. I remember my mother pulling it on a kennel once, and explaining it that way, but didn't say what agriculture was, except that it was synonymous with intramural incandescence; and a dozen times a day Mrs Gray and Sadie would tell the tale to newcomers, and say I risked my life to save the baby's, and both of us had burns to prove it, and then the company would pass me around and pet me and exclaim about me, and you could see the pride in the eyes of Sadie and her mother; and when the people wanted to know what made me limp, they looked ashamed and changed the subject, and sometimes when people hunted them this way and that way with questions about it, it looked to me as if they were going to cry.

And this was not all the glory; no, the master's friends came, a whole twenty of the most distinguished people, and had me in the laboratory, and discussed me as if I was a kind of discovery; and some of them said it was wonderful in a dumb beast, the finest exhibition of instinct they could call to mind; but the master said, with vehemence, 'It's far above instinct; it's *reason*, and many a man, privileged to be saved and go with you and me to a better world by right of its possession, has less of it than this poor silly quadruped that's foreordained to perish'; and then he laughed, and said: 'Why, look at me – I'm a sarcasm! bless you, with all my grand intelligence, the only thing I inferred was that the dog had gone mad and was destroying the child, whereas but for the beast's intelligence – its *reason*, I tell you! – the child would have perished!'

They disputed and disputed, and *I* was the very center and subject of it all, and I wished my mother could know that this grand honor had come to me; it would have made her proud.

Then they discussed optics, as they called it, and whether a certain injury to the brain would produce blindness or not, but they could not agree about it, and said they must test it by experiment by and by; and next they discussed plants, and that interested me, because in the summer Sadie and I had planted seed – I helped her dig the holes, you know – and after days and days a little shrub or a flower came up there, and it was a wonder how that could happen; but it did, and I wished I could talk – I would have told those people about it and shown them how much I knew, and been all alive with the subject; but I didn't care for the optics; it was dull, and when they came back to it again it bored me, and I went to sleep.

Pretty soon it was spring, and sunny and pleasant and lovely, and the sweet mother and the children patted me and the puppy good-by, and went away on a journey and a visit to their kin, and the master wasn't any company for us, but we played together and had good times, and the servants were kind and friendly, so we got along quite happily and counted the days and waited for the family.

And one day those men came again, and said, now for the test, and they took the puppy to the laboratory, and I limped three-leggedly along, too, feeling proud, for any attention shown the puppy was a pleasure to me, of course. They discussed and experimented, and then suddenly the puppy shrieked, and they set him on the floor, and he went staggering around, with his head all bloody, and the master clapped his hands and shouted:

'There, I've won – confess it! He's as blind as a bat!'

And they all said:

'It's so – you've proved your theory, and suffering humanity owes you a great debt from henceforth,' and they crowded around him, and wrung his hand cordially and thankfully, and praised him.

But I hardly saw or heard these things, for I ran at once to my little darling, and snuggled close to it where it lay, and licked the blood, and it put its head against mine, whimpering softly, and I knew in my heart it was a comfort to it in its pain and trouble to feel its mother's touch, though it could not see me. Then it dropped down, presently, and its little velvet nose rested upon the floor, and it was still, and did not move any more.

Soon the master stopped discussing a moment, and rang in the footman, and said, 'Bury it in the far corner of the garden,' and then went on with the discussion, and I trotted after the footman, very happy and grateful, for I knew the puppy was out of its pain now, because it was asleep. We went far down the garden to the farthest end, where the children and the nurse and the puppy and I used to play in the summer in the shade of a great elm, and there the footman dug a hole, and I saw he was going to plant the puppy, and I was glad, because it would grow and come up a fine handsome dog, like Robin Adair, and be a beautiful surprise for the family when they came home; so I tried to help him dig, but my lame leg was no good, being stiff, you know, and you have to have two, or it is no use. When the footman had finished and covered little Robin up, he patted my head, and there were tears in his eyes, and he said: 'Poor little doggie, you SAVED *his* child.'

I have watched two whole weeks, and he doesn't come up! This last week a fright has been stealing upon me. I think there is something terrible about this. I do not know what it is, but the fear makes me sick, and I cannot eat, though the servants bring me the best of food; and they pet me so, and even come in the night, and cry, and say, 'Poor doggie – do give it up and come home; *don't* break our hearts!' and all this terrifies me the more, and makes me sure something has happened. And I am so weak; since yesterday I cannot stand on my feet any more. And within this hour the servants, looking toward the sun where it was sinking out of sight and the night chill coming on, said things I could not understand but they carried something cold to my heart.

'Those poor creatures! They do not suspect. They will come home in the morning, and eagerly ask for the little doggie that did the brave deed, and who of us will be strong enough to say the truth to them: "The humble little friend is gone where go the beasts that perish." '

JAMES THURBER

JOSEPHINE HAS HER DAY

THE DICKINSONS' PUP was a failure. A bull-terrier, a female, and a failure. With all of life before her, she had suddenly gone into a decline.

'She is pining away,' said Dick, 'like a mid-Victorian lady whose cavalier rode off and never came back.'

'No,' said Ellen, 'there's nothing romantic about her. She looks like a servant girl who has been caught stealing a bar pin.'

The failure, which was spiritual as well as physical, was unaccountable. Three weeks before, the pup had been bright and waggly and rotund. Ellen, discovering it in a bird store yapping at the virulent green tail of an indignant lady parrot, had called it not only a little plum-plum, but also a little umpsy-dumpsy.

Thus one thing had led to another, including moment-ary forgetfulness of their original intention to buy a Scotch-terrier, mitigation of the crime being a female and a bull-terrier, and eventual purchase of the puppy. And now here she had been shipped to their summer cottage in the Adiron-dacks, covered with gloom and sulphur, the shadow of her former self. They sat above her, the first hour of her arrival, in grim judgment.

'Maybe she's just growing,' said Dick hopefully.

'An idiot could see she's shrinking,' said Ellen. 'Of course, you would have a bull-terrier.'

'I don't think it is a bull-terrier, now,' said Dick.

'Well, it *was* a bull-terrier. And a female, too! What ever possessed us!'

'You called her a little plum-plum,' murmured Dick.

'And you bought her,' retorted Ellen. 'Well, she'll have to be fed, I suppose. There wasn't a thing to eat in that shipping box.' She swooped up the little dog. Now that it was so thin and its excess skin so wrinkly, a curious black edging around its eyes and jaw completed an effect of the most profound melancholy.

The puppy gave only two depressed laps at the milk-soaked bread placed before her, and then wobbled over to the stove in the sitting room, revolved uncertainly three times, and closed her eyes with a pessimistic sigh.

'Well, sir, she's a nice doggy,' said Dick generously, starting over to her, 'yes, sir, she's a nice doggy.' But his wife intervened.

'Mustn't do that,' she warned. 'It says in the puppy book not to disturb them at their normal sleeping hours.' Mrs Dickinson had bought a lovely puppy book, illustrated with pictures of bright and waggly puppies.

When they went to bed the puppy was sleeping soundly on a bed they fixed for it in a corner of the kitchen, apparently glad to rest after the long, jolting ride. This gladness, however, did not carry her through the night. When the stars were still bright the Dickinsons were aroused from sleep by a clamorous yelping, a wonderfully able and lusty yelping for such a despondent puppy.

'Good Lord!' groaned Dickinson. 'Now what?'

'They are bound to yelp the first few nights,' said his wife, sleepily.

'Doesn't it say anything in the book about their not disturbing us at our normal sleeping hours?' demanded Dickinson. 'Can't I go out and shut her up, do you suppose?'

'No. It would encourage her to expect a response every time she howled, and if you humor them that way they would soon get the upper hand.'

'Well, if she keeps this up she'll get it anyway,' grumbled Dick as he stuffed the ends of his pillow into his ears. 'The National Association of Puppies probably hired the man to write that book.'

The next morning at his typewriter Dickinson felt his mind being drawn, slowly but relentlessly, away from the necessary concentration on his work. Something was striking into his brain like the measured thud of a distant drum. 'Come . . . come . . . come.'

It was his wife's voice emerging from the 'secluded room'. Gradually a note of exasperation crept in. It was followed by the sound of a slight scratching body being dragged across the floor. There were more 'comes', a silence, and more scratching. Then very insistent 'comes', but no scratching.

'Is she dead, dear?' called out Dick hopefully.

His wife came into the room, carrying the pessimistic-looking puppy, still saffron with the sulphur that, Dick hazarded, had been showered upon her in the interest of 'bug prevention'.

'She seems listless,' said Mrs Dickinson. 'Do you suppose she was the runt of a litter? The book says to avoid the runts.'

'Napoleon was a runt,' observed Dick sagely.

'But not of a litter,' responded his wife.

'By golly,' exclaimed Dick suddenly. 'I've got a name for her, anyway! We'll call her Josephine!'

'Josephine?'

'Yes. After the wife of Napoleon, the famous runt. She started well, but got sort of "down and out".'

Mrs Dickinson dropped wearily into a chair and put the puppy on the floor. 'Well, I've tried to make this thing come to me all morning, and she just sits and studies the floor with that darned frown.'

'Maybe she just doesn't want to come,' said Dick.

'That's no reason why she shouldn't. The book says it is almost certain – wait a minute, I'll read it to you.' She opened the puppy book which she carried in one hand. 'Here: "It is almost certain that you will be unexpectedly delighted during the very first lesson by their sudden scampering comprehension and that you will perceive they accept your word as law."'

They watched the little dog study the carpet with incurious attention.

'Lawless little beast,' mused Dick. 'Look out if she begins to trace the design of the carpet with her paw. It's a sure sign of the end.'

'No such luck,' said Ellen with some bitterness.

Dick leaned down nearer the puppy. 'Josephine!' he cried loudly but firmly. The puppy looked up at him as a little old lady on a train, constantly afraid of being carried past her station, might look at her carefree traveling companions. 'She knows her name, anyway, and if she didn't have this awful thing on her mind she might scamper with comprehension, or whatever it is they do.'

'Oh, I don't think she has any mind,' cried Mrs Dickinson, irritably. 'But there – the book says that calmness, toleration, and self-control are essential in training a puppy.'

'That book certainly says a lot for such a little book,' commented Dick.

'And for such a little puppy,' said his wife scornfully, as she picked up Josephine and carried her outdoors.

As the days went on, Josephine seemed to have taken the stigma of runt literally, as a thing to be religiously lived up to.

She remained undeveloped physically and, Mrs Dickinson declared, mentally, too. She declined, with stolid indifference, in her lesson hour, to adhere to any of the rules of the puppy book. The gay enterprise of 'fetch' seemed to create in her no emotion save perhaps a vague wonder as to why the bit of rolled-up paper was tossed about so often.

At length came a cold, drizzly Monday when the Dickinsons gave up. They had had the empress more than three weeks, and her favorite occupation was to sit near the stove, frowning dejectedly and quivering. Once she turned over a cold wood ash with her paw. But that was all.

'Let's give her away to some family around here,' said Dick, finally. 'They all have lots of kids who would be crazy to have her.'

'Yes, and they all have lots of dogs,' said Ellen, 'big, virile, happy dogs. Besides, no one wants anything but a hound dog, a hunter, in this country.'

'I still think we might find some family that would take her. Someone's dog may have died.'

'Everybody has two or three dogs. They wouldn't all die.'

'They might,' said Dick, hopefully. 'They might have been playing with the shotgun, not knowing it was loaded.'

'Nobody would look at a runt, a female whatnot. They would laugh just to see us walking along with her.'

'We won't walk – we'll hire the Blanchards' flivver and tour around hunting a home for her,' said Dick, enlarging on his plan.

So the next morning, which dawned with a promising sun, they started off with Josephine, the condemned puppy that wouldn't grow and wouldn't learn, shivering and frowning at the wind in dismay. Every house they passed for several miles had a hound dog, or two or three, big-pawed, long-eared creatures, nosing about the grounds. At last, however, when they tried their luck on a dirt byroad, they saw a small brown house hanging on a hillside, from whose environs came no mournful baying.

Dick stopped the car a little way down the road, bundled the puppy in his arms and got out. There he paused. The bright sun had been overcome by one of those rapidly driving caravans of dark clouds that ride the ranges of the north in the springtime. It began to rain. Dick put up his coat collar.

'Why shall I say we don't want her?' he asked his wife.

'Oh, just act bighearted,' she laughed cheerily. 'They might think you are Santa Claus.'

But Dick's confidence in his own scheme melted rapidly in the rain as he carried the distressed and quivering puppy toward the front gate of the silent, weathered house. As he reached the slate-colored mail box, which winds and rain had beaten to a dejected slant, the puppy began to behave in a singular fashion. Her insides, as Dick described it later, began to go up and down. He turned and carried Josephine quickly back to Mrs Dickinson.

'She's dying,' he said, handing her to his wife.

'Hiccups, silly,' said Ellen. 'She'll get over them. It's nothing.'

'No decent family would want a dog with hiccups,' said Dick, firmly.

So they decided to wait until the paroxysms were over. This meant an unusually long wait. Josephine proved to be an accomplished hiccuper. If an interval was so protracted as to give hope of cessation, the next hiccup was so violent as to threaten indefinite continuance. At length Dick knocked the ashes from his pipe determinedly, got out of the car and lifted Josephine down after him. He set her in the road. Then suddenly he leaped at her and barked.

The puppy plunged down into the ditch by the roadside, her ears flatly inside out in abject terror. Dick hurried after her and retrieved a very wet and very muddy Josephine.

'Have you lost your mind?' exclaimed his wife. But Dickinson held up Josephine and examined her carefully. There were no more hiccups.

'By golly,' he said, 'these home remedies are the goods.'

He started for the house again, briskly, the dog under his arm. After a long time the door on which he gingerly knocked opened just wide enough to frame the hard, spare face of a woman.

'Well, what do you want?' she growled ominously. Josephine growled ominously, too.

'I – us –' began Dick. 'That is ... er ... a ... can you tell me how far it is to Dale?'

Dale was the town on the outskirts of which the Dickinsons lived, the town from which they had just come. The woman jerked her thumb.

'Two mile,' she grunted.

Josephine growled. The woman slammed the door. Dick walked back to his wife.

'She said her husband won't have a dog about the place,' he told her. 'Seems his father was bitten by one and the boys all inherited this dread.'

The kind-faced lady who came to the door of the next place lifted her hands in polite refusal. Land! she already had two dogs! And Rex had a sore on his leg. Did the gentleman know what to do for sores on the leg? Dick said proudly that Josephine never had sores on the leg. 'Maybe Eli Madden, the storekeeper in Dale, would take it,' added the lady after a moment. 'His dog was gored by a bull a week back – well, no – two weeks come Monday. You might try there. Sometimes we think Rex was bit by a woodchuck.' Dick said

137

Josephine had never been bitten by a woodchuck, and thanked the lady.

They whirled back over the road to Madden's place, which was not far from their cottage. It happened that school was letting out and the streets were filled with children. They seemed suddenly with economy of movement to surround the Dickinsons as they got out of the car and put Josephine on the ground to stretch. She studied the insurmountable problem of dust with furrowed brow.

'Lookut the lion,' yelled one boy. 'Woo! woo!'

'What kind of a dog it it, mister?' asked another.

'Aw, that ain't no dog,' jeered a third.

'This,' said Dick, 'is a very wonderful dog. We are walking around the world with it. It eats keys.'

'Dick!' said his wife.

'Eats keys?' exclaimed the children in a grand chorus.

'Trunk keys, door keys, padlock keys – any kind of keys,' said Dick. 'It shakes them well before eating.'

Mrs Dickinson indignantly picked up Josephine and led the way into Madden's store. 'Heavens!' she said to her husband as the door shut out the parting jeers of the skeptical children. 'Don't ever do that again. It's bad enough to have such a dog without summoning spectators.'

She walked to the counter as Eli Madden came into the store from a back room. 'We understand,' she said sweetly, 'that you lost your dog recently and would like to have another one.'

'Gored by a bull,' said Madden.

'We have a splendid puppy here, an American hound terrier,' pursued Mrs Dickinson brightly. Dick coughed loudly and hurriedly.

'That is – a bull-terrier, an American bull-terrier,' he said. 'It's yours for the taking.'

'I tell you,' said Madden, picking up the dog and examining it as if it were a motor car part, 'it's too young a dog for me to bother with. But Floyd Timmons might take her. Never seen a stray yit he wouldn't. If you say so I'll take her up when I go this evening. I drive right past Floyd's place.'

'If you don't mind,' said Mrs Dickinson eagerly.

Just then Josephine sneezed.

'She ain't sick, is she?' asked Madden suspiciously.

'She never did that before,' exclaimed Mrs Dickinson.

'May be distemper,' said Madden, spitting. Josephine sniffled and looked miserable.

'Well, has she got a cold?' cooed Mrs Dickinson, picking her up. 'Has she got a little cold?'

They arranged with Madden to bring the dog back when it was quite over its cold. But for a week Josephine sneezed and sniffled at frequent intervals and her nose remained very warm. Mrs Dickinson fixed a warmer bed for her, heated the shawl on which she slept, and placed a blanket under that; she fed her meat broth every day and studied the puppy book carefully for further suggestions. On the eighth day Josephine was over her sniffling and seemed much brighter than she had ever been. She even romped a bit and tugged at an apron string that Mrs Dickinson playfully shook in front of her. 'That's a real bulldog trait,' said Dick admiringly.

They took her out into the front yard and the puppy scampered about a little on the grass, and even barked, a plaintive bark, at a vagrant scrap of paper. While they were watching her with amusement a man drove up to the end of the walk in a buggy.

'Have you got a dog here you don't want?' he sang out cheerfully. 'My name's Timmons.' The Dickinsons rose from where they were sitting on the porch.

'Oh, yes,' said Dickinson cordially, 'yes – sure.'

The man got out of his buggy and came toward the house. And immediately Josephine retreated a step toward her master and mistress and growled, a tiny, funny growl.

'Quite a watchdog,' said the man. 'Here, pup.' He stooped down and picked her up. She yielded with a wild look at Mrs Dickinson. 'You still want to part with her?'

'We really want a Scotch-terrier,' Dick told him. 'That's the reason we are giving her up.'

'I see,' said the man. He shifted the dog to an easier position.

'Be sure she has a warm place to sleep,' said Mrs Dickinson, following Timmons to his buggy. 'We aren't letting her sleep outdoors yet. She doesn't stand cold very well. She has had a cold and just got over it. Maybe you would want to take along the bed she has been using?'

'Oh, we got plenty of warm stuff we can bed her down in. We'll keep her in the kitchen of nights until it warms up a bit.'

'She shouldn't be fed much cooked meat,' went on Mrs Dickinson. 'If you could see that she got some broth now and then and some lean meat, well cut up. Milk isn't so good for her, so we don't give her much of it.'

Timmons tucked the dog into the robe by his side. Josephine peered with questioning eyes first at her new owner and then at her recent mistress.

'Now, I'd be willing to pay you a little something for her. You see, a bull-terrier will come in handy with the cows when my other dogs git too old, or die off.'

'Not at all,' said Dick.

'Oh, no,' said Mrs Dickinson. 'Her name is Josephine,' she added.

'Oh, that's all right,' said Timmons largely. He clucked to

his horse and the buggy moved off. They had a glimpse of Josephine peering back from one end of the seat, and then a hand took her out of sight.

'Well, there's a big bother off your hands,' said Dick cheerfully, and Mrs Dickinson nodded assent.

Scarcely an hour of the next few days went by, however, without some remembrance of Josephine coming up between them. There was, for one thing, the puppy book, rather useless now; and the little bed in the corner to stumble over; and the stick with a piece of paper tied on one end that Mrs Dickinson had made for a plaything; and puppy biscuits scattered about the house and grounds. After a week, however, Dickinson, absorbed in his work, had almost forgotten the dog. Then one noon at luncheon he was outlining to his wife a plot for a story. It was a tale of motored action, set in the mountain ways, with rumrunners and deputy sheriffs and a girl in a red roadster driving madly through it.

'Then,' explained Dick, 'as they near the old house, which they suppose abandoned, a dog suddenly barks—'

'I do hope he will feed her the right things,' said Mrs Dickinson.

Dick put the brakes to his careening motor cars.

'Who will feed what?'

'Josephine,' said his wife.

'Still thinking of the empress, eh?'

'You know a man is so likely to be careless. I wish I could have spoken to his wife about her.'

'She'll be all right,' said Dick brightly, pushing the dish of strawberry jam nearer to Ellen. 'And when we get that Scotty in New York this fall you'll forget all about her and be glad we got her a good home.'

'She was mighty bright and fine that last day,' mused his

wife. 'And she growled at him. But still, I suppose she would never grow.'

'Never,' agreed Dick. 'She would have been cut dead by all the best dogs in New York.'

'You know,' said Ellen, after a time, as she began to stack up the dishes, 'maybe it was because I nursed her through that sick spell. . . .' She sighed. Dick knew that sigh.

'How about running up to this chap's farm and finding out how she's getting along?' he asked. 'We wouldn't have to let her see us.'

'All right,' said Ellen quickly. 'We could just stop and ask how she is doing and I could tell his wife about the broth and lean meat.'

So one afternoon they hired the Blanchards' machine again, stopped at Eli Madden's store to ask the way to Timmons' farm, and drove up the road until they sighted his name on a gray mailbox in front of a large, rambling farmhouse.

Timmons was kneeling in a small room of the barns, sorting over some implements, when Dickinson found him.

'Hello, Timmons,' he said, with a worried crease in his forehead, 'I just dropped in to ask about the dog.'

'Darned if Norb Gibbs didn't take her,' said Timmons, rising. 'He stopped up here one day and he had a little likker on him. Norb's a mean man. He's the orneriest cuss in these parts. Well, sir, your dog was runnin' 'round in front of the house and Norb took a fancy to her. I said I didn't want to sell, seein' as she'd bin give to us, and he kidded me, like, and said well, no, you wouldn't want to sell a gift dog – he'd just take her. And he did. Laughed when I tried to stop him.'

'Can't you have the sheriff or someone get the dog?' asked Dick.

'Sheriff's 'way off to the county seat and his deputy here

is a little thick with Gibbs. Nobody ever crosses him much. He's a hard man.'

With a gesture of annoyance Dickinson finally asked the farmer to say nothing of the dog's disappearance. It wouldn't do for the thing to be talked about in the village. Then he went back to rejoin his wife.

'Did you see her?' She smiled wistfully.

'No,' said Dick, with a great effort at lightness. 'But she's doing fine, Timmons said.'

'I'm sure she is,' said Mrs Dickinson. 'I've told Mrs Timmons all about her idiosyncrasies. Well . . . I guess we must be getting back home. It looks a lot like rain.'

And it did rain, a slow, depressing drizzle, as they returned, Dick hard put to it to affect an easy cheerfulness while his mind turned over and over the quandary into which Josephine – and he – had fallen. Perhaps it might be an easy matter to buy her back for Timmons. But how was he to arrange a meeting without his wife's knowing? Through his speculations ran alternately an undercurrent of exasperation at all this bother about an undesirable pup, a thin-lipped anger at the unknown brute's action, and a faint feeling of dread.

Schemes for recovering the puppy for Timmons kept formulating in his brain. He was still thinking of the problem when, next day, he walked to Madden's store to replenish his supply of tobacco. He decided to query the storekeeper about the haunts and habits of the unseen man who never left his thoughts.

'Norb Gibbs?' asked Madden. 'Right there.' He jerked his thumb.

Dickinson turned to observe a group of three men in one corner of the store, talking haltingly in low tones, two of them pulling at pipes, the third leaning idly against a counter.

'Oh, Norb!' called Madden.

Before Dickinson could arrange his thoughts or formulate a mode of procedure, one of the smokers turned slightly and looked at the storekeeper.

'Feller here wants to see you,' continued Madden.

Dick felt his heart begin to beat rapidly and his hands at the fingertips became a little cold. The man who slouched over to him, scowling, was heavy and stockily set, with a great round face, scarred on one cheek. He was dressed in a corduroy suit, with leather boots laced to the knees. He was tremendously thick through the chest, and his wrists, where they showed under the sleeves, were scraggly black with hair. Dick stuffed his half-filled pipe into his pocket.

'You want me?' asked Gibbs, scratching his neck with big fingers of his right hand.

'Why –' began Dick. 'I – yes. That is – you have a little dog I'd like to buy from you if I could.'

'What dog?' demanded Gibbs.

'A puppy I believe you got from Mr Timmons,' said Dick with a wry attempt at a smile and a feeling that his voice was a little weak and that his tongue moved thickly.

'I got a pup from him,' said Gibbs. 'Yes.' He planted his feet apart, put his pipe in one corner of his mouth, and pushed his hat a little from his forehead. 'What about it?'

'Well,' said Dickinson, 'I gave him to Timmons and now he – that is – I – my wife and I believe we would like to have him – I mean *her* – back. How is she getting along?' He felt the question was a bit silly and out of place.

'Right well,' drawled the big man. 'I reckon she'll make me a good dog. Nope. Can't say I want to get shed of her.'

'You wouldn't sell her?' asked Dick.

'Nope.'

'How about fifty dollars?' Dick hazarded hopefully. The

thought went through his mind that maybe Timmons would agree to help buy back the dog. He had offered to pay something for it.

'Don't need no money,' said Gibbs curtly.

'I – I want the dog very much,' said Dick.

'Well s'posin' you come get her,' said Gibbs, his voice rising. 'And when you come, come big.'

He turned and looked at his companions, as if inviting them to enjoy the scene. They listened silently. Madden, weighing out some nails on a scale, looked up with lifted brows.

'I got a lot o' handy cordwood around the place I use on them as I don't want prowlin' about,' continued Gibbs. With a loud laugh he walked back and rejoined his friends. Madden resumed weighing his nails. Dick felt his face grow hot.

'You won't give her up, then?' he asked thickly.

'I said you come and get her,' glowered Gibbs, thumbing some tobacco into his short pipe and leaning against the counter. One of his friends moved over and made more room for him.

'Maybe I will,' said Dick. He was quivering slightly and his legs felt strangely strained under him.

'And maybe you'll git a clout like I've had to give yer damn dog now and again,' laughed the man, brutally, showing his teeth in a grin at his companions.

Things grew a little hazy in front of Dickinson – a little hazy and red. He realized, with something like a flash of fire in his brain, that this strange brute had beaten his dog . . . Josephine. . . .

In two bounds he was across the room, for he was lithe and quick, if no match for the other in strength. Before Gibbs could remove one ankle from the other, as he lounged against the counter – before he could take the pipe from his hand, Dickinson struck him full in the mouth with all the force of a long right swing.

They will talk about the fight that followed for many years to come. Gibbs, knocked to a sitting position between a bushel of potatoes and a heavy unopened barrel, was hampered by his weight and his heavy clothing, but when he got to his feet he rushed for Dickinson like an injured bull. The swoop of the oncoming giant was powerful. Dickinson turned and, in sheer fright, ran to the door. But there he suddenly whirled. With a quick, mad, desperate movement he hurled himself straight at the feet of the charging form. Not for nothing had he dived like that at football dummies in his school days, battering his body at the swinging stuffed moleskins as a member of the scrub team – the fighting scrubs. He struck the man just above the ankles.

Gibbs went toppling clumsily over him and hit the floor with a terrific crash. He fell near a newly opened box of hammers, glistening with blue steel heads and white-labeled handles. Dick rolled over and picked himself up as the man grasped a hammer and turned on his knees. His throw was wild. The hammer crashed into an unlighted lamp high above a counter, and glass tinkled sharply as the lamp swung and creaked dismally. As Gibbs staggered to his feet, Dick jumped for a chair behind the large stove near one corner of the store. Apparently the man, another hammer in his hand, expected Dickinson to hide behind the stove, for he moved toward him with a triumphant leer on his lips.

But Dickinson did not hide. The fever of battle was on him. He darted out straight at his foe, swinging the chair up from the floor as he came. Gibbs, somewhat startled, brought his hammer stroke down squarely on the upturned legs of the chair, two of which caught him solidly under the arm. He swore and the hammer flew from his hand. His other hand went to an injured elbow as the chair dropped to the floor. He lurched for it, but Dick tackled him again and Gibbs went down on the upturned chair. Dick was behind him. With a well-directed shove of his foot he sent Gibbs into an even more ludicrous entanglement with the piece of furniture. After which he leaped upon him, hammering blows into the back of his head.

'Get up!' yelled Dick in a frenzy. 'Get up, you dog stealer, you dog beater, you—!'

The man struggled to a sitting posture and rubbed blood with his sleeve from a gash under his eye. Only his unusually slow movements, his handicap of heaviness, prevented him from closing with Dick before the latter got over his frenzy of yelling, while he stood above the defenseless man, his arms flailing about him.

But now the fellow was on his knees, his heavy hands flat on the floor, and Dickinson's reason returned. He lurched for a counter and began to hurl things at the slowly moving terror. He threw boxes, cans, racks – everything he could get his hands on. Grapefruit and tomatoes began to fly. A can of peaches plumped roundly into Gibbs' chest. A seed rack bounded from his shoulders as the swishing packets clattered about the floor. The scoop of nails which the awestruck Madden had abandoned for the floor behind the counter sang a rattling song past Gibbs' ear and spattered like shot over walls and floor. But Gibbs got to his feet and, warding off more missiles with the chair, moved forward – relentless, grim, terrible. 'I'll kill ye!' he grunted in spasmodic breaths. 'I'll break ye in two!'

'Come on!' howled Dick, a challenge that was half wild fear, for the counter was bare of anything else to throw. He backed rapidly for the door. His feet struck the overturned box of hammers and he sat down. Madly he reached out and picked up a hammer and threw it. It went wide. Gibbs, seeing his foe on the floor before him, towered high, flung the chair against the stove with a clanging crash and rushed. And Dick's second hammer, flung with all his remaining strength and a rasping sob in his throat, struck Norb Gibbs directly over the eye. With a look of surprise, he fell to the floor in a heap.

The next thing Dickinson knew, the store was filled with people. He was aware that a hundred questions were being asked by a hundred forms moving in and out around him. Then abruptly the crowd made way for a figure that moved hurriedly through the door.

'Sheriff Griggsby! It's the sheriff!'

The crazy thought went through Dickinson's mind that this must be a movie. Then he fainted.

When he came to, he found himself firmly held in the arm of the law. His eyes widened and a question formed in his mind. Had he killed Gibbs?

'You're going to take a ride with me,' said the sheriff grimly. Dick shivered. 'You and me,' continued the sheriff, 'are going up after that female bitch now. I like a man 'll fight all hell for his dog, even if it *ain't* his.'

Late one October day, when the western windows of houses were burning with orange fire, the Dickinsons stopped on a bench in Central Park and sat down. A sturdy little terrier with a sleek brown coat and very bright eyes, whose ancestry, however, would admittedly have been difficult to trace, jumped up and sat down between them.

Presently a lady went by, leading in leash a handsome and well-groomed Scotch-terrier, of evident aristocracy.

'There, but for the grace of Gibbs,' mused Dickinson, 'goes our Scotty.'

His wife patted the little terrier by her side and looked after the retreating Scotty.

'Oh,' she said, 'it makes a good enough dog of its kind.'

ANTON CHEKHOV

KASHTANKA

I

Misbehaviour

A YOUNG DOG, a reddish mongrel, between a dachshund and a 'yard-dog', very like a fox in face, was running up and down the pavement looking uneasily from side to side. From time to time she stopped and, whining and lifting first one chilled paw and then another, tried to make up her mind how it could have happened that she was lost.

She remembered very well how she had passed the day, and how, in the end, she had found herself on this unfamiliar pavement.

The day had begun by her master Luka Alexandritch's putting on his hat, taking something wooden under his arm wrapped up in a red handkerchief, and calling: 'Kashtanka, come along!'

Hearing her name the mongrel had come out from under the work-table, where she slept on the shavings, stretched herself voluptuously and run after her master. The people Luka Alexandritch worked for lived a very long way off, so that, before he could get to any one of them, the carpenter had several times to step into a tavern to fortify himself. Kashtanka remembered that on the way she had behaved extremely improperly. In her delight that she was being taken for a walk she jumped about, dashed barking after the trains, ran into yards, and chased other dogs. The carpenter was continually losing sight of her, stopping, and angrily shouting at her. Once he had even, with an expression of fury in his face, taken her fox-like ear in his fist, smacked her, and said emphatically: 'Pla-a-ague take you, you pest!'

After having left the work where it had been bespoken, Luka Alexandritch went into his sister's and there had something to eat and drink; from his sister's he had gone to see a bookbinder he knew; from the bookbinder's to a tavern, from the tavern to another crony's, and so on. In short, by the time Kashtanka found herself on the unfamiliar pavement, it was getting dusk, and the carpenter was as drunk as a cobbler. He was waving his arms and, breathing heavily, muttered:

'In sin my mother bore me! Ah, sins, sins! Here now we are walking along the street and looking at the street lamps, but when we die, we shall burn in a fiery Gehenna. . . .'

Or he fell into a good-natured tone, called Kashtanka to him, and said to her: 'You, Kashtanka, are an insect of a creature, and nothing else. Beside a man, you are much the same as a joiner beside a cabinet-maker. . . .'

While he talked to her in that way, there was suddenly a burst of music. Kashtanka looked round and saw that a regiment of soldiers was coming straight towards her. Unable to endure the music, which unhinged her nerves, she turned round and round and wailed. To her great surprise, the carpenter, instead of being frightened, whining and barking, gave a broad grin, drew himself up to attention, and saluted with all his five fingers. Seeing that her master did not protest, Kashtanka whined louder than ever, and dashed across the road to the opposite pavement.

When she recovered herself, the band was not playing and the regiment was no longer there. She ran across the road to the spot where she had left her master, but alas, the carpenter was no longer there. She dashed forward, then back again and ran across the road once more, but the carpenter seemed to have vanished into the earth. Kashtanka began sniffing the pavement, hoping to find her master by the scent of his tracks, but some wretch had been that way just before in new rubber galoshes, and now all delicate scents were mixed with an acute stench of india-rubber, so that it was impossible to make out anything.

Kashtanka ran up and down and did not find her master, and meanwhile it had got dark. The street lamps were lighted on both sides of the road, and lights appeared in the windows. Big, fluffy snowflakes were falling and painting white the pavement, the horses' backs and the cabmen's caps, and the darker the evening grew the whiter were all these objects. Unknown customers kept walking incessantly to and fro, obstructing her field of vision and shoving against her with their feet. (All mankind Kashtanka divided into two uneven parts: masters and customers; between them there was an essential difference: the first had the right to beat her, and the second she had the right to nip by the calves of their legs.) These customers were hurrying off somewhere and paid no attention to her.

When it got quite dark, Kashtanka was overcome by despair and horror. She huddled up in an entrance and began whining piteously. The long day's journeying with Luka Alexandritch had exhausted her, her ears and her paws were freezing, and, what was more, she was terribly hungry. Only twice in the whole day had she tasted a morsel: she had eaten a little paste at the bookbinder's, and in one of the taverns she had found a sausage skin on the floor, near the counter – that was all. If she had been a human being she would have certainly thought: 'No, it is impossible to live like this! I must shoot myself!'

II

A Mysterious Stranger

But she thought of nothing, she simply whined. When her head and back were entirely plastered over with the soft feathery snow, and she had sunk into a painful doze of exhaustion, all at once the door of the entrance clicked, creaked, and struck her on the side. She jumped up. A man belonging to the class of customers came out. As Kashtanka whined and got under his feet, he could not help noticing her. He bent down to her and asked:

'Doggy, where do you come from? Have I hurt you? O, poor thing, poor thing. . . . Come, don't be cross, don't be cross. . . . I am sorry.'

Kashtanka looked at the stranger through the snow-flakes that hung on her eyelashes, and saw before her a short, fat little man, with a plump, shaven face wearing a top hat and a fur coat that swung open.

'What are you whining for?' he went on, knocking the snow off her back with his fingers. 'Where is your master? I suppose you are lost? Ah, poor doggy! What are we going to do now?'

Catching in the stranger's voice a warm, cordial note, Kashtanka licked his hand, and whined still more pitifully.

'Oh, you nice funny thing!' said the stranger. 'A regular fox! Well, there's nothing for it, you must come along with me! Perhaps you will be of use for something. . . . Well!'

He clicked with his lips, and made a sign to Kashtanka with his hand, which could only mean one thing: 'Come along!' Kashtanka went.

Not more than half an hour later she was sitting on the floor in a big, light room, and, leaning her head against her side, was looking with tenderness and curiosity at the stranger who was sitting at the table, dining. He ate and threw pieces to her. . . . At first he gave her bread and the green rind of cheese, then a piece of meat, half a pie and chicken bones, while through hunger she ate so quickly that she had not time to distinguish the taste, and the more she ate the more acute was the feeling of hunger.

'Your masters don't feed you properly,' said the stranger, seeing with what ferocious greediness she swallowed the morsels without munching them. 'And how thin you are! Nothing but skin and bones. . . .'

Kashtanka ate a great deal and yet did not satisfy her hunger, but was simply stupefied with eating. After dinner she lay down in the middle of the room, stretched her legs and, conscious of an agreeable weariness all over her body, wagged her tail. While her new master, lounging in an easy-chair, smoked a cigar, she wagged her tail and considered the question, whether it was better at the stranger's or at the carpenter's. The stranger's surroundings were poor and ugly; besides the easy-chairs, the sofa, the lamps and the rugs, there was nothing, and the room seemed empty. At the carpenter's the whole place was stuffed full of things: he had a table, a bench, a heap of shavings, planes, chisels, saws, a cage with a goldfinch, a basin. . . . The stranger's room smelt of nothing, while there was always a thick fog in the carpenter's room, and a glorious smell of glue, varnish, and shavings. On the other hand, the stranger had one great superiority – he gave her a great deal to eat and, to do him full justice, when Kashtanka sat facing the table and looking wistfully at him, he did not once hit or kick her, and did not once shout: 'Go away, damned brute!'

When he had finished his cigar her new master went out, and a minute later came back holding a little mattress in his hands.

'Hey, you dog, come here!' he said, laying the mattress in the corner near the dog. 'Lie down here, go to sleep!'

Then he put out the lamp and went away. Kashtanka lay down on the mattress and shut her eyes; the sound of a bark rose from the street, and she would have liked to answer it, but all at once she was overcome with unexpected melancholy. She thought of Luka Alexandritch, of his son Fedyushka, and her snug little place under the bench.... She remembered on the long winter evenings, when the carpenter was planing or reading the paper aloud, Fedyushka usually played with her.... He used to pull her from under the bench by her hind legs, and play such tricks with her, that she saw green before her eyes, and ached in every joint. He would make her walk on her hind legs, use her as a bell, that is, shake her violently by the tail so that she squealed and barked, and give her tobacco to sniff.... The following trick was particularly agonizing: Fedyushka would tie a piece of meat to a thread and give it to Kashtanka, and then, when she had swallowed it he would, with a loud laugh, pull it back again from her stomach, and the more lurid were her memories the more loudly and miserably Kashtanka whined.

But soon exhaustion and warmth prevailed over melancholy. She began to fall asleep. Dogs ran by in her imagination: among them a shaggy old poodle, whom she had seen that day in the street with a white patch on his eye and tufts of wool by his nose. Fedyushka ran after the poodle with a chisel in his hand, then all at once he too was covered with shaggy wool, and began merrily barking beside Kashtanka. Kashtanka and he good-naturedly sniffed each other's noses and merrily ran down the street....

III

New and Very Agreeable Acquaintances

When Kashtanka woke up it was already light, and a sound rose from the street, such as only comes in the day-time. There was not a soul in the room. Kashtanka stretched, yawned and, cross and ill-humoured, walked about the room. She sniffed the corners and the furniture, looked into the passage and found nothing of interest there. Besides the door that led into the passage there was another door. After thinking a little Kashtanka scratched on it with both paws, opened it, and went into the adjoining room. Here on the bed, covered with a rug, a customer, in whom she recognized the stranger of yesterday, lay asleep.

'Rrrrr . . .' she growled, but recollecting yesterday's dinner, wagged her tail, and began sniffing.

She sniffed the stranger's clothes and boots and thought they smelt of horses. In the bedroom was another door, also closed. Kashtanka scratched at the door, leaned her chest against it, opened it, and was instantly aware of a strange and very suspicious smell. Foreseeing an unpleasant encounter, growling and looking about her, Kashtanka walked into a little room with a dirty wall-paper and drew back in alarm. She saw something surprising and terrible. A grey gander came straight towards her, hissing, with its neck bowed down to the floor and its wings outspread. Not far from him, on a little mattress, lay a white tom-cat; seeing Kashtanka, he jumped up, arched his back, wagged his tail with his hair standing on end and he, too, hissed at her. The dog was frightened in earnest, but not caring to betray her alarm, began barking loudly and dashed at the cat. . . . The cat arched his back more than ever, mewed and gave Kashtanka a smack on the head with his paw. Kashtanka jumped back, squatted on all four paws, and craning her nose towards the cat, went off into loud, shrill barks; meanwhile the gander came up behind and gave her a painful peck in the back. Kashtanka leapt up and dashed at the gander.

'What's this?' They heard a loud angry voice, and the stranger came into the room in his dressing-gown, with a cigar between his teeth. 'What's the meaning of this? To your places!'

He went up to the cat, flicked him on his arched back, and said:

'Fyodor Timofeyitch, what's the meaning of this? Have you got up a fight? Ah, you old rascal! Lie down!'

And turning to the gander he shouted: 'Ivan Ivanitch, go home!'

The cat obediently lay down on his mattress and closed his eyes. Judging from the expression of his face and whiskers, he was displeased with himself for having lost his temper and got into a fight.

Kashtanka began whining resentfully, while the gander craned his neck and began saying something rapidly, excitedly, distinctly, but quite unintelligibly.

'All right, all right,' said his master, yawning. 'You must live in peace and friendship.' He stroked Kashtanka and went on: 'And you, redhair, don't be frightened. . . . They are capital company, they won't annoy you. Stay, what are we to call you? You can't go on without a name, my dear.'

The stranger thought a moment and said: 'I tell you what . . . you shall be Auntie. . . . Do you understand? Auntie!'

And repeating the word 'Auntie' several times he went out. Kashtanka sat down and began watching. The cat sat motionless on his little mattress, and pretended to be asleep. The gander, craning his neck and stamping, went on talking rapidly and excitedly about something. Apparently it was a very clever gander; after every long tirade, he always stepped back with an air of wonder and made a show of being highly delighted with his own speech. . . . Listening to him and answering 'R-r-r-r,' Kashtanka fell to sniffing the corners. In one of the corners she found a little trough in which she saw some soaked peas and a sop of rye crusts. She tried the peas; they were not nice; she tried the sopped bread and began eating it. The gander was not at all offended that the strange dog was eating his food, but, on the contrary, talked even more excitedly, and to show his confidence went to the trough and ate a few peas himself.

IV

Marvels on a Hurdle

A little while afterwards the stranger came in again, and brought a strange thing with him like a hurdle, or like the figure II. On the crosspiece on the top of this roughly made wooden frame hung a bell, and a pistol was also tied to it; there were strings from the tongue of the bell, and the trigger of the pistol. The stranger put the frame in the middle of the room, spent a long time tying and untying something, then looked at the gander and said: 'Ivan Ivanitch, if you please!'

The gander went up to him and stood in an expectant attitude.

'Now then,' said the stranger, 'let us begin at the very beginning. First of all, bow and make a curtsey! Look sharp!'

Ivan Ivanitch craned his neck, nodded in all directions, and scraped with his foot.

'Right. Bravo. . . . Now die!'

The gander lay on his back and stuck his legs in the air.

After performing a few more similar, unimportant tricks, the stranger suddenly clutched at his head, and assuming an expression of horror, shouted: 'Help! Fire! We are burning!'

Ivan Ivanitch ran to the frame, took the string in his beak, and set the bell ringing.

The stranger was very much pleased. He stroked the gander's neck and said:

'Bravo, Ivan Ivanitch! Now pretend that you are a jeweller selling gold and diamonds. Imagine now that you go to your shop and find thieves there. What would you do in that case?'

The gander took the other string in his beak and pulled it, and at once a deafening report was heard. Kashtanka was highly delighted with the bell ringing, and the shot threw her into so much ecstasy that she ran round the frame barking.

'Auntie, lie down!' cried the stranger; 'be quiet!'

Ivan Ivanitch's task was not ended with the shooting. For a whole hour afterwards the stranger drove the gander round him on a cord, cracking a whip, and the gander had to jump over barriers and through hoops; he had to rear, that is, sit on his tail and wave his legs in the air. Kashtanka could not take her eyes off Ivan Ivanitch, wriggled with delight, and several times fell to running after him with shrill barks. After exhausting the gander and himself, the stranger wiped the sweat from his brow and cried:

'Marya, fetch Havronya Ivanovna here!'

A minute later there was the sound of grunting. Kashtanka growled, assumed a very valiant air, and to be on the safe side, went nearer to the stranger. The door opened, an old woman looked in, and, saying something, led in a black and very ugly sow. Paying no attention to Kashtanka's growls, the sow lifted up her little hoof and grunted good-humouredly.

Apparently it was very agreeable to her to see her master, the cat, and Ivan Ivanitch. When she went up to the cat and gave him a light tap on the stomach with her hoof, and then made some remark to the gander, a great deal of good-nature was expressed in her movements, and the quivering of her tail. Kashtanka realized at once that to growl and bark at such a character was useless.

The master took away the frame and cried, 'Fyodor Timofeyitch, if you please!'

The cat stretched lazily, and reluctantly, as though performing a duty, went up to the sow.

'Come, let us begin with the Egyptian pyramid,' began the master.

He spent a long time explaining something, then gave the word of command, 'One ... two ... three!' At the word 'three' Ivan Ivanitch flapped his wings and jumped on to the sow's back. ... When, balancing himself with his wings and his neck, he got a firm foothold on the bristly back, Fyodor Timofeyitch listlessly and lazily, with manifest disdain, and with an air of scorning his art and not caring a pin for it, climbed on to the sow's back, then reluctantly mounted on to the gander, and stood on his hind legs. The result was what the stranger called the Egyptian pyramid. Kashtanka yapped with delight, but at that moment the old cat yawned and, losing his balance, rolled off the gander. Ivan Ivanitch lurched and fell off too. The stranger shouted, waved his hands, and began explaining something again. After spending an hour over the pyramid their indefatigable master proceeded to teach Ivan Ivanitch to ride on the cat, then began to teach the cat to smoke, and so on.

The lesson ended in the stranger's wiping the sweat off his brow and going away. Fyodor Timofeyitch gave a disdainful sniff, lay down on his mattress, and closed his eyes;

Ivan Ivanitch went to the trough, and the pig was taken away by the old woman. Thanks to the number of her new impressions, Kashtanka hardly noticed how the day passed, and in the evening she was installed with her mattress in the room with the dirty wall-paper, and spent the night in the society of Fyodor Timofeyitch and the gander.

V

Talent! Talent!

A month passed.

Kashtanka had grown used to having a nice dinner every evening, and being called Auntie. She had grown used to the stranger too, and to her new companions. Life was comfortable and easy.

Every day began in the same way. As a rule, Ivan Ivanitch was the first to wake up, and at once went up to Auntie or to the cat, twisting his neck, and beginning to talk excitedly and persuasively, but, as before, unintelligibly. Sometimes he would crane up his head in the air and utter a long monologue. At first Kashtanka thought he talked so much because he was very clever, but after a little time had passed, she lost all her respect for him; when he went up to her with his long speeches she no longer wagged her tail, but treated him as a tiresome chatterbox, who would not let anyone sleep and, without the slightest ceremony, answered him with 'R-r-r-r!'

Fyodor Timofeyitch was a gentleman of a very different sort. When he woke he did not utter a sound, did not stir, and did not even open his eyes. He would have been glad not to wake, for, as was evident, he was not greatly in love with life. Nothing interested him, he showed an apathetic

and nonchalant attitude to everything, he disdained everything and, even while eating his delicious dinner, sniffed
contemptuously.

When she woke Kashtanka began walking about the room
and sniffing the corners. She and the cat were the only ones
allowed to go all over the flat; the gander had not the right
to cross the threshold of the room with the dirty wall-paper,
and Havronya Ivanovna lived somewhere in a little out-
house in the yard and made her appearance only during the
lessons. Their master got up late, and immediately after
drinking his tea began teaching them their tricks. Every day
the frame, the whip, and the hoop were brought in, and every
day almost the same performance took place. The lesson
lasted three or four hours, so that sometimes Fyodor Timofeyitch was so tired that he staggered about like a drunken
man, and Ivan Ivanitch opened his beak and breathed
heavily, while their master became red in the face and could
not mop the sweat from his brow fast enough.

The lesson and the dinner made the day very interesting,
but the evenings were tedious. As a rule, their master went
off somewhere in the evening and took the cat and the
gander with him. Left alone, Auntie lay down on her little
mattress and began to feel sad.

Melancholy crept on her imperceptibly and took possession of her by degrees, as darkness does of a room. It began
with the dog's losing every inclination to bark, to eat, to run
about the rooms, and even to look at things; then vague
figures, half dogs, half human beings, with countenances
attractive, pleasant, but incomprehensible, would appear in
her imagination; when they came Auntie wagged her tail, and
it seemed to her that she had somewhere, at some time, seen
them and loved them. And as she dropped asleep, she always
felt that those figures smelt of glue, shavings, and varnish.

When she had grown quite used to her new life, and from a thin, long mongrel, had changed into a sleek, well-groomed dog, her master looked at her one day before the lesson and said:

'It's high time, Auntie, to get to business. You have kicked up your heels in idleness long enough. I want to make an artiste of you. . . . Do you want to be an artiste?'

And he began teaching her various accomplishments. At the first lesson he taught her to stand and walk on her hind legs, which she liked extremely. At the second lesson she had to jump on her hind legs and catch some sugar, which her teacher held high above her head. After that, in the following lessons she danced, ran tied to a cord, howled to music, rang the bell, and fired the pistol, and in a month could successfully replace Fyodor Timofeyitch in the 'Egyptian Pyramid'. She learned very eagerly and was pleased with her own success; running with her tongue out on the cord, leaping through the hoop, and riding on old Fyodor Timofeyitch, gave her the greatest enjoyment. She accompanied every successful trick with a shrill, delighted bark, while her teacher wondered, was also delighted, and rubbed his hands.

'It's talent! It's talent!' he said. 'Unquestionable talent! You will certainly be successful!'

And Auntie grew so used to the word talent, that every time her master pronounced it, she jumped up as if it had been her name.

VI
An Uneasy Night

Auntie had a doggy dream that a porter ran after her with a broom, and she woke up in a fright.

It was quite dark and very stuffy in the room. The fleas

were biting. Auntie had never been afraid of darkness before, but now, for some reason, she felt frightened and inclined to bark.

Her master heaved a loud sigh in the next room, then soon afterwards the sow grunted in her sty, and then all was still again. When one thinks about eating one's heart grows lighter, and Auntie began thinking how that day she had stolen the leg of a chicken from Fyodor Timofeyitch, and had hidden it in the drawing-room, between the cupboard and the wall, where there were a great many spiders' webs and a great deal of dust. Would it not be as well to go now and look whether the chicken leg were still there or not? It was very possible that her master had found it and eaten it. But she must not go out of the room before morning, that was the rule. Auntie shut her eyes to go to sleep as quickly as possible, for she knew by experience that the sooner you go to sleep the sooner the morning comes. But all at once there was a strange scream not far from her which made her start and jump up on all four legs. It was Ivan Ivanitch, and his cry was not babbling and persuasive as usual, but a wild, shrill, unnatural scream like the squeak of a door opening. Unable to distinguish anything in the darkness, and not understanding what was wrong, Auntie felt still more frightened and growled: 'R-r-r-r. . . .'

Some time passed, as long as it takes to eat a good bone; the scream was not repeated. Little by little Auntie's uneasiness passed off and she began to doze. She dreamed of two big black dogs with tufts of last year's coat left on their haunches and sides; they were eating out of a big basin some swill, from which there came a white steam and a most appetizing smell; from time to time they looked round at Auntie, showed their teeth and growled: 'We are not going to give you any!' But a peasant in a fur-coat ran out of the house and drove them away with a whip; then Auntie went up to the basin and began eating, but as soon as the peasant went out of the gate, the two black dogs rushed at her growling, and all at once there was again a shrill scream.

'K-gee! K-gee-gee!' cried Ivan Ivanitch.

Auntie woke, jumped up and, without leaving her mattress, went off into a yelping bark. It seemed to her that it was not Ivan Ivanitch that was screaming but someone else, and for some reason the sow again grunted in her sty.

Then there was the sound of shuffling slippers, and the master came into the room in his dressing-gown with a candle in his hand. The flickering light danced over the dirty wall-paper and the ceiling, and chased away the darkness. Auntie saw that there was no stranger in the room. Ivan Ivanitch was sitting on the floor and was not asleep. His wings were spread out and his beak was open, and altogether he looked as though he were very tired and thirsty. Old Fyodor Timofeyitch was not asleep either. He, too, must have been awakened by the scream.

'Ivan Ivanitch, what's the matter with you?' the master asked the gander. 'Why are you screaming? Are you ill?'

The gander did not answer. The master touched him on the neck, stroked his back, and said: 'You are a queer chap. You don't sleep yourself, and you don't let other people. . . .'

When the master went out, carrying the candle with him, there was darkness again. Auntie felt frightened. The gander did not scream, but again she fancied that there was some stranger in the room. What was most dreadful was that this stranger could not be bitten, as he was unseen and had no shape. And for some reason she thought that something very bad would certainly happen that night. Fyodor Timofeyitch was uneasy too.

Auntie could hear him shifting on his mattress, yawning and shaking his head.

Somewhere in the street there was a knocking at a gate and the sow grunted in her sty. Auntie began to whine, stretched out her front-paws and laid her head down upon them. She fancied that in the knocking at the gate, in the grunting of the sow, who was for some reason awake, in the darkness and the stillness, there was something as miserable and dreadful as in Ivan Ivanitch's scream. Everything was in agitation and anxiety, but why? Who was the stranger who could not be seen? Then two dim flashes of green gleamed for a minute near Auntie. It was Fyodor Timofeyitch, for the first time of their whole acquaintance coming up to her. What did he want? Auntie licked his paw, and not asking why he had come, howled softly and on various notes.

'K-gee!' cried Ivan Ivanitch. 'K-g-ee!'

The door opened again and the master came in with a candle.

The gander was sitting in the same attitude as before, with his beak open, and his wings spread out, his eyes were closed.

'Ivan Ivanitch!' his master called him.

The gander did not stir. His master sat down before him on the floor, looked at him in silence for a minute, and said:

'Ivan Ivanitch, what is it? Are you dying? Oh, I remember now, I remember!' he cried out, and clutched at his head. 'I know why it is! It's because the horse stepped on you today! My God! My God!'

Auntie did not understand what her master was saying, but she saw from his face that he, too, was expecting something dreadful. She stretched out her head towards the dark window, where it seemed to her some stranger was looking in, and howled.

'He is dying, Auntie!' said her master, and wrung his

hands. 'Yes, yes, he is dying! Death has come into your room. What are we to do?'

Pale and agitated, the master went back into his room, sighing and shaking his head. Auntie was afraid to remain in the darkness, and followed her master into his bedroom. He sat down on the bed and repeated several times: 'My God, what's to be done?'

Auntie walked about round his feet, and not understanding why she was wretched and why they were all so uneasy, and trying to understand, watched every movement he made. Fyodor Timofeyitch, who rarely left his little mattress, came into the master's bedroom too, and began rubbing himself against his feet. He shook his head as though he wanted to shake painful thoughts out of it, and kept peeping suspiciously under the bed.

The master took a saucer, poured some water from his wash-stand into it, and went to the gander again.

'Drink, Ivan Ivanitch!' he said tenderly, setting the saucer before him; 'drink, darling.'

But Ivan Ivanitch did not stir and did not open his eyes. His master bent his head down to the saucer and dipped his beak into the water, but the gander did not drink, he spread his wings wider than ever, and his head remained lying in the saucer.

'No, there's nothing to be done now,' sighed his master. 'It's all over. Ivan Ivanitch is gone!'

And shining drops, such as one sees on the window-pane when it rains, trickled down his cheeks. Not understanding what was the matter, Auntie and Fyodor Timofeyitch snuggled up to him and looked with horror at the gander.

'Poor Ivan Ivanitch!' said the master, sighing mournfully. 'And I was dreaming I would take you in the spring into the country, and would walk with you on the green grass. Dear creature, my good comrade, you are no more! How shall I do without you now?'

It seemed to Auntie that the same thing would happen to her, that is, that she too, there was no knowing why, would close her eyes, stretch out her paws, open her mouth, and everyone would look at her with horror. Apparently the same reflections were passing through the brain of Fyodor Timofeyitch. Never before had the old cat been so morose and gloomy.

It began to get light, and the unseen stranger who had so frightened Auntie was no longer in the room. When it was quite daylight, the porter came in, took the gander, and carried him away. And soon afterwards the old woman came in and took away the trough.

Auntie went into the drawing-room and looked behind the cupboard: her master had not eaten the chicken bone, it was lying in its place among the dust and spiders' webs. But Auntie felt sad and dreary and wanted to cry. She did not even sniff at the bone, but went under the sofa, sat down there, and began softly whining in a thin voice.

VII

An Unsuccessful Début

One fine evening the master came into the room with the dirty wall-paper, and, rubbing his hands, said:

'Well. . . .'

He meant to say something more, but went away without saying it. Auntie, who during her lessons had thoroughly studied his face and intonations, divined that he was agitated, anxious and, she fancied, angry. Soon afterwards he came back and said:

'Today I shall take with me Auntie and Fyodor Timofeyitch. Today, Auntie, you will take the place of poor Ivan Ivanitch in the "Egyptian Pyramid". Goodness knows how it will be! Nothing is ready, nothing has been thoroughly studied, there have been few rehearsals! We shall be disgraced, we shall come to grief!'

Then he went out again, and a minute later, came back in his fur-coat and top hat. Going up to the cat he took him by the fore-paws and put him inside the front of his coat, while Fyodor Timofeyitch appeared completely unconcerned, and did not even trouble to open his eyes. To him it was apparently a matter of absolute indifference whether he remained lying down, or were lifted up by his paws, whether he rested on his mattress or under his master's fur-coat.

'Come along, Auntie,' said her master.

Wagging her tail, and understanding nothing, Auntie followed him. A minute later she was sitting in a sledge by her master's feet and heard him, shrinking with cold and anxiety, mutter to himself:

'We shall be disgraced! We shall come to grief!'

The sledge stopped at a big strange-looking house, like a soup-ladle turned upside down. The long entrance to this house, with its three glass doors, was lighted up with a dozen brilliant lamps. The doors opened with a resounding noise and, like jaws, swallowed up the people who were moving to and fro at the entrance. There were a great many people, horses, too, often ran up to the entrance, but no dogs were to be seen.

The master took Auntie in his arms and thrust her in his coat, where Fyodor Timofevitch already was. It was dark and stuffy there, but warm. For an instant two green sparks flashed at her; it was the cat, who opened his eyes on being disturbed by his neighbour's cold rough paws. Auntie licked his ear, and, trying to settle herself as comfortably as possible, moved uneasily, crushed him under her cold paws, and casually poked her head out from under the coat, but at once growled angrily, and tucked it in again. It seemed to her that she had seen a huge, badly lighted room, full of monsters; from behind screens and gratings, which stretched on both sides of the room, horrible faces looked out: faces of horses with horns, with long ears, and one fat, huge countenance with a tail instead of a nose, and two long gnawed bones sticking out of his mouth.

The cat mewed huskily under Auntie's paws, but at that moment the coat was flung open, the master said, 'Hop!' and Fyodor Timofeyitch and Auntie jumped to the floor. They were now in a little room with grey plank walls; there was no other furniture in it but a little table with a looking-glass on it, a stool, and some rags hung about the corners, and instead of a lamp or candles, there was a bright fan-shaped light attached to a little pipe fixed in the wall. Fyodor Timofeyitch licked his coat which had been ruffled by Auntie, went under the stool, and lay down. Their master, still agitated and rubbing his hands, began undressing.... He undressed as he usually did at home when he was preparing to get under the rug, that is, took off everything but his underlinen, then he sat down on the stool, and, looking in the looking-glass, began playing the most surprising tricks with himself.... First of all he put on his head a wig, with a parting and with two tufts of hair standing up like horns, then he smeared his face thickly with something white, and over the white colour painted his eyebrows, his moustaches, and red on his cheeks. His antics did not end with that. After smearing his face and neck, he began putting himself into an extraordinary and incongruous costume, such as Auntie had never seen before, either in houses or in the street. Imagine very full trousers, made of chintz covered with big flowers, such as is used in working-class houses for curtains and covering furniture, trousers which buttoned up just under his armpits. One trouser leg was made of brown chintz, the other of bright yellow. Almost lost in these, he then put on a short chintz jacket, with a big scalloped collar, and a gold star on the back, stockings of different colours, and green slippers.

Everything seemed going round before Auntie's eyes and in her soul. The white-faced, sack-like figure smelt like her master, its voice, too, was the familiar master's voice, but there were moments when Auntie was tortured by doubts, and then she was ready to run away from the parti-coloured figure and to bark. The new place, the fan-shaped light, the smell, the transformation that had taken place in her master – all this aroused in her a vague dread and a foreboding that she would certainly meet with some horror such as the big face with the tail instead of a nose. And then, somewhere through the wall, some hateful band was playing, and from time to time she heard an incomprehensible roar. Only one thing reassured her – that was the imperturbability of Fyodor Timofeyitch. He dozed with the utmost tranquillity under the stool, and did not open his eyes even when it was moved.

A man in a dress coat and a white waistcoat peeped into the little room and said:

'Miss Arabella has just gone on. After her – you.'

Their master made no answer. He drew a small box from under the table, sat down, and waited. From his lips and his hands it could be seen that he was agitated, and Auntie could hear how his breathing came in gasps.

'Monsieur George, come on!' someone shouted behind the door. Their master got up and crossed himself three times, then took the cat from under the stool and put him in the box.

'Come, Auntie,' he said softly.

Auntie, who could make nothing out of it, went up to his hands, he kissed her on the head, and put her beside Fyodor Timofeyitch. Then followed darkness. . . . Auntie trampled on the cat, scratched at the walls of the box, and was so frightened that she could not utter a sound, while the box swayed and quivered, as though it were on the waves. . . .

'Here we are again!' her master shouted aloud: 'here we are again!'

Auntie felt that after that shout the box struck against something hard and left off swaying. There was a loud deep roar, someone was being slapped, and that someone, probably the monster with the tail instead of a nose, roared and laughed so loud that the locks of the box trembled. In response to the roar, there came a shrill, squeaky laugh from her master, such as he never laughed at home.

'Ha!' he shouted, trying to shout above the roar. 'Honoured friends! I have only just come from the station! My granny's kicked the bucket and left me a fortune! There is something very heavy in the box, it must be gold, ha! ha! I bet there's a million here! We'll open it and look. . . .'

The lock of the box clicked. The bright light dazzled Auntie's eyes, she jumped out of the box, and, deafened by the roar, ran quickly round her master, and broke into a shrill bark.

'Ha!' exclaimed her master. 'Uncle Fyodor Timofeyitch! Beloved Aunt, dear relations! The devil take you!'

He fell on his stomach on the sand, seized the cat and Auntie, and fell to embracing them. While he held Auntie tight in his arms, she glanced round into the world into which fate had brought her and, impressed by its immensity, was for a minute dumbfounded with amazement and delight, then jumped out of her master's arms, and to express the intensity of her emotions, whirled round and round on one spot like a top. This new world was big and full of bright light; wherever she looked, on all sides, from floor to ceiling there were faces, faces, faces, and nothing else.

'Auntie, I beg you to sit down!' shouted her master. Remembering what that meant, Auntie jumped on to a chair, and sat down. She looked at her master. His eyes looked at her gravely and kindly as always, but his face, especially his mouth and teeth, were made grotesque by a broad immovable grin. He laughed, skipped about, twitched his shoulders, and made a show of being very merry in the presence of the thousands of faces. Auntie believed in his merriment, all at once felt all over her that those thousands of faces were looking at her, lifted up her fox-like head, and howled joyously.

'You sit there, Auntie,' her master said to her, 'while Uncle and I will dance the Kamarinsky.'

Fyodor Timofeyitch stood looking about him indifferently, waiting to be made to do something silly. He danced listlessly, carelessly, sullenly, and one could see from his movements, his tail and his ears, that he had a profound contempt for the crowd, the bright light, his master and himself. When he had performed his allotted task, he gave a yawn and sat down.

'Now, Auntie!' said her master, 'we'll have first a song, and then a dance, shall we?'

He took a pipe out of his pocket, and began playing. Auntie, who could not endure music, began moving uneasily in her chair and howled. A roar of applause rose from all sides. Her master bowed, and when all was still again, went on playing. . . . Just as he took one very high note, someone high up among the audience uttered a loud exclamation:

'Auntie!' cried a child's voice, 'why it's Kashtanka!'

'Kashtanka it is!' declared a cracked drunken tenor. 'Kashtanka! Strike me dead, Fedyushka, it is Kashtanka. Kashtanka! here!'

Someone in the gallery gave a whistle, and two voices, one a boy's and one a man's, called loudly: 'Kashtanka! Kashtanka!'

Auntie started, and looked where the shouting came from. Two faces, one hairy, drunken and grinning, the other chubby, rosy-cheeked and frightened-looking, dazed her eyes as the bright light had dazed them before.... She remembered, fell off the chair, struggled on the sand, then jumped up, and with a delighted yap dashed towards those faces. There was a deafening roar, interspersed with whistles and a shrill childish shout: 'Kashtanka! Kashtanka!'

Auntie leaped over the barrier, then across someone's shoulders. She found herself in a box: to get into the next tier she had to leap over a high wall. Auntie jumped, but did not jump high enough, and slipped back down the wall. Then she was passed from hand to hand, licked hands and faces, kept mounting higher and higher, and at last got into the gallery....

Half an hour afterwards, Kashtanka was in the street, following the people who smelt of glue and varnish. Luka Alexandritch staggered and instinctively, taught by experience, tried to keep as far from the gutter as possible.

'In sin my mother bore me,' he muttered. 'And you, Kashtanka, are a thing of little understanding. Beside a man, you are like a joiner beside a cabinet-maker.'

Fedyushka walked beside him, wearing his father's cap. Kashtanka looked at their backs, and it seemed to her that she had been following them for ages, and was glad that there had not been a break for a minute in her life.

She remembered the little room with dirty wall-paper, the gander, Fyodor Timofeyitch, the delicious dinners, the lessons, the circus, but all that seemed to her now like a long, tangled, oppressive dream.

G. K. CHESTERTON

THE ORACLE
OF THE DOG

'YES,' SAID FATHER BROWN, 'I always like a dog so long as he isn't spelt backwards.'

Those who are quick in talking are not always quick in listening. Sometimes even their brilliancy produces a sort of stupidity. Father Brown's friend and companion was a young man with a stream of ideas and stories, an enthusiastic young man named Fiennes, with eager blue eyes and blond hair that seemed to be brushed back, not merely with a hair-brush, but with the wind of the world as he rushed through it. But he stopped in the torrent of his talk in a momentary bewilderment before he saw the priest's very simple meaning.

'You mean that people make too much of them?' he said. 'Well, I don't know. They're marvellous creatures. Sometimes I think they know a lot more than we do.'

Father Brown said nothing, but continued to stroke the head of the big retriever in a half-abstracted but apparently soothing fashion.

'Why,' said Fiennes, warming again to his monologue, 'there was a dog in the case I've come to see you about; what they call the "Invisible Murder Case", you know. It's a strange story, but from my point of view the dog is about the strangest thing in it. Of course, there's the mystery of the crime itself, and how old Druce can have been killed by somebody else when he was all alone in the summer house—'

The hand stroking the dog stopped for a moment in its rhythmic movement; and Father Brown said calmly, 'Oh, it was a summer house, was it?'

'I thought you'd read all about it in the papers,' answered Fiennes. 'Stop a minute; I believe I've got a cutting that will give you all the particulars.' He produced a strip of newspaper from his pocket and handed it to the priest, who began to read it, holding it close to his blinking eyes with one hand while the other continued its half-conscious caress of the dog. It looked like the parable of a man not letting his right hand know what his left hand did.

Many mystery stories, about men murdered behind locked doors and windows, and murderers escaping without means of entrance and exit, have come true in the course of the extraordinary events at Cranston on the coast of Yorkshire, where Colonel Druce was found stabbed from behind by a dagger that has entirely disappeared from the scene, and apparently even from the neighbourhood.

The summer house in which he died was indeed accessible at one entrance, the ordinary doorway which looked down the central walk of the garden towards the house. But by a combination of events almost to be called a coincidence, it appears that both the path and the entrance were watched during the crucial time, and there is a chain of witnesses who confirm each other. The summer house stands at the extreme end of the garden, where there is no exit or entrance of any kind. The central garden path is a lane between two ranks of tall delphiniums, planted so close that any stray step off the path would leave its traces; and both path and plants run right up to the very mouth of the summer house, so that no straying from the straight path could fail to be observed, and no other mode of entrance can be imagined.

Patrick Floyd, secretary of the murdered man, testified that he had been in a position to overlook the whole garden from the time when Colonel Druce last appeared alive in the doorway to the time when he was found dead; as he, Floyd, had been on the top of a stepladder clipping the garden hedge. Janet Druce, the dead man's daughter, confirmed this, saying that she had sat on the terrace of the house throughout that time and had seen Floyd at his work. Touching some part of the time, this is again supported by Donald Druce, her brother, who overlooked the garden standing at his bedroom window in his dressing gown, for he had risen late. Lastly the account is consistent with that given by Dr Valentine, a neighbour, who called for a time to talk with Miss Druce on the terrace, and by the colonel's solicitor, Mr Aubrey Traill, who was apparently the last to see the murdered man alive – presumably with the exception of the murderer.

All are agreed that the course of events was as follows: about half past three in the afternoon, Miss Druce went down the path to ask her father when he would like tea; but he said he did not want any and was waiting to see Traill, his lawyer, who was to be sent to him in the summer house. The girl then came away and met Traill coming down the path; she directed him to her father and he went in as directed. About half an hour afterwards he came out again, the colonel coming with him to the door and showing himself to all appearance in health and even high spirits. He had been somewhat annoyed earlier in the day by his son's irregular hours, but seemed to recover his temper in a perfectly normal fashion, and had been rather markedly genial in receiving other visitors, including two of his nephews who came over for the day. But as these were out walking during the whole period of the tragedy, they had no evidence to give. It is said, indeed, that the colonel was not on very good terms with Dr Valentine, but that gentleman only had a brief interview with the daughter of the house, to whom he is supposed to be paying serious attentions.

Traill, the solicitor, says he left the colonel entirely alone in the summer house, and this is confirmed by Floyd's bird's-eye view of the garden, which showed nobody else passing the only entrance. Ten minutes later Miss Druce again went down the garden and had not reached the end of the path when she saw her father, who was conspicuous by his white linen coat, lying in a heap on the floor. She uttered a scream which brought others to the spot, and on entering the place they found the colonel lying dead beside his basket-chair, which was also upset. Dr Valentine, who was still in the immediate neighbourhood, testified that the wound was made by some sort of stiletto, entering under the shoulder blade and piercing the heart. The police have searched the neighbourhood for such a weapon, but no trace of it can be found.

'So Colonel Druce wore a white coat, did he?' said Father Brown as he put down the paper.

'Trick he learnt in the tropics,' replied Fiennes with some wonder. 'He'd had some queer adventures there, by his own account; and I fancy his dislike of Valentine was connected with the doctor coming from the tropics too. But it's all an infernal puzzle. The account there is pretty accurate; I didn't see the tragedy, in the sense of the discovery; I was out walking with the young nephews and the dog – the dog I wanted to tell you about. But I saw the stage set for it as described: the straight lane between the blue flowers right up to the dark entrance, and the lawyer going down it in his blacks and his silk hat, and the red head of the secretary showing high above the green hedge as he worked on it with his shears. Nobody could have mistaken that red head at any distance; and if people say they saw it there all the time, you may be sure they did. This red-haired secretary Floyd is quite a character: breathless, bounding sort of fellow, always doing everybody's work as he was doing the gardener's. I think he is an American; he's certainly got the American way of life; what they call the viewpoint, bless 'em.'

'What about the lawyer?' asked Father Brown.

There was a silence and then Fiennes spoke quite slowly for him. 'Traill struck me as a singular man. In his fine black clothes he was almost foppish, yet you can hardly call him fashionable. For he wore a pair of long, luxuriant black whiskers such as haven't been seen since Victorian times. He had rather a fine grave face and a fine grave manner, but every now and then he seemed to remember to smile. And when he showed his white teeth he seemed to lose a little of his dignity and there was something faintly fawning about him. It may have been only embarrassment, for he would also fidget with his cravat and his tie-pin, which were at once handsome and unusual, like himself. If I could think of anybody – but what's the good, when the whole thing's impossible? Nobody knows who did it. Nobody knows how it could be done. At least there's only one exception I'd make, and that's why I really mentioned the whole thing. The dog knows.'

Father Brown sighed and then said absently, 'You were there as a friend of young Donald, weren't you? He didn't go on your walk with you?'

'No,' replied Fiennes, smiling. 'The young scoundrel had gone to bed that morning and got up that afternoon. I went with his cousins, two young officers from India, and our conversation was trivial enough. I remember the elder, whose name I think is Herbert Druce and who is an authority on horse breeding, talked about nothing but a mare he had bought and the moral character of the man who sold her; while his brother Harry seemed to be brooding on his bad luck at Monte Carlo. I only mention it to show you, in the light of what happened on our walk, that there was nothing psychic about us. The dog was the only mystic in our company.'

'What sort of a dog was he?' asked the priest.

'Same breed as that one,' answered Fiennes. 'That's what started me off on the story, your saying you didn't believe in believing in a dog. He's a big black retriever named Nox, and a suggestive name too; for I think what he did a darker mystery than the murder. You know Druce's house and garden are by the sea; we walked about a mile from it along the sands and then turned back, going the other way. We passed a rather curious rock called the Rock of Fortune, famous in the neighbourhood because it's one of those examples of one stone barely balanced on another, so that a touch would knock it over. It is not really very high, but the hanging outline of it makes it look a little wild and sinister; at least it made it look so to me, for I don't imagine my jolly young companions were afflicted with the picturesque. But it may be that I was beginning to feel an atmosphere; for just then the question arose of whether it was time to go back to tea, and even then I think I had a premonition that time counted for a good deal in the business. Neither Herbert Druce nor I had a watch, so we called out to his brother, who was some paces behind, having stopped to light his pipe under the hedge. Hence it happened that he shouted out the hour, which was twenty past four, in his big voice through the growing twilight; and somehow the loudness of it made it sound like the proclamation of something tremendous. His unconsciousness seemed to make it all the more so; but that was always the way with omens; and particular ticks of the clock were really very ominous things that afternoon. According to Dr Valentine's testimony, poor Druce had actually died just about half past four.

'Well, they said we needn't go home for ten minutes and we walked a little farther along the sands, doing nothing in particular – throwing stones for the dog and throwing sticks into the sea for him to swim after. But to me the twilight seemed to grow oddly oppressive and the very shadow of the top-heavy Rock of Fortune lay on me like a load. And then the curious thing happened. Nox had just brought back Herbert's walking stick out of the sea and his brother had thrown his in also. The dog swam out again, but just about what must have been the stroke of the half hour, he stopped swimming. He came back again on to the shore and stood in front of us. Then he suddenly threw up his head and sent up a howl or wail of woe, if ever I heard one in the world.

' "What the devil's the matter with the dog?" asked Herbert; but none of us could answer. There was a long silence after the brute's wailing and whining died away on the desolate shore; and then the silence was broken. As I live, it was broken by a faint and far-off shriek, like the shriek of a woman from beyond the hedges inland. We didn't know what it was then; but we knew afterwards. It was the cry the girl gave when she first saw the body of her father.'

'You went back, I suppose,' said Father Brown patiently. 'What happened then?'

'I'll tell you what happened then,' said Fiennes with a grim emphasis. 'When we got back into that garden the first thing we saw was Traill the lawyer; I can see him now with his black hat and black whiskers relieved against the perspective of the blue flowers stretching down to the summer house, with the sunset and the strange outline of the Rock of Fortune in the distance. His face and figure were in shadow against the sunset; but I swear the white teeth were showing in his head and he was smiling.

'The moment Nox saw that man, the dog dashed forward and stood in the middle of the path barking at him madly, murderously, volleying out curses that were almost verbal in their dreadful distinctness of hatred. And the man doubled up and fled along the path between the flowers.'

Father Brown sprang to his feet with a startling impatience.

'So the dog denounced him, did he?' he cried. 'The oracle of the dog condemned him. Did you see what birds were flying, and are you sure whether they were on the right hand or the left? Did you consult the augurs about the sacrifices? Surely you didn't omit to cut open the dog and examine his entrails. That is the sort of scientific test you heathen humanitarians seem to trust, when you are thinking of taking away the life and honour of a man.'

Fiennes sat gaping for an instant before he found breath to say, 'Why, what's the matter with you? What have I done now?'

A sort of anxiety came back into the priest's eyes – the anxiety of a man who has run against a post in the dark and wonders for a moment whether he has hurt it.

'I'm most awfully sorry,' he said with sincere distress. 'I beg your pardon for being so rude; pray forgive me.'

Fiennes looked at him curiously. 'I sometimes think you are more of a mystery than any of the mysteries,' he said.

'But anyhow, if you don't believe in the mystery of the dog, at least you can't get over the mystery of the man. You can't deny that at the very moment when the beast came back from the sea and bellowed, his master's soul was driven out of his body by the blow of some unseen power that no mortal man can trace or even imagine. And as for the lawyer, I don't go only by the dog; there are other curious details too. He struck me as a smooth, smiling, equivocal sort of person; and one of his tricks seemed like a sort of hint. You know the doctor and the police were on the spot very quickly; Valentine was brought back when walking away from the house, and he telephoned instantly. That, with the secluded house, small numbers, and enclosed space, made it pretty possible to search everybody who could have been near; and everybody was thoroughly searched – for a weapon. The whole house, garden, and shore were combed for a weapon. The disappearance of the dagger is almost as crazy as the disappearance of the man.'

'The disappearance of the dagger,' said Father Brown, nodding. He seemed to have become suddenly attentive.

'Well,' continued Fiennes, 'I told you that man Traill had a trick of fidgeting with his tie and tie-pin – especially his tie-pin. His pin, like himself, was at once showy and old-fashioned. It had one of those stones with concentric coloured rings that look like an eye; and his own concentration on it got on my nerves, as if he had been a Cyclops with one eye in the middle of his body. But the pin was not only large but long; and it occurred to me that his anxiety about its adjustment was because it was even longer than it looked; as long as a stiletto in fact.'

Father Brown nodded thoughtfully. 'Was any other instrument ever suggested?' he asked.

'There was another suggestion,' answered Fiennes, 'from

one of the young Druces – the cousins, I mean. Neither Herbert nor Harry Druce would have struck one at first as likely to be of assistance in scientific detection; but while Herbert was really the traditional type of heavy dragoon, caring for nothing but horses and being an ornament to the Horse Guards, his younger brother Harry had been in the Indian Police and knew something about such things. Indeed in his own way he was quite clever; and I rather fancy he had been too clever; I mean he had left the police through breaking some red-tape regulations and taking some sort of risk and responsibility of his own. Anyhow, he was in some sense a detective out of work, and threw himself in this business with more than the ardour of an amateur. And it was with him that I had an argument about the weapon – an argument that led to something new. It began by his countering my description of the dog barking at Traill; and he said that a dog at his worst didn't bark, but growled.'

'He was quite right there,' observed the priest.

'This young fellow went on to say that, if it came to that, he'd heard Nox growling at other people before then; and among others at Floyd the secretary. I retorted that his own argument answered itself; for the crime couldn't be brought home to two or three people, and least of all to Floyd, who was as innocent as a harum-scarum schoolboy, and had been seen by everybody all the time perched above the garden hedge with his fan of red hair as conspicuous as a scarlet cockatoo. "I know there's difficulties anyhow," said my colleague, "but I wish you'd come with me down the garden a minute. I want to show you something I don't think anyone else has seen." This was on the very day of the discovery, and the garden was just as it had been: the stepladder was still standing by the hedge, and just under the hedge my guide stooped and disentangled something from the deep grass. It was the shears used for clipping the hedge, and on the point of one of them was a smear of blood.'

There was a short silence, and then Father Brown said suddenly, 'What was the lawyer there for?'

'He told us the colonel sent for him to alter his will,' answered Fiennes. 'And, by the way, there was another thing about the business of the will that I ought to mention. You see, the will wasn't actually signed in the summer house that afternoon.'

'I suppose not,' said Father Brown; 'there would have to be two witnesses.'

'The lawyer actually came down the day before and it was signed then; but he was sent for again next day because the old man had a doubt about one of the witnesses and had to be reassured.'

'Who were the witnesses?' asked Father Brown.

'That's just the point,' replied his informant eagerly, 'the witnesses were Floyd the secretary and this Dr Valentine, the foreign sort of surgeon or whatever he is; and the two had a quarrel. Now I'm bound to say that the secretary is something of a busybody. He's one of those hot and headlong people whose warmth of temperament has unfortunately turned mostly to pugnacity and bristling suspicion; to distrusting people instead of to trusting them. That sort of red-haired red-hot fellow is always either universally credulous or universally incredulous; and sometimes both. He was not only a jack-of-all-trades, but he knew better than all tradesmen. He not only knew everything, but he warned everybody against everybody. All that must be taken into account in his suspicions about Valentine; but in that particular case there seems to have been something behind it. He said the name of Valentine was not really Valentine. He said he had seen him elsewhere known by the name of De Villon.

He said it would invalidate the will; of course he was kind enough to explain to the lawyer what the law was on that point. They were both in a frightful wax.'

Father Brown laughed. 'People often are when they are to witness a will,' he said. 'For one thing it means that they can't have any legacy under it. But what did Dr Valentine say? No doubt the universal secretary knew more about the doctor's name than the doctor did. But even the doctor might have some information about his own name.'

Fiennes paused a moment before he replied.

'Dr Valentine took it in a curious way. Dr Valentine is a curious man. His appearance is rather striking but very foreign. He is young but wears a beard cut square; and his face is very pale and dreadfully serious. His eyes have a sort of ache in them, as if he ought to wear glasses or had given himself a headache thinking; but he is quite handsome and always very formally dressed, with a top hat and dark coat and a little red rosette. His manner is rather cold and haughty, and he has a way of staring at you which is very disconcerting. When thus charged with having changed his name, he merely stared like a sphinx and then said with a little laugh that he supposed Americans had no names to change. At that I think the colonel also got into a fuss and said all sorts of angry things to the doctor; all the more angry because of the doctor's pretensions to a future place in his family. But I shouldn't have thought much of that but for a few words that I happened to hear later, early in the afternoon of the tragedy. I don't want to make a lot of them, for they weren't the sort of words on which one would like, in the ordinary way, to play the eavesdropper. As I was passing out towards the front gate with my two companions and the dog, I heard voices which told me that Dr Valentine and Miss Druce had withdrawn for a moment into the shadow of the house, in an angle behind a row of flowering plants, and were talking to each other in passionate whisperings – sometimes almost like hissings; for it was something of a lovers' quarrel as well as a lovers' tryst. Nobody repeats the sorts of things they said for the most part; but in an unfortunate business like this I'm bound to say that there was repeated more than once a phrase about killing somebody. In fact, the girl seemed to be begging him not to kill somebody, or saying that no provocation could justify killing anybody; which seems an unusual sort of talk to address to a gentleman who has dropped in to tea.'

'Do you know,' asked the priest, 'whether Dr Valentine seemed to be very angry after the scene with the secretary and the colonel – I mean about witnessing the will?'

'By all accounts,' replied the other, 'he wasn't half so angry as the secretary was. It was the secretary who went away raging after witnessing the will.'

'And now,' said Father Brown, 'what about the will itself?'

'The colonel was a very wealthy man, and his will was important. Traill wouldn't tell us the alteration at that stage, but I have since heard, only this morning in fact, that most of the money was transferred from the son to the daughter. I told you that Druce was wild with my friend Donald over his dissipated hours.'

'The question of motive has been rather overshadowed by the question of method,' observed Father Brown thoughtfully. 'At that moment, apparently, Miss Druce was the immediate gainer by the death.'

'Good God! What a cold-blooded way of talking,' cried Fiennes, staring at him. 'You don't really mean to hint that she—'

'Is she going to marry that Dr Valentine?' asked the other.

'Some people are against it,' answered his friend. 'But he

is liked and respected in the place and is a skilled and devoted surgeon.'

'So devoted a surgeon,' said Father Brown, 'that he had surgical instruments with him when he went to call on the young lady at teatime. For he must have used a lancet or something, and he never seems to have gone home.'

Fiennes sprang to his feet and looked at him in a heat of inquiry. 'You suggest he might have used the very same lancet—'

Father Brown shook his head. 'All these suggestions are fancies just now,' he said. 'The problem is not who did it or what did it, but how it was done. We might find many men and even many tools – pins and shears and lancets. But how did a man get into the room? How did even a pin get into it?'

He was staring reflectively at the ceiling as he spoke, but as he said the last words his eye cocked in an alert fashion as if he had suddenly seen a curious fly on the ceiling.

'Well, what would you do about it?' asked the young man. 'You have a lot of experience; what would you advise now?'

'I'm afraid I'm not much use,' said Father Brown with a sigh. 'I can't suggest very much without having ever been near the place or the people. For the moment you can only go on with local inquiries. I gather that your friend from the Indian Police is more or less in charge of your inquiry down there. I should run down and see how he is getting on. See what he's been doing in the way of amateur detection. There may be news already.'

As his guests, the biped and the quadruped, disappeared, Father Brown took up his pen and went back to his interrupted occupation of planning a course of lectures on the encyclical *Rerum Novarum*. The subject was a large one and he had to recast it more than once, so that he was somewhat similarly employed some two days later when the big black dog again came bounding into the room and sprawled all over him with enthusiasm and excitement. The master who followed the dog shared the excitement if not the enthusiasm. He had been excited in a less pleasant fashion, for his blue eyes seemed to start from his head and his eager face was even a little pale.

'You told me,' he said abruptly and without preface, 'to find out what Harry Druce was doing. Do you know what he's done?'

The priest did not reply, and the young man went on in jerky tones: 'I'll tell you what's he's done. He's killed himself.'

Father Brown's lips moved only faintly, and there was nothing practical about what he was saying – nothing that has anything to do with this story or this world.

'You give me the creeps sometimes,' said Fiennes. 'Did you – expect this?'

'I thought it possible,' said Father Brown; 'that was why I asked you to go and see what he was doing. I hoped you might not be too late.'

'It was I who found him,' said Fiennes rather huskily. 'It was the ugliest and most uncanny thing I ever knew. I went down that old garden again and I knew there was something new and unnatural about it besides the murder. The flowers still tossed about in blue masses on each side of the black entrance into the old grey summer house; but to me the blue flowers looked like devils dancing before some dark cavern of the underworld. I looked all round; everything seemed to be in its ordinary place. But the queer notion grew on me that there was something wrong with the very shape of the sky. And then I saw what it was. The Rock of Fortune always rose in the background beyond the garden hedge and against the sea. And the Rock of Fortune was gone.'

Father Brown had lifted his head and was listening intently.

'It was as if a mountain had walked away out of a landscape or a moon fallen from the sky; though I knew, of course, that a touch at any time would have tipped the thing over. Something possessed me and I pushed down that garden path like the wind and went crashing through that hedge as if it were a spider's web. It was a thin hedge really, though its undisturbed trimness had made it serve all the purposes of a wall. On the shore I found the loose rock fallen from its pedestal; and poor Harry Druce lay like a wreck underneath it. One arm was thrown round it in a sort of embrace as if he had pulled it down on himself; and on the broad brown sands beside it, in large crazy lettering, he had sprawled the words "The Rock of Fortune falls on the Fool".'

'It was the Colonel's will that did that,' observed Father Brown. 'The young man had staked everything on profiting himself by Donald's disgrace, especially when his uncle sent for him on the same day as the lawyer, and welcomed him with so much warmth. Otherwise he was alone; he'd lost his police job; he was beggared at Monte Carlo. And he killed himself when he found he'd killed his kinsman for nothing.'

'Here, stop a minute!' cried the staring Fiennes. 'You're going too fast for me.'

'Talking about the will, by the way,' continued Father Brown calmly, 'before I forget it, or we go on to bigger things, there was a simple explanation, I think, of all that business about the doctor's name. I rather fancy I have heard both names before somewhere. The doctor is really a French nobleman with the title of the Marquis de Villon. But he is also an ardent Republican and has abandoned his title and fallen back on the forgotten family surname. "With your Citizen Requetti you have puzzled Europe for ten days."'

'What is that?' asked the young man blankly.

'Never mind,' said the priest. 'Nine times out of ten it is a rascally thing to change one's name; but this was a piece of fine fanaticism. That's the point of his sarcasm about Americans having no names – that is, no titles. Now in England the Marquis of Hartington is never called Mr Hartington; but in France the Marquis de Villon is called Monsieur de Villon. So it might well look like a change of names. As for the talk about killing, I fancy that also was a point of French etiquette. The doctor was talking about challenging Floyd to a duel, and the girl was trying to dissuade him.'

'Oh, I *see*,' cried Fiennes slowly. 'Now I understand what she meant.'

'And what is that about?' asked his companion, smiling.

'Well,' said the young man, 'it was something that happened to me just before I found that poor fellow's body; only the catastrophe drove it out of my head. I suppose it's hard to remember a little romantic idyll when you've just come on top of a tragedy. But as I went down the lanes leading to the colonel's old place, I met his daughter walking with Dr Valentine. She was in mourning of course, and he always wore black as if he were going to a funeral; but I can't say that their faces were very funereal. Never have I seen two people looking in their way more respectably radiant and cheerful. They stopped and saluted me and then she told me they were married and living in a little house on the outskirts of the town, where the doctor was continuing his practice. This rather surprised me, because I knew that her old father's will had left her his property; and I hinted at it delicately by saying I was going along to her father's old place and had half expected to meet her there. But she only laughed and said, "Oh, we've given up all that. My husband doesn't like heiresses." And I discovered with some astonishment that they really had insisted on restoring the property to poor Donald; so I hope he's had a healthy shock and will treat it sensibly. There was never much really the matter with him; he was very young and his father was not very wise. But it was in connection with that that she said something I didn't understand at the time; but now I'm sure it must be as you say. She said with a sort of sudden and splendid arrogance that was entirely altruistic, "I hope it'll stop that red-haired fool from fussing any more about the will. Does he think my husband, who has given up a crest and a coronet as old as the Crusades for his principles, would kill an old man in a summer house for a legacy like that?" Then she laughed again and said, "My husband isn't killing anybody except in the way of business. Why, he didn't even ask his friends to call on the secretary." Now, of course, I see what she meant.'

'I see part of what she meant, of course,' said Father Brown. 'What did she mean exactly by the secretary fussing about the will?'

Fiennes smiled as he answered, 'I wish you knew the secretary, Father Brown. It would be a joy to you to watch him make things hum, as he calls it. He made the house of mourning hum. He filled the funeral with all the snap and zip of the brightest sporting event. There was no holding him, after something had really happened. I've told you how he used to oversee the gardener as he did the garden, and how he instructed the lawyer in the law. Needless to say, he also instructed the surgeon in the practice of surgery; and as the surgeon was Dr Valentine, you may be sure it ended in accusing him of something worse than bad surgery. The secretary got it fixed in his red head that the doctor had committed the crime; and when the police arrived he was perfectly sublime. Need I say that he became on the spot the greatest of all amateur detectives? Sherlock Holmes never towered over Scotland Yard with more titanic intellectual pride and scorn than Colonel Druce's private secretary over the police investigating Colonel Druce's death. I tell you it was a joy to see him. He strode about with an abstracted air, tossing his scarlet crest of hair and giving curt impatient replies. Of course it was his demeanour during these days that made Druce's daughter so wild with him. Of course he had a theory. It's just the sort of theory a man would have in a book; and Floyd is the sort of man who ought to be in a book. He'd be better fun and less bother in a book.'

'What was his theory?' asked the other.

'Oh, it was full of pep,' replied Fiennes gloomily. 'It would have been glorious copy if it could have held together for ten minutes longer. He said the colonel was still alive when they found him in the summer house and the doctor killed him with the surgical instrument on pretence of cutting the clothes.'

'I see,' said the priest. 'I suppose he was lying flat on his face on the mud floor as a form of siesta.'

'It's wonderful what hustle will do,' continued his informant. 'I believe Floyd would have got his great theory into the papers at any rate, and perhaps had the doctor arrested, when all these things were blown sky high as if by dynamite by the discovery of that dead body lying under the Rock of Fortune. And that's what we come back to after all. I suppose the suicide is almost a confession. But nobody will ever know the whole story.'

There was a silence, and then the priest said modestly, 'I rather think I know the whole story.'

Fiennes stared. 'But look here,' he cried; 'how do you come to know the whole story, or to be sure it's the true story? You've been sitting here a hundred miles away writing a sermon; do you mean to tell me you really know what happened already? If you've really come to the end, where in the world do you begin? What started you off with your own story?'

Father Brown jumped up with a very unusual excitement and his first exclamation was like an explosion.

'The dog!' he cried. 'The dog, of course! You had the whole story in your hands in the business of the dog on the beach, if you'd only noticed the dog properly.'

Fiennes stared still more. 'But you told me just now that my feelings about the dog were all nonsense, and the dog had nothing to do with it.'

'The dog had everything to do with it,' said Father Brown, 'as you'd have found out, if you'd only treated the dog as a dog and not as God Almighty, judging the souls of men.'

He paused in an embarrassed way for a moment, and then said, with a rather pathetic air of apology:

'The truth is, I happen to be awfully fond of dogs. And it seemed to me that in all this lurid halo of dog superstitions nobody was really thinking about the poor dog at all. To begin with a small point, about barking at the lawyer or growling at the secretary. You asked how I guess things a hundred miles away; but honestly it's mostly to your credit, for you described people so well that I know the types. A man like Traill who frowns usually and smiles suddenly, a man who fiddles with things, especially at his throat, is a nervous, easily embarrassed man. I shouldn't wonder if Floyd, the efficient secretary, is nervy and jumpy too; those Yankee hustlers often are. Otherwise he wouldn't have cut his fingers on the shears and dropped them when he heard Janet Druce scream.

'Now dogs hate nervous people. I don't know whether they make the dog nervous too; or whether, being after all a brute, he is a bit of a bully; or whether his canine vanity (which is colossal) is simply offended by not being liked. But anyhow there was nothing in poor Nox protesting against those people except that he disliked them for being afraid of him. Now I know you're awfully clever, and nobody of sense sneers at cleverness. But I sometimes fancy, for instance, that you are too clever to understand animals. Sometimes you are too clever to understand men, especially when they act almost as simply as animals. Animals are very literal; they live in a world of truisms. Take this case; a dog barks at a man and a man runs away from a dog. Now you do not seem to be quite simple enough to see the fact; that the dog barked because he disliked the man and the man fled because he was frightened of the dog. They had no other motives and they needed none. But you must read psychological mysteries into it and suppose the dog had supernormal vision, and was a mysterious mouthpiece of doom. You must suppose the man was running away, not from the dog, but from the hangman. And yet, if you come to think of it, all this deeper psychology is exceedingly improbable. If the dog really could completely and consciously realize the murderer of his master, he wouldn't stand yapping as he might at a curate at a tea party; he's much more likely to fly at his throat. And on the other hand, do you really think a man who had hardened his heart to murder an old friend and then walk about smiling at the old friend's family, under the eyes of his old friend's daughter and post mortem doctor – do you think a man like that could be doubled up by mere remorse because a dog barked? He might feel the tragic irony of it; it might shake his soul, like any other tragic trifle. But he wouldn't rush madly the length of a garden to escape from the only witness whom he knew to be unable to talk. People have a panic like that when they are frightened, not of tragic ironies, but of teeth. The whole thing is simpler than you can understand. But when we come to that business by the seashore, things are much more interesting. As you stated them, they were much more puzzling. I didn't understand that tale of the dog going in and out of the water; it didn't seem to me a doggy thing to do. If Nox had been very much upset about something else, he might possibly have refused to go after the stick at all. He'd probably go off nosing in whatever direction he suspected the mischief. But when once a dog is actually chasing a thing, a stone or a stick or a rabbit, my experience is that he won't stop for anything but the most peremptory command, and not always for that. That he should turn because his mood changed seems to me unthinkable.'

'But he did turn round,' insisted Fiennes, 'and came back without the stick.'

'He came back without the stick for the best reason in the world,' replied the priest. 'He came back because he couldn't find it. He whined because he couldn't find it. That's the sort of thing a dog really does whine about. A dog is a devil of a ritualist. He is as particular about the precise routine of a game as a child about the precise repetition of a fairy tale. In this case something had gone wrong with the game. He came back to complain seriously of the conduct of the stick. Never had such a thing happened before. Never had an eminent and distinguished dog been so treated by a rotten old walking stick.'

'Why, what had the walking stick done?' inquired the young man.

'It had sunk,' said Father Brown.

Fiennes said nothing, but continued to stare, and it was the priest who continued:

'It had sunk because it was not really a stick, but a rod of steel with a very thin shell of cane and a sharp point. In other words, it was a sword stick. I suppose a murderer never got rid of a bloody weapon so oddly and yet so naturally as by throwing it into the sea for a retriever.'

'I begin to see what you mean,' admitted Fiennes; 'but even if a sword stick was used, I have no guess of how it was used.'

'I had a sort of guess,' said Father Brown, 'right at the beginning when you said the words "summer house". And another when you said that Druce wore a white coat. As long as everybody was looking for a short dagger, nobody thought of it; but if we admit a rather long blade like a rapier, it's not so impossible.'

He was leaning back, looking at the ceiling, and began like one going back to his own first thoughts and fundamentals.

'All that discussion about detective stories like the Yellow Room, about a man found dead in sealed chambers which no one could enter, does not apply to the present case, because it is a summer house. When we talk of a Yellow Room, or any room, we imply walls that are really homogeneous and impenetrable. But a summer house is not made like that; it is often made, as it was in this case, of closely interlaced but still separate boughs and strips of wood, in which there are chinks here and there. There was one of them just behind Druce's back as he sat in his chair up against the wall. But just as the room was a summer house, so the chair was a basket-chair. That also was a lattice of loopholes. Lastly, the summer house was close up under the hedge; and you have just told me that it was really a thin hedge. A man standing outside it could easily see, amid a network of twigs and branches and canes, one white spot of the colonel's coat as plain as the white of a target.

'Now, you left the geography a little vague; but it was

possible to put two and two together. You said the Rock of Fortune was not really high; but you said it could be seen dominating the garden like a mountain peak. In other words, it was very near the end of the garden, though your walk had taken you a long way round to it. Also, it isn't likely the young lady really howled so as to be heard half a mile. She gave an ordinary involuntary cry and yet you heard it on the shore. And among other interesting things that you told me, may I remind you that you said Harry Druce had fallen behind to light his pipe under a hedge.'

Fiennes shuddered slightly. 'You mean he drew his blade there and sent it through the hedge at the white spot. But surely it was a very odd chance and a very sudden choice. Besides, he couldn't be certain the old man's money had passed to him, and as a fact it hadn't.'

Father Brown's face animated.

'You misunderstand the man's character,' he said, as if he himself had known the man all his life. 'A curious but not unknown type of character. If he had really *known* the money would come to him, I seriously believe he wouldn't have done it. He would have seen it as the dirty thing it was.'

'Isn't that rather paradoxical?' asked the other.

'This man was a gambler,' said the priest, 'and a man in disgrace for having taken risks and anticipated orders. It was probably for something pretty unscrupulous, for every imperial police is more like a Russian secret police than we like to think. But he had gone beyond the line and failed. Now, the temptation of that type of man is to do a mad thing precisely because the risk will be wonderful in retrospect. He wants to say, "Nobody but I could have seized that chance or seen that it was then or never. What a wild and wonderful guess it was, when I put all those things together: Donald in disgrace; and the lawyer being sent for; and Herbert and

I sent for at the same time – and then nothing more but the way the old man grinned at me and shook hands. Anybody would say I was mad to risk it; but that is how fortunes are made, by the man mad enough to have a little foresight." In short, it is the vanity of guessing. It is the megalomania of the gambler. The more incongruous the coincidence, the more instantaneous the decision, the more likely he is to snatch the chance. The accident, the very triviality, of the white speck and the hole in the hedge intoxicated him like a vision of the world's desire. Nobody clever enough to see such a combination of accidents could be cowardly enough not to use them! That is how the devil talks to the gambler. But the devil himself would hardly have induced that un-happy man to go down in a dull, deliberate way and kill an old uncle from whom he'd always had expectations. It would be too respectable.'

He paused a moment; and then went on with a certain quiet emphasis.

'And now try to call up the scene, even as you saw it your-self. As he stood there, dizzy with his diabolical opportunity, he looked up and saw that strange outline that might have been the image of his own tottering soul – the one great crag poised perilously on the other like a pyramid on its point – and remembered that it was called the Rock of Fortune. Can you guess how such a man at such a moment would read such a signal? I think it strung him up to action and even to vigilance. He who would be a tower must not fear to be a toppling tower. Anyhow he acted; his next difficulty was to cover his tracks. To be found with a sword stick, let alone a blood-stained sword stick, would be fatal in the search that was certain to follow. If he left it anywhere, it would be found and probably traced. Even if he threw it into the sea the action might be noticed, and thought noticeable – unless indeed he could think of some more natural way of covering the action. As you know, he did think of one, and a very good one. Being the only one of you with a watch, he told you it was not yet time to return, strolled a little farther, and started the game of throwing in sticks for the retriever. But how his eyes must have rolled darkly over all that desolate seashore before they alighted on the dog!'

Fiennes nodded, gazing thoughtfully into space. His mind seemed to have drifted back to a less practical part of the narrative.

'It's queer,' he said, 'that the dog really was in the story after all.'

'The dog could almost have told you the story, if he could talk,' said the priest. 'All I complain of is that because he couldn't talk, you made up his story for him, and made him talk with the tongues of men and angels. It's part of something I've noticed more and more in the modern world, appearing in all sorts of newspaper rumours and conversational catchwords; something that's arbitrary without being authoritative. People readily swallow the untested claims of this, that, or the other. It's drowning all your old rationalism and scepticism, it's coming in like a sea; and the name of it is superstition.' He stood up abruptly, his face heavy with a sort of frown, and went on talking almost as if he were alone. 'It's the first effect of not believing in God that you lose your common sense, and can't see things as they are. Anything that anybody talks about, and says there's a good deal in it, extends itself indefinitely like a vista in a nightmare. And a dog is an omen and a cat is a mystery and a pig is a mascot and a beetle is a scarab, calling up all the menagerie of polytheism from Egypt and old India; Dog Anubis and great green-eyed Pasht and all the holy howling Bulls of Bashan; reeling back to the bestial gods of the beginning, escaping into elephants and snakes and crocodiles; and all because you are frightened of four words: "He was made Man." '

The young man got up with a little embarrassment, almost as if he had overheard a soliloquy. He called to the dog and left the room with vague but breezy farewells. But he had to call the dog twice, for the dog had remained behind quite motionless for a moment, looking up steadily at Father Brown as the wolf looked at Saint Francis.

BRAD WATSON

SEEING EYE

THE DOG CAME to the curb's edge and stopped. The man holding on to his halter stopped beside him. Across the street, the signal flashed the words 'Don't Walk'. The dog saw the signal but paid little notice. He was trained to see what mattered: the absence of moving traffic. The signal kept blinking. The cars kept driving through the intersection. He watched the cars, listened to the intensity of their engines, the arid whine of their tires. He listened for something he'd become accustomed to hearing, the buzz and tumbling of switches from the box on the pole next to them. The dog associated it with the imminent stopping of the cars. He looked back over his right shoulder at the man, who stood with his head cocked, listening to the traffic.

A woman behind them spoke up.

'Huh,' she said. 'The light's stuck.'

The dog looked at her, then turned back to watch the traffic, which continued to rush through the intersection without pause.

'I'm going down a block,' the woman said. She spoke to the man. 'Would you like me to show you a detour? No telling how long this light will be.'

'No, thank you,' the man said. 'We'll just wait a little bit. Right, Buck?' The dog looked back over his shoulder at the man, then watched the woman walk away.

'Good luck,' the woman said. The dog's ears stood up and he stiffened for just a second.

'She said "luck", not "Buck",' the man said, laughing easily and reaching down to scratch the dog's ears. He gripped the loose skin on Buck's neck with his right hand and gave it an affectionate shake. He continued to hold the halter guide loosely with his left.

The dog watched the traffic rush by.

'We'll just wait here, Buck,' the man said. 'By the time we go a block out of our way, the light will've fixed itself.' He cleared his throat and cocked his head, as if listening for something. The dog dipped his head and shifted his shoulders in the halter.

The man laughed softly.

'If we went down a block, I'll bet that light would get stuck, too. We'd be following some kind of traveling glitch across town. We could go for miles, and then end up in some field, and a voice saying, "I suppose you're wondering why I've summoned you here."'

It was the longest they'd ever stood waiting for traffic to stop. The dog saw people across the street wait momentarily, glance around, then leave. He watched the traffic. It began to have a hypnotic effect upon him: the traffic, the blinking crossing signal. His focus on the next move, the crossing, on the implied courses of the pedestrians around them and those still waiting at the opposite curb, on the potential obstructions ahead, dissolved into the rare luxury of wandering attention.

The sounds of the traffic grinding through the intersection were diminished to a small aural dot in the back of his mind, and he became aware of the regular bleat of a slow-turning box fan in an open window of the building behind them. Odd scents distinguished themselves in his nostrils and blended into a rich funk that swirled about the pedestrians who stopped next to them, a secret aromatic history that eddied about him even as the pedestrians muttered among themselves and moved on.

The hard clean smell of new shoe leather seeped from the air-conditioned stores, overlaying the drift of worn leather and grime that eased from tiny musty pores in the sidewalk. He snuffled at them and sneezed. In a trembling confusion he was aware of all that was carried in the breeze, the strong odor of tobacco and the sharp rake of its smoke, the gasoline and exhaust fumes and the stench of aging rubber, the fetid waves that rolled through it all from garbage bins in the alleys and on the backstreet curbs.

He lowered his head and shifted his shoulders in the harness like a boxer.

'Easy, Buck,' the man said.

Sometimes in their room the man paced the floor, and seemed to say his words in time with his steps until he became like a lulling clock to Buck as he lay resting beneath the dining table. He dozed to the man's mumbling and the sifting sound of his fingers as they grazed the pages of his book. At times in their dark room the man sat on the edge of his cot and scratched Buck's ears and spoke to him. 'Panorama, Buck,' he would say. 'That's the most difficult to recall. I can see the details, with my hands, with my nose, my tongue. It brings them back. But the big picture. I feel like I must be replacing it with something phony, like a Disney movie or something.' Buck looked up at the man's shadowed face in the dark room, at his small eyes in their sallow depressions.

On the farm where he'd been raised before his training at the school, Buck's name had been Pete. The children and the old man and the woman had tussled with him, thrown sticks, said, 'Pete! Good old Pete.' They called out to him, mumbled the name into his fur. But now the man always said 'Buck' in the same tone of voice, soft and gentle. As if the man were speaking to himself. As if Buck were not really there.

'I miss colors, Buck,' the man would say. 'It's getting harder to remember them. The blue planet. I remember that. Pictures from space. From out in the blackness.'

Looking up from the intersection, Buck saw birds dart through the sky between buildings as quickly as they slipped past the open window at dawn. He heard their high-pitched cries so clearly that he saw their beady eyes, their barbed tongues flicking between parted beaks. He salivated at the dusky taste of a dove once he'd held in his mouth. And in his most delicate bones he felt the murmur of some incessant activity, the low hum beyond the visible world. His hackles rose and his muscles tingled with electricity.

There was a metallic whirring, like a big fat June bug stuck on its back, followed by the dull clunk of the switch in the traffic control box. Cars stopped. The lane opened up before them, and for a moment no one moved, as if the empty-eyed vehicles were not to be trusted, restrained only by some fragile miracle of faith. He felt the man carefully regrip the leather harness. He felt the activity of the world spool down into the tight and rifled tunnel of their path.

'Forward, Buck,' said the man.

He leaned into the harness and moved them into the world.

TOBIAS WOLFF

HER DOG

WHEN GRACE FIRST got Victor, she and John walked him on the beach most Sundays. Then a Chow-Chow bit some kid and the parks department restricted dogs to the slough behind the dunes. Grace took Victor there for years, and after she died John stepped in and maintained the custom, though he hated it back there. The mushy trail hedged with poison oak. Baking flats of cracked mud broken by patches of scrub. The dunes stifled the sea breeze, leaving the air still and rank and seething with insects.

But Victor came alive here in spite of himself. At home he slept and grieved, yet grief could not deaden the scent of fallow deer and porcupine, of rabbits and rats and the little gray foxes that ate them. Dogs were supposed to be kept on the leash for the sake of the wildlife, but Grace had always left Victor free to follow his nose, and John couldn't bring himself to rein him in now. Anyway, Victor was too creaky and cloudy-eyed to chase anything; if he did catch some movement in the brush he'd lean forward and maybe, just to keep his dignity, raise a paw – *Eh? That's right, run along there!* – and then go back to smelling things. John didn't hurry him. He lingered, waving away the mosquitoes and flies that swarmed around his head, until the hint of some new fragrance pulled Victor farther along the trail.

Victor was drawn to the obvious delights – putrefying carcasses, the regurgitations of hawks and owls – but he could just as easily get worked up over a clump of shrubbery that seemed no different than the one beside it. He had his nose stuck deep in swamp grass one damp morning when John saw a dog emerge from the low-hanging mist farther up the trail. It was a barrel-chested dog with a short brindled coat and a blunt pink snout, twice Victor's size, as big as a lab but of no breed familiar to John. When it caught sight of Victor it stopped for a moment, then advanced on stiffened legs.

'Scram!' John said, and clapped his hands.

Victor looked up from the grass. As the dog drew near he took a step in its direction, head craned forward, blinking like a mole. *Huh? Huh? Who's there? Somebody there?*

John took him by the collar. 'Beat it!' he said. 'Go away.'

The dog kept coming.

'Go!' John shouted again. But the dog came on, slowly now, almost mincing, with an unblinking intentness. It kept its yellow eyes on Victor and ignored John altogether. John stepped in front of Victor, to break the dog's gaze and force himself on its attention, but instead it left the trail and began to circle around him, eyes still fixed on Victor. John moved to stay between them. He put his free hand out, palm facing the dog. Victor gave a grumble and strained forward against his collar. The dog came closer. Too close, too intent, it seemed to be gathering itself. John reached down and scooped Victor up and turned his back on the dog. He rarely had occasion to lift Victor and was always surprised at his lightness. Victor lay still for a moment, then began struggling as the dog moved around to face them. 'Go away, damn you,' John said.

'Bella! Whoa, Bella.' A man's voice: sharp, nasal. John looked up the trail and saw him coming, shaved head, wraparound sunglasses, bare arms sticking out of a leather vest. He was taking his sweet time. The dog kept circling John.

Victor complained and squirmed impatiently. *Put me down, put me down.*

'Get that dog away from us,' John said.

'Bella? He won't hurt you.'

'If he touches my dog I'll kill him.'

'Whoa, Bella.' The man sauntered up behind the dog and took a leash from his back pocket. He reached for the dog but it dodged him and cut back in front of John, keeping Victor in view. 'Shame, Bella! Shame on you. Come back here – right now!' The man put his hands on his hips and stared at the dog. His arms were thick and covered with tattoos, and more tattoos rose up his neck like vines. His chest was bare and pale under the open vest. Beads of sweat glistened on the top of his head.

'Get control of that dog,' John said. He turned again, Victor still fidgeting in his arms, the dog following.

'He just wants to make friends,' the man said. He waited until the dog's orbit brought him closer, then made a lunge and caught him by the collar. 'Bad Bella!' he said, snapping on the leash. 'You just have to be everybody's friend, don't you?'

John set Victor down and leashed him and walked him farther up the trail. His hands were shaking. 'That dog is a menace,' he said. '*Bella.* Jesus.'

'It means "handsome".'

'No, actually, it means "pretty". Like a girl.'

The man looked at John through his bubbly black shades. How did he see anything? It was irritating, like the display of his uselessly muscled, illustrated arms. 'I thought it meant "handsome",' he said.

'Well it doesn't. The ending is feminine.'

'What are you, a teacher or something?'

The dog suddenly lunged against its leash.

'We're going,' John said. 'Keep your dog away from us.'

'So, are you a teacher?'

'No,' John lied. 'I'm a lawyer.'

'You shouldn't have said that about killing Bella. I could sue you, right?'

'Not really, no.'

'Okay, but still, you didn't have to get all belligerent. Do you have a card? This friend of mine had his film script totally ripped off by Steven Spielberg.'

'I don't do that kind of law.'

'You should talk to him. Like, D-day? You know, all those guys on the beach? Exactly the way my friend described it. *Exactly.*'

'D-day happened,' John said. 'Your friend didn't make it up.'

'Okay, sure. But still.'

'Anyway, that movie was years ago.'

'So you're saying statute of limitations?'

The opening notes of 'Ode to Joy' shrilled out. 'Hang on,' the man told him. He took a cell phone from his pocket and said, 'Hey, lemme call you back, I'm in kind of a legal conference here.'

'No!' John said. 'No, you can talk. Just please keep Bella on the leash, okay?'

The man gave the thumbs-up and John led Victor away, up into the mist the other two had come out of. Right away his skin felt clammy. The bugs were loud around his ears. He was still shaking.

Victor stopped to squeeze out a few turds, then looked up at John. *My savior. I guess I should be panting with gratitude. Licking your hand.*

No need.

How'd you put it? I'll kill him if he touches my dog. What devotion! Almost canine. Victor finished and made a show of kicking back some dirt. He raised his head and tested the air like a connoisseur before starting up the trail, feathery tail aloft. *I could've handled him.*

Maybe so.

He wasn't going to do anything. Anyway, since when do you care? It's not like you even wanted me. If it hadn't been for Grace, those guys at the pound would've killed me.

It wasn't you I didn't want – you in particular. I just wasn't ready for a dog.

I guess not. The way you carried on when Grace brought me home. What a brat.

I know.

All your little conditions for keeping me. I was her dog. All the feeding, all the walking, picking up poop, baths, trips to the vet, arrangements with the kennel when you went out of town – her responsibility.

I know.

Her dog, her job to keep me out of the living room, out of the study, off the couch, off the bed, off the Persian rug. No barking, even when someone came right past the house – right up to the door!

I know, I know.

And when they kicked me off the beach, remember that? No way you were going to get stuck back here. No, Grace had to walk me in the swamp while you walked along the ocean. I hope you enjoyed it.

I didn't. I felt mean and foolish.

But you made your point! Her dog, her responsibility. You let her walk me in the rain once when she had a cold.

She insisted.

Then you should've insisted more.

Yes. That's what I think, too, now.

I miss her! I miss her! I miss my Grace!

So do I.

Not like me. Did I ever bark at her?

No.

You did.

And she barked back. We disagreed sometimes. All couples do.

Not Grace and Victor. Grace and Victor never disagreed. Did I ignore her?

No.

You ignored her. She would call your name and you would go on reading your paper, or watching TV and pretend you hadn't heard. Did she ever have to call my name twice? No! Once and I'd be there, looking up at her, ready for anything. Did I ever want another mistress?

No.

You did. You looked at them in the park, on the beach, in other cars as we drove around.

Men do that. It didn't mean I wanted anyone but Grace.

Yes, you did.

Maybe for an hour. For a night. No longer.

Then I loved her more than you. I loved her with all my heart.

You had no choice. You can't be selfish. But we men – it's a wonder we forget ourselves long enough to buy a birthday card. As for love . . . we *can* love, but we're always forgetting.

I didn't forget, not once.

That's true. But then you missed out on being forgiven. You never knew how it feels to be welcomed home after you've wandered off. Without forgiveness we're lost. Can't do it for ourselves. Can't take ourselves back in.

I never wandered off.

No. You're a good dog. You always were.

Victor left the trail to inspect a heap of dirt thrown up by some tunneling creature. He yanked at the leash in his excitement. John unclipped him and waited as Victor circled the mound, sniffing busily, then stuck his nose in the burrow and began to dig around it. To watch him in his forgetfulness of everything else was John's pleasure, and this is where he found it, Sundays in the bog with Victor. He looked up through a haze of insects. A buzzard was making lazy circles high overhead, riding the sea breeze John could not feel down here, though he could faintly make out the sounds it carried from beyond the dunes, of crying gulls and crashing waves and the shrieking children who fled before them. Victor panted madly, hearing none of this. He worked fast for an old fellow, legs a blur, pawing back clumps of black earth. He lifted his dirty face from the hole to give a hunter's yelp, then plunged back in.

LYDIA MILLET

SIR HENRY

THE DOG WAS SERIOUS, always had been. No room for levity. Those around him might be lighthearted. Often they laughed, sometimes even at his expense – the miniature size, bouncing gait, flopping ears. He was a dachshund. Not his fault. You were what you were. He would have preferred the aspect of an Alsatian, possibly a Norwegian elkhound. He viewed himself as one of these large and elegant breeds.

This much could be seen with the naked eye, and the dogwalker saw it. The dogwalker was also serious – a loner, except for dogs. He prided himself on his work. He had no patience for moonlighters, for the giddy girls talking on their cell phones as they tottered through Sheep Meadow with seven different-size purebreds on as many leashes, jerking them this way and that and then screeching in indignation when the dogs became confused. He had once seen such a girl get two fingers ripped off. He'd called 911 himself. It was an ugly scene. The paramedics recovered the fingers, snarled up in leather and nylon, but the hand had been twisted so roughly they predicted it would never work right. The girl herself had passed out long before the ambulance got there. Turned out she was premed at Columbia.

Two of the dogs were also injured. Their mutual aggression had caused the accident in the first place; he had seen it coming all the way from the carousel – the dogs straining and nipping at each other, the girl on her phone with the leashes tangled around her left hand.

Himself, he was a professional with exacting standards. He made an excellent living. He had subcontractors, yes, but all of them were vet techs, trainers or groomers at the very least. None were college girls who took the job literally, expecting it to be a simple walk in the park.

The dogwalker gave his charges respect as he saw fit. Some did not deserve it, and they did not receive it. To these frivolous or problem dogs he gave only the curt nod of discipline. His favorite dogs had a sense of dignity. Theirs was a mutual approbation. Sir Henry was one of these.

The owner traveled constantly, often in Europe, Asia or South America. All over. He was a performer of some kind, in show business. When he was in town he spent most of his time at the gym, maintaining his physique, tanning, shopping or seeking photo opportunities. The dogwalker barely registered him. The dogwalker went to get Sir Henry three times a day, rain or shine. Henry seldom went out otherwise – the odd trip with one of the girls when they were home from school, or the wife on the rare occasion when she was not, like the entertainer, at the gym or shopping. Now and then, if he found himself at loose ends for twenty minutes or so, the entertainer paraded with Sir Henry personally, scoping the park for other celebs to do the meet and greet with. In the puppy days he had taken Sir Henry out frequently, but the puppy days had passed.

There was an older dachshund, Precious, also owned by the entertainer, but Precious had been virtually adopted by one of the domestics, an illegal from Haiti if the dogwalker was not mistaken. The Haitian took Precious out on her cigarette breaks. But not Sir Henry.

The dogwalker walked Sir Henry alone or with one particular other dog, a small poodle belonging to a dying violinist. The poodle was stately, subtle and, like the dachshund, possessed of a poise that elevated it beyond its miniature stature. The two seemed to have an understanding. The poodle marked first and with great discretion; the dachshund marked second. They trotted happily beside each other at an identical pace, despite the fact that the poodle's legs were almost twice as long. They listened to the dogwalker acutely and responded promptly to his commands. It was their pleasure to serve.

Did they serve him? No, and he would not have it so. They served decorum, the order of things.

At times the dogwalker enjoyed resting with them; he would settle down on a park bench and the dogs would sit at his feet, paws together neatly, looking forward with an appearance of vigilance. Their heads turned in unison as other dogs passed.

When it was morning, noon and night, of course, as it was with Sir Henry, it was no longer merely walking. The dogwalker was in loco parentis. It was he who had discovered the bladder infection, the flea eggs. It was he who had recommended a vet, a diet, routine. In the economy of dogwalkers he was top tier; only the exceptionally wealthy could afford him, those who did not even notice that their dogwalking fees exceeded rents in Brooklyn. His personal service included a commitment of the heart, for which the megarich were willing to pay through the nose. About his special charges he was not workmanlike in the least. He was professional, operating by a mature code with set rules for all of his employees, but he was not slick. He did not cultivate in himself the distancing practiced by pediatric oncologists and emergency-room surgeons. His clients sensed this, and where their pets were concerned, his fond touch soothed the conscience.

He began with respect and often ended with love. When

a dog was taken from him – a move, a change of fortune or, in one painful case, a spontaneous gifting – he felt it deeply. His concern for a lost dog, as he thought of them, would keep him up for many nights after one of these incidents. When a young Weimaraner was lost to him with not even a chance to say good-bye, he remained deeply angry for weeks. The owner, a teenage heiress often featured in the local tabloids, had given his charge away on the spur of the moment to a Senegalese dancer she met at a restaurant. He had no doubt that drug use was involved. The dog, a timid, damaged animal of great gentleness and forbearance, was on a plane to Africa by the time he found out about it the next day.

The loss was hard for him. He was tormented by thoughts of the sweet-natured bitch cowering, subjected to the whims of an unkind owner or succumbing to malnutrition. Of course, there was a chance the new owner was thoughtful, attentive, nurturing – but he had no reason to expect such a happy outcome. In his work he saw shockingly few people who were fit for their dogs.

Walking Sir Henry and the poodle up Cherry Hill, he remembered the Weimaraner, and a pang of grief and regret glanced through him. It had been almost three years ago; where was the good creature now? He had looked up Senegal on the Internet after she was taken. 'Senegal is a mainly low-lying country, with a semidesert area to the north . . .' He had never been to Africa, and in his mind the Weimaraner lived alternately in the squalor of dusty famine, scrabbling for scraps of food among fly-eyed hungry children, or in the cool white majesty of minarets. There were obdurate camels and palm trees near the Weimaraner, or there were UN cargo planes dropping crates of rice.

In less colorful moments, he was quietly certain the Weimaraner was dead. The incident had taught him a valuable lesson, one he firmly believed he should have learned earlier: in the client-selection process, people must be subjected to far greater scrutiny than their dogs. He no longer contracted with unreliable owners. If he had reason to suspect an owner or family was not prepared to keep a dog for its lifetime, he did not take the job.

It could be difficult. Sometimes a dog owned by one of these irresponsible persons had powerful appeal – grace, sensitivity, an air of loneliness. But the risk was too great. He made himself walk away from these dogs.

Sir Henry emitted one short bark and he and the poodle stopped and stood, tails wagging, pointing to the left. The dogwalker stopped too. There was the violinist, wrapped in blankets, seated under a tree in his wheelchair with his attendant and an oxygen tank. The dogwalker was surprised. As far as he knew, the violinist, who was at the end stage of a long cancer, never came out of his penthouse anymore. The place had a large wraparound terrace from which the East River could be seen; there were potted trees and even a small lawn on this terrace, where the poodle spent much of its time.

'Blackie,' said the violinist in his weak, rasping voice, and the dogwalker obediently let the two dogs approach.

'A surprise,' said the dogwalker. He was not skilled at small talk.

'Figured I should take one last stroll in the park,' said the violinist, and smiled. 'Come here, Blackie.'

The dogwalker handed the poodle's leash to the attendant and Blackie jumped up into his owner's lap. The old man winced but petted the poodle with a bone-stiff hand.

'I need to know what will happen to her,' said the violinist. 'When I die.'

The dogwalker felt embarrassed. Death was an intimate

subject. Yet it was close, and the violinist was quite right to plan for his dog.

'Difficult,' he offered.

'I wonder if, if I were to establish a trust ... ample provisions, financially ... would you consider –?'

The dogwalker, surprised again, looked to the attendant who was holding the leash. She had a beseeching look on her face, and for a minute he did not know how to take this. Finally he decided the look meant the violinist would not be able to bear a flat-out refusal.

'Let me think,' he said, stalling.

It was not in his code.

'Think fast,' said the violinist, though he was still smiling.

'I will think about it overnight,' said the dogwalker.

'You like Blackie,' said the violinist, a quaver in his voice. 'Right? Don't you like her?'

The dogwalker felt a terrible pity enfold him.

'Of course I do,' he said quickly. 'She is among my favorites.'

The violinist, on the brink of tears, bent his head to his dog, petting her softly and rapidly as she patiently withstood the onslaught. His attendant shaded her own eyes and blinked into the distance.

'I am very attached to Blackie,' the dogwalker bumbled on. 'But the adoption of dogs is against my policy. Please give me till tomorrow.'

'OK,' said the violinist, and attempted to smile again. 'I'll try not to kick the bucket before then.'

'I would take her,' explained the attendant, apologetic. 'But I just can't.'

She handed back the leash and Blackie jumped off the lap.

'We'll see you back at the apartment,' called the attendant after him.

232

They had more than half an hour left on the circuit. As the dogs trotted in front of him, he saw Sir Henry turn back to the violinist, checking up on him.

If he accepted the dog, in a clear violation of established protocol, would his principles erode? Would he end up an eccentric with an apartment full of abandoned pets? By preferring dogs to humans he put himself at risk – myopia on the part of his fellow citizens of course, since dogs were so clearly their moral superiors. Still, he did not wish to be stigmatized.

As they neared the 72nd Street entrance he saw children approaching, delighted. Children were a matter of policy also. He allowed only quiet ones to touch his charges, and he preferred the females. Males made sudden movements, capered foolishly and often taunted.

He stopped now, for these were two melancholy slips of girls with round eyes.

'May I pet him, please?' asked one of them, and suspended a hand in the air over Sir Henry's head.

Sir Henry welcomed it. Girls reminded him of the entertainer's daughters, the dogwalker thought, two blond girls who had caressed him constantly when he was only three months old but now seemed unaware of his existence.

Himself, he was preoccupied; this was a critical decision. His mind wandered as the girls leaned down. He gazed in their direction but he did not see them clearly – bent pink forms with sunlight on wavy hair . . . if he owned the poodle himself he could walk the dogs like this every day, the dachshund and Blackie. Sir Henry was most contented in the poodle's presence.

'You get *away*,' said a woman harshly to the girls. She wore tight leather pants and held a phone to her ear. 'They could bite. They're dirty.'

'They are cleaner than you are,' said the dogwalker softly. 'And they never bite nice little girls. Only mean old witches.'

'Right *now*,' snapped the woman.

'Thanks, mister,' said the elder girl, and looked with longing at Sir Henry as the woman tugged at her arm.

He was often grateful that dogs had little use for language; still, they understood tone. The leather-pants woman had slightly offended them, he suspected – a tell-tale lowering of their heads as they made for the gate. Dogs had an ear for the meaning in voice.

'Oh my God,' said a fat man in front of them on the path, pointing, and laughed. 'It's David Hasselhoff.'

He turned to see the entertainer advancing, talking into his telephone and wearing what appeared to be gaudy jogging attire, a jacket with purple details that matched purple pants. No doubt he was on his way home from the gym.

Never before had the dogwalker run into two owners on a single walk.

'Yeah. Yeah,' said David Hasselhoff on the phone. 'Yeah. Yeah. Yeah.' As he passed them he winked at the dogwalker, then swooped down, not stopping, to chuck Sir Henry on the chin. 'Hey there, little buddy.'

The dogwalker watched his back receding, ogled by various passersby. With his free hand the entertainer saluted them jauntily.

'The *Hoff*,' said one, smirking.

'They love him in Germany,' said another.

The dogwalker recalled hearing people on the sidewalk discuss the violinist also. 'He did a recording for Deutsche Grammophon, the Tchaikovsky *Concerto in D*, that actually broke my heart.' It was rare that he considered the lives of owners beyond their animals. To him they were dog neglecters most of all. And yet where would he be without this neglect?

The violinist, of course, could not be blamed in the least. He had insisted on walking Blackie himself when he was submitting to a barrage of chemotherapy that would have felled lesser men. The dogwalker respected the violinist, though it was unpleasant to see him in his wretchedness. A dog in his state would have been euthanized long ago.

In fact that was how he had met the violinist; the violinist had not gone through the usual channels. The dogwalker had come upon him struggling to keep up with Blackie on a path near Turtle Pond. Two kids on skateboards had almost run them over, and the old man had begun to tremble violently. His bones were like porcelain. Worse, one of the kids had called Blackie a 'faggot dog' as he swooped away on his board. (At that time the poodle had sported an unfortunate Continental Clip with Hip Rosettes. Later, the dogwalker had persuaded the violinist to switch to a basic Lamb.)

But the skateboarder had infuriated him. Not the words, but what was behind them – malice directed at the dog. A senseless meanness of spirit. The poodle had never done anything to hurt the kid.

He had guided the frail old man to a ledge where he could sit, and from then on the poodle had been one of his charges.

He imagined telling the violinist he could not take Blackie. In his mind he went over the conversation as he stood with the dogs. They were waiting for a walk signal.

'I am sorry,' he would say. 'But if I took in all the dogs, even all the dogs I like best, I would be a pet shelter, not a dogwalker.'

The violinist would gaze at him sadly with his watery blue eyes. In his youth, the attendant had said once, the violinist had been quite handsome, and she'd shown him a black-and-white photograph. The violinist had survived a death camp, Stalin. Now his skin was like paper, his teeth yellow.

'Can't you make an exception?' the violinist might ask.

'I would like nothing more than to take Blackie in,' he could say. 'But all I can do is help find a new family for him. Allow me to do that, at least.'

What bothered him was that the violinist had been so good to his dog. Such goodness should be rewarded.

If he did not take the poodle, chances were he would never see him again, once the violinist was out of the picture. The poodle would live out the rest of his days with someone who did not care for him as the violinist had. Blackie would be brokenhearted and Sir Henry would be bereft.

Of course even he, the dogwalker, could not promise to bestow upon the poodle the violinist's brand of solitary, desperate cherishing. But with him at least the poodle would be assured of a dignified life, a steady stream of affection.

At his feet the poodle looked up at him.

'I should be talking to *you* about this,' said the dogwalker. 'It's not right, is it? You don't have a say in the matter at all.'

No, he did not. Dogs were the martyrs of the human race.

The light turned and the three of them stepped into the crosswalk. Forward. The brightness of the day was upon them … he was lucky, he thought, with a sudden soar of hope. Here he was with his two favorite dogs, walking them at a perfect pace for all three. Neatly they jumped up onto the curb. They did not pull him and he did not pull them. Could you go forward forever, with your dogs at your side? What if he just kept going? Across the city, over the bridge, walking perfectly until darkness fell over the country. Sometimes he wished he could gather all the dogs he loved most and walk off the end of the world with them.

When a dog was put to sleep its chin simply dropped softly onto its paws. It looked up at you with the same trusting eyes it had fixed on you since it was very young.

At the violinist's building he nodded at the doorman. There was a noisy crowd in the elevator, a birthday party of children with conical hats and clownish face paint. He let them cluster and hug the dogs; the dogs licked them.

The attendant opened the penthouse door for him.

'You beat me here,' he told her. Usually he did not attempt these minor exchanges, but he was nervous and needed to fill the space.

'Poor Blackie,' she said, as he unclipped the leash and hung it. She knelt down and leaned her face against the dog's curly flank. 'My husband's allergic to dogs. It's really bad – I mean, he breaks out in rashes, he gets asthma attacks, nothing helps. Otherwise . . . I feel so bad I can't keep Blackie in the family.'

The dogwalker stared at her, a realization dawning. It was almost two years now that he had worked for them, and it had never occurred to him that she was the violinist's daughter.

He had assumed she was paid for her services.

'What's wrong?' asked the daughter. 'Is something the matter?'

'Oh no,' he said, and shook his head. 'Nothing. I am going to sleep on it.'

This time the elevator was empty. It had mirrors on every wall and he watched the long line of reflections as they descended, he and Sir Henry. In the mirror he saw infinite dogs lie down.

MADISON SMARTT BELL

BARKING MAN

A GRACIOUS DAY of early spring began it. The weather was kind, soft, annealing, and the animals were powerfully aware of it. They felt it in their muscle and bone and it made them happy and active – the most cheerful animals Alf had ever seen inside a zoo. He moved from enclosure to enclosure, his books in a nylon backpack depending from a single strap that dragged down his left shoulder, and looked in. A pair of gorillas sat in lotus position on the lush green grass the winter rains had fed, combing each other's fur with their big rubbery fingers. A warm broad beam of sunshine lapped across them. Of a sudden they both heeled over to one side and rolled over and over, closed in an embrace at first, then separating. Then they sat up again and resumed the long luxurious strokes of their grooming.

Across a concrete moat the elephants were bathing, a baby elephant and an adult, perhaps the mother? The pool was generously large and deep, and when the elephants went in their hides turned from dusty brown to a slick slate gray. The baby elephant went under the roiled surface altogether and after a moment erected a few inches of his little trunk to breathe; he could have stayed submerged forever if he'd cared to. The mother elephant snorted and made a move to leave the pool, then turned and floundered in again, sinking to one side with a huffing sound, throwing up a gleaming sheet of water that curved and dropped to rejoin its own surface.

The lions were sluggish, having just eaten, and yet they

seemed quite content, lacking the air of morose and silent desperation that most zoo lions exuded. They resembled the lions one saw in films of Africa, resting on the veldt after a kill and gorge. Adjacent, the tigers basked in the sun, fully stretched on their mappined terraces, each apparently content as a housecat on a window sill. Only one of the big males moved, with a kind of mechanical restlessness, loping back and forth on a track of his own devising, his yellow eyes hot and even a little crazed. He'd conceived some smaller circle inside his actual containment, and whenever he reached its limit he reversed his limber steps, conforming to a barrier which no one but himself could see.

The bottom of the zoo was bordered by an iron rail fence a little better than waist high, beyond which expanded the wide greensward of Regent's Park. On an impulse Alf climbed over this fence instead of going out by the South Gate. It was easily low enough for a vault, but his backpack dragged him slightly off balance, and a rail's tip caught his trousers on the inner thigh and made a neat right-angular tear. Alf stooped over to examine it and straightened up again. Big Brother would not be pleased, but possibly he wouldn't ever know about it. Possibly Hazel could mend it so it wouldn't show. He hitched up the pack and stepped out across the grass. A cool triangle lay on the inside of his leg where the cloth was torn. On to the south, farther than he could see or hear, well past the flowers of Queen Mary's Garden, he knew the traffic on Marylebone Road would be whisking back and forth like the multiple blades of some gigantic meat slicer. He stopped, turned in his traces and looked back.

Later, after a long time and much catastrophe, when Alf had passed into the care of others, he began to feel relaxed and calm. He looked at a dark spot on the wall, and his eyelids grew heavier and heavier; they grew so leaden that he could scarcely keep them open. His eyes were closed. His eyes were closed now, his breath was deep and slow. His limbs were warm and soft and tingling, his arms so heavy that he could not lift or move them. It was utterly beyond his power to open his eyes or move his arms or legs. His heartbeat slowed to requiem time. He descended a set of thirty steps into a dark place of warm and total relaxation. Asked to recollect the source of his affliction, he began to talk about the zoo, easily continuing the story of that afternoon up to the point where he had hesitated on the lawn.

'Yesssss . . .' The resonant voice of the hypnotist came from very far above, high in the mouth of the deep well into which Alf had lowered himself. 'Yes. That is very good. You are a *good* subject. You are doing *very* well. What did you think about the animals?'

Responding to some foreign motive power, Alf's hands began to twist and gnarl, his fingers twining into tangles on his lap. His breath came fast, and he could feel his features screwing up like the face of a child about to cry. Real tears were pricking the backs of his locked eyelids, though he did not know why.

'I envied them,' he said at last. 'I wanted to go back.'

Breakfast was transpiring in the flat's large airy kitchen. Big Brother was eating a soft-boiled egg with annihilating concentration. *Tap, tap, tap* went the edge of his spoon around the little end of his egg, creating a perfectly even fault line. He removed the eggshell dome and placed it on the left side of his plate, penetrated the egg white, lifted a portion and inserted it between his lips. His wrist revolved and the wristwatch on its sharkskin band presented itself briefly to his eye.

Alf choked on a bite of the scone he'd been consuming, coughed, belatedly covered his mouth with his hand and cleared his throat behind it. Big Brother lowered the spoon from his second bite of egg and raised his fishy eyes from the eggcup. The spoon's bowl connected to the plate with a minute click. For a suspended silent moment he faced Alf down the long checked range of the blue oilcloth.

'You eat like a yobbo off the street,' he said at length. 'Choice of diet and manners too. Inclusively.'

Alf's gaze broke and fell to the crumbles of scone on his plate. Once more Big Brother began to ply his spoon. He had three bites remaining; it *invariably* took him five to eat an egg. Hazel, sitting half the table's length between them, turned and shot Alf a surreptitious wink, which he returned as he reached over for the butter. Big Brother finished his strong black coffee in two tidy sips and arose from his place.

'Good-bye, Love,' he said. 'I expect to be in by seven.'

Hazel set her hands on her tight waist and arched back in her chair, lifting her face up toward him. The heavy blond braid of her hair hung down over the chair back like a plumb weight.

'Good-bye, Love,' Hazel said. 'There'll be fish for dinner. I'll see you in the evening.'

Big Brother nodded to her and passed in the direction of the hallway.

'Big-big Bang,' Alf said suddenly. 'Pow, knock'm dead, Bee Bee.'

Big Brother gave him an eerie look but continued his course without pause. There was a whetting sound as he lifted his sharkskin briefcase from the hall stand, then the tumbling of the door's many locks. Hazel stood up and curved her torso in Alf's direction. The morning sunshine

244

rushed in through the kitchen's south windows to lighten the green of her eyes.

'More tea?' she said, and stroked the rounded belly of the teapot.

'No thanks, well yes, ah, I guess I will.' Alf pushed his cup in the direction of the spout.

'Don't let me make you late for school,' said Hazel. 'What is it you have Tuesday mornings?'

'Supercalifragilisticmacroeconomics,' Alf said.

Hazel threw back her head and laughed a laugh that reminded him of someone pouring a delicious drink.

In the usual London style the sunshine failed him as soon as he hit the street. Underneath the damp gray sky he walked a block across Fulham Road and turned. His shoulder sagged under the strap of the weighty bookbag. It had given him a seemingly permanent crick in his neck. He circumambulated the South Kensington tube stop, watching the rush of people in and out from the far side of the street. There was no reason for him to enter, nowhere he urgently had to go. He had actually succeeded in forgetting in which quarter of the city the London School of Economics was to be found, and indeed was rather proud of this feat.

A few raindrops patted up and down the sidewalk; Alf sniffed and squinted at the sky. A six-month sequence of dissembling had taxed his talent for killing time. His budget did not allow him long periods in cinemas or pubs, and he had dawdled through every museum in the city at least a dozen times. Spring should have opened up more outdoor distractions, but the difference in the weather appeared most days to be only a few degrees of temperature. Give him another good day at the zoo for choice, but it was a long way, and he doubted he'd enjoy it in the rain.

He took the umbrella from his pack and shot it up and turned south in the direction of the King's Road. He shambled from one shop to the next, standing before the various clothes racks, revolving his few blunt pound coins in his pocket. Alf's interest in clothes was nil, but clothes stores did have doors and roofs. Whenever he felt an attendant's eye upon him, he departed and moved on to the next shop. When the pubs opened he went into one and had a pork pie and a half of Courage. Yobbo's lunch. The other yobs, punks and skinheads that frequented the area, jostled him up and down the counter, somehow always managing to show him only their backs.

By the time he left the pub the rain had stopped, though the sky remained dull. He walked to Saint Luke's and sat on a bench in the church garden, trying to remember his ostensible school schedule. As always, the flowers were immaculate in every elaborate bed. The gardeners had timed the bulbs so that every few weeks the color scheme underwent a magical change. Alf slouched lower on the bench, pushing his pack away from him. He would have preferred to return to the flat, but he wasn't sure if that would be plausible.

A woman in a beige suit came clipping down the walk, one of those London women who, though on close examination were clearly in their twenties, contrived to convey by their dress and demeanor the impression of being nearer forty-five. A small brown terrier was leading her along at the end of a white leash. Halfway down the walk she stooped and slipped the catch from the collar, then sat down on a bench and watched the little dog run free, sniffing along the line of displaced tombstones propped against the churchyard's western fence.

The woman took a compact from her bulky handbag and began to examine herself in its mirror, her lips pursed uncomfortably tight. She had a weak chin, but a powerful nose to compensate. The terrier turned from the fence and locked its nose to some trace of scent and began to execute geometric figures around the bench where Alf was slouched.

'The little dog laughed to see such sport,' Alf suggested. 'And the dish ran away with the spoon.' The terrier stopped and looked skeptically up at him.

'Please do not permit your dog to foul the amenity area,' Alf intoned, quoting loosely from the several green placards planted here and there on the lawn. The terrier sat back on its haunches and let out a little yip.

'– oof,' Alf replied, falsetto.

'riffrirf,' the terrier said, jumping up and smiling.

'aarffooorffurfurfiiiii!' said Alf, somewhat louder. Across the walk the woman snapped her compact shut with a cross click and stood up, shaking the leash.

At the head of the stairs of the maisonette flat, Hazel and Big Brother had their bedroom, and next to it Big Brother occupied what Hazel optimistically referred to as his study. In fact, it was a sort of electronic cockpit, packed with computers, printers, monitors, fax machines and modems hooked up to New York and Japan. Here, after nourishing himself from his exertions in the City, Big Brother would repair to continue trying to figure out every conceivable ramification of Big Bang for a good part of each night. From the windows of both of these rooms could be seen the Natural History Museum, the domes of the V&A, the Queen's Tower and other features of the skyline, though Alf doubted if Big Brother ever raised his eyes to them.

His own room was at the other end of a longish hall, right beside the bathroom, a location which admitted him to privacies of which he might have preferred to remain ignorant.

As the spring continued, Alf spent much of his *out of class* time seated at the small desk before the windows, staring out across the binding of some textbook at the children playing in the trapezoidal courtyard of the council houses below. After the evening meal he'd most often retreat to this same position, staring inattentively at his own faint reflection in the darkened window panes.

'All's well, Love?' Hazel's voice came from down the hall; she must have opened the door to look in on Big Brother, for Alf could also hear that munching sound the computers liked to make as they gobbled information. He couldn't hear the Beeb's reply, if he made any, only a drop in the hum of the machines as the door closed. He propped his elbows on the pages of his book and shut his eyes to dream of Spain. For several weeks he'd been considering that he might claim a holiday after his *long year of study*, and though he didn't speak the language the excursion fares to Spain were cheap. Hazel was coming down the hall, though he wasn't sure just how he knew it. Her bare feet made no sound on the carpet runner; it was more like a small breeze passing by. There came some groans and gurgles from the bathroom pipes, then her reflection appeared in Alf's window pane, framed by his open doorway.

'Still hitting the books this late at night?'

Alf flipped the pristine textbook shut and swiveled in his chair. The lights flickered and dimmed for an instant as the computers engorged some great mass of news. Hazel had let down her hair – it descended in a warm current parted by the oval of her face, rejoining on the rise of her bosom, where one hand smoothed it absently against her nightgown's cotton weave.

'The two of you,' she said, smiling. 'Seems like you never stop.'

'Ah,' Alf said, and stopped with his mouth open. Conscious of this, he shaped the opening into a sort of smile and began to scrape his fingers across his scalp.

'Hmm, well, *I'm* going to bed,' Hazel said, and shook her head to toss her hair back onto her shoulder blades. 'Sweet dreams, Alfie . . .' She pushed herself out of the doorway and swung his door half shut.

Alf turned back to face the window, pulled his hand loose from his head and looked down at it. His fingers were wrapped with stiff black hairs, indubitably his own. He lifted his forelock and leaned toward the window to examine his hairline. No doubt that it really was receding. A short harsh sound came out of him, something like a cough.

Hazel was leaning over the small gas stove top, rolling *kofta* meatballs and dropping them to sizzle in a pan of oil. She turned suddenly to reach for something and collided with Alf, who'd been peeping over her shoulder.

'Good Lord, you're always *right* behind me,' Hazel said. Her face was pink and humid from the burners on the stove.

She made a shooing motion and Alf retreated, slinking along the edge of the table, which was laden with trays of tiny salmon and caviar sandwiches for the cocktail party that evening. He sniffed and cleared his throat with a rasping sound, then picked up a tray and started down the long hall with it toward the living room.

'Where do you think you're going with that?' Hazel called after him. 'Just bring it back, it's way too soon, they won't be here for *hours*.'

Alf reversed his steps and put the tray back where he'd found it. He began to turn an uneasy circle between the table and the stove.

'Well, I'm sorry,' Hazel said. 'Well, you're just underfoot, that's all. Haven't you got a class to go to? Then just go out and get some air, go on now, scat!' The kitchen steamed and she steamed with it; she had sweated nearly through her blouse. She smiled at him gaily through the vapors, and flapped her hands to send him away.

He walked up Exhibition Road to its end, went into Hyde Park and continued as far as the lower end of the Serpentine. Two men were fishing where he paused, their long poles leveled over the dank surface of the water. The concrete bank was littered with goose down and slimy green goose droppings. An unpleasant idea came to Alf completely of its own accord. Many years before when he was small and they still lived on the farm outside Cedar Rapids, he and his older brother had taken the BB gun to the little pond and whiled away an afternoon shooting toads. When he remembered the *phttt* sound the BBs made going through toad bellies, two voices separated in his mind.

It was Tom's idea, he was the oldest, claimed the first, and the second answered, *No no, Alfie, it was* you, *it was your idea from the beginning. If not for you it never would have happened* ... The thing was that it didn't actually kill the toads, at least not right away, just left them drearily flopping around with drooling puncture wounds through their slack stomachs.

'RURRRRFFAAARRRH,' Alf cried, and discovered the subject had been instantly wiped from his mind. One of the fishermen looked up at him sharply, then away.

Alf couldn't get his bow tie right and finally decided to leave it with one end bigger than the other. Leaning into the mirror, he pulled the loose skin of his cheeks down into bloodhound jowls, then let it snap back with a wet smack. He passed a hand across his head, wiped the loose hairs on the edge of the sink and went downstairs to survey the situation.

An assortment of pinstriped Big Bangers and a smaller number of their fretful wives were circulating through the two front rooms. Big Brother, sharkskin Filofax in hand, appeared to be rearranging his appointments. A somewhat scurvy-looking gent, Hazel's water-color teacher, stood alone, snapping salmon sandwiches into his mouth, glancing around after each gulp to see if anyone was observing him. Hazel stood with a gay hairdresser called Neddy who'd be-friended her at the painting class. Alf ate a caviar and cracker and began to eddy up toward their conversation. She wore some sort of pseudo-Victorian velvet dress, fastened with a thousand tiny buttons down the back. Though it conformed to no current fashion it made the most of her bee shape; the swell of her rear and the arch of her back even suggested a bustle. Alf drifted in a little nearer. Hazel's hair was scooped up into a smooth blond orb, exposing the fine down on the back of her neck.

'. . . then a body perm, and Bob's your uncle,' he overheard Neddy saying. 'Just whip a comb through it in the morning and you're off!'

Hazel plucked at her lower lip with a finger. 'It does take a lot of time to look after . . . ,' she said musingly.

Alf felt some rough obstruction rising in his throat.

'But after all,' said Hazel, half turning to include him in the subject, 'what else have I really got to do?'

A steely clasp shut on Alf's upper arm and he felt himself inexorably drawn away.

'Mr Thracewell, my brother Alfred,' Big Brother said. 'Alf, fetch Mr Thracewell a gin and French.' He passed Alf an empty glass and leaned to whisper in his ear, 'Jesus *Christ*, your tie's not straight.'

As Alf receded into the hallway, he thought he heard the murmured invocation *London School of Economics*, and he swallowed against that plaguey roughness in his gullet. The kitchen was empty and he snatched up the gin bottle, carried it into the pantry and shut the door after him. With the bottle upended over his jaws, he squinted up at its butt end until he saw four bubbles rise, then lowered it and gasped. Gin and French? He sniffed the glass the Beeb had given him, but the scent was unenlightening. He fixed a gin and tonic with a lot of ice and headed back toward the front of the flat. En route he toppled a tower of bowler hats from the hall stand, made an abortive move to gather them, then decided to let them lie. Deep in conversation with Big Brother, Thracewell took the drink unconsciously and tasted it without looking. Alf watched his mouth shrivel to the surface of the glass, and at that very instant the vast bubble of gin he'd swallowed burst inside him with a soft explosion.

'*iirrrfffooorrrffffaaarrrROOOOORF OOOO OOOO!!!*' he howled. All around the room he could hear vertebrae popping with the speed of the turning heads.

'Your *younger* brother this is, you say?' Mr Thracewell murmured. 'My word, a most original chap.'

The Spanish holiday did not materialize and now that school was out Alf was at looser ends than ever. Though the weather had turned generally fine, he tended to loiter around the flat, tracking Hazel from room to room till she was inspired to invent some errand for him. He went down Elystan Street to the newsagent on the little square and joined the queue of all the old ladies of Chelsea, each waiting patiently for a lovely chat with the brick-faced woman behind the postal grille at the rear. Often he came here to buy stamps for Hazel. The fat lady behind the candy counter glowered at Alf and only Alf, who was a foot taller and forty years younger than anyone else present, the only man and, to be sure, the only foreigner. He shifted nervously from leg to leg, trying not to think of how soon Big Brother was likely to discover that he had set foot in the London School of Economics only once or twice ten months before. The tiny lady immediately ahead of him, ancient and brittle as a bit of dry-rotted antique lace, had with the help of a complicated-looking walker made her way up to the grille. She conducted some sort of savings transaction and asked for a television stamp. Television stamp? Alf rocked forward and peered to see what that might be.

'What do you *mean?*' the brick-faced woman hissed. 'Turn round, you. Turn *right* round. I shan't go on till you turn right round.'

Alf unfroze himself and turned around and stood staring out over the heads of the others behind him, into the blinding square of sunlight at the door. When permission was given to approach, he made his purchase wordlessly, fumbling the change with his slightly trembling fingers, and went out. Halfway back up Elystan Street the enlargement of his throat surpassed containment.

'wurf! Wurf! WurrrfffaaarrrhhOOORRRHHHrrrr,' he barked. A bobby looked at him sternly from the opposite side of the street. With an additional swallowed snarl tightly wrapped around his tonsils, Alf averted his eyes and went resolutely on.

Hazel seemed to grow a little restless too; she swept more and more activities into her schedule, adding to the water-color sessions a class in yoga and another in French conversation. Her shopping expeditions moved farther afield; she undertook riverboat trips and excursions to outlying villages. Alone in the flat, Alf turned the television on and off, flipped through books and magazines and furtively prowled from room to room; the areas he found the most attractive were those where he had no good reason to be. A time or two he breached the sanctity of Big Brother's electronic office, tiptoeing in and standing on the little throw rug before the desk. All around him on their long shelves the machines blinked and flickered, pooped and wheeped, and every so often they spontaneously crunched out some document. Alf could not rid himself of the superstitious fear that somehow they were recording his own activity to report to Big Brother on his return.

In the bedroom, Hazel and Big Brother's bedroom, there was an indefinable smell of lilac, a natural scent as from dried petals, though Alf could find no bowl of potpourri. Atop the bureau was a wedding picture in a silver frame. Big Brother's long neck was loose in the high stock of his tuxedo; he looked a little frightened, perhaps startled by the flash, but Hazel wore an easy, merry smile, and looked straight out of the frame at Alf, who set the picture down. He opened a drawer at random and discovered Big Brother's starched white shirts laid out in rigid rows. Another held a tangled nest of Hazel's jewelry.

The bed was a platform on short legs, low and broad, with two unremarkable nightstands on either side of it. On Hazel's was a ragged copy of *Time Out*. Big Brother's was bare except for the coaster where he set his water glass at night. The bed was spread with a quilted eiderdown, emerald green, with feather pillows mounded on it at the headboard. When Alf leaned down and touched the surface of the quilt, his fingers somehow would not come away. He was drawn farther, farther down, his shoulder tucking as he dropped. He curled up on his side and dreamed.

* * *

'I don't know why,' he said. 'I just don't know.' His arms were pasted to the leather arms of the deep dark chair, his head lolled, his eyeballs spiraled behind their lids.

'You know,' the hypnotist murmured softly. 'Oh yes, you know very well.'

'I didn't *want* to know,' said Alf. 'What would have been the use of that?'

'Knowledge is power,' the hypnotist suggested.

A galvanic shudder emerged from the reaches of Alf's autonomic nervous system and shook him to his finger ends.

'No it's not,' he said loudly. 'Not when you know everything and can't change any of it.'

No matter how deep his daydreams took him, Alf remained alive to the sound of Hazel's key entering the downstairs lock. He'd roll from the eiderdown, land on his hands and knees and scamper out, coming erect again some distance down the hallway toward his own bedroom. Until the day some deeper sleep overtook him and he woke to find Hazel standing in the doorway, looking down. She wore her loose black sweatsuit, her face was patchily flushed from yoga, and a forefinger pulled down her plump red lower lip in her familiar gesture of perplexity.

'oooOORF!' barked Alf in sheer alarm. He flipped from the bed onto all fours and barked again, 'urrrrrfffffff-OOOHRRRFF *RRAAAARRFFFF!*'

Hazel's eyes lit up, she swirled in the doorway and ran down the hall. Alf pursued her as quickly as he could on his knees and elbows, barking happy ringing barks. She ran a little awkwardly, her loose hair flagging out behind her, looking back over her shoulder in mock fright. He chased her around his room, back down the hall and down the stairs and up again, yapping hysterically at her heels. Hazel fled back into her bedroom, dove onto the bed and rolled onto her back, shuddering with wave upon wave of laughter. Her knees drew up toward her stomach, her sweatshirt rode up to the bottoms of her breasts, her head thrashed back and forth on the wide silky spread of her hair. Too breathless to bark anymore at all, Alf put his forepaws on the quilt between her feet and raised himself to look at her. She was warm with a radiant heat, an intoxicating scent poured out of her, she was rich with her own beauty (he put his hind paws on the bed and bunched himself for his next move) – she was his *brother's wife*.

Hazel turned stone pale and sat up quickly on the edge of the bed. She clapped her knees together, wrapped her arms around herself, bit down on her lip till it went white, and began to shake all over. Alf got up too and stood with his hands hanging, dead little lumps against his thighs. After a moment he picked up her hairbrush from the bureau, turned her slightly with the least touch on her shoulder and started to brush her hair. Supporting the whole sweep of it over his left forearm, he brushed it out till every auburn highlight gleamed beyond perfection. After a few minutes her back loosened and her breath began to ease and deepen.

'Thank you, Alf,' she said. 'Thank you, that feels good. That was very nice. You can stop now, please.'

Alf walked away and set down the brush, turned and propped himself on the bureau's edge. Hazel gathered her hair in one hand and drew it forward over her shoulder. She put an end of it into her mouth and wet it into a point, then took it out and stared at it round-eyed.

'I'm thinking of getting all this cut off,' she said.

'Don't do it,' said Alf. 'What for?'

'It's a lot of trouble to take care of.'

'It took you twenty years to grow it.'

'Neddy said he'd style it for me free, said he'd come to the house and do it.'

'What, that slimy little shrimp? Don't you let him touch your hair.'

'*He'd* like it if I looked a little more contemporary,' Hazel said, jerking her head toward Big Brother's nightstand.

'Don't do it,' Alf said as he walked out of the room. 'You'll be sorry if you do.' He hadn't been so sure of anything all year.

Big Brother had been working too hard – well, that much was no secret. But Hazel wanted a good night out, she wanted a date with her husband, in fact, and that wasn't so unreasonable, was it, once every couple of months or so? They went to the theater and to a champagne supper afterward. Alf fell dead asleep on the eiderdown and didn't wake up till he heard them giggling outside the bedroom door.

There was time, just barely time, for him to make it under the bed. He lay frozen in a mummy's pose, admiring its simple but ingenious construction. There were many slender wooden slats, and these were surely what made it so comfortable to lie on. He heard the sound of buttons and zippers, drawers opening and closing upon articles put away.

'Love?'

'Yes, Love . . .'

A great soft weight settled itself over him. He began a mental chant: *Don't bark, Alfie, you mustn't bark, quiet now, good dog, good dog* . . . and by some mercy this drowned out every sound. Three fifths of the way down the length of the bed, a group of slats began to flex, slowly at first, then faster and faster and FASTER . . . Then it stopped.

*   *   *

Big Brother unlocked the door, came in, set down his shark-skin briefcase, locked the door, picked up his sharkskin brief-case and snapped his fingers. Alf, who'd been basking in the glow of the BBC in the front room, raised his head slightly from a couch cushion.

'A word with you, young Alfred,' Big Brother said brittlely. 'Upstairs, if you please.'

Alf stood on the little throw rug in the glow of the various video terminals. The phrase 'called on the carpet' distantly presented itself to his mind. Big Brother, strangely inarticulate, swiveled to and fro in his desk chair, compul-sively flicking the edge of his sharkskin calculator case with a fingernail. Finally he stopped in midrotation and stared up at Alf.

'My hair is brown,' he remarked. 'Yours, on the other hand, is black.'

'This much is true,' Alf said. 'Always the wizard of percep-tion, Bee Bee.'

'I have a name,' Big Brother said bleakly. 'My name is Tom. You are familiar with it, I believe. Why don't you ever call me by my name?'

After the ensuing silence had accomplished itself, Big Brother spoke again.

'Well,' he said. 'Right.' He reached into a tea mug on his desk and pulled out a little snarl of something. 'This is hair.'

Alf nodded.

'Black hair.'

'That's so,' said Alf.

'There's quite a bit of it, wouldn't you say?' Big Brother said. 'I've been collecting it for about a week. Off my pillow, in point of fact.'

Huskily, Alf cleared his throat.

'Well then, I'd like to know what you've been playing at.'

'When exactly was it you started talking like a freaking Englishman?'

'When in Rome ...,' Big Brother said. 'Don't try to change the subject.'

'Okay,' Alf said. 'You're concerned that I've been climbing on your furniture.'

'Yes, I suppose you could put it that way.'

'At least I'm housebroken,' Alf said. 'That's something to be thankful for.'

In the weird light of the computer screens, Big Brother's sudden change of complexion looked purely fantastic.

'What the hell is the matter with you?!' he cried, half rising from his seat. Alf barked at him several times and left the room.

He sat with his elbows on the table, watching a bug walk around the little blue squares of the oilcloth. They didn't have cockroaches in the flat, and this bug didn't much look like one; however, it didn't look much like anything else either. After a long time Hazel came down and made a pot of tea. When she brought it to the table, Alf could see the dark circles around her eyes.

'It's been a tough year for him too,' she said. 'You need to try and understand that, Alfie. He's more of a small-town type of person, really. We all are, I suppose.'

Alf leaned back and raised his eyebrows toward the ceiling.

'I had to make him take a pill,' Hazel said. 'Zonko.'

'I see,' said Alf. 'Well, here we are.'

'It's really hard for him at work,' she said. 'The English snub him all the time. But they don't know *any* of the stuff he knows. Till this year they did their whole stock market with pen and ink and big black books, supposedly.' She gave her braid a yank and dropped it. 'But it worries him that he doesn't fit in. *He* thinks *they* think *I* look like some kind of a pioneer woman off the prairie . . .'

Alf scalded his mouth on a gulp of tea.

'You two were close when you were children, I know that,' Hazel said. 'He used to talk about that a lot.'

'That's right,' Alf said. 'But ever since we got to London he's been acting like a goddamn microchip.'

'He's really scared about it all sometimes,' Hazel said. 'He's afraid the whole balloon is going to pop. He says people used to worry when their assets were only on paper, but now they're not even on *paper* anymore.'

Alf watched the bug walk over the edge of the table out of sight.

'He's worried about you too, Alf,' she said. 'He's pretty upset about you, in fact.'

'He doesn't think—'

'No, not that. Thank God, he never even thought of that . . . He knows you didn't go to school, though. But he doesn't know what to do about it.'

The bug reappeared in the vicinity of Alf's tea mug. He turned the mug around and around and watched the amber liquid swirl.

'He's worried maybe you're going nuts,' Hazel said. 'He doesn't know how to handle that either. Alfie, you know he'd do anything for you, but what is it he can do?'

Alf reached over and snapped his finger at the bug, which rebounded from the Delft tile around the kitchen fireplace and fell down into the shadows below.

'He was crying, actually,' Hazel said.

'roorrrfff!' said Alf. 'aaaarrhhhhwwwOOO*OOORFF-OOOOOOOOO!!!*'

'For God's sake, will you stop that ridiculous barking,' Hazel said, and slammed her palms flat down against the table.

As he retreated further and further into the world of the canine, Alf's sense of smell became increasingly acute, so that on the final day he was faintly apprehensive of disaster from the moment he got onto the lift. The aroma, at first indefinable, became more vivid and more complex as soon as he had entered the flat. Hanging over everything was the odor of neutralizer and the bright ammoniac smell of the perm fluid. Mingled with this was a whiff of Neddy's after-shave and, most alarming of all, the smell of Hazel's tears.

He went down the hall with his hackles rising. Hazel, barely recognizable by sight, sat at the kitchen table, weeping over a small square mirror. The inch or two of hair remaining to her had been strangled into tiny ringlets which resembled scrambled eggs. The balance of her face was wrecked and her features looked heavy and bovine. It appeared that she had been crying for a long time without even trying to wipe her face. Her eyes were ridged with stiff red veins and her tears were pooling on the mirror.

'Well, there's no need for you to keep grieving so,' Neddy said a little crossly. He had stretched Hazel's severed hair out on the table and was securing each end of it with a bit of black ribbon. 'What if it *is* a little tight? It'll relax in a day or so, you'll see if it doesn't . . .' He took a cloth tape from his pocket, measured the coil of hair and tucked it away in a leather bag. 'And if you *really* decide you don't fancy it, why, in just a few years you can grow it all back. So brace up, eh? There's a duck . . .'

Alf dropped to all fours on the kitchen floor and bounced springily on all of his paws.

'Here now, Hazel, look who's come,' Neddy said with a nervous titter. Hazel cried intently on, as if she were incapable of hearing.

'It's your little brother who's mad,' said Neddy.

'*rrrrrRRRRRR,*' said Alf. He bristled. His lips pulled back from his incisors.

'*Hazel,*' Neddy said. 'Your brother's off his bloody head—'

'*rrrrRRRRR,*' Alf said, and moved a little closer in, his hindquarters taut and trembling. Neddy took a long step backward into a complicated corner of the fireplace and the kitchen walls.

'Here now, Alf,' Neddy said. 'Let's be reasonable, old chum. There's a good fellow, I mean, *keep away, you! Just you keep off!*' But Alf was no longer able to hear or understand his speech. In fact, he was aware of nothing at all but the vibrating fabric of Neddy's trouser leg and the odor, texture and taste of the blood and meat inside.

'No,' the hypnotist said thoughtfully. 'No, I do not think you can believe that you were justified. Undoubtedly what you did was very wrong. And it is true, as you have heard, that human bites are very dangerous . . .'

Limp in the deep dark chair, Alf commenced to twitch and whimper.

'However,' the hypnotist went on, 'you will remember that it has all been satisfactorily resolved. The gentleman in question has accepted your brother's settlement. Moreover, he has not been lamed or hurt in any permanent way. It is *not* true, and never was, that you have rabies. And so, though naturally you will regret your unwise action, you will feel no permanent guilt. You will forgive yourself for what you did. Indeed, you have already done so.'

Alf twitched again and faintly yipped a time or two.

'And now,' the hypnotist said, 'and *now*, you are let off your leash. You have slipped your collar, Alfie, you are free. You are running away from the house and into the barnyard. You feel the soft damp grass of the lawn between your toes, you feel the dust and the little stones of the barnyard. When you have run into the hall of the barn, you pause and sniff – you smell the hay, you smell the grain ... and something else too, another odor. Rats, Alfie! *rrrRRRATS!*'

'rirfff!' yelped Alf from the chair. His body tensed and then relaxed.

'You leave the barnyard,' the hypnotist said, 'and you go into the field. You are capering among the hog huts, you run past the slow and lazy hogs until you reach that farthest fence. Feel the wire rub hard across your back as you squirm underneath. And now you have come through the screen of trees to reach the little pond. You are very warm from the sunshine and from running, and so you splash into the water, you feel the cool water soaking into your hot fur, and you look up and see how the little white duck you startled is flying far away in the blue sky.

'And now you are lying on the warm soft grass, Alfie, with your eyes closed and all four legs stretched out. Feel how the warm sun dries your fur, feel how the little breeze ruffles it. You doze, you are sleeping very deeply, yes. You dream.

'And now you are running into the forest, deeper and deeper into the trees. You see all the woodland sights, you hear all the woodland sounds, and you are in a very special world of *smells*, Alfie, which only you can understand and navigate. There are many, many smells, Alfie, but one of them is more important than all the rest. What is it, Alfie? What is that you smell? rrr ... *rrrrrr* ...'

Alf's mouth came slightly open as he whined; he salivated on the leather of the chair.

'*rrrrrRRRRABBIT!*' said the hypnotist. 'You *smell* the *rabbit!* You smell the rabbit *very* near! And now you *see* the rabbit! And now you *chase* the rabbit!'

Alf's arms and legs began to pump in rhythmic running motions as his neck stretched out and out.

'And now you *catch* the rabbit in your jaws, you *bite* through the fur and skin into the tender flesh and the hot blood, you *crush* the rabbit's little bones, and you swallow every part of it. And now, Alfie, now that you are satisfied, you rest. Rest now, Alf. You are sleeping very deeply now.

'And now you hear voices, Alfie, voices calling out your name from far away across the fields. *Alfie, Alfie*, they are calling. They are calling you to go home to your house, Alf, and you go. You will obey the calling voices, you are going now. On the back porch of your house you see your family waiting for you – your mother, your father, your elder brother Tom, your sister-in-law Hazel, she is there too. It is they who have been calling you, Alfie, because they need you to come home. They feed you your dinner, Alf, and when you have eaten, they pat your head and they rub your ears the way you love it so. They have prepared a soft mat near the warmth of the kitchen stove, Alf, where you stretch out and rest from your doggy, doggy day. You have no worries, Alf. You have no responsibilities at all . . . but still, something is missing. What is it, Alf? What is it that you lack?'

Alf shifted, coming more nearly upright in the chair. He trembled a little, but he didn't bark. His hands settled on his knees and he assumed a posture of attention. The hypnotist leaned a little closer to him.

'*Dogs don't love*,' the hypnotist whispered. 'They haven't got the capability. They *feel*, yes, but they don't love.'

'That,' said Alf, 'is a debatable point.'

'Perhaps,' the hypnotist said. 'Possibly. But in your case ... not worth debating, I shouldn't think.'

Alf whined and pricked his ears, then let them lower.

'Come on, Alf,' the hypnotist said. 'Come on, boy. Come on out. Are you coming, now?'

BRET HARTE

A YELLOW DOG

I NEVER KNEW WHY in the Western States of America a yellow dog should be proverbially considered the acme of canine degradation and incompetency, nor why the possession of one should seriously affect the social standing of its possessor. But the fact being established, I think we accepted it at Rattlers Ridge without question. The matter of ownership was more difficult to settle; and although the dog I have in my mind at the present writing attached himself impartially and equally to everyone in camp, no one ventured to exclusively claim him; while, after the perpetration of any canine atrocity, everybody repudiated him with indecent haste.

'Well, I can swear he hasn't been near our shanty for weeks,' or the retort, 'He was last seen comin' out of *your* cabin,' expressed the eagerness with which Rattlers Ridge washed its hands of any responsibility. Yet he was by no means a common dog, nor even an unhandsome dog; and it was a singular fact that his severest critics vied with each other in narrating instances of his sagacity, insight, and agility which they themselves had witnessed.

He had been seen crossing the 'flume' that spanned Grizzly Canyon at a height of nine hundred feet, on a plank six inches wide. He had tumbled down the 'shoot' to the South Fork, a thousand feet below, and was found sitting on the riverbank 'without a scratch, 'cept that he was lazily givin' himself with his off hind paw'. He had been forgotten in a snowdrift on a Sierran shelf, and had come home in the early spring with the conceited complacency of an Alpine traveler and a plumpness alleged to have been the result of an exclusive diet of buried mail bags and their contents. He was generally believed to read the advance election posters, and disappear a day or two before the candidates and the brass band – which he hated – came to the Ridge. He was suspected of having overlooked Colonel Johnson's hand at poker, and of having conveyed to the Colonel's adversary, by a succession of barks, the danger of betting against four kings.

While these statements were supplied by wholly unsupported witnesses, it was a very human weakness of Rattlers Ridge that the responsibility of corroboration was passed to the dog himself, and *he* was looked upon as a consummate liar.

'Snoopin' round yere, and *callin'* yourself a poker sharp, are ye! Scoot, you yaller pizin!' was a common adjuration whenever the unfortunate animal intruded upon a card party. 'Ef thar was a spark, an *atom* of truth in *that dog*, I'd believe my own eyes that I saw him sittin' up and trying to magnetize a jay bird off a tree. But wot are ye goin' to do with a yaller equivocator like that?'

I have said that he was yellow – or, to use the ordinary expression, 'yaller'. Indeed, I am inclined to believe that much of the ignominy attached to the epithet lay in this favorite pronunciation. Men who habitually spoke of a '*yellow* bird', a '*yellow*-hammer', a '*yellow* leaf', always alluded to him as a '*yaller* dog'.

He certainly *was* yellow. After a bath – usually compulsory – he presented a decided gamboge streak down his back, from the top of his forehead to the stump of his tail, fading in his sides and flank to a delicate straw color. His breast, legs, and feet – when not reddened by 'slumgullion', in which

he was fond of wading – were white. A few attempts at orna-
mental decoration from the India-ink pot of the storekeeper
failed, partly through the yellow dog's excessive agility, which
would never give the paint time to dry on him, and partly
through his success in transferring his markings to the
trousers and blankets of the camp.

The size and shape of his tail – which had been cut off
before his introduction to Rattlers Ridge – were favorite
sources of speculation to the miners, as determining both his
breed and his moral responsibility in coming into camp in
that defective condition. There was a general opinion that
he couldn't have looked worse with a tail, and its removal
was therefore a gratuitous effrontery.

His best feature was his eyes, which were a lustrous Van-
dyke brown, and sparkling with intelligence; but here again
he suffered from evolution through environment, and their
original trustful openness was marred by the experience of
watching for flying stones, sods, and passing kicks from the
rear, so that the pupils were continually reverting to the outer
angle of the eyelid.

Nevertheless, none of these characteristics decided the
vexed question of his *breed*. His speed and scent pointed to
a 'hound', and it is related that on one occasion he was laid
on the trail of a wildcat with such success that he followed it
apparently out of the State, returning at the end of two weeks
footsore, but blandly contented.

Attaching himself to a prospecting party, he was sent
under the same belief, 'into the brush' to drive off a bear, who
was supposed to be haunting the campfire. He returned in a
few minutes *with* the bear, *driving it into* the unarmed circle
and scattering the whole party. After this the theory of his
being a hunting dog was abandoned. Yet it was said – on the
usual uncorroborated evidence – that he had 'put up' a quail;

and his qualities as a retriever were for a long time accepted, until, during a shooting expedition for wild ducks, it was discovered that the one he had brought back had never been shot, and the party were obliged to compound damages with an adjacent settler.

His fondness for paddling in the ditches and 'slumgullion' at one time suggested a water spaniel. He could swim, and would occasionally bring out of the river sticks and pieces of bark that had been thrown in; but as *he* always had to be thrown in with them, and was a good-sized dog, his aquatic reputation faded also. He remained simply 'a yaller dog'. What more could be said? His actual name was 'Bones' – given to him, no doubt, through the provincial custom of confounding the occupation of the individual with his quality, for which it was pointed out precedent could be found in some old English family names.

But if Bones generally exhibited no preference for any particular individual in camp, he always made an exception in favor of drunkards. Even an ordinary roistering bacchanalian party brought him out from under a tree or a shed in the keenest satisfaction. He would accompany them through the long straggling street of the settlement, barking his delight at every step or misstep of the revelers, and exhibiting none of that mistrust of eye which marked his attendance upon the sane and the respectable. He accepted even their uncouth play without a snarl or a yelp, hypocritically pretending even to like it; and I conscientiously believe would have allowed a tin can to be attached to his tail if the hand that tied it on were only unsteady, and the voice that bade him 'lie still' were husky with liquor. He would 'see' the party cheerfully into a saloon, wait outside the door – his tongue fairly lolling from his mouth in enjoyment – until they reappeared, permit them even to tumble over him with pleasure, and then gambol away before them, heedless of awkwardly projected stones and epithets. He would afterward accompany them separately home, or lie with them at crossroads until they were assisted to their cabins. Then he would trot rakishly to his own haunt by the saloon stove, with the slightly conscious air of having been a bad dog, yet of having had a good time.

We never could satisfy ourselves whether his enjoyment arose from some merely selfish conviction that he was more *secure* with the physically and mentally incompetent, from some active sympathy with active wickedness, or from a grim sense of his own mental superiority at such moments. But the general belief leant toward his kindred sympathy as a 'yaller dog' with all that was disreputable. And this was supported by another very singular canine manifestation – the 'sincere flattery' of simulation or imitation.

'Uncle Billy' Riley for a short time enjoyed the position of being the camp drunkard, and at once became an object of Bones' greatest solicitude. He not only accompanied him everywhere, curled at his feet or head according to Uncle Billy's attitude at the moment, but, it was noticed, began presently to undergo a singular alteration in his own habits and appearance. From being an active, tireless scout and forager, a bold and unovertakable marauder, he became lazy and apathetic; allowed gophers to burrow under him without endeavoring to undermine the settlement in his frantic endeavors to dig them out, permitted squirrels to flash their tails at him a hundred yards away, forgot his usual caches, and left his favorite bones unburied and bleaching in the sun. His eyes grew dull, his coat lusterless, in proportion as his companion became blear-eyed and ragged; in running, his usual arrowlike directness began to deviate, and it was not unusual to meet the pair together, zigzagging up the hill.

Indeed, Uncle Billy's condition could be predetermined by Bones' appearance at times when his temporary master was invisible. 'The old man must have an awful jag on today,' was casually remarked when an extra fluffiness and imbecility was noticeable in the passing Bones. At first it was believed that he drank also, but when careful investigation proved this hypothesis untenable, he was freely called a 'derned time-servin', yaller hypocrite'. Not a few advanced the opinion that if Bones did not actually lead Uncle Billy astray, he at least 'slavered him over and coddled him until the old man got conceited in his wickedness'. This undoubtedly led to a compulsory divorce between them, and Uncle Billy was happily dispatched to a neighboring town and a doctor.

Bones seemed to miss him greatly, ran away for two days, and was supposed to have visited him, to have been shocked at his convalescence, and to have been 'cut' by Uncle Billy in his reformed character; and he returned to his old active life again, and buried his past with his forgotten bones. It was said that he was afterward detected in trying to lead an intoxicated tramp into camp after the methods employed by a blind man's dog, but was discovered in time by the – of course – uncorroborated narrator.

I should be tempted to leave him thus in his original and picturesque sin, but the same veracity which compelled me to transcribe his faults and iniquities obliges me to describe his ultimate and somewhat monotonous reformation, which came from no fault of his own.

It was a joyous day at Rattlers Ridge that was equally the advent of his change of heart and the first stagecoach that had been induced to diverge from the highroad and stop regularly at our settlement. Flags were flying from the post office and Polka saloon, and Bones was flying before the brass band that he detested, when the sweetest girl in the county – Pinkey Preston – daughter of the county judge and hopelessly beloved by all Rattlers Ridge, stepped from the coach which she had glorified by occupying as an invited guest.

'What makes him run away?' she asked quickly, opening her lovely eyes in a possibly innocent wonder that anything could be found to run away from her.

'He don't like the brass band,' we explained eagerly.

'How funny,' murmured the girl; 'is it as out of tune as all that?'

This irresistible witticism alone would have been enough to satisfy us – we did nothing but repeat it to each other all the next day – but we were positively transported when we saw her suddenly gather her dainty skirts in one hand and trip off through the red dust toward Bones, who, with his eyes over his yellow shoulder, had halted in the road, and half-turned in mingled disgust and rage at the spectacle of the descending trombone. We held our breath as she approached him. Would Bones evade her as he did us at such moments, or would he save our reputation, and consent, for the moment, to accept her as a new kind of inebriate? She came nearer; he saw her; he began to slowly quiver with excitement – his stump of a tail vibrating with such rapidity that the loss of the missing portion was scarcely noticeable. Suddenly she stopped before him, took his yellow head between her little hands, lifted it, and looked down in his handsome brown eyes with her two lovely blue ones. What passed between them in that magnetic glance no one ever knew. She returned with him; said to him casually: 'We're not afraid of brass bands, are we?' to which he apparently acquiesced, at least stifling his disgust of them while he was near her – which was nearly all the time.

During the speechmaking her gloved hand and his yellow

head were always near together, and at the crowning ceremony – her public checking of Yuba Bill's 'waybill' on behalf of the township, with a gold pencil presented to her by the Stage Company – Bones' joy, far from knowing no bounds, seemed to know nothing but them, and he witnessed it apparently in the air. No one dared to interfere. For the first time a local pride in Bones sprang up in our hearts – and we lied to each other in his praises openly and shamelessly.

Then the time came for parting. We were standing by the door of the coach, hats in hand, as Miss Pinkey was about to step into it; Bones was waiting by her side, confidently looking into the interior, and apparently selecting his own seat on the lap of Judge Preston in the corner, when Miss Pinkey held up the sweetest of admonitory fingers. Then, taking his head between her two hands, she again looked into his brimming eyes, and said, simply, '*Good* dog,' with the gentlest of emphasis on the adjective, and popped into the coach.

The six bay horses started as one, the gorgeous green and gold vehicle bounded forward, the red dust rose behind, and the yellow dog danced in and out of it to the very' outskirts of the settlement. And then he soberly returned.

A day or two later he was missed – but the fact was afterward known that he was at Spring Valley, the county town where Miss Preston lived, and he was forgiven. A week afterward he was missed again, but this time for a longer period, and then a pathetic letter arrived from Sacramento for the storekeeper's wife.

'Would you mind,' wrote Miss Pinkey Preston, 'asking some of your boys to come over here to Sacramento and bring back Bones? I don't mind having the dear dog walk out with me at Spring Valley, where everyone knows me; but here he *does* make one so noticeable, on account of *his color*. I've got scarcely a frock that he agrees with. He don't go with my pink muslin, and that lovely buff tint he makes three shades lighter. You know yellow is *so* trying.'

A consultation was quickly held by the whole settlement, and a deputation sent to Sacramento to relieve the unfortunate girl. We were all quite indignant with Bones – but, oddly enough, I think it was greatly tempered with our new pride in him. While he was with us alone, his peculiarities had been scarcely appreciated, but the recurrent phrase 'that yellow dog that they keep at the Rattlers' gave us a mysterious importance along the countryside, as if we had secured a 'mascot' in some zoological curiosity.

This was further indicated by a singular occurrence. A new church had been built at the crossroads, and an eminent divine had come from San Francisco to preach the opening sermon. After a careful examination of the camp's wardrobe, and some felicitous exchange of apparel, a few of us were deputed to represent 'Rattlers' at the Sunday service. In our white ducks, straw hats, and flannel blouses, we were sufficiently picturesque and distinctive as 'honest miners' to be shown off in one of the front pews.

Seated near the prettiest girls, who offered us their hymn books – in the cleanly odor of fresh pine shavings, and ironed muslin, and blown over by the spices of our own woods through the open windows, a deep sense of the abiding peace of Christian communion settled upon us. At this supreme moment someone murmured in an awe-stricken whisper:

' *Will* you look at Bones?'

We looked. Bones had entered the church and gone up in the gallery through a pardonable ignorance and modesty; but, perceiving his mistake, was now calmly walking along the gallery rail before the astounded worshipers. Reaching the end, he paused for a moment, and carelessly looked down. It was about fifteen feet to the floor below – the simplest jump in the world for the mountain-bred Bones. Daintily, gingerly, lazily, and yet with a conceited airiness of manner, as if, humanly speaking, he had one leg in his pocket and were doing it on three, he cleared the distance, dropping just in front of the chancel, without a sound, turned himself around three times, and then lay comfortably down.

Three deacons were instantly in the aisle, coming up before the eminent divine, who, we fancied, wore a restrained smile. We heard the hurried whispers: 'Belongs to them.' 'Quite a local institution here, you know.' 'Don't like to offend sensibilities'; and the minister's prompt 'By no means,' as he went on with his service.

A short month ago we would have repudiated Bones; today we sat there in slightly supercilious attitudes, as if to indicate that any affront offered to Bones would be an insult to ourselves, and followed by our instantaneous withdrawal in a body.

All went well, however, until the minister, lifting the large Bible from the communion table and holding it in both hands before him, walked toward a reading stand by the altar rails. Bones uttered a distinct growl. The minister stopped.

We, and we alone, comprehended in a flash the whole situation. The Bible was nearly the size and shape of one of those soft clods of sod which we were in the playful habit of launching at Bones when he lay half-asleep in the sun, in order to see him cleverly evade it.

We held our breath. What was to be done? But the opportunity belonged to our leader, Jeff Briggs – a confoundedly good-looking fellow, with the golden mustache of a northern viking and the curls of an Apollo. Secure in his beauty and bland in his self-conceit, he rose from the pew, and stepped before the chancel rails.

'I would wait a moment, if I were you, sir,' he said, respectfully, 'and you will see that he will go out quietly.'

'What is wrong?' whispered the minister in some concern.

'He thinks you are going to heave that book at him, sir, without giving him a fair show, as we do.'

The minister looked perplexed, but remained motionless, with the book in his hands. Bones arose, walked halfway down the aisle, and vanished like a yellow flash!

With this justification of his reputation, Bones disappeared for a week. At the end of that time we received a polite note from Judge Preston, saying that the dog had become quite domiciled in their house, and begged that the camp, without yielding up their valuable *property* in him, would allow him to remain at Spring Valley for an indefinite time; that both the judge and his daughter – with whom Bones was already an old friend – would be glad if the members of the camp would visit their old favorite whenever they desired, to assure themselves that he was well cared for.

I am afraid that the bait thus ingenuously thrown out had a good deal to do with our ultimate yielding. However, the reports of those who visited Bones were wonderful and marvelous. He was residing there in state, lying on rugs in the drawing-room, coiled up under the judicial desk in the judge's study, sleeping regularly on the mat outside Miss Pinkey's bedroom door, or lazily snapping at flies on the judge's lawn.

'He's as yaller as ever,' said one of our informants, 'but it don't somehow seem to be the same back that we used to break clods over in the old time, just to see him scoot out of the dust.'

And now I must record a fact which I am aware all lovers of dogs will indignantly deny, and which will be furiously bayed at by every faithful hound since the days of Ulysses.

Bones not only *forgot*, but absolutely *cut us*! Those who called upon the judge in 'store clothes' he would perhaps casually notice, but he would sniff at them as if detecting and resenting them under their superficial exterior. The rest he simply paid no attention to. The more familiar term of 'Bonesy' – formerly applied to him, as in our rare moments of endearment – produced no response. This pained, I think, some of the more youthful of us; but, through some strange human weakness, it also increased the camp's respect for him. Nevertheless, we spoke of him familiarly to strangers at the very moment he ignored us. I am afraid that we also took some pains to point out that he was getting fat and unwieldy, and losing his elasticity, implying covertly that his choice was a mistake and his life a failure.

A year after, he died, in the odor of sanctity and respectability, being found one morning coiled up and stiff on the mat outside Miss Pinkey's door. When the news was conveyed to us, we asked permission, the camp being in a prosperous condition, to erect a stone over his grave. But when it came to the inscription we could only think of the two words murmured to him by Miss Pinkey, which we always believe effected his conversion:

'*Good* Dog!'

DORIS LESSING

THE STORY OF
TWO DOGS

GETTING A NEW DOG turned out to be more difficult than we thought, and for reasons rooted deep in the nature of our family. For what, on the face of it, could have been easier to find than a puppy once it had been decided: 'Jock needs a companion, otherwise he'll spend his time with those dirty Kaffir dogs in the compound'? All the farms in the district had dogs who bred puppies of the most desirable sort. All the farm compounds owned miserable beasts kept hungry so that they would be good hunters for their meat-starved masters; though often enough puppies born to the cage-ribbed bitches from this world of mud huts were reared in white houses and turned out well. Jacob our builder heard we wanted another dog, and came up with a lively puppy on the end of a bit of rope. But we tactfully refused. The thin flea-bitten little object was not good enough for Jock, my mother said; though we children were only too ready to take it in.

Jock was a mongrel himself, a mixture of Alsatian, Rhodesian ridgeback, and some other breed – terrier? – that gave him ears too cocky and small above a long melancholy face. In short, he was nothing to boast of, outwardly: his qualities were all intrinsic or bestowed on him by my mother who had given this animal her heart when my brother went off to boarding school.

In theory Jock was my brother's dog. Yet why give a dog to a boy at that moment when he departs for school and will be away from home two-thirds of the year? In fact my brother's dog was his substitute; and my poor mother, whose children were always away being educated, because we were farmers, and farmers' children had no choice but to go to the cities for their schooling – my poor mother caressed Jock's too-small intelligent ears and crooned: 'There, Jock! There, old boy! There, good dog, yes, you're a *good* dog, Jock, you're such a *good* dog. . . .' While my father said, uncomfortably: 'For goodness' sake, old girl, you'll ruin him, that isn't a house pet, he's not a lapdog, he's a farm dog.' To which my mother said nothing, but her face put on a most familiar look of mis-understood suffering, and she bent it down close so that the flickering red tongue just touched her cheeks, and sang to him: 'Poor old Jock then, yes, you're a poor old dog, you're not a rough farm dog, you're a good dog, and you're not strong, no you're delicate.'

At this last word my brother protested; my father pro-tested; and so did I. All of us, in our different ways, had refused to be 'delicate' – had escaped from being 'delicate' – and we wished to rescue a perfectly strong and healthy young dog from being forced into invalidism, as we all, at different times, had been. Also of course we all (and we knew it and felt guilty about it) were secretly pleased that Jock was now absorbing the force of my mother's pathetic need for some-thing 'delicate' to nurse and protect.

Yet there was something in the whole business that was a reproach to us. When my mother bent her sad face over the animal, stroking him with her beautiful white hands on which the rings had grown too large, and said 'There, good dog, yes Jock, you're such a gentleman –' well, there was something in all this that made us, my father, my brother and myself, need to explode with fury, or to take Jock away and make him run over the farm like the tough young brute he was, or go away ourselves forever so that we didn't have to hear the awful yearning intensity in her voice. Because it was entirely our fault that note was in her voice at all; if we had allowed ourselves to be delicate, and good, or even gentlemen or ladies, there would have been no need for Jock to sit between my mother's knees, his loyal noble head on her lap, while she caressed and yearned and suffered.

It was my father who decided there must be another dog, and for the expressed reason that otherwise Jock would be turned into a 'sissy'. (At this word, reminder of a hundred earlier battles, my brother flushed, looked sulky, and went right out of the room.) My mother would not hear of another dog until her Jock took to sneaking off to the farm compound to play with the Kaffir dogs. 'Oh you bad dog, Jock,' she said sorrowfully, 'playing with those nasty dirty dogs, how could you, Jock!' And he would playfully, but in an agony of remorse, snap and lick at her face, while she bent the whole force of her inevitably betrayed self over him, crooning: 'How could you, oh how could you, Jock?'

So there must be a new puppy. And since Jock was (at heart, despite his temporary lapse) noble and generous and above all well-bred, his companion must also possess these qualities. And which dog, where in the world, could possibly be good enough? My mother turned down a dozen puppies; but Jock was still going off to the compound, slinking back to gaze soulfully into my mother's eyes. This new puppy was to be my dog. I decided this: if my brother owned a dog, then it was only fair that I should. But my lack of force in claiming this puppy was because I was in the grip of abstract justice only. The fact was I didn't want a good noble and well-bred dog. I didn't know what I did want, but the idea of such a dog bored me. So I was content to let my mother turn down puppies, provided she kept her terrible maternal energy on Jock, and away from me.

Then the family went off for one of our long visits in another part of the country, driving from farm to farm to stop a night, or a day, or a meal, with friends. To the last place we were invited for the weekend. A distant cousin of my father, 'a Norfolk man' (my father was from Essex), had married a woman who had nursed in the war (First World War) with my mother. They now lived in a small brick and iron house surrounded by granite *kopjes* that erupted everywhere from thick bush. They were as isolated as any people I've known, eighty miles from the nearest railway station. As my father said, they were 'not suited', for they quarreled or sent each other to Coventry all the weekend. However, it was not until much later that I thought about the pathos of these two people, living alone on a minute pension in the middle of the bush, and 'not suited'; for that weekend I was in love.

It was night when we arrived, about eight in the evening, and an almost full moon floated heavy and yellow above a stark granite-bouldered *kopje*. The bush around was black and low and silent, except that the crickets made a small incessant din. The car drew up outside a small boxlike structure whose iron roof glinted off moonlight. As the engine stopped, the sound of crickets swelled up, the moonlight's cold came in a breath of fragrance to our faces; and there was the sound of a mad wild yapping. Behold, around the corner of the house came a small black wriggling object that hurled itself towards the car, changed course almost on touching it, and hurtled off again, yapping in a high delirious yammering which, while it faded behind the house, continued faintly, our ears, or at least mine, straining after it.

'Take no notice of that puppy,' said our host, the man from Norfolk. 'It's been stark staring mad with the moon every night this last week.'

We went into the house, were fed, were looked after; I was

put to bed so that the grown-ups could talk freely. All the time came the mad high yapping. In my tiny bedroom I looked out onto a space of flat white sand that reflected the moon between the house and the farm buildings, and there hurtled a mad wild puppy, crazy with joy of life, or moonlight, weaving back and forth, round and round, snapping at its own black shadow and tripping over its own clumsy feet – like a drunken moth around a candle flame, or like ... like nothing I've ever seen or heard of since.

The moon, large and remote and soft, stood up over the trees, the empty white sand, the house which had unhappy human beings in it; and a mad little dog yapping and beating its course of drunken joyous delirium. That, of course, was my puppy; and when Mr Barnes came out from the house saying: 'Now, now, come now, you lunatic animal ...' finally almost throwing himself on the crazy creature, to lift it in his arms still yapping and wriggling and flapping around like a fish, so that he could carry it to the packing case that was its kennel, I was already saying, as anguished as a mother watching a stranger handle her child: Careful now, careful, that's my dog.

Next day, after breakfast, I visited the packing case. Its white wood oozed out resin that smelled tangy in hot sunlight, and its front was open and spilling out soft yellow straw. On the straw a large beautiful black dog lay with her head on outstretched forepaws. Beside her a brindled pup lay on its fat back, its four paws sprawled every which way, its eyes rolled up, as ecstatic with heat and food and laziness as it had been the night before from the joy of movement. A crust of mealie porridge was drying on its shining black lips that were drawn slightly back to show perfect milk teeth. His mother kept her eyes on him, but her pride was dimmed with sleep and heat.

I went inside to announce my spiritual ownership of the puppy. They were all around the breakfast table. The man from Norfolk was swapping boyhood reminiscences (shared in space, not time) with my father. His wife, her eyes still red from the weeping that had followed a night quarrel, was gossiping with my mother about the various London hospitals where they had ministered to the wounded of the War they had (apparently so enjoyably) shared.

My mother at once said: 'Oh my dear, no, not that puppy, didn't you see him last night? We'll never train him.'

The man from Norfolk said I could have him with pleasure.

My father said he didn't see what was wrong with the dog, if a dog was healthy that was all that mattered: my mother dropped her eyes forlornly, and sat silent.

The man from Norfolk's wife said she couldn't bear to part with the silly little thing, goodness knows there was little enough pleasure in her life.

The atmosphere of people at loggerheads being familiar to me, it was not necessary for me to know *why* they disagreed, or in what ways, or what criticisms they were going to make about my puppy. I only knew that inner logics would in due course work themselves out and the puppy would be mine. I left the four people to talk about their differences through a small puppy, and went to worship the animal, who was now sitting in a patch of shade beside the sweet-wood-smelling packing case, its dark brindled coat glistening, with dark wet patches on it from its mother's ministering tongue. His own pink tongue absurdly stuck out between white teeth, as if he had been too careless or lazy to withdraw it into its proper place under his equally pink wet palate. His brown buttony beautiful eyes ... but enough, he was an ordinary mongrelly puppy.

Later I went back to the house to find out how the battle balanced: my mother had obviously won my father over, for he said he thought it was wiser not to have that puppy: 'Bad blood tells, you know.'

The bad blood was from the father, whose history delighted my fourteen-year-old imagination. This district being wild, scarcely populated, full of wild animals, even leopards and lions, the four policemen at the police station had a tougher task than in places nearer town; and they had bought half a dozen large dogs to (a) terrorize possible burglars around the police station itself and (b) surround themselves with an aura of controlled animal savagery. For the dogs were trained to kill if necessary. One of these dogs, a big ridgeback, had 'gone wild'. He had slipped his tether at the station and taken to the bush, living by himself on small buck, hares, birds, even stealing farmers' chickens. This dog, whose proud lonely shape had been a familiar one to farmers for years, on moonlit nights, or in gray dawns and dusks, standing aloof from human warmth and friendship, had taken Stella, my puppy's mother, off with him for a week of sport and hunting. She simply went away with him one morning; the Barneses had seen her go; had called after her; she had not even looked back. A week later she returned home at dawn and gave a low whine outside their bedroom window, saying: I'm home; and they woke to see their errant Stella standing erect in the paling moonlight, her nose pointed outwards and away from them towards a great powerful dog who seemed to signal to her with his slightly moving tail before fading into the bush. Mr Barnes fired some futile shots into the bush after him. Then they both scolded Stella who in due time produced seven puppies, in all combinations of black, brown and gold. She was no pure-bred herself, though of course her owners thought she was or ought to be, being their dog. The night the puppies were born, the man from Norfolk and his wife heard a sad wail or cry, and arose from their beds to see the wild police dog bending his head in at the packing-case door. All the bush was flooded with a pinkish-gold dawn light, and the dog looked as if he had an aureole of gold around him. Stella was half wailing, half growling her welcome, or protest, or fear at his great powerful reappearance and his thrusting muzzle so close to her seven helpless pups. They called out, and he turned his outlaw's head to the window where they stood side by side in striped pajamas and embroidered pink silk. He put back his head and howled, he howled, a mad wild sound that gave them gooseflesh, so they said; but I did not understand that until years later when Bill the puppy 'went wild' and I saw him that day on the antheap howling his pain of longing to an empty listening world.

The father of her puppies did not come near Stella again; but a month later he was shot dead at another farm, fifty miles away, coming out of a chicken run with a fine white Leghorn in his mouth; and by that time she had only one pup left, they had drowned the rest. It was bad blood, they said, no point in preserving it, they had only left her that one pup out of pity.

I said not a word as they told this cautionary tale, merely preserved the obstinate calm of someone who knows she will get her own way. Was right on my side? It was. Was I owed a dog? I was. Should anybody but myself choose my dog? No, but ... very well then, I had chosen. I chose this dog. I chose it. Too late, I *had* chosen it.

Three days and three nights we spent at the Barneses' place. The days were hot and slow and full of sluggish emotions; and the two dogs slept in the packing case. At nights, the four people stayed in the living room, a small brick place heated unendurably by the paraffin lamp whose oily yellow glow attracted moths and beetles in a perpetual whirling halo of small moving bodies. They talked, and I listened for the mad far yapping, and then I crept out into the cold moon-light. On the last night of our stay the moon was full, a great perfect white ball, its history marked on a face that seemed close enough to touch as it floated over the dark cricket-singing bush. And there on the white sand yapped and danced the crazy puppy, while his mother, the big beautiful animal, sat and watched, her intelligent yellow eyes slightly anxious as her muzzle followed the erratic movements of her child, the child of her dead mate from the bush. I crept up beside Stella, sat on the still-warm cement beside her, put my arm around her soft furry neck, and my head beside her alert moving head. I adjusted my breathing so that my rib cage moved up and down beside hers, so as to be closer to the warmth of her barrelly furry chest, and together we turned our eyes from the great staring floating moon to the tiny black hurtling puppy who shot in circles from near us, so near he all but crashed into us, to two hundred yards away where he just missed the wheels of the farm wagon. We watched, and I felt the chill of moonlight deepen on Stella's fur, and on my own silk skin, while our ribs moved gently up and down together, and we waited until the man from Norfolk came to first shout, then yell, then fling him-self on the mad little dog and shut him up in the wooden box where yellow bars of moonlight fell into black dog-smelling shadow. 'There now, Stella girl, you go in with your puppy,' said the man, bending to pat her head as she obediently went inside. She used her soft nose to push her puppy over. He was so exhausted that he fell and lay, his four legs stretched out and quivering like a shot dog, his breath squeezed in and out of him in small regular wheezy pants like whines. And so I left them, Stella and her puppy, to go to my bed in the little brick house which seemed literally crammed with hateful emotions. I went to sleep, thinking of the hurtling little dog, now at last asleep with exhaustion, his nose pushed against his mother's breathing black side, the slits of yellow moonlight moving over him through the boards of fragrant wood.

We took him away next morning, having first locked Stella in a room so that she could not see us go.

It was a three-hundred-mile drive, and all the way Bill yapped and panted and yawned and wriggled idiotically on his back on the lap of whoever held him, his eyes rolled up, his big paws lolling. He was a full-time charge for myself and my mother, and, after the city, my brother, whose holidays were starting. He, at first sight of the second dog, reverted to the role of Jock's master, and dismissed my animal as altogether less valuable material. My mother, by now Bill's slave, agreed with him, but invited him to admire the adorable wrinkles on the puppy's forehead. My father demanded irritably that both dogs should be 'thoroughly trained'.

Meanwhile, as the nightmare journey proceeded, it was noticeable that my mother talked more and more about Jock, guiltily, as if she had betrayed him. 'Poor little Jock, what will he say?'

Jock was in fact a handsome young dog. More Alsatian than anything, he was a low-standing, thick-coated animal of a warm gold color, with a vestigial 'ridge' along his spine, rather wolflike, or foxlike, if one looked at him frontways, with his sharp cocked ears. And he was definitely not 'little'. There was something dignified about him from the moment he was out of puppyhood, even when he was being scolded by my mother for his visits to the compound.

The meeting, prepared for by us all with trepidation, went off in a way which was a credit to everyone, but particularly Jock, who regained my mother's heart at a stroke. The puppy was released from the car and carried to where Jock sat, noble and restrained as usual, waiting for us to greet him. Bill at once began weaving and yapping around the rocky space in front of the house. Then he saw Jock, bounded up to him, stopped a couple of feet away, sat down on his fat backside and yelped excitedly. Jock began a yawning, snapping movement of his head, making it go from side to side in half-snarling, half-laughing protest, while the puppy crept closer, right up, jumping at the older dog's lifted wrinkling muzzle. Jock did not move away; he forced himself to remain still, because he could see us all watching. At last he lifted up his paw, pushed Bill over with it, pinned him down, examined him, then sniffed and licked him. He had accepted him, and Bill had found a substitute for his mother who was presumably mourning his loss. We were able to leave the child (as my mother kept calling him) in Jock's infinitely patient care. 'You are such a good dog, Jock,' she said, overcome by this scene, and the other touching scenes that followed, all marked by Jock's extraordinary forbearance for what was, and even I had to admit it, an intolerably destructive little dog.

Training became urgent. But this was not at all easy, due, like the business of getting a new puppy, to the inner nature of the family.

To take only one difficulty: dogs must be trained by their masters, they must owe allegiance to one person. And who was Jock to obey? And Bill: I was his master, in theory. In practice, Jock was. Was I to take over from Jock? But even to state it is to expose its absurdity: what I adored was the graceless puppy, and what did I want with a well-trained dog? Trained for *what*?

A watchdog? But all our dogs were watchdogs. 'Natives' – such was the article of faith – were by nature scared of dogs. Yet everyone repeated stories about thieves poisoning fierce dogs, or making friends with them. So apparently no one really believed that watchdogs were any use. Yet every farm had its watchdog.

Throughout my childhood I used to lie in bed, the bush not fifty yards away all around the house, listening to the cry of the nightjar, the owls, the frogs and the crickets; to the tom-toms from the compound; to the mysterious rustling in the thatch over my head, or the long grass it had been cut from down the hill; to all the thousand noises of the night on the veld; and every one of these noises was marked also by the house dogs, who would bark and sniff and investigate and growl at all these; and also at starlight on the polished surface of a leaf, at the moon lifting itself over the mountains, at a branch cracking behind the house, at the first rim of hot red showing above the horizon – in short at anything and everything. Watchdogs, in my experience, were never asleep; but they were not so much a guard against thieves (we never had any thieves that I can remember) as a kind of instrument designed to measure or record the rustlings and movements of the African night that seemed to have an enormous life of its own, but a collective life, so that the falling of a stone, or a star shooting through the Milky Way, the grunt of a wild pig, and the wind rustling in the mealie field were all evidences and aspects of the same truth.

How did one 'train' a watchdog? Presumably to respond only to the slinking approach of a human, black or white. What use is a watchdog otherwise? But even now, the most powerful memory of my childhood is of lying awake listening to the sobbing howl of a dog at the inexplicable appearance of the yellow face of the moon; of creeping to the window to see the long muzzle of a dog pointed black against a great bowl of stars. We needed no moon calendar with those dogs, who were like traffic in London: to sleep at all, one had to learn not to hear them. And if one did not hear them, one would not hear the stiff warning growl that (presumably) would greet a marauder.

At first Jock and Bill were locked up in the dining room at night. But there were so many stirrings and yappings and rushings from window to window after the rising sun or moon, or the black shadows which moved across whitewashed walls from the branches of the trees in the garden, that soon we could no longer stand the lack of sleep, and they were turned out onto the verandah. With many hopeful injunctions from my mother that they were to be 'good dogs': which meant that they should ignore their real natures and sleep from sundown to sunup. Even then, when Bill was just out of puppyhood, they might be missing altogether in the early mornings. They would come guiltily up the road from the lands at breakfast time, their coats full of grass seeds, and we knew they had rushed down into the bush after an owl, or a grazing animal, and, finding themselves farther from home than they had expected in a strange nocturnal world, had begun nosing and sniffing and exploring in practice for their days of wildness soon to come.

So they weren't watchdogs. Hunting dogs perhaps? My brother undertook to train them, and we went through a long and absurd period of 'Down, Jock', 'To heel, Bill', while sticks of barley sugar balanced on noses, and paws were offered to be shaken by human hands, etc., etc. Through all this Jock suffered, bravely, but saying so clearly with every part of him that he would do anything to please my mother – he would send her glances half proud and half apologetic all the time my brother drilled him, that after an hour of training my brother would retreat, muttering that it was too hot, and Jock bounded off to lay his head on my mother's lap. As for Bill, he never achieved anything. Never did he sit still with the golden lumps on his nose, he ate them at once. Never did he stay to heel. Never did he remember what he was supposed to do with his paw when one of us offered him a hand. The truth was, I understood then, watching the training sessions, that Bill was stupid. I pretended of course that he despised being trained, he found it humiliating; and that Jock's readiness to go through with the silly business showed his lack of spirit. But alas, there was no getting around it, Bill simply wasn't very bright.

Meanwhile he had ceased to be a fat charmer; he had become a lean young dog, good-looking, with his dark brindled coat, and his big head that had a touch of New-foundland. He had a look of puppy about him still. For just as Jock seemed born elderly, had respectable white hairs on his chin from the start; so Bill kept something young in him; he was a young dog until he died.

The training sessions did not last long. Now my brother said the dogs would be trained on the job: this to pacify my father, who kept saying that they were a disgrace and 'not worth their salt'.

There began a new regime, my brother, myself, and the two dogs. We set forth each morning, first my brother, earnest with responsibility, his rifle swinging in his hand, at his heels the two dogs. Behind this time-honored unit, myself, the girl, with no useful part to play in the serious masculine business, but necessary to provide admiration. This was a very old role for me indeed: to walk away on one side of the scene, a small fierce girl, hungry to be part of it, but knowing she never would be, above all because the heart that had been put to pump away all her life under her ribs was not only critical and intransigent, but one which longed so bitterly to melt into loving acceptance. An uncomfortable combination, as she knew even then – yet I could not remove the sulky smile from my face. And it *was* absurd: there was my brother, so intent and serious, with Jock the good dog just behind him; and there was Bill the bad dog intermittently behind him, but more often than not sneaking off to enjoy some side path. And there was myself, unwillingly following, my weight shifting from hip to hip, bored and showing it.

I knew the route too well. Before we reached the sullen thickets of the bush where game and birds were to be found, there was a long walk up the back of the *kopje* through a luxuriant pawpaw grove, then through sweet potato vines that tangled our ankles, and tripped us, then past a rubbish heap whose sweet rotten smell was expressed in a heave of glittering black flies, then the bush itself. Here it was all dull green stunted trees, miles and miles of the smallish, flattish *msasa* trees in their second growth: they had all been cut for mine furnaces at some time. And over the flat ugly bush a large overbearing blue sky.

We were on our way to get food. So we kept saying. Whatever we shot would be eaten by 'the house', or by the house's servants, or by 'the compound'. But we were hunting according to a newer law than the need for food, and we knew it and that was why we were always a bit apologetic about these expeditions, and why we so often chose to return empty-handed. We were hunting because my brother had been given a new and efficient rifle that would bring down (infallibly, if my brother shot) birds, large and small; and small animals, and very often large game like koodoo and sable. We were hunting because we owned a gun. And because we owned a gun, we should have hunting dogs, it made the business less ugly for some reason.

We were on our way to the Great Vlei, as distinct from the Big Vlei, which was five miles in the other direction. The Big Vlei was burnt out and eroded, and the waterholes usually dried up early. We did not like going there. But to reach the Great Vlei, which was beautiful, we had to go through the ugly bush 'at the back of the *kopje*'. These ritual names for parts of the farm seemed rather to be names for regions in our minds. 'Going to the Great Vlei' had a fairy-tale quality about it, because of having to pass through the region of sour ugly frightening bush first. For it did frighten us, always, and without reason: we felt it was hostile to us and we walked through it quickly, knowing that we were earning by this danger the water-running peace of the Great Vlei. It was only partly on our farm; the boundary between it and the next farm ran invisibly down its center, drawn by the eye from this outcrop to that big tree to that pothole to that antheap. It was a grassy valley with trees standing tall and spreading on either side of the watercourse, which was a half-mile width of intense greenness broken by sky-reflecting brown pools. This was old bush, these trees had never been cut: the Great Vlei had the inevitable look of natural bush – that no branch, no shrub, no patch of thorn, no outcrop, could have been in any other place or stood at any other angle.

The potholes here were always full. The water was stained clear brown, and the mud bottom had a small movement of creatures, while over the brown ripples skimmed blue jays and hummingbirds and all kinds of vivid flashing birds we did not know the names of. Along the lush verges lolled pink and white water lilies on their water-gemmed leaves.

This paradise was where the dogs were to be trained.

During the first holidays, long ones of six weeks, my brother was indefatigable, and we set off every morning after breakfast. In the Great Vlei I sat on a pool's edge under a thorn tree, and daydreamed to the tune of the ripples my swinging feet set moving across the water, while my brother, armed with the rifle, various sizes of stick, and lumps of sugar and biltong, put the two dogs through their paces. Sometimes, roused perhaps because the sun that fell through the green lace of the thorn was burning my shoulders, I turned to watch the three creatures, hard at work a hundred yards off on an empty patch of sand. Jock, more often than not, would be a dead dog, or his nose would be on his paws while his attentive eyes were on my brother's face. Or he would be sitting up, a dog statue, a golden dog, admirably obedient. Bill, on the other hand, was probably balancing on his spine, all four paws in the air, his throat back so that he was flat from nose to tail tip, receiving the hot sun equally over his brindled fur. I would hear, through my own lazy thoughts: 'Good dog, Jock, yes, good dog. Idiot Bill, fool dog, why don't you work like Jock?' And my brother, his face reddened and sweaty, would come over to flop beside me, saying: 'It's all Bill's fault, he's a bad example. And of course Jock doesn't see why he should work hard when Bill just plays all the time.' Well, it probably was my fault that the training failed. If my earnest and undivided attention had been given, as I knew quite well was being demanded of me, to this business of the boy and the two dogs, perhaps we would have ended up with a brace of efficient and obedient animals, ever ready to die, to go to heel, and to fetch it. Perhaps.

By next holidays, moral disintegration had set in. My father complained the dogs obeyed nobody, and demanded training, serious and unremitting. My brother and I watched our mother petting Jock and scolding Bill, and came to an unspoken agreement. We set off for the Great Vlei but once there we loafed up and down the waterholes, while the dogs did as they liked, learning the joys of freedom.

The uses of water, for instance. Jock, cautious as usual, would test a pool with his paw, before moving in to stand chest deep, his muzzle just above the ripples, licking at them with small yaps of greeting or excitement. Then he walked gently in and swam up and down and around the brown pool in the green shade of the thorn trees. Meanwhile Bill would have found a shallow pool and be at his favorite game. Starting twenty yards from the rim of a pool he would hurl himself, barking shrilly, across the grass, then across the pool, not so much swimming across it as bouncing across it. Out the other side, up the side of the vlei, around in a big loop, then back, and around again . . . and again and again and again. Great sheets of brown water went up into the sky above him, crashing back into the pool while he barked his exultation.

That was one game. Or they chased each other up and down the four-mile-long valley like enemies, and when one caught the other there was a growling and a snarling and a fighting that sounded genuine enough. Sometimes we went to separate them, an interference they suffered; and the moment we let them go one or another would be off, his hindquarters pistoning, with the other in pursuit, fierce and silent. They might race a mile, two miles, before one leaped at the other's throat and brought him down. This game, too, over and over again, so that when they did go wild, we knew how they killed the wild pig and the buck they lived on.

On frivolous mornings they chased butterflies, while my brother and I dangled our feet in a pool and watched. Once, very solemnly, as it were in parody of the ridiculous business (now over, thank goodness) of 'fetch it' and 'to heel', Jock brought us in his jaws a big orange-and-black butterfly, the delicate wings all broken, and the orange bloom smearing his furry lips. He laid it in front of us, held the still fluttering creature flat with a paw, then lay down, his nose pointing at it. His brown eyes rolled up, wickedly hypocritical, as if to say: 'Look, a butterfly, I'm a *good* dog.' Meanwhile, Bill leaped and barked, a small brown dog hurling himself up into the great blue sky after floating colored wings. He had taken no notice at all of Jock's captive. But we both felt that Bill was much more likely than Jock to make such a seditious comment, and in fact my brother said: 'Bill's corrupted Jock. I'm sure Jock would never go wild like this unless Bill was showing him. It's the blood coming out.' But alas, we had no idea yet of what 'going wild' could mean. For a couple of years yet it still meant small indisciplines, and mostly Bill's.

For instance, there was the time Bill forced himself through a loose plank in the door of the store hut, and there ate and ate, eggs, cake, bread, a joint of beef, a ripening guinea fowl, half a ham. Then he couldn't get out. In the morning he was a swollen dog, rolling on the floor and whining with the agony of his overindulgence. 'Stupid dog, Bill, Jock would never do a thing like that, he'd be too intelligent not to know he'd swell up if he ate so much.'

Then he ate eggs out of the nest, a crime for which on a farm a dog gets shot. Very close was Bill to this fate. He had actually been seen sneaking out of the chicken run, feathers on his nose, egg smear on his muzzle. And there was a mess of oozing yellow and white slime over the straw of the nests. The fowls cackled and raised their feathers whenever Bill came near. First he was beaten, by the cook, until his howls shook the farm. Then my mother blew eggs and filled them with a solution of mustard and left them in the nests. Sure enough, next morning, a hell of wild howls and shrieks: the beatings had taught him nothing. We went out to see a brown dog running and racing in agonized circles with his tongue hanging out, while the sun came up red over black mountains – a splendid backdrop to a disgraceful scene.

My mother took the poor inflamed jaws and washed them in warm water and said: 'Well now, Bill, you'd better learn, or it's the firing squad for you.'

He learned, but not easily. More than once my brother and I, having arisen early for the hunt, stood in front of the house in the dawn hush, the sky a high, far gray above us, the edge of the mountains just reddening, the great spaces of silent bush full of the dark of the night. We sniffed at the small sharpness of the dew, and the heavy somnolent night-smell off the bush, felt the cold heavy air on our cheeks. We stood, whistling very low, so that the dogs would come from wherever they had chosen to sleep. Soon Jock would appear, yawning and sweeping his tail back and forth. No Bill – then we saw him, sitting on his haunches just outside the chicken run, his nose resting in a loop of the wire, his eyes closed in, yearning for the warm delicious ooze of fresh egg. And we would clap our hands over our mouths and double up with heartless laughter that had to be muffled so as not to disturb our parents.

On the mornings when we went hunting, and took the dogs, we knew that before we'd gone half a mile either Jock or Bill would dash off barking into the bush; the one left would look up from his own nosing and sniffing and rush away too. We would hear the wild double barking fade away with the crash and the rush of the two bodies, and, often enough, the subsidiary rushings away of other animals who had been asleep or resting and just waiting until we had gone away. Now we could look for something to shoot, which probably we would never have seen at all had the dogs been there. We could settle down for long patient stalks, circling around a grazing koodoo, or a couple of duikers. Often enough we would lie watching them for hours, afraid only that Jock and Bill would come back, putting an end to this

302

particular pleasure. I remember once we caught a glimpse of a duiker grazing on the edge of a farmland that was still half dark. We got onto our stomachs and wriggled through the long grass, not able to see if the duiker was still there. Slowly the field opened up in front of us, a heaving mass of big black clods. We carefully raised our heads, and there, at the edge of the clod sea, a couple of arms' lengths away, were three little duikers, their heads turned away from us to where the sun was about to rise. They were three black, quite motionless silhouettes. Away over the other side of the field, big clods became tinged with reddish gold. The earth turned so fast toward the sun that the light came running from the tip of one clod to the next across the field like flames leaping along the tops of long grasses in front of a strong wind. The light reached the duikers and outlined them with warm gold. They were three glittering little beasts on the edge of an imminent sunlight. They then began to butt each other, lifting their hindquarters and bringing down their hind feet in clicking leaps like dancers. They tossed their sharp little horns and made short half-angry rushes at each other. The sun was up. Three little buck danced on the edge of the deep green bush where we lay hidden, and there was a weak sunlight warming their gold hides. The sun separated itself from the line of the hills, and became calm and big and yellow; a warm yellow color filled the world, the little buck stopped dancing, and walked slowly off, frisking their white tails and tossing their pretty heads, into the bush.

We would never have seen them at all, if the dogs hadn't been miles away.

In fact, all they were good for was their indiscipline. If we wanted to be sure of something to eat, we tied ropes to the dogs' collars until we actually heard the small clink-clink-clink of guinea fowl running through the bush. Then we untied them. The dogs were at once off after the birds, who rose clumsily into the air, looking like flying shawls that sailed along, just above grass level, with the dogs' jaws snapping underneath them. All they wanted was to land unobserved in the long grass, but they were always forced to rise painfully into the trees, on their weak wings. Sometimes, if it was a large flock, a dozen trees might be dotted with the small black shapes of guinea fowl outlined against dawn or evening skies. They watched the barking dogs, took no notice of us. My brother or I – for even I could hardly miss in such conditions – planted our feet wide for balance, took aim at a chosen bird and shot. The carcass fell into the worrying jaws beneath. Meanwhile a second bird would be chosen and shot. With the two birds tied together by their feet, the rifle, justified by utility, proudly swinging, we would saunter back to the house through the sun-scented bush of our enchanted childhood. The dogs, for politeness' sake, escorted us part of the way home, then went off hunting on their own. Guinea fowl were very tame sport for them, by then.

It had come to this, that if we actually wished to shoot something, or to watch animals, or even to take a walk through bush where every animal for miles had not been scared away, we had to lock up the dogs before we left, ignoring their whines and their howls. Even so, if let out too soon, they would follow. Once, after we had walked six miles or so, a leisurely morning's trek toward the mountains, the dogs arrived, panting, happy, their pink wet tongues hot on our knees and forearms, saying how delighted they were to have found us. They licked and wagged for a few moments – then off they went, they vanished, and did not come home until evening. We were worried. We had not known that they went so far from the farm by themselves. We spoke of how bad it would be if they took to frequenting other farms –

perhaps other chicken runs? But it was all too late. They were too old to train. Either they had to be kept permanently on leashes, tied to trees outside the house, and for dogs like these it was not much better than being dead – either that, or they must run free and take their chances.

We got news of the dogs in letters from home and it was increasingly bad. My brother and I, at our respective boarding schools where we were supposed to be learning discipline, order, and sound characters, read: 'The dogs went away a whole night, they only came back at lunchtime.' 'Jock and Bill have been three days and nights in the bush. They've just come home, worn out.' 'The dogs must have made a kill this time and stayed beside it like wild animals, because they came home too gorged to eat, they just drank a lot of water and fell off to sleep like babies. . . .' 'Mr Daly rang up yesterday to say he saw Jock and Bill hunting along the hill behind his house. They've been chasing his oxen. We've got to beat them when they get home because if they don't learn, they'll get themselves shot one of these dark nights. . . .'

They weren't there at all when we went home for the holidays. They had already been gone for nearly a week. But, or so we flattered ourselves, they sensed our return, for back they came, trotting gently side by side up the hill in the moonlight, two low black shapes moving above the accompanying black shapes of their shadows, their eyes gleaming red as the shafts of lamplight struck them. They greeted us, my brother and me, affectionately enough, but at once went off to sleep. We told ourselves that they saw us as creatures like them, who went off on long exciting hunts: but we knew it was sentimental nonsense, designed to take the edge off the hurt we felt because our animals, *our* dogs, cared so little about us. They went away again that night, or rather, in the first dawnlight. A week later they came home. They smelled

305

foul, they must have been chasing a skunk or a wildcat. Their fur was matted with grass seeds and their skin lumpy with ticks. They drank water heavily, but refused food: their breath was foetid with the smell of meat.

They lay down to sleep and remained limp while we, each taking an animal, its sleeping head heavy in our laps, removed ticks, grass seeds, blackjacks. On Bill's forepaw was a hard ridge which I thought was an old scar. He sleep-whimpered when I touched it. It was a noose of plaited grass, used by Africans to snare birds. Luckily it had snapped off. 'Yes,' said my father, 'that's how they'll end, both of them, they'll die in a trap, and serve them both right, they won't get any sympathy from me!'

We were frightened into locking them up for a day; but we could not stand their misery, and let them out again.

We were always springing gametraps of all kinds. For the big buck, the sable, the eland, the koodoo, the Africans bent a sapling across a path, held it by light string, and fixed on it a noose of heavy wire cut from a fence. For the smaller buck there were low traps with nooses of fine baling wire or plaited tree fiber. And at the corners of the cultivated fields or at the edges of waterholes, where the birds and hares came down to feed, were always a myriad tiny tracks under the grass, and often across every track hung a small noose of plaited grass. Sometimes we spent whole days destroying these snares.

In order to keep the dogs amused, we took to walking miles every day. We were exhausted, but they were not, and simply went off at night as well. Then we rode bicycles as fast as we could along the rough farm tracks, with the dogs bounding easily beside us. We wore ourselves out, trying to please Jock and Bill, who, we imagined, knew what we were doing and were trying to humor us. But we stuck at it. Once, at the end of a glade, we saw the skeleton of a large animal hanging from a noose. Some African had forgotten to visit his traps. We showed the skeleton to Jock and Bill, and talked and warned and threatened, almost in tears, because human speech was not dogs' speech. They sniffed around the bones, yapped a few times up into our faces – out of politeness, we felt; and were off again into the bush.

At school we heard that they were almost completely wild. Sometimes they came home for a meal, or a day's sleep, 'treating the house', my mother complained, 'like a hotel'.

Then fate struck, in the shape of a bucktrap.

One night, very late, we heard whining, and went out to greet them. They were crawling toward the front door, almost on their bellies. Their ribs stuck out, their coats stared, their eyes shone unhealthily. They fell on the food we gave them; they were starved. Then on Jock's neck, which was bent over the food bowl, showed the explanation: a thick strand of wire. It was not solid wire, but made of a dozen twisted strands, and had been chewed through, near the collar. We examined Bill's mouth: chewing the wire through must have taken a long time, days perhaps: his gums and lips were scarred and bleeding, and his teeth were worn down to stumps, like an old dog's teeth. If the wire had not been stranded, Jock would have died in the trap. As it was, he fell ill, his lungs were strained, since he had been half strangled with the wire. And Bill could no longer chew properly, he ate uncomfortably, like an old person. They stayed at home for weeks, reformed dogs, barked around the house at night, and ate regular meals.

Then they went off again, but came home more often than they had. Jock's lungs weren't right: he would lie out in the sun, gasping and wheezing, as if trying to rest them. As for Bill, he could only eat soft food. How, then, did they manage when they were hunting?

One afternoon we were shooting, miles from home, and we saw them. First we heard the familiar excited yapping coming toward us, about two miles off. We were in a large vlei, full of tall whitish grass which swayed and bent along a fast regular line: a shape showed, it was a duiker, hard to see until it was close because it was reddish brown in color, and the vlei had plenty of the pinkish feathery grass that turns a soft intense red in strong light. Being near sunset, the pale grass was on the verge of being invisible, like wires of white light; and the pink grass flamed and glowed; and the fur of the little buck shone red. It swerved suddenly. Had it seen us? No, it was because of Jock who had made a quick maneuvering turn from where he had been lying in the pink grass, to watch the buck, and behind it, Bill, pistoning along like a machine. Jock, who could no longer run fast, had turned the buck into Bill's jaws. We saw Bill bound at the little creature's throat, bring it down and hold it until Jock came in to kill it: his own teeth were useless now.

We walked over to greet them, but with restraint, for these two growling snarling creatures seemed not to know us, they raised eyes glazed with savagery, as they tore at the dead buck. Or rather, as Jock tore at it. Before we went away we saw Jock pushing over lumps of hot steaming meat toward Bill, who otherwise would have gone hungry.

They were really a team now; neither could function without the other. So we thought.

But soon Jock took to coming home from the hunting trips early, after one or two days, and Bill might stay out for a week or more. Jock lay watching the bush, and when Bill came, he licked his ears and face as if he had reverted to the role of Bill's mother.

Once I heard Bill barking and went to see. The telephone line ran through a vlei near the house to the farm over the hill. The wires hummed and sang and twanged. Bill was underneath the wires, which were a good fifteen feet over his head, jumping and barking at them: he was playing, out of exuberance, as he had done when a small puppy. But now it made me sad, seeing the strong dog playing all alone, while his friend lay quiet in the sun, wheezing from damaged lungs.

And what did Bill live on, in the bush? Rats, birds' eggs, lizards, anything *soft* enough? That was painful, too, thinking of the powerful hunters in the days of their glory.

Soon we got telephone calls from neighbors: Bill dropped in, he finished off the food in our dog's bowl. . . . Bill seemed hungry, so we fed him. . . . Your dog Bill is looking very thin, isn't he? . . . Bill was around our chicken run – I'm sorry, but if he goes for the eggs, then . . .

Bill had puppies with a pedigreed bitch fifteen miles off: her owners were annoyed: Bill was not good enough for them, and besides there was the question of his 'bad blood'. All the puppies were destroyed. He was hanging around the house all the time, although he had been beaten, and they had even fired shots into the air to scare him off. Was there anything we could do to keep him at home? they asked; for they were tired of having to keep their bitch tied up.

No, there was nothing we could do. Rather, there was nothing we *would* do; for when Bill came trotting up from the bush to drink deeply out of Jock's bowl, and to lie for a while nose to nose with Jock, well, we could have caught him and tied him up, but we did not. 'He won't last long anyway,' said my father. And my mother told Jock that he was a sensible and intelligent dog; for she again sang praises of his nature and character, just as if he had never spent so many glorious years in the bush.

I went to visit the neighbor who owned Bill's mate. She

was tied to a post on the verandah. All night we were disturbed by a wild sad howling from the bush, and she whimpered and strained at her rope. In the morning I walked out into the hot silence of the bush, and called to him: Bill, Bill, it's me. Nothing, no sound. I sat on the slope of an antheap in the shade, and waited. Soon Bill came into view, trotting between the trees. He was very thin. He looked gaunt, stiff, wary – an old outlaw, afraid of traps. He saw me, but stopped about twenty yards off. He climbed halfway up another anthill and sat there in full sunlight, so I could see the harsh patches on his coat. We sat in silence, looking at each other. Then he lifted his head and howled, like the howl dogs give to the full moon, long, terrible, lonely. But it was morning, the sun calm and clear, and the bush without mystery. He sat and howled his heart out, his muzzle pointed away toward where his mate was chained. We could hear the faint whimperings she made, and the clink of her metal dish as she moved about. I couldn't stand it. It made my flesh cold, and I could see the hairs standing up on my forearm. I went over to him and sat by him and put my arm around his neck as once, so many years ago, I had put my arm around his mother that moonlit night before I stole her puppy away from her. He put his muzzle on my forearm and whimpered, or rather cried. Then he lifted it and howled.... 'Oh, my God, Bill, don't do that, please don't, it's not the slightest use, please, dear Bill....' But he went on, until suddenly he leaped up in the middle of a howl, as if his pain were too strong to contain in sitting, and he sniffed at me, as if to say: That's you, is it, well, good-bye – then he turned his wild head to the bush and trotted away.

Very soon he was shot, coming out of a chicken run early one morning with an egg in his mouth.

Jock was quite alone now. He spent his old age lying in

the sun, his nose pointed out over the miles and miles of bush between our house and the mountains where he had hunted all those years with Bill. He was really an old dog, his legs were stiff, and his coat was rough, and he wheezed and gasped. Sometimes, at night, when the moon was up, he went out to howl at it, and we would say: He's missing Bill. He would come back to sit at my mother's knee, resting his head so that she could stroke it. She would say: 'Poor Jock, poor old boy, are you missing that bad dog Bill?'

Sometimes, when he lay dozing, he started up and went trotting on his stiff old legs through the house and the out-houses, sniffing everywhere and anxiously whining. Then he stood, upright, one paw raised, as he used to do when he was young, and gazed over the bush and softly whined. And we would say: 'He must have been dreaming he was out hunting with Bill.'

He got ill. He could hardly breathe. We carried him in our arms up the hill into the bush, and my mother stroked and patted him while my father put the gun barrel to the back of his head and shot him.

RICK BASS

THE HERMIT'S STORY

AN ICE STORM, following seven days of snow; the vast fields
and drifts of snow turning to sheets of glazed ice that shine
and shimmer blue in the moonlight, as if the color is being
fabricated not by the bending and absorption of light but by
some chemical reaction within the glossy ice; as if the source
of all blueness lies somewhere up here in the north – the core
of it beneath one of those frozen fields; as if blue is a thing
that emerges, in some parts of the world, from the soil itself,
after the sun goes down.

Blue creeping up fissures and cracks from depths of several
hundred feet; blue working its way up through the gleaming
ribs of Ann's buried dogs; blue trailing like smoke from the
dogs' empty eye sockets and nostrils – blue rising as if from
deep-dug chimneys until it reaches the surface and spreads
laterally and becomes entombed, or trapped – but still alive,
and drifting – within those moonstruck fields of ice.

Blue like a scent trapped in the ice, waiting for some soft
release, some thawing, so that it can continue spreading.

It's Thanksgiving. Susan and I are over at Ann and Roger's
house for dinner. The storm has knocked out all the power
down in town – it's a clear, cold, starry night, and if you were
to climb one of the mountains on snowshoes and look forty
miles south toward where town lies, instead of seeing the
usual small scatterings of light – like fallen stars, stars sunken
to the bottom of a lake, but still glowing – you would see
nothing but darkness – a bowl of silence and darkness in

balance for once with the mountains up here, rather than opposing or complementing our darkness, our peace.

As it is, we do not climb up on snowshoes to look down at the dark town – the power lines dragged down by the clutches of ice – but can tell instead just by the way there is no faint glow over the mountains to the south that the power is out: that this Thanksgiving, life for those in town is the same as it always is for us in the mountains, and it is a good feeling, a familial one, coming on the holiday as it does – though doubtless too the townspeople are feeling less snug and cozy about it than we are.

We've got our lanterns and candles burning. A fire's going in the stove, as it will all winter long and into the spring. Ann's dogs are asleep in their straw nests, breathing in that same blue light that is being exhaled from the skeletons of their ancestors just beneath and all around them. There is the faint smell of cold-storage meat – slabs and slabs of it – coming from down in the basement, and we have just finished off an entire chocolate pie and three bottles of wine. Roger, who does not know how to read, is examining the empty bottles, trying to read some of the words on the labels. He recognizes the words *the* and *in* and *USA*. It may be that he will never learn to read – that he will be unable to – but we are in no rush; he has all of his life to accomplish this. I for one believe that he will learn.

Ann has a story for us. It's about a fellow named Gray Owl, up in Canada, who owned half a dozen speckled German shorthaired pointers and who hired Ann to train them all at once. It was twenty years ago, she says – her last good job.

She worked the dogs all summer and into the autumn, and finally had them ready for field trials. She took them back up to Gray Owl – way up in Saskatchewan – driving all day and night in her old truck, which was old even then, with dogs piled up on top of one another, sleeping and snoring: dogs on her lap, dogs on the seat, dogs on the floorboard.

Ann was taking the dogs up there to show Gray Owl how to work them: how to take advantage of their newfound talents. She could be a sculptor or some other kind of artist, in that she speaks of her work as if the dogs are rough blocks of stone whose internal form exists already and is waiting only to be chiseled free and then released by her, beautiful, into the world.

Basically, in six months the dogs had been transformed from gangling, bouncing puppies into six wonderful hunters, and she needed to show their owner which characteristics to nurture, which ones to discourage. With all dogs, Ann said, there was a tendency, upon their leaving her tutelage, for a kind of chitinous encrustation to set in, a sort of oxidation, upon the dogs leaving her hands and being returned to someone less knowledgeable and passionate, less committed than she. It was as if there were a tendency for the dogs' greatness to disappear back into the stone.

So she went up there to give both the dogs and Gray Owl a checkout session. She drove with the heater on and the windows down; the cold Canadian air was invigorating, cleaner. She could smell the scent of the fir and spruce, and the damp alder and cottonwood leaves beneath the many feet of snow. We laughed at her when she said it, but she told us that up in Canada she could taste the fish in the water as she drove alongside creeks and rivers.

She got to Gray Owl's around midnight. He had a little guest cabin but had not heated it for her, uncertain as to the day of her arrival, so she and the six dogs slept together on a cold mattress beneath mounds of elk hides: their last night together. She had brought a box of quail with which to work

317

the dogs, and she built a small fire in the stove and set the box of quail next to it.

The quail muttered and cheeped all night and the stove popped and hissed and Ann and the dogs slept for twelve hours straight, as if submerged in another time, or as if everyone else in the world were submerged in time – and as if she and the dogs were pioneers, or survivors of some kind: upright and exploring the present, alive in the world, free of that strange chitin.

She spent a week up there, showing Gray Owl how his dogs worked. She said he scarcely recognized them afield, and that it took a few days just for him to get over his amazement. They worked the dogs both individually and, as Gray Owl came to understand and appreciate what Ann had crafted, in groups. They traveled across snowy hills on snowshoes, the sky the color of snow, so that often it was like moving through a dream, and, except for the rasp of the snowshoes beneath them and the pull of gravity, they might have believed they had ascended into some sky-place where all the world was snow.

They worked into the wind – north – whenever they could. Ann would carry birds in a pouch over her shoulder and from time to time would fling a startled bird out into that dreary, icy snowscape. The quail would fly off with great haste, a dark feathered buzz bomb disappearing quickly into the teeth of cold, and then Gray Owl and Ann and the dog, or dogs, would go find it, following it by scent only, as always.

Snot icicles would be hanging from the dogs' nostrils. They would always find the bird. The dog, or dogs, would point it, Gray Owl or Ann would step forward and flush it, and the beleaguered bird would leap into the sky again, and once more they would push on after it, pursuing that bird toward the horizon as if driving it with a whip. Whenever the bird wheeled and flew downwind, they'd quarter away from it, then get a mile or so downwind from it and push it back north.

When the quail finally became too exhausted to fly, Ann would pick it up from beneath the dogs' noses as they held point staunchly, put the tired bird in her game bag, and replace it with a fresh one, and off they'd go again. They carried their lunch in Gray Owl's daypack, as well as emergency supplies – a tent and some dry clothes – in case they should become lost, and around noon each day (they could rarely see the sun, only an eternal ice-white haze, so that they relied instead only on their internal rhythms) they would stop and make a pot of tea on the sputtering little gas stove. Sometimes one or two of the quail would die from exposure, and they would cook that on the stove and eat it out there in the tundra, tossing the feathers up into the wind as if to launch one more flight, and feeding the head, guts, and feet to the dogs.

Seen from above, their tracks might have seemed aimless and wandering rather than with the purpose, the focus that was burning hot in both their and the dogs' hearts. Perhaps someone viewing the tracks could have discerned the pattern, or perhaps not, but it did not matter, for their tracks – the patterns, direction, and tracing of them – were obscured by the drifting snow, sometimes within minutes after they were laid down.

Toward the end of the week, Ann said, they were finally running all six dogs at once, like a herd of silent wild horses through all that snow, and as she would be going home the next day there was no need to conserve any of the birds she had brought, and she was turning them loose several at a time: birds flying in all directions; the dogs, as ever, tracking them to the ends of the earth.

It was almost a whiteout that last day, and it was hard to keep track of all the dogs. Ann was sweating from the exertion as well as the tension of trying to keep an eye on, and evaluate, each dog, and the sweat was freezing on her as if she were developing an ice skin. She jokingly told Gray Owl that next time she was going to try to find a client who lived in Arizona, or even South America. Gray Owl smiled and then told her that they were lost, but no matter, the storm would clear in a day or two.

They knew it was getting near dusk – there was a faint dulling to the sheer whiteness, a kind of increasing heaviness in the air, a new density to the faint light around them – and the dogs slipped in and out of sight, working just at the edges of their vision.

The temperature was dropping as the north wind increased – 'No question about which way south is,' Gray Owl said, 'so we'll turn around and walk south for three hours, and if we don't find a road, we'll make camp' – and now the dogs were coming back with frozen quail held gingerly in their mouths, for once the birds were dead, the dogs were allowed to retrieve them, though the dogs must have been puzzled that there had been no shots. Ann said she fired a few rounds of the cap pistol into the air to make the dogs think she had hit those birds. Surely they believed she was a goddess.

They turned and headed south – Ann with a bag of frozen birds over her shoulder, and the dogs, knowing that the hunt was over now, once again like a team of horses in harness, though wild and prancy.

After an hour of increasing discomfort – Ann's and Gray Owl's hands and feet numb, and ice beginning to form on the dogs' paws, so that the dogs were having to high-step – they came in day's last light to the edge of a wide clearing: a terrain that was remarkable and soothing for its lack of hills. It was a frozen lake, which meant – said Gray Owl – they had drifted west (or perhaps east) by as much as ten miles.

Ann said that Gray Owl looked tired and old and guilty, as would any host who had caused his guest some unasked-for inconvenience. They knelt down and began massaging the dogs' paws and then lit the little stove and held each dog's foot, one at a time, over the tiny blue flame to help it thaw out.

Gray Owl walked out to the edge of the lake ice and kicked at it with his foot, hoping to find fresh water beneath for the dogs; if they ate too much snow, especially after working so hard, they'd get violent diarrhea and might then become too weak to continue home the next day, or the next, or whenever the storm quit.

Ann said that she had barely been able to see Gray Owl's outline through the swirling snow, even though he was less than twenty yards away. He kicked once at the sheet of ice, the vast plate of it, with his heel, then disappeared below the ice.

Ann wanted to believe that she had blinked and lost sight of him, or that a gust of snow had swept past and hidden him, but it had been too fast, too total: she knew that the lake had swallowed him. She was sorry for Gray Owl, she said, and worried for his dogs – afraid they would try to follow his scent down into the icy lake and be lost as well – but what she had been most upset about, she said – to be perfectly honest – was that Gray Owl had been wearing the little daypack with the tent and emergency rations. She had it in her mind to try to save Gray Owl, and to try to keep the dogs from going through the ice, but if he drowned, she was going to have to figure out how to try to get that daypack off of the drowned man and set up the wet tent in the blizzard on the snowy prairie and then crawl inside and survive. She would have to go into the water naked, so that when she came back out – if she came back out – she would have dry clothes to put on.

The dogs came galloping up, seeming as large as deer or elk in that dim landscape against which there was nothing else to give the viewer a perspective, and Ann whoaed them right at the lake's edge, where they stopped immediately, as if they had suddenly been cast with a sheet of ice.

Ann knew the dogs would stay there forever, or until she released them, and it troubled her to think that if she drowned, they too would die – that they would stand there motionless, as she had commanded them, for as long as they could, until at some point – days later, perhaps – they would lie down, trembling with exhaustion – they might lick at some snow, for moisture – but that then the snows would cover them, and still they would remain there, chins resting on their front paws, staring straight ahead and unseeing into the storm, wondering where the scent of her had gone.

Ann eased out onto the ice. She followed the tracks until she came to the jagged hole in the ice through which Gray Owl had plunged. She was almost half again lighter than he, but she could feel the ice crackling beneath her own feet. It sounded different, too, in a way she could not place – it did not have the squeaky, percussive resonance of the lake-ice back home – and she wondered if Canadian ice froze differently or just sounded different.

She got down on all fours and crept closer to the hole. It was right at dusk. She peered down into the hole and dimly saw Gray Owl standing down there, waving his arms at her. He did not appear to be swimming. Slowly, she took one glove off and eased her bare hand down into the hole. She could find no water, and, tentatively, she reached deeper.

Gray Owl's hand found hers and he pulled her down in. Ice broke as she fell, but he caught her in his arms. She could smell the wood smoke in his jacket from the alder he burned in his cabin. There was no water at all, and it was warm beneath the ice.

'This happens a lot more than people realize,' he said. 'It's not really a phenomenon; it's just what happens. A cold snap comes in October, freezes a skin of ice over the lake – it's got to be a shallow one, almost a marsh. Then a snowfall comes, insulating the ice. The lake drains in fall and winter – percolates down through the soil' – he stamped the spongy ground beneath them – 'but the ice up top remains. And nobody ever knows any different. People look out at the surface and think, *Aha, a frozen lake.*' Gray Owl laughed.

'Did you know it would be like this?' Ann asked.

'No,' he said. 'I was looking for water. I just got lucky.'

Ann walked back to shore beneath the ice to fetch her stove and to release the dogs from their whoa command. The dry lake was only about eight feet deep, but it grew shallow quickly closer to shore, so that Ann had to crouch to keep from bumping her head on the overhead ice, and then crawl; and then there was only space to wriggle, and to emerge she had to break the ice above her by bumping and then battering it with her head and elbows, struggling like some embryonic hatchling; and when she stood up, waist-deep amid sparkling shards of ice – it was night-time now – the dogs barked ferociously at her, but they remained where she had ordered them. She was surprised at how far off course she was when she climbed out; she had traveled only twenty feet, but already the dogs were twice that far away from her. She knew humans had a poorly evolved, almost nonexistent sense of direction, but this error – over such a short distance – shocked her. It was as if there were in us a thing – an impulse, a catalyst – that denies our ever going straight to another thing. Like dogs working left and right into the wind, she thought, before converging on the scent.

Except that the dogs would not get lost, while she could easily imagine herself and Gray Owl getting lost beneath the lake, walking in circles forever, unable to find even the simplest of things: the shore.

She gathered the stove and dogs. She was tempted to try to go back in the way she had come out – it seemed so easy – but she considered the consequences of getting lost in the other direction, and instead followed her original tracks out to where Gray Owl had first dropped through the ice. It was true night now, and the blizzard was still blowing hard, plastering snow and ice around her face like a mask. The dogs did not want to go down into the hole, so she lowered them to Gray Owl and then climbed gratefully back down into the warmth herself.

The air was a thing of its own – recognizable as air, and breathable as such, but with a taste and odor, an essence, unlike any other air they'd ever breathed. It had a different density to it, so that smaller, shallower breaths were required; there was very much the feeling that if they breathed in too much of the strange, dense air, they would drown.

They wanted to explore the lake, and were thirsty, but it felt like a victory simply to be warm – or rather, not cold – and they were so exhausted that instead they made pallets out of the dead marsh grass that rustled around their ankles, and they slept curled up on the tiniest of hammocks, to keep from getting damp in the pockets and puddles of water that still lingered here and there.

All eight of them slept as if in a nest, heads and arms

draped across other ribs and hips; and it was, said Ann, the best and deepest sleep she'd ever had – the sleep of hounds, the sleep of childhood. How long they slept, she never knew, for she wasn't sure, later, how much of their subsequent time they spent wandering beneath the lake, and then up on the prairie, homeward again, but when they awoke, it was still night, or night once more, and clearing, with bright stars visible through the porthole, their point of embarkation; and even from beneath the ice, in certain places where, for whatever reasons – temperature, oxygen content, wind scour – the ice was clear rather than glazed, they could see the spangling of stars, though more dimly; and strangely, rather than seeming to distance them from the stars, this phenomenon seemed to pull them closer, as if they were up in the stars, traveling the Milky Way, or as if the stars were embedded in the ice.

It was very cold outside – up above – and there was a steady stream, a current like a river, of the night's colder, heavier air plunging down though their porthole – as if trying to fill the empty lake with that frozen air – but there was also the hot muck of the earth's massive respirations breathing out warmth and being trapped and protected beneath that ice, so that there were warm currents doing battle with the lone cold current.

The result was that it was breezy down there, and the dogs' noses twitched in their sleep as the images brought by these scents painted themselves across their sleeping brains in the language we call dreams but which, for the dogs, was reality: the scent of an owl *real*, not a dream; the scent of bear, cattail, willow, loon, *real*, even though they were sleeping, and even though those things were not visible, only over the next horizon.

The ice was contracting, groaning and cracking and

squeaking up tighter, shrinking beneath the great cold – a concussive, grinding sound, as if giants were walking across the ice above – and it was this sound that awakened them. They snuggled in warmer among the rattly dried yellowing grasses and listened to the tremendous clashings, as if they were safe beneath the sea and were watching waves of star-light sweeping across their hiding place; or as if they were in some place, some position, where they could watch mountains being born.

After a while the moon came up and washed out the stars. The light was blue and silver and seemed, Ann said, to be like a living thing. It filled the sheet of ice just above their heads with a shimmering cobalt light, which again rippled as if the ice were moving, rather than the earth itself, with the moon tracking it – and like deer drawn by gravity getting up in the night to feed for an hour or so before settling back in, Gray Owl and Ann and the dogs rose from their nests of straw and began to travel.

'You didn't – you know – *engage*?' Susan asks, a little mischievously.

Ann shakes her head. 'It was too cold,' she says.

'But you would have, if it hadn't been so cold, right?' Susan asks, and Ann shrugs.

'He was an old man – in his fifties – he seemed old to me then, and the dogs were around. But yeah, there was something about it that made me think of . . . those things,' she says, careful and precise as ever.

They walked a long way, Ann continues, eager to change the subject. The air was damp down there, and whenever they'd get chilled, they'd stop and make a little fire out of a bundle of dry cattails. There were little pockets and puddles of swamp gas pooled in place, and sometimes a spark from the cattails would ignite one of those, and those little pockets of gas would light up like when you toss gas on a fire – explosions of brilliance, like flashbulbs, marsh pockets igniting like falling dominoes, or like children playing hopscotch – until a large enough flash-pocket was reached – sometimes thirty or forty yards away – that the puff of flame would blow a chimney-hole through the ice, venting the other pockets, and the fires would crackle out, the scent of grass smoke sweet in their lungs, and they could feel gusts of warmth from the little flickering fires, and currents of the colder, heavier air sliding down through the new vent-holes and pooling around their ankles. The moonlight would strafe down through those rents in the ice, and shards of moon-ice would be glittering and spinning like diamond-motes in those newly vented columns of moonlight; and they pushed on, still lost, but so alive.

The small explosions were fun, but they frightened the dogs, so Ann and Gray Owl lit twisted bundles of cattails and used them for torches to light their way, rather than building warming fires, though occasionally they would still pass though a pocket of methane and a stray ember would fall from their torches, and the whole chain of fire and light would begin again, culminating once more with a vent-hole being blown open and shards of glittering ice tumbling down into their lair . . .

What would it have looked like, seen from above – the orange blurrings of their wandering trail beneath the ice; and what would the sheet of lake-ice itself have looked like that night – throbbing with ice-bound, subterranean blue and orange light of moon and fire? But again, there was no one to view the spectacle: only the travelers themselves, and they had no perspective, no vantage from which to view or judge themselves. They were simply pushing on from one fire to the next, carrying their tiny torches.

They knew they were getting near a shore – the southern shore, they hoped, as they followed the glazed moon's lure above – when the dogs began to encounter shore birds that had somehow found their way beneath the ice through small fissures and rifts and were taking refuge in the cattails. Small winter birds – juncos, nuthatches, chickadees – skittered away from the smoky approach of their torches; only a few late-migrating (or winter-trapped) snipe held tight and steadfast; and the dogs began to race ahead of Gray Owl and Ann, working these familiar scents – blue and silver ghost-shadows of dog muscle weaving ahead through slants of moonlight.

The dogs emitted the odor of adrenaline when they worked, Ann said – a scent like damp, fresh-cut green hay – and with nowhere to vent, the odor was dense and thick around them, so that Ann wondered if it too might be flammable, like the methane – if in the dogs' passions they might literally immolate themselves.

They followed the dogs closely with their torches. The ceiling was low – about eight feet – so that the tips of their torches' flames seared the ice above them, leaving a drip behind them and transforming the milky, almost opaque cobalt and orange ice behind them, wherever they passed, into wandering ribbons of clear ice, translucent to the sky – a script of flame, or buried flame, ice-bound flame – and they hurried to keep up with the dogs.

Now the dogs had the snipe surrounded, as Ann told it, and one by one the dogs went on point, each dog freezing as it pointed to the birds' hiding places, and Gray Owl moved in to flush the birds, which launched themselves with vigor against the roof of the ice above, fluttering like bats; but the snipe were too small, not powerful enough to break through those frozen four inches of water (though they could fly four

328

thousand miles to South America each year and then back to Canada six months later – is freedom a lateral component, or a vertical one?), and as Gray Owl kicked at the clumps of frost-bent cattails where the snipe were hiding and they burst into flight, only to hit their heads on the ice above them, they came tumbling back down, raining limp and unconscious back to their soft grassy nests.

The dogs began retrieving them, carrying them gingerly, delicately – not caring for the taste of snipe, which ate only earthworms – and Ann and Gray Owl gathered the tiny birds from the dogs, placed them in their pockets, and continued on to the shore, chasing that moon, the ceiling lowering to six feet, then four, then to a crawlspace, and after they had bashed their way out and stepped back out into the frigid air, they tucked the still-unconscious snipe into little crooks in branches, up against the trunks of trees and off the ground, out of harm's way, and passed on, south – as if late in their own migration – while the snipe rested, warm and terrified and heart-fluttering, but saved, for now, against the trunks of those trees.

Long after Ann and Gray Owl and the pack of dogs had passed through, the birds would awaken, their bright, dark eyes luminous in the moonlight, and the first sight they would see would be the frozen marsh before them, with its chain of still-steaming vent-holes stretching back across all the way to the other shore. Perhaps these were birds that had been unable to migrate owing to injuries, or some genetic absence. Perhaps they had tried to migrate in the past but had found either their winter habitat destroyed or the path so fragmented and fraught with danger that it made more sense – to these few birds – to ignore the tuggings of the stars and seasons and instead to try to carve out new lives, new ways of being, even in such a stark and severe landscape: or rather, in a stark and severe period – knowing that lushness and bounty were still retained with that landscape, that it was only a phase, that better days would come. That in fact (the snipe knowing these things with their blood, ten million years in the world) the austere times were the very thing, the very imbalance, that would summon the resurrection of that frozen richness within the soil – if indeed that richness, that magic, that hope, did still exist beneath the ice and snow. Spring would come like its own green fire, if only the injured ones could hold on.

And what would the snipe think or remember, upon reawakening and finding themselves still in that desolate position, desolate place and time, but still alive, and with hope?

Would it seem to them that a thing like grace had passed through, as they slept – that a slender winding river of it had passed through and rewarded them for their faith and endurance?

Believing, stubbornly, that that green land beneath them would blossom once more. Maybe not soon; but again.

If the snipe survived, they would be among the first to see it. Perhaps they believed that the pack of dogs, and Gray Owl's and Ann's advancing torches, had only been one of winter's dreams. Even with the proof – the scribings – of grace's passage before them – the vent-holes still steaming – perhaps they believed it was a dream.

Gray Owl, Ann, and the dogs headed south for half a day until they reached the snow-scoured road on which they'd parked. The road looked different, Ann said, buried beneath snowdrifts, and they didn't know whether to turn east or west. The dogs chose west, and Gray Owl and Ann followed them. Two hours later they were back at their truck, and that night they were back at Gray Owl's cabin; by the next night Ann was home again.

She says that even now she still sometimes has dreams about being beneath the ice – about living beneath the ice – and that it seems to her as if she was down there for much longer than a day and a night; that instead she might have been gone for years.

It was twenty years ago, when it happened. Gray Owl has since died, and all those dogs are dead now, too. She is the only one who still carries – in the flesh, at any rate – the memory of that passage.

Ann would never discuss such a thing, but I suspect that it, that one day and night, helped give her a model for what things were like for her dogs when they were hunting and when they went on point: how the world must have appeared to them when they were in that trance, that blue zone, where the odors of things wrote their images across the dogs' hot brainpans. A zone where sight, and the appearance of things – *surfaces* – disappeared, and where instead their essence – the heat molecules of scent – was revealed, illuminated, circumscribed, possessed.

I suspect that she holds that knowledge – the memory of that one day and night – especially since she is now the sole possessor – as tightly, and securely, as one might clench some bright small gem in one's fist: not a gem given to one by some favored or beloved individual but, even more valuable, some gem found while out on a walk – perhaps by happenstance, or perhaps by some unavoidable rhythm of fate – and hence containing great magic, great strength.

Such is the nature of the kinds of people living, scattered here and there, in this valley.

THOMAS McGUANE

FLIGHT

DURING BIRD SEASON, dogs circle each other in my kitchen, shell vests are piled in the mudroom, all drains are clogged with feathers, and hunters work up hangover remedies at the icebox. As a diurnal man, I gloat at these presences, estimating who will and who will not shoot well.

This year was slightly different in that Dan Ashaway arrived seriously ill. Yet this morning, he was nearly the only clear-eyed man in the kitchen. He helped make the vast breakfast of grouse hash, eggs, juice, and coffee. Bill Upton and his brother, Jerry, who were miserable, loaded dogs and made a penitentially early start. I pushed away some dishes and lit a breakfast cigar. Dan refilled our coffee and sat down. We've hunted birds together for years. I live here and Dan flies in from Philadelphia. Anyway, this seemed like the moment.

'How bad off are you?' I asked.

'I'm afraid I'm not going to get well,' said Dan directly, shrugging and dropping his hands to the arms of his chair. That was that. 'Let's get started.'

We took Dan's dogs at his insistence. They jumped into the aluminum boxes on the back of the truck when he said 'Load': Betty, a liver-and-white female, and Sally, a small bitch with a banded face. These were – I should say *are* – two dead-broke pointers who found birds and retrieved without much handling. Dan didn't even own a whistle.

As we drove toward Roundup, the entire pressure of my

335

thoughts was of how remarkable it was to be alive. It seemed a strange and merry realization.

The dogs rode so quietly I had occasion to remember when Betty was a pup and yodeled in her box, drawing stares in all the towns. Since then she had quieted down and grown solid at her job. She and Sally had hunted everywhere from Albany, Georgia, to Wilsall, Montana. Sally was born broke but Betty had the better nose.

We drove between two ranges of desertic mountains, low ranges without snow or evergreens. Section fences climbed infrequently and disappeared over the top or into blue sky. There was one little band of cattle trailed by a cowboy and a dog, the only signs of life. Dan was pressing sixteen-gauge shells into the elastic loops of his cartridge belt. He was wearing blue policeman's suspenders and a brown felt hat, a businessman's worn-out Dobbs.

We watched a harrier course the ground under a bluff, sharptail grouse jumping in his wake. The harrier missed a half dozen, wheeled on one wingtip, and nailed a bird in a pop of down and feathers. As we resumed driving, the hawk was hooded over its prey, stripping meat from the breast.

Every time the dirt road climbed to a new vantage point, the country changed. For a long time, a green creek in a tunnel of willows was alongside us; then it went off under a bridge, and we climbed away to the north. When we came out of the low ground, there seemed no end to the country before us: a great wide prairie with contours as unquestionable as the sea. There were buttes pried up from its surface and yawning coulees with streaks of brush where the springs were. We had to abandon logic to stop and leave the truck behind. Dan beamed and said, 'Here's the spot for a big nap.' The remark frightened me.

'Have we crossed the stagecoach road?' Dan asked.

'Couple miles back.'

'Where did we jump all those sage hens in 1965?'

'Right where the stagecoach road passed the old hotel.'

Dan had awarded himself a little English sixteen-gauge for graduating from the Wharton School of Finance that year. It was in the gun rack behind our heads now, the bluing gone and its hinge pin shot loose.

'It's a wonder we found anything,' said Dan from afar, 'with the kind of run-off dog we had. Señor Jack. You had to preach religion to Señor Jack every hundred yards or he'd leave us. Remember? It's a wonder we fed that common bastard.' Señor Jack was a dog with no talent, loyalty, or affection, a dog we swore would drive us to racquet sports. Dan gave him away in Georgia.

'He found the sage hens.'

'But when we got on the back side of the Little Snowies, remember? He went right through all those sharptails like a train. We should have had deer rifles. A real wonder dog. I wonder where he is. I wonder what he's doing. Well, it's all an illusion, a very beautiful illusion, a miracle which is taking place before our very eyes. 1965. I'll be damned.'

The stagecoach road came in around from the east again, and we stopped: two modest ruts heading into the hills. We released the dogs and followed the road around for half an hour. It took us past an old buffalo wallow filled with water. Some teal got up into the wind and wheeled off over the prairie.

About a mile later the dogs went on point. It was hard to say who struck game and who backed. Sally catwalked a little, relocated, and stopped; then Betty honored her point. So we knew we had moving birds and got up on them fast. The dogs stayed staunch, and the long covey rise went off like something tearing. I killed a going-away and Dan made

337

a clean left and right. It was nice to be reminded of his strong heads-up shooting. I always crawled all over my gun and lost some quickness. It came of too much waterfowling when I was young. Dan had never really been out of the uplands and had speed to show for it.

Betty and Sally picked up the birds; they came back with eyes crinkled, grouse in their mouths. They dropped the birds and Dan caught Sally with a finger through her collar. Betty shot back for the last bird. She was the better marking dog.

We shot another brace in a ravine. The dogs pointed shoulder to shoulder and the birds towered. We retrieved those, walked up a single, and headed for a hillside spring with a bar of bright buckbrush, where we nooned up with the dogs. The pretty bitches put their noses in the cold water and lifted their heads to smile when they got out of breath drinking. Then they pitched down for a rest. We broke the guns open and set them out of the way. I laid a piece of paper down and arranged some sandwiches and tangy apples from my own tree. We stretched out on one elbow, ate with a free hand, and looked off over the prairie, to me the most beautiful thing in the world. I wish I could see all the grasslands, while we still have them.

Then I couldn't stand it. 'What do you mean you're not going to get better?'

'It's true, old pal. It's quite final. But listen, today I'm not thinking about it. So let's not start.'

I was a little sore at myself. We've all got to go, I thought. It's like waiting for an alarm to go off, when it's too dark to read the dial. Looking at Dan's great chest straining his policeman's suspenders, it was fairly unimaginable that anything predictable could turn him to dust. I was quite wrong about that too.

A solitary antelope buck stopped to look at us from a great distance. Dan put his hat on the barrels of his gun and decoyed the foolish animal to thirty yards before it snorted and ran off. We had sometimes found antelope blinds the Indians had built, usually not far from the eagle traps, clever things made by vital hands. There were old cartridge cases next to the spring, lying in the dirt, 45–70s; maybe a fight, maybe an old rancher hunting antelope with a cavalry rifle. Who knows. A trembling mirage appeared to the south, blue and banded with hills and distance. All around us the prairie creaked with life. I tried to picture the Indians, the soldiers. I kind of could. Were they gone or were they not?

'I don't know if I want to shoot a limit.'

'Let's find them first,' I said. I would have plenty of time to think about that remark later.

Dan thought and then said, 'That's interesting. We'll find them and decide if we want to limit out or let it stand.' The pointers got up, stretched their backs, glanced at us, wagged once, and lay down again next to the spring. I had gotten a queer feeling. Dan went quiet. He stared off. After a minute, a smile shot over his face. The dogs had been watching for that, and we were all on our feet and moving.

'This is it,' Dan said, to the dogs or to me; I was never sure which. Betty and Sally cracked off, casting into the wind, Betty making the bigger race, Sally filling in with meticulous groundwork. I could sense Dan's pleasure in these fast and beautiful bracemates.

'When you hunt these girls,' he said, 'you've got to step up their rations with hamburger, eggs, bacon drippings – you know, mixed in with that kibble. On real hot days, you put electrolytes in their drinking water. Betty comes into heat in April and October; Sally, March and September. Sally runs a little fever with her heat and shouldn't be hunted in hot weather for the first week and a half. I always let them stay in the house. I put them in a roading harness by August first to get them in shape. They've both been roaded horseback.'

I began to feel dazed and heavy. Maybe life wasn't something you lost at the end of a long fight. But I let myself off and thought, These things can go on and on.

Sally pitched over the top of a coulee. Betty went in and up the other side. There was a shadow that crossed the deep grass at the head of the draw. Sally locked up on point just at the rim, and Dan waved Betty in. She came in from the other side, hit the scent, sank into a running slink, and pointed.

Dan smiled at me and said, 'Wish me luck.' He closed his gun, walked over the rim, and sank from sight. I sat on the ground until I heard the report. After a bit the covey started to get up, eight dusky birds that went off on a climbing course. I whistled the dogs in and started for my truck.

JAMES SALTER

MY LORD YOU

THERE WERE CRUMPLED napkins on the table, wine-glasses still with dark remnant in them, coffee stains, and plates with bits of hardened Brie. Beyond the bluish windows the garden lay motionless beneath the birdsong of summer morning. Daylight had come. It had been a success except for one thing: Brennan.

They had sat around first, drinking in the twilight, and then gone inside. The kitchen had a large round table, fireplace, and shelves with ingredients of every kind. Deems was well known as a cook. So was his somewhat unknowable girlfriend, Irene, who had a mysterious smile though they never cooked together. That night it was Deems's turn. He served caviar, brought out in a white jar such as makeup comes in, to be eaten from small silver spoons.

– The only way, Deems muttered in profile. He seldom looked at anyone. Antique silver spoons, Ardis heard him mistakenly say in his low voice, as if it might not have been noticed.

She was noticing everything, however. Though they had known Deems for a while, she and her husband had never been to the house. In the dining room, when they all went in to dinner, she took in the pictures, books, and shelves of objects including one of perfect, gleaming shells. It was foreign in a way, like anyone else's house, but half-familiar.

There'd been some mix-up about the seating that Irene

tried vainly to adjust amid the conversation before the meal began. Outside, darkness had come, deep and green. The men were talking about camps they had gone to as boys in piny Maine and about Soros, the financier. Far more interesting was a comment Ardis heard Irene make, in what context she did not know,

– I think there's such a thing as sleeping with one man too many.

– Did you say 'such a thing' or 'no such thing'? she heard herself ask.

Irene merely smiled. I must ask her later, Ardis thought. The food was excellent. There was cold soup, duck, and a salad of young vegetables. The coffee had been served and Ardis was distractedly playing with melted wax from the candles when a voice burst out loudly behind her,

– I'm late. Who's this? Are these the beautiful people?

It was a drunken man in a jacket and dirty white trousers with blood on them, which had come from nicking his lip while shaving two hours before. His hair was damp, his face arrogant. It was the face of a Regency duke, intimidating, spoiled. The irrational flickered from him.

– Do you have anything to drink here? What is this, wine? Very sorry I'm late. I've just had seven cognacs and said goodbye to my wife. Deems, you know what that's like. You're my only friend, do you know that? The only one.

– There's some dinner in there, if you like, Deems said, gesturing toward the kitchen.

– No dinner. I've had dinner. I'll just have something to drink. Deems, you're my friend, but I'll tell you something, you'll become my enemy. You know what Oscar Wilde said – my favorite writer, my favorite in all the world. Anyone can choose his friends, but only the wise man can choose his enemies.

344

He was staring intently at Deems. It was like the grip of a madman, a kind of fury. His mouth had an expression of determination. When he went into the kitchen they could hear him among the bottles. He returned with a dangerous glassful and looked around boldly.

– Where is Beatrice? Deems asked.

– Who?

– Beatrice, your wife.

– Gone, Brennan said.

He searched for a chair.

– To visit her father? Irene asked.

– What makes you think that? Brennan said menacingly. To Ardis's alarm he sat down next to her.

– He's been in the hospital, hasn't he?

– Who knows where he's been, Brennan said darkly. He's a swine. Lucre, gain. He's a slum owner, a criminal. I would hang him myself. In the fashion of Gomez, the dictator, whose daughters are probably wealthy women.

He discovered Ardis and said to her, as if imitating someone, perhaps someone he assumed her to be,

– 'N 'at funny? 'N 'at wonderful?

To her relief he turned away.

– I'm their only hope, he said to Irene. I'm living on their money and it's ruinous, the end of me. He held out his glass and asked mildly, Can I have just a tiny bit of ice? I adore my wife. To Ardis he confided, Do you know how we met? Unimaginable. She was walking by on the beach. I was unprepared. I saw the ventral, then the dorsal, I imagined the rest. Bang! We came together like planets. Endless fornication. Sometimes I just lie silent and observe her. *The black panther lies under his rose-tree*, he recited. *J'ai eu pitié des autres* . . .

He stared at her.

345

– What is that? she asked tentatively.

– ... *but that the child walk in peace in her basilica,* he intoned.

– Is it Wilde?

– You can't guess? Pound. The sole genius of the century. No, not the sole. I am another: a drunk, a failure, and a great genius. Who are you? he said. Another little housewife?

She felt the blood leave her face and stood to busy herself clearing the table. His hand was on her arm.

– Don't go. I know who you are, another priceless woman meant to languish. Beautiful figure, he said as she managed to free herself, pretty shoes.

As she carried some plates into the kitchen she could hear him saying,

– Don't go to many of these parties. Not invited.

– Can't imagine why, someone murmured.

– But Deems is my friend, my very closest friend.

– Who is he? Ardis asked Irene in the kitchen.

– Oh, he's a poet. He's married to a Venezuelan woman and she runs off. He's not always this bad.

They had quieted him down in the other room. Ardis could see her husband nervously pushing his glasses up on his nose with one finger. Deems, in a polo shirt and with rumpled hair, was trying to guide Brennan toward the back door. Brennan kept stopping to talk. For a moment he would seem reformed.

– I want to tell you something, he said. I went past the school, the one on the street there. There was a poster. The First Annual Miss Fuck Contest. I'm serious. This is a fact.

– No, no, Deems said.

– It's been held, I don't know when. Question is, are they coming to their senses finally or losing them? A tiny bit more, he begged; his glass was empty. His mind doubled back. Seriously, what do you think of that?

In the light of the kitchen he seemed merely dishevelled, like a journalist who has been working hard all night. The unsettling thing was the absence of reason in him, his glare. One nostril was smaller than the other. He was used to being ungovernable. Ardis hoped he would not notice her again. His forehead had two gleaming places, like nascent horns. Were men drawn to you when they knew they were frightening you?

She could feel his eyes. There was silence. She could feel him standing there like a menacing beggar.

– What are you, another bourgeois? he said to her. I know I've been drinking. Come and have dinner, he said. I've ordered something wonderful for us. Vichyssoise. Lobster. S. G. Always on the menu like that, *selon grosseur*.

He was talking in an easy way, as if they were in the casino together, chips piled high before them, as if it were a shrewd discussion of what to bet on and her breasts in the dark T-shirt were a thing of indifference to him. He calmly reached out and touched one.

– I have money, he said. His hand remained where it was, cupping her. She was too stunned to move. Do you want me to do more of that?

– No, she managed to say.

His hand slipped down to her hip. Deems had taken an arm and was drawing him away.

– Ssh, Brennan whispered to her, don't say anything. The two of us. Like an oar going into the water, gliding.

– We have to go, Deems insisted.

– What are you doing? Is this another of your ruses? Brennan cried. Deems, I shall end up destroying you yet!

347

As he was herded to the door, he continued. Deems was the only man he didn't loathe, he said. He wanted them all to come to his house, he had everything. He had a phonograph, whisky! He had a gold watch!

At last he was outside. He walked unsteadily across the finely cut grass and got into his car, the side of which was dented in. He backed away in great lurches.

– He's headed for Cato's, Deems guessed. I ought to call and warn them.

– They won't serve him. He owes them money, Irene said.

– Who told you that?

– The bartender. Are you all right? she asked Ardis.

– Yes. Is he actually married?

– He's been married three or four times, Deems said.

Later they started dancing, some of the women together. Irene pulled Deems onto the floor. He came unresisting. He danced quite well. She was moving her arms sinuously and singing.

– Very nice, he said. Have you ever entertained?

She smiled at him.

– I do my best, she said.

At the end she put her hand on Ardis's arm and said again,

– I'm so embarrassed at what happened.

– It was nothing. I'm all right.

– I should have taken him and thrown him out, her husband said on the way home. Ezra Pound. Do you know about Ezra Pound?

– No.

– He was a traitor. He broadcast for the enemy during the war. They should have shot him.

– What happened to him?

– They gave him a poetry prize.

They were going down a long empty stretch where on a

348

corner, half hidden in trees, a small house stood, the gypsy house, Ardis thought of it as, a simple house with a water pump in the yard and occasionally in the daytime a girl in blue shorts, very brief, and high heels, hanging clothes on a line. Tonight there was a light on in the window. One light near the sea. She was driving with Warren and he was talking.

– The best thing is to just forget about tonight.

– Yes, she said. It was nothing.

Brennan went through a fence on Hull Lane and up on to somebody's lawn at about two that morning. He had missed the curve where the road bent left, probably because his headlights weren't on, the police thought.

She took the book and went over to a window that looked out on the garden behind the library. She read a bit of one thing or another and came to a poem some lines of which had been underlined, with pencilled notes in the margin. It was 'The River-Merchant's Wife'; she had never heard of it. Outside, the summer burned, white as chalk.

At fourteen I married My Lord you, she read.
I never laughed, being bashful . . .

There were three old men, one of them almost blind, it appeared, reading newspapers in the cold room. The thick glasses of the nearly blind man cast white moons onto his cheeks.

The leaves fall early this autumn, in wind.
The paired butterflies are already yellow with August
Over the grass in the West garden;
They hurt me. I grow older.

She had read poems and perhaps marked them like this, but that was in school. Of the things she had been taught she remembered only a few. There had been one My Lord though she did not marry him. She'd been twenty-one, her first year in the city. She remembered the building of dark brown brick on Fifty-eighth Street, the afternoons with their slitted light, her clothes in a chair or fallen to the floor, and the damp, mindless repetition, to it, or him, or who knew what: oh, God, oh, God, oh, God. The traffic outside so faint, so far away . . .

She'd called him several times over the years, believing that love never died, dreaming foolishly of seeing him again, of his returning, in the way of old songs. To hurry, to almost run down the noontime street again, the sound of her heels on the sidewalk. To see the door of the apartment open . . .

If you are coming down the narrows of the river Kiang,
Please let me know beforehand,
And I will come out to meet you.
*   As far as Chô-fu-Sa*

There she sat by the window with her young face that had a weariness in it, a slight distaste for things, even, one might imagine, for oneself. After a while she went to the desk.

– Do you happen to have anything by Michael Brennan? she asked.

– Michael Brennan, the woman said. We've had them, but he takes them away because unworthy people read them, he says. I don't think there're any now. Perhaps when he comes back from the city.

– He lives in the city?

– He lives just down the road. We had all of his books at one time. Do you know him?

She would have liked to ask more but she shook her head.

– No, she said. I've just heard the name.

– He's a poet, the woman said.

On the beach she sat by herself. There was almost no one. In her bathing suit she lay back with the sun on her face and knees. It was hot and the sea calm. She preferred to lie up by the dunes with the waves bursting, to listen while they crashed like the final chords of a symphony except they went on and on. There was nothing as fine as that.

She came out of the ocean and dried herself like the gypsy girl, ankles caked with sand. She could feel the sun burnishing her shoulders. Hair wet, deep in the emptiness of days, she walked her bicycle up to the road, the dirt velvety beneath her feet.

She did not go home the usual way. There was little traffic. The noon was bottle-green, large houses among the trees and wide farmland, like a memory, behind.

She knew the house and saw it far off, her heart beating strangely. When she stopped, it was casually, with the bike tilting to one side and she half-seated on it as if taking a rest. How beautiful a lone woman is, in a white summer shirt and bare legs. Pretending to adjust the bicycle's chain she looked at the house, its tall windows, water stains high on the roof. There was a gardener's shed, abandoned, saplings growing in the path that led to it. The long driveway, the sea porch, everything was empty.

Walking slowly, aware of how brazen she was, she went toward the house. Her urge was to look in the windows, no more than that. Still, despite the silence, the complete stillness, that was forbidden.

She walked farther. Suddenly someone rose from the side porch. She was unable to utter a sound or move.

It was a dog, a huge dog higher than her waist, coming toward her, yellow-eyed. She had always been afraid of dogs, the Alsatian that had unexpectedly turned on her college roommate and torn off a piece of her scalp. The size of this one, its lowered head and slow, deliberate stride.

Do not show fear, she knew that. Carefully she moved the bicycle so that it was between them. The dog stopped a few feet away, its eyes directly on her, the sun along its back. She did not know what to expect, a sudden short rush.

– Good boy, she said. It was all she could think of. Good boy.

Moving cautiously, she began wheeling the bicycle toward the road, turning her head away slightly so as to appear unworried. Her legs felt naked, the bare calves. They would be ripped open as if by a scythe. The dog was following her, its shoulders moving smoothly, like a kind of machine. Somehow finding the courage, she tried to ride. The front wheel wavered. The dog, high as the handlebars, came nearer.

– No, she cried. No!

After a moment or two, obediently, he slowed or veered off. He was gone.

She rode as if freed, as if flying through blocks of sunlight and high, solemn tunnels of trees. And then she saw him again. He was following – not exactly following, since he was some distance ahead. He seemed to float along in the fields, which were burning in the midday sun, on fire. She turned onto her own road. There he came. He fell in behind her. She could hear the clatter of his nails like falling stones. She looked back. He was trotting awkwardly, like a big man running in the rain. A line of spittle trailed from his jaw. When she reached her house he had disappeared.

That night in a cotton robe she was preparing for bed, cleaning her face, the bathroom door ajar. She brushed her hair with many rapid strokes.

– Tired? her husband asked as she emerged.

It was his way of introducing the subject.

– No, she said.

So there they were in the summer night with the far-off sound of the sea. Among the things her husband admired that Ardis possessed was extraordinary skin, luminous and smooth, a skin so pure that to touch it would make one tremble.

– Wait, she whispered, – not so fast.

Afterward he lay back without a word, already falling into deepest sleep, much too soon. She touched his shoulder. She heard something outside the window.

– Did you hear that?

– No, what? he said drowsily.

She waited. There was nothing. It had seemed faint, like a sigh.

The next morning she said,

– Oh! There, just beneath the trees, the dog lay. She could see his ears – they were small ears dashed with white.

– What is it? her husband asked.

– Nothing, she said. A dog. It followed me yesterday.

– From where? he said, coming to see.

– Down the road. I think it might be that man's. Brennan's.

– Brennan?

– I passed his house, she said, and afterward it was following me.

– What were you doing at Brennan's?

– Nothing. I was passing. He's not even there.

– What do you mean, he's not there?

– I don't know. Somebody said that.

He went to the door and opened it. The dog – it was a deerhound – had been lying with its forelegs stretched out in front like a sphinx, its haunches round and high. Awkwardly it rose and after a moment moved, reluctantly it

353

seemed, wandering slowly across the fields, never looking back.

In the evening they went to a party on Mecox Road. Far out toward Montauk, winds were sweeping the coast. The waves exploded in clouds of spray. Ardis was talking to a woman not much older than herself, whose husband had just died of a brain tumor at the age of forty. He had diagnosed it himself, the woman said. He'd been sitting in a theater when he suddenly realized he couldn't see the wall just to his right. At the funeral, she said, there had been two women she did not recognize and who did not come to the reception afterward.

– Of course, he was a surgeon, she said, and they're drawn to surgeons like flies. But I never suspected. I suppose I'm the world's greatest fool.

The trees streamed past in the dark as they drove home. Their house rose in the brilliant headlights. She thought she had caught sight of something and found herself hoping her husband had not. She was nervous as they walked across the grass. The stars were numberless. They would open the door and go inside, where all was familiar, even serene.

After a while they would prepare for bed while the wind seized the corners of the house and the dark leaves thrashed each other. They would turn out the lights. All that was outside would be left in wildness, in the glory of the wind.

It was true. He was there. He was lying on his side, his whitish coat ruffled. In the morning light she approached slowly. When he raised his head his eyes were hazel and gold. He was not that young, she saw, but his power was that he was unbowed. She spoke in a natural voice.

– Come, she said.

She took a few steps. At first he did not move. She glanced back again. He was following.

It was still early. As they reached the road a car passed, drab and sun-faded. A girl was in the back seat, head fallen wearily, being driven home, Ardis thought, after the exhausting night. She felt an inexplicable envy.

It was warm but the true heat had not risen. Several times she waited while he drank from puddles at the edge of the road, standing in them as he did, his large, wet toenails gleaming like ivory.

Suddenly from a porch rushed another dog, barking fiercely. The great hound turned, teeth bared. She held her breath, afraid of the sight of one of them limp and bleeding, but violent as it sounded they kept a distance between them. After a few snaps it was over. He came along less steadily, strands of wet hair near his mouth.

At the house he went to the porch and stood waiting. It was plain he wanted to go inside. He had returned. He must be starving, she thought. She looked around to see if there was anyone in sight. A chair she had not noticed before was out on the grass, but the house was as still as ever, not even the curtains breathing. With a hand that seemed not even hers she tried the door. It was unlocked.

The hallway was dim. Beyond it was a living room in disorder, couch cushions rumpled, glasses on the tables, papers, shoes. In the dining room there were piles of books. It was the house of an artist, abundance, disregard.

There was a large desk in the bedroom, in the middle of which, among paper clips and letters, a space had been cleared. Here were sheets of paper written in an almost illegible hand, incomplete lines and words that omitted certain vowels. *Deth of fathr*, she read, then indecipherable things and something that seemed to be *carrges sent empty*, and at the bottom, set apart, two words, *anew, anew*. In a different hand was the page of a letter, *I deeply love you.*

I admire you. I love you and admire you. She could not read anymore. She was too uneasy. There were things she did not want to know. In a hammered silver frame was the photograph of a woman, face darkened by shadow, leaning against a wall, the unseen white of a villa somewhere behind. Through the slatted blinds one could hear the soft clack of palm fronds, the birds high above, in the villa where he had found her, where her youth had been bold as a declaration of war. No, that was not it. He had met her on a beach, they had gone to the villa. What is powerful is a glimpse of a truer life. She read the slanting inscription in Spanish, *Tus besos me destierran.* She put the picture down. A photograph was sacrosanct, you were excluded from it, always. So that was the wife. *Tus besos*, your kisses.

She wandered, nearly dreaming, into a large bathroom that looked out on the garden. As she entered, her heart almost stopped – she caught sight of somebody in the mirror. It took a second before she realized it was herself and, as she looked more closely, a not wholly recognizable, even an illicit self, in soft, grainy light. She understood suddenly, she accepted the fate that meant she was to be found here, that Brennan would be returning and discover her, having stopped for the mail or bread. Out of nowhere she would hear the paralyzing sound of footsteps or a car. Still, she continued to look at herself. She was in the house of the poet, the demon. She had entered forbidden rooms. *Tus besos* ... the words had not died. At that moment the dog came to the door, stood there, and then fell to the floor, his knowing eyes on her, like an intimate friend. She turned to him. All she had never done seemed at hand.

Deliberately, without thinking, she began to remove her clothes. She went no further than the waist. She was dazzled by what she was doing. There in the silence with the sunlight outside she stood slender and half-naked, the missing image of herself, of all women. The dog's eyes were raised to her as if in reverence. He was unbetraying, a companion like no other. She remembered certain figures ahead of her at school. Kit Vining, Nan Boudreau. Legendary faces and reputations. She had longed to be like them but never seemed to have the chance. She leaned forward to stroke the beautiful head.

– You're a big fellow. The words seemed authentic, more authentic than anything she had said for a long time. A very big fellow.

His long tail stirred and with faint sound brushed the floor. She kneeled and stroked his head again and again.

There was the crackling of gravel beneath the tires of a car. It brought her abruptly to her senses. Hurriedly, almost in panic, she threw on her clothes and made her way to the kitchen. She would run along the porch if necessary and then from tree to tree.

She opened the door and listened. Nothing. As she was going quickly down the back steps, by the side of the house she saw her husband. Thank God, she thought helplessly.

They approached each other slowly. He glanced at the house.

– I brought the car. Is anyone here?

There was a moment's pause.

– No, no one. She felt her face stiffen, as if she were telling a lie.

– What were you doing? he asked.

– I was in the kitchen, she said. I was trying to find something to feed him.

– Did you find it?

– Yes. No, she said.

He stood looking at her and finally said,

– Let's go.

As they backed out, she caught sight of the dog just lying down in the shade, sprawled, disconsolate. She felt the nakedness beneath her clothes, the satisfaction. They turned onto the road.

– Somebody's got to feed him, she said as they drove. She was looking out at the houses and fields. Warren said nothing. He was driving faster. She turned back to look. For a moment she thought she saw him following, far behind.

Late that day she went shopping and came home about five. The wind, which had arisen anew, blew the door shut with a bang.

– Warren?

– Did you see him? her husband said.

– Yes.

He had come back. He was out there where the land went up slightly.

– I'm going to call the animal shelter, she said.

– They won't do anything. He's not a stray.

– I can't stand it. I'm calling someone, she said.

– Why don't you call the police? Maybe they'll shoot him.

– Why don't you do it? she said coldly. Borrow someone's gun. He's driving me crazy.

It remained light until past nine, and in the last of it, with the clouds a deeper blue than the sky, she went out quietly, far across the grass. Her husband watched from the window. She was carrying a white bowl.

She could see him very clearly, the gray of his muzzle there in the muted grass and when she was close the clear, tan eyes. In an almost ceremonial way she knelt down. The wind was blowing her hair. She seemed almost a mad person there in the fading light.

– Here. Drink something, she said.

His gaze, somehow reproachful, drifted away. He was like a fugitive sleeping on his coat. His eyes were nearly closed.

My life has meant nothing, she thought. She wanted above all else not to confess that.

They ate dinner in silence. Her husband did not look at her. Her face annoyed him, he did not know why. She could be good-looking but there were times when she was not. Her face was like a series of photographs, some of which ought to have been thrown away. Tonight it was like that.

– The sea broke through into Sag Pond today, she said dully.

– Did it?

– They thought some little girl had drowned. The fire trucks were there. It turned out she had just strayed off. After a pause, We have to do something, she said.

– Whatever happens is going to happen, he told her.

– This is different, she said. She suddenly left the room. She felt close to tears.

Her husband's business was essentially one of giving advice. He had a life that served other lives, helped them come to agreements, end marriages, defend themselves against former friends. He was accomplished at it. Its language and techniques were part of him. He lived amid disturbance and self-interest but always protected from it. In his files were letters, memorandums, secrets of careers. One thing he had seen: how near men could be to disaster no matter how secure they seemed. He had seen events turn, one ruinous thing following another. It could happen without warning. Sometimes they were able to save themselves, but there was a point at which they could not. He sometimes wondered about himself – when the blow came and the beams began to give and come apart, what would happen?

She was calling Brennan's house again. There was never an answer.

During the night the wind blew itself out. In the morning at first light, Warren could feel the stillness. He lay in bed without moving. His wife's back was turned toward him. He could feel her denial.

He rose and went to the window. The dog was still there, he could see its shape. He knew little of animals and nothing of nature but he could tell what had happened. It was lying in a different way.

– What is it? she asked. She had come up beside him. It seemed she stood there for a long time. He's dead.

She started for the door. He held her by the arm.

– Let me go, she said.

– Ardis . . .

She began to weep,

– Let me go.

– Leave him alone! he called after her. Let him be!

She ran quickly across the grass in her nightgown. The ground was wet. As she came closer she paused to calm herself, to find courage. She regretted only one thing – she had not said good-bye.

She took a step or two forward. She could sense the heavy, limp weight of him, a weight that would disperse, become something else, the sinews fading, the bones becoming light. She longed to do what she had never done, embrace him. At that moment he raised his head.

– Warren! she cried, turning toward the house. Warren!

As if the shouts distressed him, the dog was rising to his feet. He moved wearily off. Hands pressed to her mouth, she stared at the place where he had been, where the grass was flattened slightly. All night again. Again all night. When she looked, he was some distance off.

She ran after him. Warren could see her. She seemed free. She seemed like another woman, a younger woman, the kind one saw in the dusty fields by the sea, in a bikini, stealing potatoes in bare feet.

She did not see him again. She went many times past the house, occasionally seeing Brennan's car there, but never a sign of the dog, or along the road or off in the fields.

One night in Cato's at the end of August, she saw Brennan himself at the bar. His arm was in a sling, from what sort of accident she could not guess. He was talking intently to the bartender, the same fierce eloquence, and though the restaurant was crowded, the stools next to him were empty. He was alone. The dog was not outside, nor in his car, nor part of his life anymore – gone, lost, living elsewhere, his name perhaps to be written in a line someday though most probably he was forgotten, but not by her.

PENELOPE LIVELY

BLACK DOG

JOHN CASE CAME home one summer evening to find his wife huddled in the corner of the sofa with the sitting-room curtains drawn. She said there was a black dog in the garden, looking at her through the window. Her husband put his briefcase in the hall and went outside. There was no dog; a blackbird fled shrieking across the lawn and next door someone was using a mower. He did not see how any dog could get into the garden: the fences at either side were five feet high and there was a wall at the far end. He returned to the house and pointed this out to his wife, who shrugged and continued to sit hunched in the corner of the sofa. He found her there again the next evening and at the weekend she refused to go outside and sat for much of the time watching the window.

The daughters came, big girls with jobs in insurance companies, wardrobes full of bright clothes and twenty-thousand-pound mortgages. They stood over Brenda Case and said she should get out more. She should go to evening classes, they said, join a health dub, do a language course, learn upholstery, go jogging, take driving lessons. And Brenda Case sat at the kitchen table and nodded. She quite agreed, it would be a good thing to find a new interest – jogging, upholstery, French; yes, she said, she must pull herself together, and it was indeed up to her in the last resort, they were quite right. When they had gone she drew the

365

sitting-room curtains again and sat on the sofa staring at a magazine they had brought. The magazine was full of recipes the daughters had said she must try; there were huge bright glossy photographs of puddings crested with alpine peaks of cream, of dark glistening casseroles and salads like an artist's palette. The magazine costed each recipe; a four-course dinner for six worked out at £3.89 a head. It also had articles advising her on life insurance, treatment for breast cancer and how to improve her lovemaking.

John Case became concerned about his wife. She had always been a good housekeeper; now, they began to run out of things. When one evening there was nothing but cold meat and cheese for supper he protested. She said she had not been able to shop because it had rained all day; on rainy days the dog was always outside, waiting for her.

The daughters came again and spoke severely to their mother. They talked to their father separately, in different tones, proposing an autumn holiday in Portugal or the Canaries, a new three-piece for the sitting-room, a musquash coat.

John Case discussed the whole thing with his wife, reasonably. He did this one evening after he had driven the Toyota into the garage, walked over to the front door and found it locked from within. Brenda, opening it, apologized; the dog had been round at the front today, she said, sitting in the middle of the path.

He began by saying lightly that dogs have not been known to stand up on their hind legs and open doors. And in any case, he continued, there is no dog. No dog at all. The dog is something you are imagining. I have asked all the neighbours; nobody has seen a big black dog. Nobody round here owns a big black dog. There is no evidence of a dog. So you must stop going on about this dog because it does not exist. 'What is the matter?' he asked, gently. 'Something must be the matter. Would you like to go away for a holiday? Shall we have the house redecorated?'

Brenda Case listened to him. He was sitting on the sofa, with his back to the window. She sat listening carefully to him and from time to time her eyes strayed from his face to the lawn beyond, in the middle of which the dog sat, its tongue hanging out and its yellow eyes glinting. She said she would go away for a holiday if he wished, and she would be perfectly willing for the house to be redecorated. Her husband talked about travel agents and decorating firms and once he got up and walked over to the window to inspect the condition of the paintwork; the dog, Brenda saw, continued to sit there, its eyes always on her.

They went to Marrakesh for ten days. Men came and turned the kitchen from primrose to eau-de-nil and the hallway from magnolia to parchment. September became October and Brenda Case fetched from the attic a big gnarled walking stick that was a relic of a trip to the Tyrol many years ago; she took this with her every time she went out of the house which nowadays was not often. Inside the house, it was always somewhere near her – its end protruding from under the sofa, or hooked over the arm of her chair.

The daughters shook their tousled heads at their mother, towering over her in their baggy fashionable trousers and their big gay jackets. It's not fair on Dad, they said, can't you see that? You've only got one life, they said sternly, and Brenda Case replied that she realized that, she did indeed. Well then ... said the daughters, one on each side of her, bigger than her, brighter, louder, always saying what they meant, going straight to the point and no nonsense, competent with income-tax returns and contemptuous of muddle.

When she was alone, Brenda Case kept doors and windows closed at all times. Occasionally, when the dog was not there, she would open the upstairs windows to air the bed-rooms and the bathroom; she would stand with the curtains blowing, taking in great gulps and draughts. Downstairs, of course, she could not risk this, because the dog was quite unpredictable; it would be absent all day, and then suddenly there it would be squatting by the fence, or leaning hard up against the patio doors, sprung from nowhere. She would draw the curtains, resigned, or move to another room and endure the knowledge of its presence on the other side of the wall, a few yards away. When it was there she would sit doing nothing, staring straight ahead of her; silent and patient. When it was gone she moved around the house, prepared meals, listened a little to the radio, and sometimes took the old photograph albums from the bottom drawer of the bur-eau in the sitting-room. In these albums the daughters slowly mutated from swaddled bundles topped with monkey faces and spiky hair to chunky toddlers and then to spindly-limbed little girls in matching pinafores. They played on Cornish beaches or posed on the lawn, holding her hand (that same lawn on which the dog now sat on its hunkers). In the photographs, she looked down at them, smiling, and they gazed up at her or held out objects for her inspection – a flower, a sea-shell. Her husband was also in the photo-graphs; a smaller man than now, it seemed, with a curiously vulnerable look, as though surprised in a moment of privacy. Looking at herself, Brenda saw a pretty young woman who seemed vaguely familiar, like some relative not encountered for many years.

John Case realized that nothing had been changed by Marrakesh and redecorating. He tried putting the walking stick back up in the attic; his wife brought it down again. If he opened the patio doors she would simply close them as soon as he had left the room. Sometimes he saw her looking over his shoulder into the garden with an expression on her face that chilled him. He asked her, one day, what she thought the dog would do if it got into the house; she was silent for a moment and then said quietly she supposed it would eat her.

He said he could not understand, he simply did not understand, what could be wrong. It was not, he said, as though they had a thing to worry about. He gently pointed out that she wanted for nothing. It's not that we have to count the pennies any more, he said, not like in the old days.

'When we were young,' said Brenda Case. 'When the girls were babies.'

'Right. It's not like that now, is it?' He indicated the 24-inch colour TV set, the video, the stereo, the microwave oven, the English Rose fitted kitchen, the bathroom with separate shower. He reminded her of the BUPA membership, the index-linked pension, the shares and dividends. Brenda agreed that it was not, it most certainly was not.

The daughters came with their boyfriends, nicely spoken confident young men in very clean shirts, who talked to Brenda of their work in firms selling computers and Japanese cameras while the girls took John into the garden and discussed their mother.

'The thing is, she's becoming agoraphobic.'

'She thinks she sees this black dog,' said John Case.

'We know,' said the eldest daughter. 'But that, frankly, is neither here nor there. It's a mechanism, simply. A ploy. Like children do. One has to get to the root of it, that's the thing.'

'It's her age,' said the youngest.

'Of course it's her age,' snorted the eldest. 'But it's also her. She was always inclined to be negative, but this is ridiculous.'

'Negative?' said John Case. He tried to remember his wife

– his wives – who – one of whom – he could see inside the house, beyond the glass of the patio window, looking out at him from between two young men he barely knew. The reflections of his daughters, his strapping prosperous daughters, were superimposed upon their mother, so that she looked at him through the cerise and orange and yellow of their clothes.

'Negative. A worrier. Look on the bright side, *I* say, but that's not Mum, is it?'

'I wouldn't have said . . .' he began.

'She's unmotivated,' said the youngest. 'That's the real trouble. No job, no nothing. It's a generation problem, too.'

'I'm trying . . .' their father began.

'We know, Dad, we know. But the thing is, she needs help. This isn't something you can handle all on your own. She'll have to see someone.'

'No way,' said the youngest, 'will we get Mum into therapy.'

'Dad can take her to the surgery,' said the eldest. 'For starters.'

The doctor – the new doctor, there was always a new doctor – was about the same age as her daughters, Brenda Case saw. Once upon a time doctors had been older men, fatherly and reliable. This one was good-looking, in the manner of men in knitting-pattern photographs. He sat looking at her, quite kindly, and she told him how she was feeling. In so far as this was possible.

When she had finished he tapped a pencil on his desk. 'Yes,' he said. 'Yes, I see.' And then he went on, 'There doesn't seem to be any very specific trouble, does there, Mrs Case?'

She agreed.

'How do you think you would define it yourself?'

She thought. At last she said that she supposed there was

370

nothing wrong with her that wasn't wrong with – well, everyone.

'Quite,' said the doctor busily, writing now on his pad. 'That's the sensible way to look at things. So I'm giving you this . . . Three a day . . . Come back and see me in two weeks.'

When she had come out John Case asked to see the doctor for a moment. He explained that he was worried about his wife. The doctor nodded sympathetically. John told the doctor about the black dog, apologetically, and the doctor looked reflective for a moment and then said, 'Your wife is fifty-four.'

John Case agreed. She was indeed fifty-four.

'Exactly,' said the doctor. 'So I think we can take it that with some care and understanding these difficulties will . . . disappear. I've given her something,' he said, confidently; John Case smiled back. That was that.

'It will go away,' said John Case to his wife, firmly. He was not entirely sure what he meant, but it did not do, he felt sure, to be irresolute. She looked at him without expression.

Brenda Case swallowed each day the pills that the doctor had given her. She believed in medicines and doctors, had always found that aspirin cured a headache and used to frequent the surgery with the girls when they were small. She was prepared for a miracle. For the first few days it did seem to her just possible that the dog was growing a little smaller but after a week she realized that it was not. She continued to take the pills and when at the end of a fortnight she told the doctor that there was no change he said that these things took time, one had to be patient. She looked at him, this young man in his swivel chair on the other side of a cluttered desk, and knew that whatever was to be done would not be done by him, or by cheerful yellow pills like children's sweets.

The daughters came, to inspect and admonish. She said

that yes, she had seen the doctor again, and yes, she was feeling rather more ... herself. She showed them the new sewing-machine with many extra attachments that she had not used and when they left she watched them go down the front path to their cars, swinging their bags and shouting at each other, and saw the dog step aside for them, wagging its tail. When they had gone she opened the door again and stood there for a few minutes, looking at it, and the dog, five yards away, looked back, not moving.

The next day she took the shopping trolley and set off for the shops. As she opened the front gate she saw the dog come out from the shadow of the fence but she did not turn back. She continued down the street, although she could feel it behind her, keeping its distance. She spoke in a friendly way to a couple of neighbours, did her shopping and returned to the house, and all the while the dog was there, twenty paces off. As she walked to the front door she could hear the click of its claws on the pavement and had to steel herself so hard not to turn round that when she got inside she was bathed in sweat and shaking all over. When her husband came home that evening he thought her in a funny mood; she asked for a glass of sherry and later she suggested they put a record on instead of watching TV – *West Side Story* or another of those shows they went to years ago.

He was surprised at the change in her. She began to go out daily, and although in the evenings she often appeared to be exhausted, as though she had been climbing mountains instead of walking suburban streets, she was curiously calm. Admittedly, she had not appeared agitated before, but her stillness had not been natural; now, he sensed a difference. When the daughters telephoned he reported their mother's condition and listened to their complacent comments; that stuff usually did the trick, they said, all the medics were using it nowadays, they'd always known Mum would be OK soon. But when he put the telephone down and returned to his wife in the sitting-room he found himself looking at her uncomfortably. There was an alertness about her that worried him; later, he thought he heard something outside and went to look. He could see nothing at either the front or the back and his wife continued to read a magazine. When he sat down again she looked across at him with a faint smile.

She had started by meeting its eyes, its yellow eyes. And thus she had learned that she could stop it, halt its patient shadowing of her, leave it sitting on the pavement or the garden path. She began to leave the front door ajar, to open the patio window. She could not say what would happen next, knew only that this was inevitable. She no longer sweated or shook; she did not glance behind her when she was outside, and within she hummed to herself as she moved from room to room.

John Case, returning home on an autumn evening, stepped out of the car and saw light streaming through the open front door. He thought he heard his wife speaking to someone in the house. When he came into the kitchen, though, she was alone. He said, 'The front door was open,' and she replied that she must have left it so by mistake. She was busy with a saucepan at the stove and in the corner of the room, her husband saw, was a large dog basket towards which her glance occasionally strayed.

He made no comment. He went back into the hall, hung up his coat and was startled suddenly by his own face, caught unawares in the mirror by the hatstand and seeming like someone else's – that of a man both older and more burdened than he knew himself to be. He stood staring at it for a few moments and then took a step back towards the kitchen. He could hear the gentle chunking sound of his wife's wooden spoon stirring something in the saucepan and then, he thought, the creak of wickerwork.

He turned sharply and went into the sitting-room. He crossed to the window and looked out. He saw the lawn, blackish in the dusk, disappearing into darkness. He switched on the outside lights and flooded it all with an artificial glow – the grass, the little flight of steps up to the patio and the flower-bed at the top of them, from which he had tidied away the spent summer annuals at the weekend. The bare earth was marked all over, he now saw, with what appeared to be animal footprints, and as he stood gazing it seemed to him that he heard the pad of paws on the carpet behind him. He stood for a long while before at last he turned round.

ACKNOWLEDGMENTS

RICK BASS: "The Hermit's Story" from *The Hermit's Story* by Rick Bass. Copyright © 2002 by Rick Bass. Reprinted by permission of Houghton Mifflin Harcourt Publishing Company. All rights reserved.

RAY BRADBURY: "The Emissary" by Ray Bradbury. Reprinted by permission of Don Congdon Associates, Inc. Copyright © 1947 by Arkham House, renewed 1975 by Ray Bradbury.

PATRICIA HIGHSMITH: "There I Was, Stuck With Bubsy". Copyright © 1975 by Patricia Highsmith, from *The Selected Stories of Patricia Highsmith* by Patricia Highsmith. Used by permission of W. W. Norton & Company, Inc. "There I Was, Stuck With Bubsy" from: Patricia Highsmith *Kleine Mordgeschichten für Tiefreunde*. Copyright © 1979 by Diogenes Verlag AG, Zurich.

DORIS LESSING: "The Story of Two Dogs" from *A Man and Two Women* by Doris Lessing. Copyright © 1963 Doris Lessing. Reprinted by kind permission of Jonathan Clowes Limited, London, on behalf of Doris Lessing.

JONATHAN LETHEM: "Ava's Apartment" by Jonathan Lethem, originally published in *The New Yorker*. Copyright © 2009 by Jonathan Lethem. Reprinted by permission of the Richard Parks Agency.

PENELOPE LIVELEY: "Black Dog" from *A Pack of Cards*, published by Penguin. Used by permission of David Higham Associates. "Black Dog" from *A Pack of Cards*, copyright © 1978 by Penelope Lively. Used by permission of Grove/Atlantic, Inc.

377